Praise for

The Enchanted Boot: Italian Fairy Tales and Their Tellers

"What a timely and marvelous volume this is! *The Enchanted Boot* traces a much-needed trajectory for the Italian fairy-tale tradition, mapping a long and distinctive history for this unruly genre that highlights how intertwined its fantastic flights and ironies are with harsh social realities as well as with the Italian peoples' often conflicting regional and national sensibilities. Canepa's breadth and insight as a scholar of literary fairy tales and Italian culture is matched by her genuine talent as a translator keenly tuned into the brio, moods, and multiple registers of the genre in Italy from the fourteenth century to the present. Finally, a collection in English that allows for Italian fairy tales to take their rightful place in the transnational history of the genre rather than playing cameo roles in it, and it is such a pleasure to read."

—Cristina Bacchilega, professor emerita, University of Hawai'i at Mānoa, and coeditor of *Marvels & Tales: A Journal of Fairy-Tale Studies*

"Nancy Canepa has superbly translated and edited a complete collection of the most significant Italian tales from Roman times to the present. Her translations and choice of tales reveal the enchantment of Italian storytellers who deserve to be better known in the English-speaking world."

—Jack Zipes, professor emeritus, University of Minnesota

"Nancy Canepa's splendid selection of Italian fairy tales is a precious gift to all readers interested in this literary genre. Not only does this volume reveal the persistent beauty of the Italian tradition, it also offers a rigorous analysis of its historical and cultural evolution."

—Armando Maggi, Arthur and Joann Rasmussen Professor of Western Civilization, University of Chicago

"Thanks to *The Enchanted Boot*, English-speaking readers can now experience the Italian fairy tale's unique role in shaping Europe's literature of magic and wonder. Superb translations and expert commentary make Nancy Canepa's collection of Italian tales from the Middle Ages to the twenty-first century a monumental contribution to fairy-tale studies."

—Donald Haase, coeditor of *Folktales and Fairy Tales: Traditions and Texts from around the World*

THE ENCHANTED BOOT

The Donald Haase Series in Fairy-Tale Studies

Series Editor

Anne E. Duggan, Wayne State University

Founding Editor

Donald Haase, Wayne State University

Donald Haase

A complete listing of the advisory editors and the books in this series can be found online at wsupress.wayne.edu.

THE ENCHANTED BOOT

Italian Fairy Tales and Their Tellers

Edited, Translated, and Introduced by

Nancy L. Canepa

Wayne State University Press
Detroit

Library of Congress Control Number: 2022944695

ISBN 978-0-8143-3475-1 (paperback)
ISBN 978-0-8143-4920-5 (hardcover)
ISBN 978-0-8143-4921-2 (e-book)

On cover: *Resilience* by Carmelo Lettere. Cover design by Chelsea Hunter.

Wayne State University Press rests on Waawiyaataanong, also referred to as Detroit, the ancestral and contemporary homeland of the Three Fires Confederacy. These sovereign lands were granted by the Ojibwe, Odawa, Potawatomi, and Wyandot Nations, in 1807, through the Treaty of Detroit. Wayne State University Press affirms Indigenous sovereignty and honors all tribes with a connection to Detroit. With our Native neighbors, the press works to advance educational equity and promote a better future for the earth and all people.

Published with the assistance of a fund established by Thelma Gray James of Wayne State University for the publication of folklore and English studies.

Wayne State University Press
Leonard N. Simons Building
4809 Woodward Avenue
Detroit, Michigan 48201-1309

Visit us online at wsupress.wayne.edu.

Contents

Part V.
Italo Calvino's *Fiabe Italiane (Italian Folktales)*

Part VI.
Something Old, Something New: Fairy Tales for Our Times

Acknowledgments

The preparation of this volume was at times akin to one of those fairy-tale journeys with endless twists and turns, whose end seemed at one moment to be close at hand and at the next almost impossibly far-off. I am grateful to the wonderful team at Wayne State University Press for being patient and enthusiastic fellow travelers, as well as for helping me to overcome various obstacles along the way. In particular, Don Haase, the general editor of the Series in Fairy-Tale Studies until very recently, has over the years offered inspiration, insight, and generous and unwavering support in every one of my fairy-tale projects, and I thank him many times over for that.

Finally, much love to those who have inhabited the world of Italian fairy tales with me, in the process making it infinitely richer: Camilla, Gaia, and Carmelo.

Introduction

What interests me above all else are the tests that man experiences and the way he overcomes them. The form of the most remote folktales—the child abandoned in the woods or the knight who must overcome encounters with beasts and enchantments—remains the irreplaceable framework of all human stories, the design of all great exemplary novels, in which a moral personality realizes itself as it journeys through a ruthless nature or society.

—Italo Calvino, "Il midollo del leone"

Organizing our experience into words and stories is an essential human activity that gives life meaning; we fashion our lives into stories and in the process come under the transformative magic of already-existing stories. Perhaps no other genre illustrates this narrative reciprocity as well as the fairy tale. The lasting power and what Italo Calvino calls in the epigraph the "irreplaceable framework" of the seemingly simple narratives of fairy tales have to do with the way they have transformed, adapted, and been reconceived over thousands of years to meet the different needs and aspirations of individuals and communities. "Fairy tales register an effort . . . to develop maps for coping with personal anxieties, family conflicts, social frictions, and the myriad frustrations of everyday life" (Tatar xi). Whether in oral or literary form, fairy tales document the trials and triumphs of the human journey and have always had social functions—to entertain, to acculturate, but also to enforce, grapple with, and question dominant values and ideologies. Through fairy tales, human beings transpose their own worlds and reimagine new worlds, just as the stories that fairy tales tell can be creatively integrated into our own real-life trajectories. The stories that individuals, communities, and even nations tell themselves change vastly over time and space, and investigating how and why these changes occur is an important way of revisiting history.

Definitions of the fairy tale are notoriously slippery, but as a starting point we may refer to folklorist Stith Thompson's classic 1946 definition of this genre as a short narrative "involving a succession of motifs or episodes. It moves in an unreal world without definite locality or definite characters and is filled with the marvelous. In this never-never land humble heroes kill adversaries, succeed to kingdoms, and marry princesses" (Thompson 8; cit. in Haase 1:323). Scholars generally make a distinction between unauthored, orally transmitted folktales with a strong magical component (the German term *Märchen* is often used) and authored, literary tales of magic (*Kuntsmärchen*), though in reality there has always been a porous and productive back-and-forth between the two. The tales included in this volume are primarily literary and offer a vast and rich range of approaches to reimagining the materials of folk tradition.

Today we tend to associate fairy tales with children. The forms of the fairy tale that as ex-children and parents we are most familiar with, at least in the West, are the tales by the Brothers Grimm, Hans Christian Andersen, Charles Perrault; perhaps the *Arabian Nights* (in some bowdlerized form); beautifully illustrated picture books; and, of course, Disney movies. And yet the emergence, in Europe, of the modern genre of the authored, literary fairy tale from an oral tradition was initiated in the Italian Renaissance by authors such as Giovan Francecso Straparola and Giambattista Basile, far before the times of Perrault or the Brothers Grimm and far before fairy tales were written for children.

The Italian Tradition of Fairy Tales

Italy can pride itself on having one of the earliest and richest collections of literary fairy tales in Giambattista Basile's *Lo cunto de li cunti* (*The Tale of Tales*). From the early history of Italian literature in the medieval period up to today, there has been a vital and fruitful interchange between oral folkloric traditions and "official" culture, which has resulted in the incorporation of fairy-tale motifs and structures into a wide variety of works. But the seminal experimentations with the fairy tale as an independent literary genre in the Renaissance and the Baroque on the part of Straparola and Basile did not provide the impetus for the blossoming of a subsequent fairy-tale "vogue" in Italy, as was the case in eighteenth-century France or during the Romantic period throughout Europe; and Basile's *Tale of Tales*, though for centuries recognized by scholars as an artistic and folkloric masterpiece, never achieved the status of beloved national treasure that Perrault's or the Brothers Grimm's collections did. Even if in the nineteenth century Italians were once again at the forefront of collecting and authoring tales, only relatively recently, with Italo Calvino's *Fiabe italiane* (*Italian Folktales*, 1956), did Italy come to have its own "master collection" of fairy tales akin to those published in other European countries in the nineteenth century. Moreover, although a number of folklorists and other scholars have begun to research the vast storehouse of dialect tales deriving from oral tradition that came to light in the nineteenth century (still, however, in part unfamiliar to the modern reading public), the development of the literary fairy tale as genre in Italy is, with few exceptions, a largely unexplored topic. At the same time, innovative Italian fabulists continue to this day to reinvent the fairy tale as expression of both collective identities and individual sensibilities. For a student of Italian culture, an understanding of the history of the Italian fairy tale contributes to the understanding of the evolution, over the centuries, of the rich spectrum of Italian identities and cultures; for a student of fairy tales, it offers a tantalizing look at some of the best-kept secrets in literary history.

Fairy-Tale Motifs in Early Italian Literature

Although fairy tales as we know them today made their debut in early modern Italy, both authored texts and oral folkloric narratives had long incorporated fairy-tale material. As a number of recent studies have convincingly shown, fairy-tale motifs and themes populated texts from classical antiquity through the Middle Ages (see, e.g., Anderson; Ziolkowski). One of the most famous forebears of the fairy tale is "Cupid and Psyche," a mythological tale embedded in Apuleius's second-century BCE Latin novel *The Golden Ass* and a version of ATU tale type 425 (The Search for the Lost Husband), closely related to the later Beauty and the Beast variant. During the subsequent millennium, we may suppose that oral tales continued to circulate in the same fashion that they had for hundreds, if not thousands, of years, but there were few further experiments with the fairy tale as literary genre, even if medieval local and religious legends shared motifs and structuring devices with the fairy tale. This hiatus was due to various factors, principal among them the lack of a secular literate culture.

With the advent of European vernacular culture, especially from the thirteenth century on, the novella became a predominant literary genre, and the presence of fairy-tale functions and motifs such as lack and villainy, magical helpers and objects, marvelous transformations, and near-impossible tasks and quests made their way, more and more, into short narrative, even if it would be three centuries before the first integral fairy tales appeared. The eclectic anonymous late thirteenth-century *Il Novellino* (*The Novellino, or One Hundred Ancient Tales*), for example, incorporates in its hundred tales materials from diverse cultural traditions and thematic areas. Although many of the tales have the structure of medieval exempla, the collection also includes animal fables and fantastic motifs; in general, however, the exemplum flavor of many of these earliest novellas did not allow for the full expression of the secular supernatural and marvelous that permeates the fairy tale.

In Giovanni Boccaccio's works we find what is perhaps the first explicit postclassical reference to fairy tales, together with an early vernacular use of fairy-tale motifs. In chapter 10 of book 14 of his treatise on ancient mythology, *Genealogia deorum gentilium* (*The Genealogy of the Pagan Gods*, 1350–74), he offers a theoretical affirmation of the importance of fairy tales, maintaining that although the deepest wisdom lies in the works of great poets like Virgil, Dante, and Petrarch, popular oral narratives also have something to say to us. In a discussion of four types of fiction in terms of their "truth value," he considers fairy tales, "the invention of crazy old women," as the lowest of these but later recognizes their pedagogical and allegorical potential: "not even the craziest old crone keeping vigil around the hearth . . . and telling some tales about the Ogre, the Fairies, and Witches . . . thinks she is not including some serious sentiment . . . with which she wants to frighten small children, or delight young ladies, or make fun of older folks, or at least show the power of Fortune" (17, 21).

Among Boccaccio's works of fiction, the *Filocolo* (1336?), a prose novel, adopts the French tale of Florio and Biancofiore's tribulated but ultimately happy-ended love story and includes such fairy-tale functions as an initial lack, the presence of antagonists and helpers, the hero's difficult quest and series of tasks, magic gifts, and the final reward and marriage. But it is above all in his most famous work, the *Decameron* (1349–50), for centuries the European model for prose storytelling, that fairy-tale functions come most significantly into play. Boccaccio had a pivotal role as mediator between the feudal-chivalric and the emerging mercantile cultures; in the *Decameron* he drew from classical literature, medieval lais and fabliaux, chansons de geste, anecdotes, and other popular narratives to create tales that often feature the triumph of ordinary protagonists over obstacles and hardships. As is well known, the entire book has a consolatory function; its frame tale, modeled on Eastern collections such as the *Arabian Nights*, recounts the physical and psychological ravages of the plague (the Black Death of 1348), from which a group of ten noble youths temporarily escape into the countryside outside Florence to amuse and comfort themselves with storytelling. The tales, offered as examples of the workings of fortune, individual enterprise, and love, in a number of cases also borrow structural elements of the fairy tale: in particular, the tales of day 2, dedicated to the workings of fortune, and day 5, love stories with happy endings. Tale 2.3, "Messer Tedaldo," for instance, is a rags-to-riches story of three brothers, and "Andreuccio of Perugia" (2.5) includes a tripartite series of trials. "Giletta of Nerbona" (3.9) features a savvy young woman who works a difficult situation to her advantage, similarly to the heroine of "Sapia," tale 5.6 of Giambattista Basile's *Tale of Tales*; "Nastagio degli Onesti" (5.8) and "Torello of Stra and the Saladino" (10.9) also incorporate fairy-tale motifs. The last tale of the *Decameron*, "Griselda and the Marquis of Saluzzo" (10.10), combines elements common to the Cinderella and Beauty and the Beast tale types in a tale of the excruciating trials of an underdog heroine married to an inhumane husband, and found later rewritings in Chaucer, Basile, and Charles Perrault.

Although Boccaccian realism continued to prevail in the novella into the Renaissance, a general interest in popular culture and folk traditions persisted. Other early novella collections incorporated fairy-tale schemes and motifs. Four of the fifty novellas of Giovanni Fiorentino's *Pecorone* (The Big Sheep, second half fourteenth century) combine realistic and marvelous elements (4.1, 4.2, 9.2, 10.1); the first of these, "The Lady of Belmonte," inspired Shakespeare's *The Merchant of Venice*. Several of Giovanni Sercambi's *Novelle*

(Novellas, 1390–1402) also make use of fairy-tale elements ("De bono facto," "De vera amicitia et caritate," and "De bona ventura"). From the second half of the fifteenth century on, there was an increasing interest in moralizing Aesopian fables, which culminated in Girolamo Morlini's Latin *Novellae, fabulae, comoedia* (Novellas, Fables, Comedy, 1520), an eclectic mix of short narratives (see pp. 45–51). In addition, fairy-tale compositional techniques inform two other genres of this period that were positioned between oral and literary spheres. The *cantari*, epic or chivalric ballads that in their early form were recited in town squares by minstrels, drew on chansons de geste, novellas, legends, exempla, and current events for their materials. Several *cantari* have an integral fairy-tale structure, such as the anonymous *Il bel Gherardino* (The Fair Gherardino), *Ponzela Gaia* (Merry Ponzela), and *Liombruno* (see pp. 31–44), each of which is structured in two "movements" and abounds in magic and other typical fairy-tale elements. *Sacre rappresentazioni*, or religious dramas, also performed in public venues or churches, had as their subject biblical stories, Christian legends, and saints' lives. Persecution of the innocent was a favorite topic of these dramas, and a number of the best-known ones share plot and structure with common fairy-tale types: *Santa Guglielma* tells of a persecuted wife; *Santa Uliva*, in which a daughter's victimhood includes having her hands cut off, finds correlates in tales by Basile, Perrault, and the Grimms; and the central motif of *Stella*—an evil stepmother—is present in innumerable fairy tales.

The *cantari* were in turn a signal influence on the authored Italian chivalric epics that emerged in this period, and fairy-tale motifs present in the former, such as witches and wizards, fairies, and enchanted objects, migrated to the latter. In Luigi Pulci's comic epic *Morgante* (1483), for instance, we find dragons and ogrish wild men; in particular, the story of Florinetta in canto 19 is quite similar to Basile's "The Flea" (1.4) and "Cannetella" (3.1). Matteo Maria Boiardo's *Orlando innamorato* (*Orlando in Love*, 1495), also a jocose interpretation of the epic tradition, is populated by miraculous animals, ogres, and fairies; Ludovico Ariosto's entire *Orlando furioso* (*The Frenzy of Orlando*, 1516–32), with its interminable search for the elusive female object of desire, is structured like an extended fairy tale.

By the mid-sixteenth century, in short, folkloric and popular motifs and stories were present at all social strata and in multiple storytelling contexts, including but not limited to the elite conversational circles of academies and literary salons. In this letter the Venetian Andrea Calmo paints a picture of what a Renaissance *veglia*, or evening of oral tale-telling attended by community members of all ages and stations, might have felt like:

> Jugs and crusts of bread are passed around, with roast eels that jump as they are cooking, and chestnuts and stewed pears. And everyone sits around swapping the most stupendous tall tales, nonsense, and fanciful stories in the world: they tell of Mother Goose, of the piper, the green bird, the wooden statue, the fairies' chest, the little pigs, the hermit donkey, the wandering mouse, the wolf who became a doctor, and so many fantastic stories that I can't even begin to tell you. (346)

The Birth of the Literary Fairy Tale in Early Modern Italy

With Giovan Francesco Straparola and, especially, Giambattista Basile, the tale types that later dominated the Western fairy-tale tradition assumed their distinctly recognizable form. How and why did a certain form of folk narrative make its way onto the literary stage at this time? Both authors partook in the European novella tradition initiated by Boccaccio, which produced thousands of tales in the centuries following the publication of the *Decameron* and which by the mid-sixteenth century, with the spread of print culture, could count on a growing reading public hungry for novelty. Yet at the same time, the Boccaccian model of generally optimistic bourgeois realism, in which "even the most adventurous and dramatic human experiences culminate in . . . catharsis or reconciliation," was giving way to a more turbulent perspective on human agency, in which "disequilibrium, dissonance, . . . the blind and uncontrolled depths of instinct prevail" (Mazzacurati 108). In this context, not only did a genre like the fairy tale appeal to publishers eager to diversify their offerings, but its consolatory narratives of magical metamorphoses also provided a corrective lens to the grimmer vision of contemporary fare put forth in works such as Matteo Bandello's *Novelle* (Novellas, 1554). Moreover, it fed the growing fascination with marvelous, extraordinary, and rare phenomena and subjects that permeated late Renaissance and Baroque culture and that was to some degree inspired by the intense geographical exploration of this period. The marvelous could also, though, reside in what was close to home, if unfamiliar: the artifacts and proto-anthropological accounts of other worlds that European explorers, colonizers, and missionaries brought back and transmitted to a curious public found a local correlate in the reevaluation of Europe's own "native exotic" folk traditions, and in the efforts of authors like Straparola and Basile (together with Rabelais, Shakespeare, and many others) to transpose folk narratives into the realm of literature. For narrators living at a time in which systems of thought, social organization, and geography were in a state of flux, the attraction to a genre whose central themes revolve around journeys of initiation toward the unknown and miraculous transformations was in many ways a natural one.

We know very little about Giovan Francesco Straparola (ca. 1480–1558), except that he was born in the northern Italian town of Caravaggio and as a young man moved to Venice. "Straparola" itself is a nickname meaning, appropriately for a storyteller, "garrulous" or "bigmouth." Straparola's present-day fame rests on the widely popular novella collection *Le piacevoli* notti (*The Pleasant Nights*), published in two volumes in 1550 and 1553. "A cabinet of literary curiosities," its seventy-four tales include approximately fifteen fairy tales; twenty-three direct translations from Morlini's *Novellae*; novellas with the familiar Boccaccian themes of trickery or amorous intrigue; assorted moral exempla, tragic and heroic tales; and more (Beecher 3). Although Straparola's versions of fairy tales are not as innovative as Basile's experiment with the genre in the following century, there is no doubt that he had a great influence not only on the latter, who reworked several of his tales, but also on Perrault and the Brothers Grimm; most of the fairy tales from *The Pleasant Nights*, in fact, find later counterparts in the above collections and others.

There are no known written sources for Straparola's fairy tales, and notwithstanding the "centuries-long pattern of literary borrowing from story traditions of the 'folk,'" his tales may be the first "hard evidence of their existence in the oral culture of the Renaissance" (Beecher 38, 39). It is not hard to imagine that in the rich culture of Renaissance storytelling, in which "every village and town had its raconteurs, . . . and stories were told at all echelons of society, from hovel to court," Straparola found an ample supply of raw material (44). At the same time, Straparola is still firmly entrenched in the novella tradition, and in his fairy tales realistic and fantastic elements uniquely merge.

If Straparola, in his role as "anthologizer of popular materials," may perhaps be considered Europe's "founder of literary ethnography" (Beecher 8, 7), his tales are no match for the spectacularly original narratives of *The Tale of Tales*, which definitively established the new narrative prototype of the literary fairy tale. The Neapolitan Giambattista Basile (1575?–1632), like many men of letters of his time, spent much of his life as an itinerant courtier and pen-for-hire and was relatively successful at it. Today, however, he is remembered for his projects devoted to the popular culture and narratives of Naples and southern Italy: *Le muse napoletane* (The Neapolitan Muses, 1635); and *Lo cunto de li cunti overo lo trattenemiento de' peccerille* (*The Tale of Tales, or Entertainment for Little Ones*), the latter today recognized as one of the standout works of the Italian seventeenth century.

Basile's rich storehouse of fairy-tale motifs, themes, and tale types includes the earliest literary versions of the now classic tale types known as Cinderella, Sleeping Beauty, Snow White, Rapunzel, Hansel and Gretel, and others and is distinctive on many fronts. It was written in the nonstandard Neapolitan dialect, a choice that underscores the collection's roots in oral culture; Basile wrote his tales in the same language he would have heard them. At the same time, Basile transformed his "raw" materials into tales distinguished by the rhetorical pyrotechnics so beloved to the Baroque aesthetic, a raunchy comic verve, and a poetics of the grotesque that frequently relies on sex, violence, and the absurd to shock and awe (as well as delight!) his readers. One of the most stunning aspects of this text is, in fact, its ability to meld high and low registers and aesthetics, to bring together the marvelous and the all too real in a thrillingly precarious balance. In addition, the encyclopedic references to the sites, customs, everyday rituals, and popular art forms of Basile's time make his collection a veritable treasure trove of anthropological information on seventeenth-century Naples and southern Italy.

Despite its subtitle of "Entertainment for Little Ones," Basile's collection was not written for children, who did not become the target audience for fairy tales until much later. The pervasive wordplay, urbane manipulation of Baroque conceit, and racy content that led Italo Calvino to call Basile "a deformed Neapolitan Shakespeare . . . in whose work the sublime blends with the coarse and the sordid" clearly begs a sophisticated audience (xiii). It is presumed, in fact, that Basile's tales initially circulated orally and/or in manuscript form in the academies and courts around Naples that he frequented and in which they were read or performed as entertainment.

Both content and style provide surprises for the first-time reader of *The Tale of Tales*. Basile's heroes, heroines, and antagonists are not the flat fairy-tale characters devoid of psychological depth that have been described by Max Lüthi and other scholars but rather flesh-and-blood creatures involved both in the affairs of daily life and in more marvelous adventures. They emote and are long-winded about it; they express affection and passion and have sex and revel in it; they are cruel and vengeful; they whine and complain, gossip, browbeat, and nag—in short, everything that we have always suspected is behind the refractive exteriors of the more famous Cinderellas and Sleeping Beauties. Nor do Basile's protagonists always present unflawed models of exemplary behavior as they make their way through a moral universe that often resembles the troubled world in which Basile himself lived. Together with the ogres, talking animals, and magic transformations endemic to fairy tales, Basile's tales feature the quests of well-identifiable types of the dog-eat-dog society of seventeenth-century Italy: backstabbing courtiers, title-buying arrivistes, deficient royals, shady innkeepers, smooth-talking thieves, and opportunists of every stripe. The fairy tale, which in some of its more familiar forms depicts "the surmounting of obstacles, the harmonious solution of all problems, . . . mastering the art of life" (Rohrich 209), finds its very foundations cracked in a striking number of Basile's tales, in which happy endings are complicated by unresolved subplots, irregular paradigms of protagonism, and the intrusion of the uncontrollable or the arbitrary.

In the murky moral world of some of Basile's tales, violence and deception may or may not prove to be winning strategies, and royals driven by unbridled desire become embroiled in cruel and petty pursuits. Other tales, though, present different paradigms. Some celebrate the inevitable force of love, youth, and sexual vitality (compare, e.g., "Petrosinella" [2.1] to the Grimms' "Rapunzel"), and noble-spirited and kind heroes populate others. But so do winning protagonists who operate according to a completely different logic, or lack of logic, and seemingly possess few redeeming qualities ("The Tale of the Ogre" [1.1]; "Peruonto" [1.3]; "Vardiello" [1.4]). On the contrary, there are a surprising number of female protagonists whose intelligence substitutes for the magic that lesser heroes need. These heroines succeed in turning events to their advantage, often in spite of hostile family members and male counterparts whose social class and power exceed their own ("Viola" [2.3]; "Sapia" [5.6]). Conventional antagonists (and in particular, ogres) naturally also figure in Basile's skewed fairy-tale universe, sometimes occupying the surprising role of enlightened commentators on the sad state of civilized society.

The authors of these experiments with a new, noncanonical form could not and did not have the same role in the "civilizing process" as did later authors such as the Brothers Grimm, who through their tales intervened in debates on national identity, popular culture, and the legacy of the "folk" but also helped to establish a canon of literature, appropriate for both adults and children, that could entertain but also educate. As fashioners of a genre yet without conventions and without a clear position in the system of literary institutions, the early fabulists, and in particular Basile, were able to engage more freely in what Jack Zipes has termed the "art of subversion." And just as the "topsy-turvy" hierarchies of *The Tale of Tales* are part and parcel of Basile's idiosyncratic brand of the marvelous, they also insinuate a vigorous dialogue with the here and now. In the words of the twentieth-century Neapolitan writer Domenico Rea, "It may look like Basile is just telling stories, but in reality he is describing the horror of our life down here. . . . There is no pleasure and no brutality that is not contemplated there" (262). The power of attraction of fairy tales like Basile's for a contemporary audience lies precisely in this: just as they document our very real human needs for directives and happy endings, their heroes and heroines are at the same time often prevented by the messy and incomplete business of living in a complicated and at times barely comprehensible world from reaching those endings, or from reaching them by conventional means.

Sleeping Beauty: The Italian Fairy Tale after Basile

In the century following its first publication, *The Tale of Tales* went through at least six reeditions. Yet even if Basile's work inspired much admiration, there were few further experiments with the genre within Italy. Italy saw no phenomenon parallel to the enormous production and popularity of fairy tales in late-seventeenth-century and eighteenth-century France, which resulted in the institutionalization of the genre and culminated in the forty-one-volume *Le Cabinet des fées* (The Cabinet of Fairies, 1785–86), a compilation of tales written and collected over the previous hundred years. Basile's contemporary and friend Giulio Cesare Cortese included several fairy-tale episodes in his *Viaggio di Parnaso* (Voyage to Parnassus, 1620), one of which closely resembles the first tale of *The Tale of Tales*, which was probably already in progress at this time. The Neapolitan Salvatore Rosa made reference to some of the themes present in Basile's collection in his *Satire* (Satires), written in midcentury, and in Lorenzo Lippi's' mock epic *Malmantile riacquistato* (Malmantile Recaptured, 1676) we also find an episode borrowed from Basile. The only other collection of fairy tales to appear in seventeenth-century Italy, though, is Pompeo Sarnelli's little-known *Posilecheata* (An Outing to Posillipo, 1684), composed of five fairy tales told in Neapolitan dialect by peasant women at the end of the country banquet that the frame story narrates.

It was nearly a century and a half after Basile before another major Italian fairy-tale opus saw the light. Perhaps influenced by the incorporation of fairy tales into Parisian *foire* theater several decades earlier, the Venetian Carlo Gozzi published, from 1760 to 1770, his ten *Fiabe teatrali* (Fairy Tales for the Theater). The particularity of Gozzi's plays lies in their juxtaposition of fairy tales and the conventions, improvisational techniques, and masks of the commedia dell'arte, a mix that, somewhat paradoxically, could result in the transformation of the humor of his sources into a more intellectual interpretation of the marvelous. Gozzi, a political conservative and literary traditionalist, wrote his satirical and moralistic plays in polemic with his archrival Carlo Goldoni's dramas of bourgeois realism and considered his own fairy-tale subjects as negligible "children's" themes chosen precisely for their distance from the everyday world depicted in Goldoni's plays, as well as for their ability to stimulate curiosity and surprise rather than psychological tension or substantial reflection. Nonetheless, Gozzi's *Fiabe* proved to be quite interesting from a theatrical point of view, as is evidenced by their subsequent adaptation in operas by Wagner, Busoni, Puccini, von Weber, and Prokofiev, among others.

The Golden Age of the Italian Fairy Tale

The early-nineteenth-century Romantic interest in archaic popular traditions, which in the eyes of scholars such as the Brothers Grimm most genuinely represented the "spirit of a nation," in Italy expressed itself primarily in the study of folk songs and oral poetry and in investigations of popular customs and beliefs. Fairy tales were generally not included in this first phase of research. Only later in the century, during the period of Italian Unification (1860–70), did tales and legends become the focus of positivistic and comparativistic scholarly studies and ethnographic collections, which began to be published in the following decade. Among the first collections of fairy tales to appear were Laura Gonzenbach's *Sicilianische Märchen* (*Sicilian Fairy Tales*, 1870) and Vittorio Imbriani's *Novellaja fiorentina* (Florentine Tales, 1871) and *Novellaja milanese* (Milanese Tales, 1872); these were followed by what is arguably the most important Italian collection of the century, the four-volume *Fiabe novelle e racconti popolari siciliani* (Sicilian Fairy Tales, Novellas, and Popular Tales, 1875) by Giuseppe Pitrè. From the last decades of the nineteenth century to the beginning of the twentieth century, many other collections followed and would later become precious documents for anthologists of Italian fairy tales such as Italo Calvino. These included Carolina Coronedi-Berti's *Novelle popolari bolognesi* (Bolognese Popular Tales, 1874), Domenico Comparetti's *Novelline popolari italiane* (Italian Popular Tales, 1875), Isaia Visentini's *Fiabe mantovane* (Mantuan Fairy Tales, 1879), Gherardo Nerucci's *Sessanta novelle popolari montalesi* (Sixty Popular Tales from Montale, 1880), Pietro Pellizzari's *Fiabe e canzoni popolari del contado di Maglie in terra d'Otranto* (Fairy Tales and Popular Songs from the Countryside of Maglie in Terra d'Otranto, 1881), Antonio De Nino's *Fiabe* (Fairy Tales, 1883), Pitré's *Novelle popolari toscane* (Tuscan Popular Tales, 1888), Domenico Giuseppe Bernoni's *Fiabe popolari veneziane* (Venetian Popular Fairy Tales, 1893), Giggi Zannazzo's *Novelle, favole e leggende romanesche* (Roman Tales, Fables, and Legends, 1907), and Letterio di Francia's *Fiabe e novelle calabresi* (Calabrian Fairy Tales and Stories, 1929–31). Most of these scholars espoused rigorous (at least for their times) standards for transcribing the material they collected in the field, and when taken together, these volumes offer a truly fascinating glimpse not only of a type of traditional storytelling that no longer survives in Italy but also, in many cases, of a "submerged" history of nineteenth-century rural and working-class Italy.

Of the important fairy-tale collectors, anthologizers, and scholars who crowded the nineteenth century, Laura Gonzenbach (1842–78) and Giuseppe Pitrè (1841–1916) are represented in this volume. Gonzenbach's and Pitrè's tales should be considered in the context of post-Unification Italy, when the "Southern Question," a constant in Italian history, was exacerbated as attempts were made to forge a precarious national identity. In a sense, these scholars' work constitutes an attempt to counter stereotypes of Sicilian and southern regional identity—as backward, fatalistic, "other"—by collecting everyday, if marvelous, tales of survival and adaptation.

Gonzenbach, who was born to a Swiss German family in Messina and lived in Sicily for most of her life, was a self-taught student of folklore and began to collect what would become the *Sicilianische Märchen* (1870) when a German scholar asked her to send him several Sicilian narratives; for this reason she transcribed the tales not into the Sicilian dialect in which she heard them but rather into High German. Gonzenbach collected the tales predominantly from lower- and middle-class women, and in many cases they offer a distinctly female perspective that features cunning heroines, cruel vendettas on men who mistreat women, and, in general, details of the daily life of women that are not as evident in other collections.

Giuseppe Pitrè, who played a central role in establishing the systematic study of folklore in Italy, cultivated a lifelong attention to the history, customs, mentalities, and, above all, cultural production of the Sicilian common people. This interest stemmed from his conviction that "the hidden history of the Sicilian folk constituted the hidden treasure of Sicilian culture" (Zipes 7) and that their tale-telling in particular formed an important, and often subversive, corrective to the master narratives of official history. He was thus particularly observant of how the Sicilian narrators whose narratives he transcribed adapted common fairy-tale motifs to fit their own particular contexts. Many of Pitrè's tales, published in the Sicilian dialect in which he heard them, model strategies for getting by under the most difficult of conditions; their protagonists do what they have to do to improve their lot by using the only resources they can truly count on, the ones that no one can steal from them: street smarts, quick wits, and a keen hunger that impels them to use these resources in the most effective way possible.

Writers in the last decades of the nineteenth century benefited from the huge amount of "prime materials" newly at their disposal to produce highly creative elaborations of fairy tales. Foremost among these is Carlo Collodi, whose initiation into fairy-tale writing took the form of his 1875 translation of tales by Perrault and other French fabulists, by that point canonical texts. Collodi's classic novel *Le avventure di Pinocchio: Storia di un burattino* (*The Adventures of Pinocchio: Story of a Puppet*, 1883) is one of the best-known and best-selling Italian works in the world. *Pinocchio* tells of how its eponymous protagonist, a wooden puppet, is induced both by the harsh socioeconomic conditions in which he lives and by his own cheerfully transgressive nature to undergo a series of perilous adventures that eventually lead to his transformation into a real boy. *Pinocchio* shares with the fairy tale its structure of a journey of initiation fraught with obstacles that ultimately leads to rebirth on the higher plane of adulthood, along with the common motifs of a fairy godmother, talking animals, magical helpers and donors, and other marvelous beings. Yet it also has much in common with the more realistic genres of the picaresque novel, the moralizing family drama so prevalent in children's literature of this period, and even the Bildungsroman, or novel of formation. And quite differently from the bowdlerized, reduced versions of *Pinocchio*, the best known of which is Disney's 1940 film, the puppet's adventures are essentially traumatic. The social world that Collodi depicts is colored by privation, violence, and indifference, and even in the more intimate, familial sphere, self-interest and cruelty often reign. *Pinocchio* has, in fact, been considered an "anti-Cinderella" tale, for even when social validation arrives through self-sacrifice and acceptance of a strict work ethic, it is far from the enchanted happy ending of fairy tales. Ultimately, though, perhaps *Pinocchio*'s lasting attraction has less to do with any satisfaction deriving from the puppet's metamorphosis into a responsible member of society than with the affirmation of the unleashed vitality and deep humanity of childhood, of which Pinocchio gives constant and poignant proof up to the very last chapter. Collodi's grand experiment with fairy-tale motifs and types was one of the first in Italy to be written explicitly for a young audience and remains an irresistible point of reference up to this day.

The birth of *Pinocchio* coincided with the publication of the Sicilian Luigi Capuana's first and most important volume of original fairy tales, *C'era una volta* (Once Upon a Time, 1882), which would later be followed by many other collections. Capuana used his familiarity with Sicilian folklore and with the work of folklorists such as Pitrè to create tales that often evoked, in tone and in structure, the formulaic oral tales of tradition. But it is his elaboration of these materials through the use of irony, humor, and whimsical fantasy that gives his tales their true flavor and makes for the creation of a fairy-tale world that is entirely and originally his own. Capuana's tales offer typical fairy-tale motifs and sequences, but they also abound in more realistic details. Sicilian landscapes and domestic scenes are lovingly depicted, even the most fantastic characters have surprisingly earthy characteristics, and humble protagonists are consumed by their primary needs of food, shelter, and good health. In the triumph of the virtues possessed by his lower-class heroes—perseverance, goodness of heart, and humility, often accompanied also by a good dose of irreverence and *furbizia* (cunning)—we may glimpse not only Capuana's own allegiances but also a dream of social compensation common to many fairy-tale writers of this time.

Emma Perodi's and Grazia Deledda's experimentations with the genre, which close the nineteenth century and open the twentieth century, also offer a more personal interpretation of the fairy-tale tradition. Perodi, who hailed from Tuscany, worked as a journalist and children's writer for most of her life and published numerous fairy-tale collections. The tales of her best-known work, *Le novelle della nonna: fiabe fantastiche* (Grandmother's Stories: Fantastic Fairy Tales, 1892), many of which draw on fairy-tale motifs, are framed by a realistic narrative centered on the life of the Marcuccis, an extended peasant family of the Casentino, in the Tuscan countryside. The first of forty-five tales is told around the family hearth on Christmas Eve by the designated storyteller, Regina, and they continue into the following October. As the tales unfold, the Marcucci family's own stories intervene; indeed, Regina often chooses her tales on the basis of the consolation or instruction that they may offer to members of the family. In Perodi's tales we find a vividly expressive style that juxtaposes domestic scenarios, uncanny fantastic topographies, and gothically tinged medieval landscapes to create an atmosphere dominated by the bizarre and the macabre. Grazia Deledda, who in 1926 was the first Italian woman to receive the Nobel Prize in Literature, was born in Sardinia, and is less known for her works based on fairy tales than as a major fiction writer of the early twentieth century. Yet she had a lifelong interest in Sardinian folklore, and her own stories that qualify as fairy tales, such as "Fairy Tale," included in this volume, are often "meta-tales" that adopt traditional motifs to weave melancholic reflections on the impossibility of attaining happy endings.

Numerous other authors, and in particular female authors, who do not appear here revisited fairy-tale tradition in suggestive ways in this period rich in rediscovery of traditional material. These include Gabriele d'Annunzio, Cesare Causa, Adriano Salani, Epaminonda Provaglio, Carolina Invernizio, Carolina Isolani, Maria Messina, and Amalia Guglielminetti. This volume includes two tales by Guido Gozzano, also of this period, best known as a poet who aspired to "little, serene things" and whose poetry was veined with themes of nostalgia and, later in his life when he was debilitated by tuberculosis, sickness and death. The fairy tales (nearly twenty-five of them) that in his later years he penned alongside of his poetry express an urgent desire for happiness that was not attainable in his own life or in the dramatic historical context in which he lived, the years around World War I.

By this time fairy tales had also spread from the stage of prose theater to become popular material for the opera, orchestra, and dance stage as well, in Italy and in other European countries. Among the many operas of Gioacchino Rossini (1792–1868) is the two-act *La Cenerentola* (Cinderella, 1817), whose libretto by Jacopo Ferretti was adapted from Charles Perrault's fairy tale. In Rossini and Ferretti's version of this tale, Angelina (Cinderella) is maltreated by her father, Don Magnifico, and her stepsisters, Clorinda and Tisbe. Prince Ramiro, disguised as his own servant, falls in love with Angelina, and the prince's tutor, Alidoro, has the role of magic helper as he assists Angelina in her attempt to go to the prince's ball. Angelina finally proves that she is the object of the prince's desire by means of a silver bracelet, a variation on the glass slipper found in Perrault's tale. The other Italian composer most engaged with fairy-tale themes was Giacomo Puccini (1858–1924), whose 1926 opera *Turandot* (libretto by Adami and Simoni) was based on Carlo Gozzi's play of the same name (1762), itself in part adapted from the *Arabian Nights*. The plot revolves around Princess Turandot's promise to marry whomever can answer the three riddles that she poses.

By the end of the nineteenth century the Italian fairy-tale landscape had richly transformed due to a number of interlinked factors: as in the rest of Europe, a new sensitivity to the role that folk and popular culture (then often understood as the mostly oral or undocumented production of the lower classes) had, and should have, in the rearticulation of national heritages; the formation of the discipline of folklore studies; the excavation of folkloric narrative traditions in the form of collecting and publishing projects and the subsequent use of this material to fuel new literary experiments; and the ongoing dialogue with what had become established as the European fairy-tale canon—which by this time included Perrault, Andersen, and the Brothers Grimm.

Italo Calvino's *Italian Folktales* and the Role of Folklore in Postwar Italy

By the start of World War I, the flurry of collection and compilation of tales had died down somewhat, although important reworkings of the genre continued, with authors such as Sto (Sergio Tofano), Antonio Baldini, and Tommaso Landolfi. In the realm of children's literature, which at this point was an established genre, fairy tales did not feature foremost during the twenty years of the fascist regime, which tended instead to feature works with a surrealist or superheroic bent.

After World War II, interest in traditional narrative resurged. The rediscovery of folklore from the various Italian regions was characterized, on the one hand, by a more painstakingly philological approach to source materials and, on the other, by an attempt to identify the distribution of tale types within cultural and/or geographical areas of Italy. In addition to the newly invigorated upsurge in folkloric research, two towering figures of twentieth-century Italian intellectual life, the philosophers Benedetto Croce and Antonio Gramsci, significantly redirected folkloric and fairy-tale scholarship, even if from very different positions. Croce, above all in his seminal studies of Basile's *Tale of Tales* published in the first decades of the century, maintained that the investigation of folktales as historical and aesthetic entities should supersede questions of origin or comparativistic analysis of motifs, and thus opened the door, especially as far as authored fairy tales were concerned, to a full-fledged literary analysis of fairy tales. Gramsci, in his 1935 essay "Observations on Folklore," put forth the idea that popular folklore expressed a "concept of the world" radically different from hegemonic worldviews present in "official" culture, especially in Italy, where, due to the particularities of its political and cultural history, an authentically national heritage based on a connection between the *popolo* and intellectuals had never come to be.

Gramsci's ideas in particular were influential in the postwar landscape, when folklorists, ethnologists, and literary scholars such as Giuseppe Cocchiara, Ernesto de Martino, Paolo Toschi, and Alberto Cirese engaged in discussions on the relation of Italian folklore to national culture. The imperative to recover and creatively reevaluate the voices of many different Italies in the form of previously marginalized folkloric heritages, after decades in which a grandiose mythology of "national culture" had been imposed from above by means of the propagandistic rhetoric and symbolic practices of fascism, was considered by many an essential ingredient of a revised model of national unity. Such a model would promote, it was hoped, a shared cultural identity that might finally be truly inclusive, providing a catalyst for increased consciousness in the subaltern classes whose active role folkloric narratives often celebrate. This sort of thinking was just as far from the nineteenth-century Romantic conceptualization of the spontaneous and genuine popular "spirit" as it was radically different from the instrumental "reinvention" and idealization of folklore during the fascist regime (e.g., by the Comitato nazionale per le tradizioni popolari), which generally aimed to "promote a compact sense of popular identity in order to form a more easily controllable collectivity" (Calabresi 3). In particular, the period 1948–55 was an extremely fertile one for the discipline of folklore, in terms of fieldwork and publishing and, in general, of discussions on how to "preserve and recodify" popular traditions. It is fascinating, moreover, how much of the ongoing conversation about the role of the committed writer in the "new," postwar Republic included discussions of folklore; in the words of Stefano Calabresi, "Folklore acquired dignity as a field of study and, above all, lent itself as an instrument with which to investigate the organicity and contradictions of the present cultural system" (2).

In Italy, the Turin publisher Einaudi was at the forefront of these initiatives. The "Classics of the Fairy Tale" series, a subset of the Einaudi "Millenni" series, was inaugurated with the publication of *The 1001 Nights* in 1948 and continued into the early 1950s with editions of the Grimms and Andersen, as well as of African, Russian, and French fairy tales. At the same time, numerous regional indices, such as G. D'Aronco's *Indice delle fiabe toscane* (Index of Tuscan Fairy Tales, 1953), facilitated consideration of the geographic specificities of the Italian tale types. Yet, differently from most other European countries at the time and notwithstanding the new tale collections and the theoretical reflections on the material contained therein, a definitive national collection of Italian tales, akin to that of the Grimms, was still lacking. This was the context in which, in 1954, Italo Calvino, by the postwar period already emerging as one of the most promising, and experimental, writers of this generation, was commissioned by Einaudi to assemble such a master collection. And thus the project of the *Fiabe italiane* (*Italian Folktales*, 1956) was born, motivated by the desire to transport tales previously dispersed in little-known collections and written in impenetrable dialects to the literary mainstream, making accessible Italy's rich heritage of folk narrative in a way that it had never been before. The two hundred tales (just as in the Grimms) of Calvino's now classic *Italian Folktales* were chosen with the criteria of offering every major tale type, of which they include about fifty, often in multiple versions, and of representing the twenty regions of Italy.

In the introduction to his collection, Calvino comments on how so many Italian folktales have as their realistic point of departure "dire need, hunger, or unemployment" and how together these tales "appear like fragments of an epic of laborers," a not so oblique reference to how pertinent this genre could be in a period—the late 1950s—that for Italy was one of intense industrialization, mass internal migration, and pressing problems of socioeconomic inequality.

Something Old, Something New: Fairy Tales for Our Times

In the introduction to *Italian Folktales*, Calvino also exhorts his readers to consult the original sources he used and scholars to publish the tales they contain. In the last half century, this challenge has been met on multiple fronts, in the form of reeditions of the classic nineteenth-century collections, new regional compilations of tales and indices of tale types, and innovative "retellings" of traditional tales by well-known contemporary authors. Comprehensive indexing tools, such as Domenic P. Rotunda's *Motif-Index of the Italian Novella in Prose* (1942, rev. 1962) and, more recently, Renato Aprile's *Indice delle fiabe popolari italiane di magia* (Index of Popular Italian Tales of Magic, 2000), have offered scholars precious resources. In the 1960s and 1970s, a regionwide initiative on the part of the State Discoteca resulted in a vast amount of new material collected in the field. In subsequent decades, Mondadori embarked on the ambitious project (1982–90) of publishing a series of sixteen volumes dedicated to the fairy tales of the various Italian regions, in each of which an author and scholar teamed up to translate and edit the material. In initiatives like this and others, "the ideological aspect of the operation," in which "the nostalgia of preserving the past by taking stock of it meets and mingles ambiguously with the commitment to stimulate the awakening of consciousness in a subaltern culture whose potentially active role is recognized," coexists with the aim of "transferring a regional or even more local cultural originality into the context of national culture" (Aristodemo and de Meijer 712). Another significant series of projects was undertaken by the composer, conductor, and ethnomusicologist Roberto De Simone, whose immensely successful *La gatta Cenerentola* (The Cinderella Cat, 1976), a musical based on Basile's seventeenth-century tale, incorporates popular songs of Basile's own time with original variations on the modern folk repertoire of the Naples area. In 1994 Simone also published *Fiabe campane: I novantanove racconti delle dieci notti* (Fairy Tales from Campania: The Ninety-Nine Tales of the Ten Nights), the result of twenty years spent tape-recording oral storytellers in the Campania region of Italy.

In the past half century there have also been noteworthy experiments with refashioning the classic fairy-tale canon for children. The children's author and pioneer of pedagogical reform Gianni Rodari included, in his groundbreaking *Grammatica della fantasia* (*The Grammar of Fantasy*, 1973), a theoretical discussion of how fairy tales could assume a creative and liberating function in the hands of both children and educators. Rodari's own most suggestive encounters with fairy tales, such as *Favole al telefono* (*Telephone Tales*, 1962), *Tante storie per giocare* (Lots of Stories for Play, 1971) and *C'era due volte il barone Lamberto* (*Lamberto, Lamberto, Lamberto*, 1978), have served as models for other authors who have, over the past decades, continued to create innovative works that take on contemporary social and political issues within the narrative framework of the fairy tale. Among these are Beatrice Solinas Donghi, whose playful approach to tradition is most evident in *Le fiabe incatenate* (Linked Fairy Tales, 1967) and *La gran fiaba intrecciata* (The Great Interlaced Fairy Tale, 1972); Bianca Pitzorno, whose revisitation of fairy-tale commonplaces focuses on the development of positive female protagonists, as in *L'incredibile storia di Lavinia* (The Incredible Story of Lavinia, 1985), *La bambola dell'alchimista* (The Alchemist's Doll, 1988), and *Streghetta mia* (My Little Witch, 1988); Roberto Piumini, whose extensive fairy-tale production includes innovative tales that engage with the social transformations and political myths of our time, such as *Il giovane che entrava nel palazzo* (The Youth Who Entered the Palace) and *Fiabe da Perserèn* (Fairy Tales from Perseren), both written in the early 1980s; and Luigi Malerba, whose *Pinocchio con gli stivali* (Pinocchio in Boots, 1977), included in this volume, is a pastiche in which a modern Pinocchio encounters classic fairy-tale characters such as Little Red Riding Hood and Cinderella. Significant have also been initiatives like the 1975 anthology *Favole su favole* (Fairy Tales upon

Fairy Tales), in which well-known contemporary writers and poets offer "free" retellings of fairy tales of their regions.

Fairy tales, ever concerned with metamorphoses, rites of initiation, and thorny familial and societal conflicts, seem a genre made to order for times of shifting identities. Their prototypical stories of young adults who leave home, undergo arduous journeys and trials, and are compelled to confront the threats and the challenges of the unknown dramatize well the departure from familiar landscapes that accompanies periods of historical and cultural upheaval. It is no coincidence, I believe, that the three most significant moments in Italian fairy-tale history occur at pivotal moments of construction, deconstruction, or reconfiguration of national identity: in Straparola's and Basile's time, the sixteenth and seventeenth centuries, a period of crisis and change when the cultural centrality of Renaissance Italy was ebbing, at the same time that the coordinates of modernity were taking shape; in Pitrè's and Collodi's time, the years around Unification in the nineteenth century, when despite its new political identity Italy still struggled to reconcile its historically diverse regional identities and to manage a generalized state of social and economic fragmentation; and in Calvino's time, the period following World War II and twenty years of fascist rule, in which questions about national identity re-presented themselves in full force. In a letter to folklorist Giuseppe Cocchiara, Calvino exclaimed, "It was me—poor me!—to whom Einaudi had assigned this task of 'unification,'" referring to the still fragile project of "making Italy" but also to the potential contribution that such a collection might make to this very project.

The distinct interface that is at the heart of the fairy tale—expression of individual and local identities but also collective, shared narrative heritage—has long made the fairy tale a special vehicle for examining and reflecting on what it means to become, and to remain part of, a larger community. If the cataloging of popular tales in the second half of the nineteenth century was in some sense a response to national unification and the inevitable weakening of local traditions that its linguistic and educational standardization would bring, so today the cultural homogenization that our late industrial, globalized society thrives on makes the need to retrieve the narrative remnants of local heritages seem even more urgent. Not out of a romantic nostalgia for preserving the past but with the hope that the cultures that produced these traditions may regain their distinct vitality and continue to tell their life-affirming tales and to reflect, across the most diverse spectrum of here and nows, on what sort of behavior may, or should, lead to a happy ending, both for the individual and for the larger community. Or to reflect on whether a happy ever after is even, at the end, the best road to follow.

About This Volume

This volume presents a translated anthology of fairy tales selected from the principal authors of the Italian fairy-tale tradition; chronologically, it covers from the fourteenth to the twenty-first centuries. It includes many tales that are easily recognizable variants of well-known tale types, however embellished (e.g., Basile), but also, especially from the nineteenth century on, original tales that utilize classic types as inspirations rather than direct models. Most of the tales included here are literary, bearing the idiosyncratic mark of an individual author, with the partial exceptions of Laura Gonzenbach's and Giuseppe Pitrè's tales. There exists an entire other corpus of tales that were collected in oral form from informants and transcribed (such as the ones published by Gonzenbach and Pitrè), which could constitute a volume onto itself. As mentioned earlier, many of these collections date from the nineteenth century, though significant initiatives of this sort appeared in the mid-twentieth century as well.

Several of the classic collections of Italian tales (Basile, Gonzenbach, Pitrè) have, over the past decades, been translated, and a new curiosity toward the Italian tradition has emerged outside of the field of Italian studies. But many works still remain untranslated and therefore inaccessible to an English-speaking public. Instructors who teach, or would like to teach, a panoramic survey course on the Italian fairy tale find themselves having to limit their choices due to what can be found in translation and/or to piece together course readers from the materials that are available in an array of volumes published at different times and translated with varying degrees of success. Making a comprehensive sampling of Italian tales accessible to an English-speaking public will also, I hope, encourage a revisitation of the fairy-tale canon (Perrault, the Grimms, Andersen, Disney, et al.) in light of some of the most fascinating material that has been excluded from it.

Each author is introduced by a short essay that builds upon the information offered in the general introduction; a list of suggested further reading that includes both primary and secondary sources concludes each section. The notes preceding and accompanying the translated texts offer explanation of cultural references, as well as information on ATU tale types and similar tales by other authors. In choosing the tales, I have tried to achieve a balance between offering a wide variety of tale types, both very familiar and less so, and including different variants of the same tale type. A general bibliography of works relevant to studying the Italian fairy tale can be found at the end of the volume.

A word on ATU classification. The acronym refers to the three-volume *The Types of International Folktales: A Classification and Bibliography* by Hans-Jörg Uther, published in 2004. Uther builds on, updates, and expands the historical and international coverage of the system previously created by Aanti Aarne in 1910 and revised by Stith Thompson in 1928 and 1961. The ATU is a catalog of familiar narrative sequences, each of which is made up of constellations of motifs: for example, ATU tale type 310 is The Maiden in the Tower, or Rapunzel; ATU 333 is Little Red Riding Hood; and so forth. Each entry in the catalog includes information on combinations (other types or episodes commonly found with the type in question), general remarks, secondary literature on the type, and worldwide variants. The index contains nearly twenty-five hundred tale types, although most of what we consider to be fairy tales are found in the "Tales of Magic" section (types 300–749); other groupings include "Animal Tales," "Religious Tales," "Realistic Tales," "Tales of the Stupid Ogre," "Anecdotes and Jokes," and "Formula Tales." The ATU system is an indispensable starting point for studies of tale types, allowing scholars to compare variants across time and space as well as across both oral and literary traditions. It is often used in tandem with the *Motif-Index of Folk-Literature*, created by Stith Thompson in 1932–36 and revised and expanded in 1955–58. The *Motif-Index* is a catalog of thousands of motifs, or the smaller building blocks of tale types (e.g., motif H36.1: "slipper test"; motif F848.1: "girl's long hair as ladder into tower"). I have included an appendix that references all the ATU tale types that appear in the volume.

Translation of so many authors with vastly different styles has presented a particular challenge. At one extreme are ultra-literary authors like

Giambattista Basile, for whom the negotiation between canonical literary tradition and the formulas of orality results in a playful but complex "hybrid" text; at the other are tales that simulate or attempt to reproduce orality. I have resisted the temptation to hyper-translate or overcorrect when the Italian text sounds unpolished to the modern ear; this may be due, for example, to the author's own stylistic quirks or to the fact that an initially nonliterary text, with its distinctive narrative norms and formulas, was transcribed or otherwise internalized. In Straparola's *Pleasant Nights*, for instance, what can seem like clumsy repetition and stylistic "roughness" is, perhaps, part and parcel with his attraction to the materials of oral folk narrative and his status as the first author to introduce fairy tales into a literary collection. On the other hand, a text like Basile's is replete with flamboyant description and metaphor; proverbial expressions referring to arcane objects or practices; and long word lists of fish, birds, children's games, and the like—all of which create an "estranging" effect that might tempt (and has tempted) a translator to "domesticate" the text. Doing so might ease a modern reader's entrance into the text, but it would also betray the text's dizzying originality. With the folktales of the nineteenth century transcribed from oral sources (such as those in Gonzenbach's and Pitrè's collections), it seemed imperative to me to preserve certain particularities of oral storytelling, such as breaking from the narrative world to address the surrounding extradiegetic audience and the use of formulaic repetitions. And twentieth-century texts written for young audiences, such as those by Rodari, adopt a creative and lighthearted play of language that has its own challenges, such as nonsensical names and puns.

When translating proper names, I have usually preserved the Italian in the case of simple names (e.g., Pietro). When a name is descriptive of certain characteristics and thus carries more specific meaning, I offer both the original and the English translation the first time it appears but usually tend to use the Italian thereafter (e.g., Piumadoro / Golden Feather).

Finally, all translations are my own, except for those of Giorgio Manganelli's "Eighty-One" and the eight tales by Italo Calvino. I am grateful to McPherson & Company for granting me the permission to use Henry Martin's wonderful translation of Manganelli's tale. Since it was not possible to obtain translation rights for Calvino, I thank Harper Collins for granting me permission to use George Martin's 1980 translations from *Italian Folktales* and William Weaver's translation of "The Forest on the Superhighway."

Works Cited

Anderson, Graham. *Fairytale in the Ancient World.* New York: Routledge, 2000.

Aristodemo, Dina, and Pieter de Meijer. "Le fiabe popolari fra cultura regionale e cultura nazionale." *Belfagor* 34, no. 6 (1979): 711–16.

Beecher, Donald. "Introduction." In Giovan Francesco Straparola, *The Pleasant Nights*, ed. Donald Beecher. Toronto: University of Toronto Press, 2012. 3–140.

Boccaccio, Giovanni. *The Genealogy of the Pagan Gods.* Trans. Suzanne Magnanini. In *Fairy Tales Framed: Early Forewords, Afterwords, and Critical Words*, ed. Ruth B. Bottigheimer. Albany: State University of New York Press, 2012. 13–21.

Calabresi, Stefano, ed. *Il folklore unplugged: Calvino, Cocchiara, De Martino, Pavese e la tradizone popolare.* Bologna: Archetipolibri, 2008.

Calmo, Andrea. "Lettera a la signora Frondosa." In *Le Lettere di Messer Andrea Calmo*, ed. Vittorio Rossi. 4 vols. Turin: Loescher, 1888. 4:345–50.

Calvino, Italo. *Fiabe italiane.* Turin: Einaudi, 1956.

Haase, Donald. "Fairy Tale." In *The Greenwood Encyclopedia of Folktales and Fairy Tales*, ed. Donald Haase. 3 vols. Westport, CT: Greenwood Press, 2008. 1:322–25.

Mazzacurati, Giancarlo. *Società e strutture narrative (dal Trecentto al Cinquecento).* Naples: Liguori, 1971.

Rea, Domenico. *Il fondaco nudo.* Milan: Rusconi, 1984.

Rohrich, Lutz. *Folktales and Reality.* Trans. Peter Tokofsky. Bloomington: Indiana University Press, 1991.

Tatar, Maria. "Introduction." In *The Classic Fairy Tales*, ed. Maria Tatar. New York: Norton, 1999. ix–xviii.

Thompson, Stith. *The Folktale.* New York: Dryden Press, 1946.

Ziolkowski, Jan. *Fairy Tales from Before Fairy Tales: The Medieval Latin Past of Wonderful Lies.* Ann Arbor: University of Michigan Press, 2009.

Zipes, Jack. "The Indomitable Giuseppe Pitrè." In *The Collected Sicilian Folk and Fairy Tales of Giuseppe Pitrè*, trans. and ed. Jack Zipes and Joseph Russo. 2 vols. New York: Routledge, 2009. 1–20.

PART I

Fairy-Tale Motifs in Early Italian Literature

1

Anonymous

Liombruno belongs to the genre of the *cantari*, oral poems composed predominantly in fourteenth- and fifteenth-century Italy for recitation in streets and squares and collected and published in numerous editions from the fifteenth to the nineteenth centuries. The subject matter of *cantari* ranged from the classic tales of the epic traditions, both ancient (stories of Rome and Troy) and more recent (chivalric material from the Arthurian and Carolingian cycles), to legends and romances, current events, and fantastic and fairy-tale material. The marvelous, abundantly present in the chivalric tradition itself in the form of magical creatures and feats, often takes center stage in the fairy-tale structures and overall atmosphere of the *cantari*. This is especially evident in the best-known examples of the genre, all anonymous: *Il bel Gherardino*, *Ponzela Gaia*, and *Liombruno*. Each of these is structured in two *canti* or "movements" containing about fifty octaves each. In *Il bel Gherardino*, the youngest of three sons squanders his inheritance and must set out to find his fortune; he arrives at the mysterious White Fairy's castle, where he spends three months. He is finally allowed to return home (Rome) with a magic gift, a glove, and the warning not to speak of what happened to him. He disobeys this order, and only by later winning a tournament is he able to be reunited with the White Fairy. *Ponzela Gaia* begins at the court of King Arthur, where there is a competition to see who can bring back the best hunting trophy. Galvano, the hero, encounters a serpent who then becomes a beautiful maiden, Ponzela Gaia, previously transformed by her mother, the Fata Morgana. Galvano returns to court with several magic objects and the prohibition to speak about his adventures, instead brags about his lover, and is condemned to death since he is unable to prove any of it. Ponzela Gaia saves him from death but is transformed back into beastly form; Galvano finally conquers the Fata Morgana and frees Ponzela Gaia.

Further Reading

Primary

Cantari novellistici dal Tre al Cinquecento. Ed. Elisabetta Benucci, R. Manetti, and F. Zabagli. Introd. Domenico de Robertis. 2 vols. Rome: Salerno, 2002. 1:302–39. [source text]

Secondary

Branca, Vittore. "Nostalgie tardogotiche e gusto del fiabesco nella tradizione narrativa dei cantari." In *Studi di varia umanita in onore di Francesco Flora*, ed. Giovanni Battista Pighi et al. Milan: Mondadori, 1963. 88–108.

Lecco, Margherita. "Per uno studio dei cantari fiabeschi italiani." *Romance Studies* 28, no. 1 (2010): 1–16.

Morabito, Raffaele. "The Italian Cantari between Orality and Writing." In *Medieval Oral Literature*, ed. Karl Reichl. Berlin: Walter de Gruyter, 2012. 371–86.

Liombruno

Liombruno *has an overall fairy-tale structure and contains many familiar fairy-tale motifs and episodes, from the poor father who sells off his youngest child to a Bluebeard-like demon; to a supernatural "beastly" creature, the fairy Lady Aquilina, who warns her visitor and then husband, Liombruno, not to stay away too long when he insists on leaving her to visit his family; to the subsequent quest for a lost wife (ATU 400); to the trio of magical objects: a wishing ring, "seven-league" boots, and a cloak of invisibility. As in ATU 425B (Cupid and Psyche), though with the genders reversed, the first part of the story (canto 1) concludes with Liombruno's transgression of Aquilina's order and her abandonment of him as a punishment for this; the second part (canto 2) is devoted to the adventures that finally lead Liombruno to find and be reconciled with her. The role of Aquilina as both antagonist and helper is particularly interesting, as she not only is a lover to Liombruno but raises him from a young age to rise above his humble origins and become a knight, as well as imparting a moral education that includes the inevitable series of trials.*

Liombruno, *like many* cantari, *as well as other epic and romance poems, contains stanzas of ottava rima, or eight verses (ABABABAB). I have opted for a prose translation, in which each paragraph corresponds to an octave. Each of the two cantos begins with an exhortation for God's help in telling the story, which I have omitted. The opening to the second canto includes the verse "I will need to depend on my heart and memory, for I am able neither to read nor to write," underlining the oral origins of the* cantari.

Canto 1

Ladies and gentlemen, I have found that on account of poverty, many people do not arrive where they wish to, and lose their freedom; and that on account of poverty, many despair. Now, if you listen to me, I will tell you, in all truth, the story of a poor man who because of his poverty encountered great peril, and was forced to give his son to the devil.

This poor man was a fisherman, and every day this unlucky man would be out fishing at all hours, for he was never able to catch fish. He no longer owned land or vineyards, but he had three sons to feed, and a wife who was fresher than a rose: he lived off of his fishing, and nothing else.

One morning the good man rose and went off to fish in his boat. He caught nothing the whole day, for which the good man grew worried. He came to a small island in the middle of the sea, where he encountered a terrible demon, who said to him, "What will you give me, if I give you some fish and a good deal of money?"

The good man said, "If you grant that I may catch some fish, I will do whatever you command." And the demon gave him this treacherous advice: "My good man, if you are willing to bring to this island one of your sons, whichever one you choose, and you promise not to trick me, in return I will give you fish, a large quantity of money, and silver and gold."

The good man was aggrieved, but his poverty forced him to give his word, and he said, "I will give you my youngest, and I will bring him to this island." And without further delay, the demon caught some fish and filled the little boat. Then he gave the man many coins to take with him, and said, "I will drown you if you trick me!"

The good man took his leave, saying, "Of course I will not trick you," and went straight home, bringing with him the fish and all that money. And then he dressed himself richly, and adorned his wife and sons in a similar manner, and filled the house with provisions. Yet his son's fate was an open wound.

He summoned the youngest son, and took him out in the little boat (but with great heartache), and after sailing for a while they reached the little island. He set him on the shore and said, "My son, wait for me here." And thus he left his son, who was barely seven years old, in this deceptive manner.

Weeping, the father departed, for he did not want to witness his son's death. Then the demon appeared before the boy, and intended to carry him away to meet that very end. When the child saw him, he was bewildered, and had no one to comfort him, but by the power of Christ he made the sign of the cross, and the demon fled.

The child stood there in great fear, and called for his father. He looked around and saw, standing on a hill, a lady who had magically taken the form of a bird. She had the semblance of an eagle, and she approached the boy, saying, "My dear heart, have no fear; I intend to take you away from this island."

The child said, "I don't want to leave, because I must wait for my father here." Then the eagle said, "I will take you to where your father is." And without further ado she picked the boy up and began to fly through the air, and she took him up so high that the child's hair began to burn from the heat.

Then she pointed out her land, far away, and her castle, also at a great distance: four hundred days of traveling, for certain, or even more, according to the books. With the child on her back, the eagle flew through the night, using her magical arts: they left the island in the evening, and the next morning they arrived at her castle.

"Wait a moment for me," said the eagle. She went into a chamber and transformed into a maiden, and she looked as if she had descended from paradise: young, fresh, and as bright as a star. Then she came back out and said to the youth, "You should know that it was I who brought you here so quickly and saved you from the terrible demon to whom your father had consigned you."

The child, who gave signs that he understood her words well, thanked her courteously, and said, "My lady, I am quite content, and will forever remain your servant." The lady said, "Have no fear, I will make you even more content." She was ten years old and he, seven; they lived together in a pure and virginal state for eight years.

In that time he devoted himself to study with an accomplished master, and was a fine student; and then he learned to fence and to joust, and grew to be so good at it that no man in the land could hold out against him. The people would openly say to each other, "His bearing is that of the son of a great nobleman!"

The squire was fifteen years old when he accomplished these feats; everyone adored him, since he was brave and full of kindness. Lady Aquilina turned eighteen at that same time, and she was a vision of loveliness: there was no woman in the world whose beauty surpassed hers.

When they had grown to this age, he was like a lily, and she a rose. One day the beautiful lady said, "My heart will never rest if my will is not done: I want to be his lawfully wedded wife. Since I was the one who raised this pleasing squire, I intend to take him for my husband."

The maiden told this to the boy, and the youth replied to Lady Aquilina with his usual discretion, "You have every reason to deserve this. You saved me when I was on the shore, and I am prepared to do as you please!" And now I will announce his name to all: the boy's name was Liombruno.

And thus it was that he wed the lady; she was his wife and he, her husband. Her castle was a stronghold, and equipped with everything they needed; it had two gates of the strongest steel, which had been magically crafted to this end: no one could enter through them unless Lady Aquilina willed it.

But Liombruno knew the enchantment, and he would pass through the gates whenever he wished; and he would often take part in tourneys and jousts, competing whenever he had the chance. His fair lady admired him more and more every day, for he was strong and full of vigor. And yet, he was most certainly in a state of great melancholy.

One day when he was most melancholy, Lady Aquilina spoke to him, and said, "My husband, my sweet bridegroom, what are the reasons for your great tribulation?" And Liombruno replied, "A heavy thought weighs upon me: I would like to see my brothers, along with my father and mother."

The lady said, "If you want to go to them, you must promise not to deceive me, and to return by the deadline that I give you: you shall be back here before one year elapses." He promised her that he would do this: "And may God save me from all mortal danger!" Then she gave the squire a precious ring to keep him safe from all danger.

And she said, "When you ask this ring for something, you will have whatever you desire: money, clothes, even food. But you must not display these things, and if you speak about them, you will lose your weapons and your horses. Make sure that before a year is up you return, and take care not to stay any longer."

Liombruno said, "Of course!" And before the squire left, the noble and pleasing lady held a court feast for three entire days. She bestowed upon him the title of knight, and a pair of golden spurs, and girded him with a polished sword; he was now called Sir Liombruno. When this was done, he bid her farewell.

It would have taken four hundred days of travel to reach his land, but the lady put a spell on him and ordered that he fall asleep, and with her magical arts commanded that he be transported to his land immediately; and that very night the valorous Liombruno was transported by magic to his land.

In the morning he looked at the ring, and first asked for a steed, as befits a knight, and some finely decorated vestments, as well as a small trunk fully stocked with clothing and as much money as served his purpose; he also asked for more men, and was given foot soldiers and cavalry.

He returned home with the men and the trunk, and was reunited with his father and his brothers, who were very happy to see him. He presented the trunk to his mother, together with all the money and the beautiful clothing, and for his kinsmen there were many precious jewels. His father and his brothers and everyone present said, "Welcome, Liombruno!"

Each member of his family asked him, "O Liombruno, where have you been?" Liombruno stood before them and replied, "I have been earning my living well; I have been with some rich merchants who have dressed and outfitted me as you see; and for my good service to them, they have named me Knight of the Golden Spur."

These gifts continued for nine more months, and he gave them with great love. He often took part in tourneys, and would always be going off to noble jousts; and even though friends and family tried to challenge him, Liombruno was always the victor. When nine months had elapsed, he said, "Without a doubt, it is time for me to leave,

since I promised the merchants that I would return within a year." His kinsmen said to him, "O Liombruno, where do you intend to go? The king of Granada has been waiting for a long time to wed his lovely daughter, and he's announced a grand tournament: he who wins will have her."

When Liombruno heard this, he wanted to try his luck. He told the ring to summon forth a fine steed and strong armor, and what he had asked for came without fail. Liombruno took up his arms fearlessly and bade farewell to his father and everyone else; his mother and his brothers were weeping.

Liombruno mounted his horse, and rode until he reached Granada, where the tournament was to take place and where many people had gathered. The following day the contenders entered the field, and the great joust began; and there was a Saracen who was so powerful that he nearly won the joust.

The Saracen was possessed with such great strength that no one was able to hold out against him; he was so strong and fierce that there was not anyone who wanted to meet him in battle. In the most noble manner, Liombruno went to him and greeted him courteously; the Saracen said, "Either you give up or, if you want to joust with me, take your place on the field!"

Liombruno said, "Gladly!" He entered the field, and drew back to the starting place. The Saracen, who was strong and fierce, mounted his noble steed, and rushed valiantly in to strike the other. Each racing toward the other, they bravely clashed in battle: you will soon hear who was most valorous.

The Saracen and Sir Liombruno were now striking each other's shields, and exchanging strong blows, but the Saracen was losing. His weapons were not worth a dried prune, for the mighty knight Liombruno pierced the Saracen's heart with his sword and his spear and sent him from his steed to the ground.

The Saracen fell dead to the ground, and Liombruno continued to strike: he knocked down every man he encountered, and they all retreated before him, and from the great blows he was dealing everyone, he clearly appeared to be the champion. Everyone was crying, "Long live the great lord; the glory of the joust is yours!"

The king called the knight over, and said to him, "Valiant baron, my daughter is your wife, and you will be my son-in-law and her husband." Liombruno replied, "Most willingly; whatever pleases you, gracious sir!" But before allowing his daughter to marry, the king went to ask his barons for counsel.

When the king had summoned his advisers, he said, "What do you think of the knight?" One of them said, "Now, listen to me: perhaps he has a wife in his own land. Really, we know nothing about his lineage, nor who his parents are; even if he is brave in arms, he does not appear to be of the same noble stock as you.

"But if you will heed my advice, order that each person here vaunt his greatest glory and present the proof of it before you." Then the king had all of the lords return to the hall, and he ordered each of them to vaunt his greatest glory and present proof of it;

and those who could not prove their glory would lose their head for that misdeed. There were those who vaunted their fine mansions, others their castles or noble steeds, some their birds and hawks, some their great falcons, and some of them vaunted their beautiful wives. After everyone had vaunted their glory, Sir Liombruno was asked for his.

The king said, "Why do you not vaunt your glory?" and Liombruno began to speak, saying, "Holy Crown, I beg your pardon!" and the king said, "You are pardoned!" Liombruno said, "Now, listen to me: my vaunt is that there is no lady in the world more beautiful than mine, and in twenty days' time I intend to prove it to you!"

"You ask me for a limit of twenty days," said the king, "but I will give you thirty!" Liombruno left, and said to the ring, "May Lady Aquilina appear before me, right here!" Then Liombruno was forced to regret what he had said, for she did not appear; and he became agitated, for in thirty days he would lose his head.

Liombruno was very worried about the vaunt that he had taken on; for this reason he wept loudly and often prayed to the ring, though his prayers were to no avail, because the lady had expressed her will. But then she was moved to pity, and disregarded his beastly behavior.

At the end of the thirty days the lady arrived, but kept outside of the city. She sent one of her maids-in-waiting, who appeared before the king and his lords. When he saw her, the king said, "Is this your lady?" to which Liombruno replied, "No, this is her maid-in-waiting!" The king marveled at this, for she was quite beautiful.

"My lady is even more lovely"; and at this the king and the others marveled. Another maid arrived, and the king looked into her face: "Is this she, so delicate in appearance?" Liombruno whispered to him, "It is none of these. This is her maid-in-waiting; she is more beautiful!"

In the meantime, Lady Aquilina appeared before the king, her face radiating splendor. She greeted him courteously, and then took her leave without delay. When the king had seen her, he said to Liombruno, "My gentle lord, accept my pardon!" and Liombruno replied, "And you accept mine!" and then bade him farewell.

As soon as he had mounted his horse, he followed straight after his lady, who was waiting for him in a pretty meadow; when he arrived, he begged for her mercy, and she said, "You false renegade! I was even feeling sorry that you might have died! I rescued you, but now it is certain that you will never see me again as long as you live!"

And using her magical arts, the lady disappeared, and left Liombruno alone, with neither weapons nor a horse. By chance he entered a wood, and came upon three thieves, each of whom looked like a rabid dog. In the next canto I will tell you about it, as befits your honor.

Canto 2

I will tell you about Sir Liombruno, ladies and gentlemen, who had lost his dear wife; if you listen to me, I will tell you in what manner he realized his desires, and how while doing so he deceived three thieves, who found themselves in this unfortunate situation because of a pair of boots and a very fine cloak they had stolen.

Those thieves had stacked three piles of florins on a flat rock. The shrewd Liombruno greeted them with flowery words, and then addressed them, saying "What brings you to these parts?" One of them answered, "We will tell you, boy, and then we want you to resolve a dispute for us."

"What sort of dispute are you speaking of?" said the squire. "Tell me, gentlemen, if you please." The eldest of the three came forward and said, "Listen, my true friend, I swear to you that our dispute, which does not allow us any peace, is because of that cloak and those boots, on account of which we have become like mortal enemies."

Liombruno said, "Out with it, then; what sort of magical power do these boots have, so that you so desire them?" The eldest began to speak: "You could not buy them for any amount of money, for they are as fast as the wind, and if you say, 'Take me to so-and-so place!' they will obey you without further ado."

When Liombruno heard of this magic power, he said, "I will never believe that unless I try them out myself or see it with my own eyes!" The eldest told him to go ahead and try them on if he liked, and take a few steps in them. And so Liombruno put on the boots; then he asked what sort of magical power the cloak had.

The eldest said, "My dear brother, it wears the royal crown of all powers. If you are in a town, a city, or a castle, among many people," he continued, "and you are wearing this cloak, no one is able to see your body, and you can go safely anyplace you want, when you are wearing this cloak here."

The noble youth, who had the boots on his feet, said to the thieves, "If it pleases you, I would gladly try this out with the cloak, just to see." The eldest said, "And my answer is that you may put it on without the least fear." Liombruno quickly put it on, and the thieves said, "We cannot see you."

"Now take off those boots," they said, "and that cloak, so that we can see you," and Liombruno did not answer, but reached his hand toward the florins, and took a good quantity from each pile. Then he said, in a low voice, "If you want these things back, you will have to come after me with your own legs!"

At that, the thieves nearly choked with anger, and each looked at the others with rancor; the two younger ones immediately went to the eldest and, without a moment of hesitation, spoke these resentful words: "Where did you have him take our things? You think that you can trick us this way? By God, you shall pay for this!"

Then their old partner replied, saying, "O my good, dear companions, since the boots, which were the mirror of our fortune, and the cloak have been taken away from us, I will see to dividing up these coins." But his companions replied, "Traitor, you are the one who ordered this!" and he replied, "No I did not, for the love of God!"

None of his excuses did any good; they continued to believe he had ordered the youth to take the boots and cloak away, and one of them—now, listen to this, good people—drew up to him and slipped him a knife, while the other twisted a sword into him so deeply that he was dead before he hit the ground.

Once their partner was dead, they were not able to come to an agreement about the florins and how to split them up, and each of them feared the worst of the other. They began to argue and complain over the florins, of which only a few were left since Liombruno had taken a part of each share, and by doing so had avenged their old partner.

And seeing the small size of each stack, the younger of the two spoke to the older one in a petulant voice, saying, "You robbed and deceived me: you took coins from my pile and stashed them away so that you can make your own house rich and prosperous!" The older one, when he heard this, replied, "No, you are the one who hid them!"

And tearing into each other, they laid hands on their sharp swords, and with loud shouts one moved toward the other, and they began to cut each other up fearlessly, wielding their swords as vigorously as if there were twenty of them. And each gave the other such a violent blow to the chest that they both fell to their grassy deathbed at the very same moment.

Let us leave them, one pierced through by the other, and return to the baron of valor, to Liombruno, our bold youth, who arrived that same day in a city. He went to an inn and encountered large numbers of merchants who had come from far-off regions; there he took off the cloak so that he could be seen.

Then he greeted the innkeeper and each of his fellow travelers. The merchants looked at him and addressed him pleasantly: they asked him from whence he came, and if he intended to do business with others. With tears running down his cheeks, Liombruno turned to them and quickly said, "I will join you, if you agree to a pact."

"Tell us what sort of a pact," they said, "and you may come with us tomorrow morning." The courtly youth then replied, "I swear to His Divine Majesty that I will come with you, if you show me the land where that gentle lass named Lady Aquilina dwells. For I have a great longing to see her."

When they heard him speak of this, the merchants thought hard; none of them had any memory of having been in such a strange place. Then they said to him, "Be not melancholy, for finding your lady is not a lost cause. Go to that other innkeeper, who lodges people from every part of the world;

people from every walk of life arrive there, those who have traveled across plains and mountains, the English Channel and the Gulf of Lion, and through all the villages of Spain. They can surely point you toward the land of the one your heart laments." And without further delay Liombruno went straight to the inn they had referred to.

There he found merchants of every station, and he greeted them cheerfully, saying, "I wish you well, companions!" and the merchants and the other people there replied, in unison, "Welcome, fair squire!" And, lovingly disposed by his greeting, they all rose to their feet and treated him with great honor.

Liombruno said to the innkeeper, "Kindly bring us some drink, and I will pay for it straightaway, without any discussion." The host said, "You do not know how much this wine costs!" and Liombruno said, "If six florins is enough for half a pitcher, then bring plenty of it!" and the innkeeper went quickly off.

Once everyone had drunk their fill, the squire paid and the innkeeper quickly took away the money. Then Liombruno spoke in this manner: "Now kindly listen to me, my good sirs: is there anyone here who might know where Lady Aquilina, the shining mirror of my soul, dwells?" An old man replied at once, saying,

"You ask of a land you could not reach even in a whole lifetime; if you ran for nine months straight, you would never arrive. I will tell you once again, and I know what I say is the truth: there is no one who can remember having ever heard of that place; if I am not mistaken, only the wind would be able to show you the way."

Tears ran down Liombruno's cheeks as he said, "Alas, I am wretched and ill-fated!" and the old man immediately called him over and said, "You seem desperate!" Then he pointed to a mountain that looked as if it was touching the sky, and said, "See if you can get to the top, where there is a hermit who might be able to show you the way,

since every evening the winds come to him in all their power, and he detains them (he does this as penance), asking them where they are going and from whence they came, and they tell him in all honesty, for Christ our blessed Lord wills that all be subject to Him.

"This hermit whom the winds visit is obliged to keep all the winds he detains in his abode from leaving; they must stay shut in all night with him. Then, in the morning each wind goes on its way as it is ordered to, and as they leave there are loud arguments. If you go up there, he will show you how to find the land you are looking for."

Liombruno delayed no longer, and set off quickly toward the mountain, as the old man had instructed him; when he was at its foot, he raised his head and said to his boots, "It is taking me too long to get to the dwelling place of the winds: take me there in a way more to my liking!"

The handsome youth got to his feet, and the magic power of the boots carried him away with nary a stop and, as was the will of the Supreme Lord Jesus, he was transported quickly and without harm. When he reached the top of the mountain, Liombruno gave many thanks to God, and went off to the hermit's.

He knocked sharply on the door of the saintly hermit's dwelling; the hermit grew alarmed when he heard the knocking, and his cautious words were, "Who is it, and how did you get here? I do believe you are the Prince of Darkness: by the grace of God, I exorcise you!"

Then Liombruno began to speak, and said, "My brother, you speak in vain. I beg you, for the love of God: do not doubt my intentions. I am a perfect and true Christian, and it is the force of love that brings me here and to even more distant places. My heart is much aggrieved, and coming here has greatly wearied me!"

The saintly hermit was reassured, and asked the charming squire, "Tell me, who showed you how to get here? And what are you searching the world for?" Liombruno said, "I have been making all efforts to find a lady who has put me in this terrible state, and I will roam, crying, 'Woe is me!' until I am in her presence."

"What is her name, then?" asked the friar. "Reveal this to me, without a moment's delay!" The kind and noble youth replied, "She is named Aquilina, and that is the truth." The friar said, "My dear brother, only the wind can show you where she is; I have never heard of her." And then an angel came to speak to the friar.

"Give that charming boy some of what I bring you to eat, and comfort him and keep him with you, so that he is not distrustful of you; when the sweet wind comes, go to the door and say, 'Come to me; there is a boy who came here for love, and the Lord God wills that you offer him help.'"

Just as the angel had commanded, the winds arrived at the house, one by one, and the hermit proceeded to ask them, "Might any of you be so worthy as to be familiar with the way to a castle guarded by fierce dragons, inside of which lives a queen by the name of Lady Aquilina?"

Seventy-one winds arrived, and each one said, "I have never been there." The hermit turned to the lad with a merciful countenance, and said, "Tell me what you will do now!" But then one of the winds spoke in this manner: "You should ask this evening as well; another wind has yet to arrive, and perhaps it can show you how to get to that place."

As he was saying this, the other wind arrived, and it looked like a burning fire; whatever it encountered, it appeared to set ablaze. The hermit said, "Listen here: why did you return after all the others from the place you were assigned? Tell me: I know that you are familiar with a certain land, and that you will be kind enough to show me where it is."

The esteemed wind replied, saying, "Which land do you want to know about?" and the hermit said, "Let it be told: I would like you to reveal the whereabouts of a lady with a rosy visage who goes by the name of Aquilina." The wind replied, without pause, "She is locked up behind two doors of steel,

and guarded by six dragons." The hermit said to the wind, "If you go back there tomorrow morning, there is a lad here who would gladly accompany you, for he is very much in love with her. If you are able, I beg you to take him with you." The wind said, "Yes, if he is able to keep up with me."

The lad, who had heard this, replied, "I will put on a pair of boots and I promise you, by God, that I will be ahead of you." The wind said, "My dear brother, if that is the case, they would be worth a thousand piles of money! Make sure that you are ready tomorrow morning when I call you, for I will not be able to wait."

The next morning, when day had come, the wind called the noble youth. Liombruno arose with a joyous countenance, and gathered his cloak around him. He prepared to take his leave, looked about, and then the hermit opened the door for him. The wind said, "Let us take this route," and Liombruno followed him.

Liombruno asked his boots if, out of love and kindness and since they were accustomed to traveling faster than the wind, they could overtake the wind. Then he spoke in this manner: "Pray tell, wind, am I going in the right direction?" The wind replied, "I cannot see you, but you seem to be going in the right direction."

As they traveled along like this, the wind marveled greatly, and would often turn and look behind to see if the squire was there; and in its mind it wondered, "What can this mean?" It seemed incredible: "He is ahead of me, and yet I never saw him get there!" And as the wind was saying this, it arrived at a mountain.

Upon reaching the mountain, the wind called to Liombruno that he should not go any farther. Liombruno removed the cloak and sat down to wait; and when it arrived, the wind said, "O Liombruno, I now intend to show you the fine palace where the woman who is the pillar of your heart lives,

the noble castle where the royal lady resides." Then Liombruno, the newly named knight, took his leave of nature's wind and said, "You will send the saintly little friar greetings from the celestial Lord." Then he most pleasantly parted from the wind, and set off toward the palace.

He put a spell on the sharp-edged door, so that it would open, and then he entered and went up the stairs, where he found the dragons, each one fiercer than the next. But no one could see him, and he reached the big hall, where he found his lovely lady. She was at the table, preparing to eat. Liombruno sat down next to her.

Liombruno was very hungry, and he began to eat; when food was put down before the lady, he quickly did away with it. At this, the lady said, "It seems that I am not eating a quarter of the food, and yet as far as I can see, I am eating it all! O Liombruno, may God save you from danger!"

And then she said, "O true God, if only he were here with me now, he who holds my heart in his hand: I mean Liombruno, who has me in his power!" Upon hearing this, Liombruno's desire grew, and he took the ring off his finger and put it on the cutting board where the meat was, at which the lady marveled greatly.

She entrusted herself to the supreme and true God, called the maidservants, and said, "Upon my word, this is the ring that was to keep Liombruno safe! This is the work of the great fire of hell, come to add to my melancholy!" Crying loudly over this great misfortune, she entered her chamber; the lad entered after her.

The lady stripped down to her shift, got into her splendid bed, and then fell asleep full of melancholy; Liombruno, who longed for her, undressed and lay by her side, and had no hesitation in doing so. When she felt him there she began to scream loudly, and her maids came; but no one could see him.

The maids said to the confused lady, "What is it, why are you thrashing around like this?" and she said, "My life is miserable, and worth no more than a miserable piece of straw! I am in shock for the fright that I just had: there was a man, Christ help me, in my presence, but I could not see him, and that is why I screamed."

He went to her in the same way two more times. When she felt him by her side the third time, she held on to him so tightly that he was not able to keep the cloak on. Then, contemplating his face, she said, "Alas, traitorous Liombruno, how did you come to this place, and light my heart like a fire?"

He replied, "I came here as God willed," and told her the whole story of the boots that he had stolen, and of the cloak, which he was still laughing about, and of the magic powers that he had acquired; and he told her of the hermit and the wind: one thing at a time, leaving nothing out.

Then the lady said to him, "My dear heart, until now I have lived in sorrow, and there was not a day when I was happy; but now that you have ended your journey, let us take our joy, my true lord, without melancholy, and be grateful to the men to whom these things belonged." They kissed, and they made peace through love.

There are no words for the great joy that the lady and the noble youth enjoyed; and they had no more use for the magic objects, even if they did keep the ring, just in case; and in truth, the boots and the cloak, too. They held great festivities to celebrate their love; and this story ends in your honor.

2

Girolamo Morlini

(SECOND HALF OF FIFTEENTH CENTURY)

Not much is known about Morlini's life, except that he studied and then taught law in Naples; presumably he was born there as well. He is known principally for his *Novellae, fabulae, comoedia* (Novellas, Fables, Comedy), first published in 1520 and written in Latin, an unusual choice at this time, when most novella writers followed Boccaccio's vernacular example. The collection lacks a frame tale and comprises eighty-one short novellas, twenty Aesopian fables, and a one-act comedy. The tales are predominantly set in Naples and environs, and they feature a less than noble cast of conmen, adulterers, and others struggling to get by or to feed their basest instincts. Morlini was influenced in his choice of materials by medieval preaching and the traditions of exempla and fabliaux, as well as by both written (e.g., Apuleius) and oral tale-telling. In 1559 Morlini's *Novellae* were placed on the *Index of Prohibited Books* for obscenity.

Further Reading

Primary

Morlini, Girolamo. *Novelle e favole*. Ed. Giovanni Villani. Rome: Salerno, 1983. 228–31, 374–77. [source text]

Secondary

Guglielminetti, Marziano. "Dalle novellae del Morlini alle favole dello Straparola." In *Medioevo e rinascimento veneto con altri studi in onore di Lino Lazzarini*, ed. Alberto Limentani. Padua: Antenore, 1979. 69–81.

The Mother Who Left Her Son to Watch the House (De matre filium domum custoditum reliquit)

This tale follows ATU 1218, Numskull Sits on Eggs to Finish the Hatching, and includes other common motifs found in "numskull" tales common in many cultures, such as the tales of the Giufà cycle (see pp. 235–38). Basile's "Vardiello" features a similar antihero.

A bad-tempered and boozy woman, who had an idiot for a son, had put some eggs under her hen to brood, hoping to derive a good part of her fortune from them. One day, when she needed to go out, she went to her son and gave him these instructions: "My son, watch over our little house, for it is our most secure refuge from poverty. Take good care of the hen and the eggs; from this moment on I am appointing you chick breeder, and confidently entrust to you all related tasks."

The woman had a jar of walnuts mixed with Hymettus honey, and since she feared that her son might gobble them down, she got him to believe that the jar contained a poison made from wolfsbane, and told him, "If you don't look after everything with the greatest care, when I return (meanwhile pointing to the jar with her index finger) you will die by means of that terrible poison!"

With that, she closed the door on its hinges and left.

But the foolish son was hungry. He grabbed a piece of bread and a bit of cheese to eat; then he thought he'd like to guzzle some wine from the barrel, and put the food down on a plate. However, while he was drawing the wine the brooding hen, driven by hunger, pinched the cheese and made a quick getaway. Then the foolish boy, leaving the spigot on the wine barrel open, tried to catch the fugitive hen, but since he wasn't able to snare her, he grabbed a club to help himself along, and ended up whacking and killing her. When he went back, he found that all the wine had spilled out; in order to hide it he covered it with flour, which he sprinkled on the floor and then smoothed over.

Then he went to the roost and began to brood like a hen. Actually, he brooded the eggs in a shitting position; and when at a certain point his knees gave out he collapsed onto the eggs, smashing them. At this point he was beside himself, because he realized he had neglected to carry out his mother's orders, and, fearing that he would be punished on her return, he decided to end things with the poison. So he took the jar of walnuts and gobbled them down.

Meanwhile, his mother returned, and when she saw all the messes he had made, she began to scold her son. To console her, he said, "O mother, I know I made some mistakes, but by God, I'll pay the penalty for my errors. In fact, I've taken every last bit of that poison; I poured the entire jar into the bowl of my stomach so that I would die quickly. So I want you to know that I plan to die as soon as possible!"

The mother recognized the innocence of her son and, laughing, blamed herself instead of him for what had happened.

This tale shows that you shouldn't trust fools any differently than you would the blind, because neither knows what they're doing.

The Brothers Who Wandered through the World and Acquired Wealth (De fratibus qui per orbem pererrando ditati sunt)

The theme of brothers who must make a life for themselves after the death of a parent, with or without the help of magic, is a common one, as is the youngest brother's "unconventional" life choice, which ultimately proves to be the winning one for all of them. Straparola recycled Morlini's tale in The Pleasant Nights *7.5.*

A needy man had three sons whom, because of his destitution, he was barely in a position to feed adequately. For this reason his famished sons, acknowledging the poverty and scant resources of their father, reached an agreement: they determined that they would free him of this burden and, in the hope that they might sniff out some earnings, roam the world with a stick and a sack in the manner of philosophers. They then knelt in a circle around their father, asking him to forgive them and promising that when a decade had passed they would return to their homeland. After leaving him with this promise, they separated at a crossroads.

The eldest wound up, by the will of fate, in a camp of enemy soldiers who were engaged in an expedition. He put himself at the service of one of the captains, and in a short time he became such an expert and vigorous soldier that in terms of valor and courage he was second to none, and was able to scale the walls of the highest fortress with only two daggers to help him along.

The second brother reached a port where ships were built, and offered his services to a carpenter who excelled above all others in preparing ship hulls;

and after being under his guidance for a short time, he progressed so quickly in the trade and became so renowned that in the region he was acclaimed as having no equals in what he did.

As for the last brother, after listening to the harmonious songs of the nightingale and becoming deeply enchanted by them, he began to follow their flight and their melancholy refrains through shaded valleys and dense woods, and down mountains into solitary, musical forests and far-off wilds. And he was so taken by the sweetness of their song that he forgot to return, and he became an inhabitant of those woods and lived there as a wild man for a decade. Thus, from his long familiarity with birdsong he learned their every language and was able to understand them perfectly, and was recognized among all the fauna as a new Feronia or Pan.

When the day of their return arrived, the first two brothers met in the arranged place. Just as they were expressing their sadness over the fate of the youngest, he came running toward them, naked, shaggy, and with a loving expression on his face. His brothers burst into tears, embraced him, and covered him with their own clothes.

Later, they were eating dinner in a tavern when a magpie landed on a poplar tree and with its raspy cry said, "You should know, fellow diners, that there is an immense treasure hidden in a corner of this tavern. It has for some time been destined to be yours: now go and get it." After saying this, it flew away. The youngest related what the bird had said, word for word, to his brothers; they began to dig, and found the treasure. Full of joy, they returned to their father as very wealthy men.

After many paternal embraces and sumptuous meals, one day the youngest brother happened to hear another bird, which said, "In the Aegean Sea lies the island of Chios. It has a perimeter of nine hundred furlongs and houses an impenetrable fortress built of Parian marble built by the daughter of Apollo, Chios.[1] Still today the entrance to the fortress is guarded by a fire- and venom-spewing serpent, with a basilisk at its side. Now, the goddess Aglaia[2] has been kept imprisoned there, with all of her amassed treasures (when she arrived at the fortress, she brought with her an incalculable amount of money), and whoever climbs the fortress and gains entrance will win Aglaia's treasure."

1. Chios is in Greek mythology a son, not a daughter, of Apollo.
2. Aglaia is one of the three Charites, or Graces.

After the bird said this, it flew away. Once the brothers had interpreted its speech, they determined that they would go: the first brother promised that he would scale the fortress with his two daggers, and the second that he would prepare a fast ship. It was not long before the ship was ready, and one fine day, with the best of omens, they hoisted the mast and aft sail, began to cut through the waves with the wind in their favor, and sailed toward Chios.

Some nights later they landed on the island just as day was about to break. The brave soldier, armed with his two daggers, scaled the fortress, recovered Aglaia, and lowered her by rope to his brothers. Then, after throwing down carbuncles, jewels, and a large quantity of gold, he left the empty fortress, climbed down, and they all returned to their homeland safe and sound.

In all truth, there was a subsequent lengthy feud among the brothers over possession of the woman. After many long disputes about which of those equal parties deserved the indivisible Aglaia, the controversy is still in the hands of Palemone.[3] For this reason I will leave you, reader, to adjudicate the matter for yourself, using the arguments that you find most suitable.

This tale shows that wits surpass strength, and that parents should make all efforts, within the limits of their resources, to ensure that their children do justice to their professions.

3. Palemone of Aetolia was one of Jason's Argonauts.

PART II

The Birth of the Literary Fairy Tale in Early Modern Italy

1

Giovan Francesco Straparola (ca. 1480–1558)

The somewhat mysterious writer and poet Giovan Francesco Straparola was born in the northern Italian town of Caravaggio and as a young man moved to Venice. Although the most important narrative model for Straparola's *Le piacevoli notti* (*The Pleasant Nights*, 1550–53) was the novella tradition descended from Giovanni Boccaccio's *Decameron*, Straparola also embarked in the innovative direction of incorporating folktales and fairy tales into his collection, and his *Nights* was the first collection in Western Europe in which the literary fairy tale occupies a place of honor.

The realistic frame tale, modeled on the *Decameron*, tells of the arrival in Venice, during Carnival season, of the historical personage Ottaviano Maria Sforza, ex-bishop of Lodi, who together with his widowed daughter Lucrezia Sforza Gonzaga has fled Milan for political reasons. He and his party proceed from Venice by boat to Murano, a nearby island, where they take refuge in a marvelously appointed palace with, despite the season, a garden in full bloom. They decide to spend the remaining nights of Carnival telling tales and summon a group of young ladies and gentlemen to form the company. It is above all the rather abstractly characterized women who narrate the tales, while the men, whose ranks include historical men of letters such as Pietro Bembo and Bernardo Cappello, listen. The seventy-four tales are divided among thirteen nights; songs and dances precede each night, and the tales end with "enigmas" or riddles. There is no well-defined thematic division of the days, as in the *Decameron*, apart from the predominance of motifs of magic in the third day. The *Nights* are an eclectic mix; besides fifteen fairy tales, they include Boccaccian novellas, exempla, tales "borrowed" from Morlini, and other forms of short narrative.

The experimentation with various narrative genres and modes of representation was not uncommon at the time when Straparola wrote, near the end of the golden age of the European novella. In particular, the attraction to the fairy tale exemplified the general interest in folk traditions present in the late Renaissance, as well as the intuition that the bourgeois protagonists of the novella were no longer the convincing paradigms they had once been. The proliferation of lower-class heroes who inhabit marvelous worlds, marry princes and princesses, and are passively aided by magic—instead of using their intelligence and enterprise to actively change the course of events—suggests how fantastic such social betterment may have seemed in the "real world" of Straparola's time.

It is thought that most of the fairy tales included in the *Nights* are of European and Eastern origin; Straparola may have invented several himself. All of these tales had significant influence on the subsequent history of the genre, and versions of them reappeared in later collections such as Giambattista Basile's *The Tale of Tales* and Jacob and Wilhelm Grimms' *Children's and Household Tales*. Yet Straparola's fairy tales have a distinct flavor with respect to his successors. It is not surprising that, with one foot still in the novella tradition, Straparola's fairy tales effectively combine realistic, earthy details with magical transformations in what are often uncanny ways, such as in "King Pig."

In 1555 the *Nights* were published in a single volume in which one of the tales was replaced by two new tales, bringing the total to seventy-five. In the course of the next half century, Straparola's work became a veritable best seller, with over twenty editions. Already in the late sixteenth century the *Nights* encountered problems with ecclesiastical censors due to the anticlerical thematics and obscenity of some of the tales, and in 1624 it was artificially doomed to a fall in popularity after being placed on the papal *Index of Prohibited Books*.

Further Reading

Primary

Straparola, Giovan Francesco. *Le piacevoli notti*. Ed. Donato Pirovano. 2 vols. Rome: Salerno, 2000. 1:95–106, 165–78, 199–215, 344–57. [source text]

Straparola, Giovan Francesco. *The Pleasant Nights*. Ed. and trans. S. Magnanini. Tempe: Iter Arizona Center for Medieval and Renaissance Studies, 2015.

Straparola, Giovan Francesco. *The Pleasant Nights*. Ed. and trans. Donald Beecher. 2 vols. Toronto: University of Toronto Press, 2012.

Secondary

Beecher, Donald. "Introduction." In Giovan Francesco Straparola, *The Pleasant Nights*, ed. and trans. Donald Beecher. 2 vols. Toronto: University of Toronto Press, 2012. 1:3–140.

Bottigheimer, Ruth B. *Fairy Godfather: Straparola, Venice, and the Fairy Tale Tradition*. Philadelphia: University of Pennsylvania Press, 2002.

Magnanini, Suzanne. *Fairy-Tale Science: Monstrous Generation in the Tales of Straparola and Basile*. Toronto: University of Toronto Press, 2008.

Magnanini, Suzanne. "Introduction." In Giovan Francesco Straparola, *The Pleasant Nights*, ed. and trans. Suzanne Magnanini. Tempe: Iter Arizona Center for Medieval and Renaissance Studies, 2015.

Pirovano, Donato. "The Literary Fairy Tale of Giovan Francesco Straparola." *Romanic Review* 99, nos. 3–4 (2008): 281–96.

King Pig (Galeotto re di Anglia ha uno figliuolo nato porco)

There are many versions of this tale, which belongs to the tale type ATU 441, Hans My Hedgehog (see, e.g., the Grimms' tale by the same name), as well as to the broader type 425A, The Animal as Bridegroom (also related to the Cupid and Psyche myth). Especially in its early modern variations, it is often read as a story about women's fears of contractual marriages to a potentially "monstrous" stranger; the perspective may be consolatory (e.g., Jeanne-Marie Leprince de Beaumont's 1756 "Beauty and the Beast") or dystopic (e.g., Catherine Bernard's 1697 "Riquet with the Tuft"). Straparola's tale has been related, by Suzanne Magnanini, even more specifically to the anxiety about the unstable boundaries between the human and the animal that is expressed in the numerous tracts on monstrosity, and in particular monstrous births, published in this period, as well as to the particularities of the Venetian marriage market of Straparola's time, in which an excess of eligible young men of the upper classes compared to women of the same class resulted in "a decline in patrician marriages," prolonged bachelorhoods, and a greater risk of behaviors associated with "disruptive sexual desire" (114). Marrying down, even if potentially risky from the patrician perspective, could be one solution to this situation. Straparola's happy ending combines social mobility and social stability so as to satisfy his hybrid reading public: he "offers his readers from the artisan classes a fantasy of social and economic betterment" yet also "renders this tale palatable for aristocratic readers by offering them a fantasy of an interclass marriage that serves to preserve both the nobility and the state" (116).

Galeotto, king of England, has a son who is born a pig. The son marries three times, and when he sheds his pigskin and becomes a magnificent young man, he is named King Pig.

You should know, my dear ladies, that Galeotto, king of England, was a man no less rich in gifts of fortune than in those of spirit. His wife, who was named Ersilia, was the daughter of Mattias, king of Hungary, and surpassed all other matrons of her time in beauty, virtue, and refinement. Galeotto ruled his kingdom so prudently that there was not a person who could with any truth complain about him. Although the two of them had lived together for a long time, fate willed it that Ersilia had never become pregnant. And this displeased the one and the other very much.

One day Ersilia was walking through her garden and picking flowers, and since she was already quite weary, a spot full of tender green grasses caught her eye, and she went over and sat down; beckoned by her sleepiness and by the birds that sang sweetly up in the green branches, she fell asleep. As luck had it, at that very moment three splendid fairies came passing through the air, and when they saw the young woman asleep, they stopped. After considering her beauty and grace, they discussed rendering her inviolable and enchanted; at the end, all three fairies were in agreement. The first one said, "I wish that she may be inviolable, and that the first night she lies with her husband she may become pregnant and that from her be born a son whose beauties have no equals in the world."

The next one said, "And I wish that no one may offend her, and that the son born from her be endowed with every virtue and kindness that can be imagined."

The third said, "And I wish that she may be the wisest and richest of all women, but that the son she conceives be born completely covered with pigskin, and that his gestures and manners all be those of a pig, and that he never be able to leave that state unless he first takes three wives."

When the three fairies had left, Ersilia awoke and arose at once, gathered up the flowers that she had picked, and returned to the palace.

Before many days had passed Ersilia became pregnant, and when she reached the desired birth, she delivered a son whose limbs were not those of a human but a pig. When this news reached the ears of the king and queen, they felt immeasurable grief. And so as to avoid the repercussions of such a birth resulting in the disgrace of the queen, who was a good and saintly woman, more than once the king resolved to have the pig killed and thrown into the sea. But then, after turning it over in his mind and thinking, with reason, that whatever this son was, he had been generated by the king and was his own blood, he lay to rest any fierce intentions that he had previously had and, embracing pity mixed with pain, decided that his son should in all regards be brought up and nourished not as a beast but as a rational animal. The child was thus diligently nourished, and would often come to his mother, rising on his hind legs and putting his little snout and trotters in her lap. His merciful mother, for her part, caressed him, putting her hands on his bristly back and hugging and kissing him no differently than if he had been a human creature. And the child curled his tail, and with very clear signs showed her how pleasing the maternal caresses were to him.

When the little piggy was more grown up, he began to speak like a human being, and to stroll around the city, and wherever there was garbage and filth, he plunged right in, as pigs do. Afterward, he would return home filthy and stinking, and when he went up to his father and mother and rubbed against their clothes, he soiled them all over with muck. But because he was their only child, they patiently put up with everything.

One day the little pig came home, filthy and dirty as usual, and, jumping all over his mother's clothes, he grunted and said to her, "My dear mother, I would like to get married." When she heard this, his mother answered, "You've got to be crazy. Who do you think would take you as a husband? You're stinky and dirty, and you think a baron or knight is going to give you his daughter?" To which he replied, grunting, that he wanted a wife at all costs. The queen, not knowing how to deal with this, said to the king, "What should we do? You can see what sort of situation we are in. Our son wants a wife, but no woman will take him for her husband." The little pig then returned to his mother and said, grunting loudly, "I want a wife, and I will continue to want one until I have the girl that I saw today, for she was most pleasing."

This girl was the daughter of a poor little woman who had three daughters, each of whom was very beautiful. When the queen heard this, she immediately sent for the poor woman together with her eldest daughter, and said to her, "Dearest mother, you are poor and laden with daughters; if you give your consent to what I ask, you come out of this rich. I have a son who is a pig, and I would like to marry him to your eldest daughter. I ask that you pay your respect not to him, since he is a pig, but to the king and me, for at the end our whole kingdom will be in her possession."

Upon hearing these words, the girl grew quite upset and, turning as red as a morning rose, said that she would not consent to such a thing under any condition. But the poor woman's pleas were so sweet that her daughter finally contented her.

When the pig returned home, all filthy, he ran to his mother, who said to him, "My son, we have found you a wife, and she will be to your satisfaction." After the bride had been dressed in the most splendid of royal clothing, the queen had her brought in, and she introduced her to the pig. When he saw how beautiful and full of grace she was, he rejoiced and, all stinky and dirty, he circled around her, pushing with his snout and hooves and giving her the most ardent caresses a pig has ever given. But because he was soiling her clothes, she pushed him away. Then the pig said to her, "Why are you pushing me away? Didn't I have that clothing made for you?" To which she, full of pride, scornfully answered, "Neither you nor your kingdom of pigs made it for me." And when it came time to go and rest, the young woman said, "What am I going to do with this stinky beast? Tonight, when he's in his first sleep, I'll kill him." The pig, who was not far off, heard these words but said nothing.

At the appointed hour the pig, all smeared with mud and other foul matter, arrived at the magnificent bed, lifted the featherlight sheets with his snout and hooves and soiled everything with fetid excrement, and then got into bed next to his bride. It wasn't long before she fell asleep. The pig, though, had only pretended to go to sleep, and with his sharp tusks he pierced her chest so violently that she immediately died.

After he arose the next morning at the usual time, he went off, according to his habit, to feed and dirty himself. The queen thought that she should go and visit her daughter-in-law, and when she found that she had been killed by the pig, she felt the greatest grief. Upon returning home and receiving a bitter reprimand from the queen, the pig replied to her that he had done to his bride what she had intended to do to him. And then he indignantly left.

Before many days had passed the pig began to goad his mother again about wanting to marry, this time the other sister. Although the queen was most contrary, he nevertheless wanted the girl at all costs, and threatened to bring everything to ruin if he could not have her. When the queen heard this, she went to the king and told him the whole story, and he said that it would be better to have the pig killed than for the pig to cause some great evil in the city. But the queen, who was his mother and nurtured a great love for him, could not suffer the thought of remaining without him, even if he was a pig. And so she summoned the poor little woman together with another of her daughters and discussed the matter at length with them. After they had much deliberated about the marriage, the second daughter consented to accept the pig for her husband.

It did not work out as she desired, however, since the pig killed the second girl as he had done with the first, after which he immediately left the house. When he returned to the palace at the appointed time covered with such filth and mud that it was impossible to get near him for the stench, he was severely rebuked by the king and queen for his excessive actions. But the pig boldly replied that he had done to his bride what she had intended to do to him.

Before long Mister Pig again began to prod his mother about wanting to marry and take the third sister for his wife, who was even more beautiful than the first and the second. When this demand was flatly denied, he pleaded even more insistently to have her, and with fearful and boorish words he threatened the queen's death if he could not have the girl as his bride. Upon hearing his foul and shameful words, the queen felt such torment in her heart that she was close to going mad. And so she put aside every other thought and summoned the poor little woman and her third daughter, who was named Meldina, and said to her, "Meldina, my dear girl, I want you to take Mister Pig for your husband, not out of respect for him but for his father and me, for if you are able to be with him in the right way, you will be the happiest and most content woman there is."

Meldina replied with a serene and clear countenance that she was extremely happy, and thanked the queen very much for deigning to accept her as her daughter-in-law. And even if she had nothing else, it would be enough that she had gone in one instant from being a poor little girl to the daughter-in-law of a powerful king. When the queen heard this grateful and loving answer, she felt such sweetness that she could not keep the tears from her eyes. But she still feared that what had happened to the other two would happen to her.

The new bride was dressed in rich clothing and precious jewels, and waited for her dear bridegroom to come home. And when Mister Pig arrived, filthier and dirtier than he had ever been, his bride received him kindly, spreading her precious dress on the ground and begging him to lie next to her. The queen told her to push him away, but she refused to do this, and said the following words to the queen:

I have heard tell of three things
Sacred, venerable, and pious crown.

For one, which is impossible to find,
The search is too great a folly.
Do not place your trust in the other,
As it leads neither to reason nor to the straight path.
The third, the precious and rare gift
That you have in your hands, make sure to hold dear.

Mister Pig, who was not sleeping but understood everything clearly, stood up and began to lick her face, throat, chest, and shoulders, and she, in exchange, caressed him and kissed him until he was all aflame with love.

When it came time to rest, the bride went off to bed and waited for her dear bridegroom to come, and it wasn't long before he approached the bed, all filthy and stinking. She lifted up the blankets and invited him to lie beside her, placing his head on the pillow. Then she covered him well and closed the bed curtains so that he would not suffer the cold.

At the break of day Mister Pig went off to pasture, leaving the mattress full of excrement. In the morning the queen went to the bride's chamber, believing that she would see what she had already seen with the other two. But instead she found her daughter-in-law cheerful and content, even if the bed was soiled with every sort of filth and foul matter. And she thanked the supreme God for this lovely gift, that her son had found a wife to his liking.

Before much time had gone by, one day, while exchanging pleasurable considerations with his lady, Mister Pig said to her, "Meldina, my darling wife, if I could believe that you would not reveal to anyone a great secret of mine, I would uncover to you, and not without your greatest happiness, something that until now I have kept hidden. Since I know that you are prudent and wise, and I see that you love me with perfect affection, I would like you to be privy to it." "Of course you may reveal your every secret to me," said Meldina. "I promise you that I will not disclose it against your wishes to anyone."

Reassured by his wife's words, Mister Pig took off his stinking and dirty skin, and there was revealed a graceful and magnificently handsome young man, and for that whole night he lay tightly embraced with his Meldina. After commanding that she not say a word about any of this, for the time was near for him to leave this miserable state, he got out of bed, collected his porcine covering, and went back to his garbage, just as he had done before. I leave it to each of you to imagine the nature and degree of Meldina's happiness at finding herself in the company of such a fair and exquisite young man.

Before long the young woman became pregnant, and when it came time to give birth, she was delivered of a beautiful baby boy. This brought great happiness to the king and the queen, most of all because he had the form of a human being and not a beast. Keeping such a sublime and marvelous matter secret was, however, a great weight on Meldina, and thus she went to her mother-in-law and said, "Most prudent queen, I believed my companion to be a beast, but the husband you gave me is the most handsome, virtuous, and well-mannered young man that nature ever created. When he comes to my chamber to lie with me, he takes off his stinking skin and places it on the ground, and there stands an elegant and fair young man. And no one could possibly believe this unless they see it with their own eyes."

The queen thought that her daughter-in-law spoke in jest, while in fact she told the truth. And when she asked her how she might see this, her daughter-in-law answered, "Come to my chamber in the early hours of the night and you will see that what I tell you is true."

Night came, and after waiting for the hour when everyone had gone to rest, the queen had torches lit, and together with the king she went to her son's chamber. Upon entering, she found the pigskin on the ground in a corner of the chamber, and, nearing the bed, she saw that her son was a magnificent young man, and that his wife, Meldina, was holding him tightly in her arms. At this sight, the king and queen rejoiced greatly, and the king ordered that before anyone left the room the skin be torn into tiny shreds; and so great was the happiness of the king and queen for their renewed son that they came close to dying of pleasure. When King Galeotto saw that he had such a son, and a grandson besides, he removed his diadem and his royal cloak, and in his place his son was crowned with great ceremony, and was named King Pig. King Pig reigned much to the satisfaction of his people, and with Meldina, his beloved wife, he lived in great happiness for a long time.

Crazy Pietro (Pietro Pazzo)

This story of a doltish hero with few redeeming qualities corresponds to ATU 675, The Lazy Boy. Another early Italian variant is Basile's "Peruonto" (1.3); it also shares many affinities with the Grimms' "Hans Dumm." A more recent version is Calvino's "The Cloven Youth."

Crazy Pietro becomes wise by virtue of a fish called tuna, which he catches and saves from death. He takes for his wife King Luciano's daughter, Luciana, who through a previous enchantment had been made pregnant by him.

On the island of Capraia, located in the Ligurian Sea and ruled by King Luciano, there once lived a poor little widow named Isotta. She had a son who was a fisherman, but it was his misfortune to be crazy, and everyone who knew him called him Crazy Pietro. Each day he would go off to fish, but fortune was so hostile to him that he never caught a thing. And each time he returned home, when he was still more than half a mile away from the house he would start shouting so loudly that everyone on the island could easily hear him. And this is what he shouted: "O Mother, bring big basins and little basins, big buckets and little buckets, big tubs and little tubs, for Pietro has a load of fish!" His poor mother had faith in her son's words and, believing what he said to be true, prepared everything for his arrival. But as soon as he reached his mother, the crazy fellow would jeer at her and make fun of her, sticking out his tongue a full palm's length.

The house of this poor little widow faced the palace of King Luciano, who had a most lovely and graceful ten-year-old daughter, to whom, as his only child, her father had given his own name, calling her Luciana. As soon as Luciana would hear Crazy Pietro say, "O Mother, bring big basins and little basins, big buckets and little buckets, big tubs and little tubs, for Pietro has caught a lot of fish," she would run to the window, and the sight of him gave her so much amusement and delight that at times she felt that she would die laughing. When he saw her laughing so immoderately, the crazy fellow was most offended, and insulted her with inappropriate words. But the more he attacked her with insulting words, the harder she laughed and acted as if it were a game, as children of a tender age are wont to do.

And so Pietro continued to go fishing day in and day out, and to foolishly repeat to his mother the aforementioned words. One day it happened that the poor boy caught a big, fat fish, commonly called by the name of tuna. This gave him such great happiness that he began to jump up and down on the shore, shouting, "Now my mother and I can have some dinner, now my mother and I can have some dinner!" And he repeated these words a number of times.

When the tuna saw that it had been caught and could in no way escape, it said to Crazy Pietro, "Pray, brother: out of courtesy, I beg you to free me from this captivity and to give me my life. Pray, dear brother: what do you want with me? Once you have eaten me, what other benefit do you expect to obtain? But on the other hand, if you spare me from death, perhaps at another time I could be of use to you."

But the good Pietro, who was more in need of eating than of words, wanted all the same to throw the fish over his shoulder and take it home, so that he could enjoy it in happiness with his mother, who also suffered from great need. Yet the tuna did not cease to beg him fervently, offering to provide him with all the fish he desired. And after that it promised to grant him whatever he asked for. However crazy he was, Pietro's heart was not a diamond, and, moved to pity, he agreed to free the tuna from its death. And he pushed it so hard with his feet and his arms that he was able to throw it back into the sea.

When the tuna saw what a great favor it had received, it did not want to appear ungrateful, and said to Pietro, "Get into your little boat, and with an oar and your body tip it over to one side so that it lets water in." Pietro climbed into the boat, and when he had caused it to curve up and lean to one side above the sea, such an abundance of fish washed into the boat that it was in the greatest danger of sinking. At the sight of this, Pietro, who esteemed the danger to be but little, grew very happy. And gathering up as much of the fish as he was able to carry on his back, he set off toward home.

When he was not far from the house, he began, in his usual fashion, to shout loudly, "O Mother, bring big basins and little basins, big buckets and little buckets, big tubs and little tubs, for Pietro has caught a lot of fish!"

His mother, who thought she was being mocked and made fun of like the other times, decided to do nothing. But the crazy fellow continued to shout even more loudly, at which his mother, fearing that he might commit some even greater act of madness if he did not find the receptacles ready, prepared everything. When Pietro reached home and his mother saw such an abundance of beautiful fish, she grew very happy, praising God that for once she had had good luck.

Hearing Pietro's loud shouts, the daughter of the king ran to the window and began to taunt and jeer at him, laughing raucously at his words. This sparked anger and fury in the poor boy, and not knowing what else to do, he ran to the shore and called out loudly to the tuna for help. When the tuna heard the voice and recognized whose it was, it swam in close to shore and, extending its head from the briny waves, asked him what his wish might be. To which the crazy fellow said, "For the moment I want nothing more than for Luciana, daughter of King Luciano, to find herself pregnant."

In less than the blink of an eye exactly what he had wished for was executed.

Before many days and months had gone by, the girl's virginal belly began to grow, so that although she had not yet reached her twelfth year, she showed all the telltale signs of being a pregnant woman. When the girl's mother saw this, she was most afflicted, and could not imagine how a girl of eleven years, who did not yet show any sign of being a woman, could become pregnant. And thinking, as is wont to happen, that the girl had instead fallen prey to some incurable disease, she insisted that she be seen by the women who are expert in such things. But after diligently examining her in great secrecy, they deemed there to be no doubt that the girl was pregnant.

The queen could not bear the weight of this excessive ignominy, and decided to share the news with King Luciano, her husband, who when he heard it felt that he would die of grief. He used every honest and covert means to conduct the investigation necessary to discover who had violated the girl, but he got nowhere at all, and he resolved to have his daughter killed in secret to avoid such a shameful humiliation. But her mother, who loved her daughter tenderly, begged the king to spare her until she gave birth, after which he could do what he wished. The king—who was, after all, her father—was moved to compassion for the girl, his only child, and acquiesced to the mother's wishes.

When the time arrived to give birth, the girl delivered a most beautiful baby boy, and he was of such supreme beauty that the king could not bear that he be killed. Instead, he ordered the queen to have him nursed and well nourished until he was one year old.

When the baby arrived at the term of one year, he had so grown in beauty that there was no other baby who could equal him, and the king decided to conduct an experiment to find the man who had fathered him. He had a public proclamation issued throughout the city, ordering that, under penalty of having his head cut from his torso, every man over the age of fourteen was obliged to present himself to His Majesty, carrying in his hands a fruit or a flower or some other thing that might excite the baby's interest. According to the king's command, everyone came to the palace bearing a fruit or a flower or one thing or another in their hands. They passed in front of the king, and then sat according to their ranks.

As a certain youth was on his way to the palace, just like everyone else was, he happened to run into Crazy Pietro, and said to him, "Where are you going, Pietro? Why don't you go to the palace, like the others, and obey the king's orders?" To which Pietro answered, "Come on, what would I do in such a crowd? Don't you see that I'm poor and naked, that I don't even have clothes to cover myself? You want me to go and present myself among all those lords and courtiers? I can't do that."

Then the youth said, jokingly, "Come with me and I'll give you some clothes; who knows, the baby might be yours!" So Pietro went off to the youth's house and was given some clothes, which he took. He put them on, and then went to the palace in the company of the youth. After going up the stairs of the palace, he placed himself behind a door, so that he could barely be seen. When everyone had been presented to the king and was seated, the king ordered the baby to be brought into the hall, thinking that if the father were present, the most visceral paternal feelings might be excited. The wet nurse took the baby in her arms and carried him into the hall, where everyone caressed him, giving him now a fruit, now a flower, now one thing, and now another. But the baby pushed it all away with his hand.

The wet nurse, who had been walking up and down the hall, at one point passed close to the palace door, at which the child immediately burst out laughing, and his head and whole body were so doubled over that he almost fell out of his nurse's arms. But she did not notice anything, and continued her course around the room. When she got back to the door again, the child was beside himself with joy, laughing and pointing at the door with his finger. The king, who had already noticed the child's actions, called the nurse over and asked her who was behind the door. The nurse answered that it was a beggar, as this was what she thought. But when the king summoned the man into his presence, he recognized him as Crazy Pietro. The child, who was right there, opened his arms and threw them around Pietro's neck, hugging him tightly. Upon seeing this, the king grew more and more distressed, and once he had politely dismissed his company, he deliberated that Pietro, his daughter, and the baby must die.

But the queen, who possessed great prudence, most wisely considered that if they were beheaded and burned alive by order of the king, this would result in no little insult and disgrace for him. And so she persuaded him to order a barrel, the biggest that could be made, and to close the three of them inside it and have it thrown to sea, so that without too much suffering they might be left to their fate. The king was greatly pleased by this counsel. He ordered the barrel and had the three of them put inside, with a basket of bread and a flask of good Vernaccia wine, as well as a bushel of figs for the child. He then had the barrel thrown onto the high seas, imagining that sooner or later it would hit a reef and break open, and they would drown.

Things went differently than what the king and queen had expected, however. When Pietro's little old mother, already oppressed by her years, heard of the curious case of her son, she was overcome by grief, and in the course of a few days she died. The miserable Luciana, under the assault of tempestuous waves in the barrel, and able to see neither the sun nor the moon, wept over her misfortune without pause. And having no milk with which to quiet the child, who would often cry, she sometimes put him to sleep by feeding him figs.

But Pietro paid no attention to any of this, and gave mind to nothing but the bread and the Vernaccia. When Luciana saw this, she said, "Alas, Pietro! You see how I suffer this punishment innocently because of you, and you laugh, eat, and drink in that senseless way, not considering for a moment our common peril." To which he answered, "We find ourselves in this situation not through any fault of mine, but because you continually mocked and made fun of me. But keep up your spirits," he said. "We'll soon leave our worries behind." "I think that you're right," said Luciana, "when you say that we'll soon leave our worries behind, since any time now the barrel will be split open by some rock and we'll all drown."

Then Pietro said, "Be quiet now, for I have a secret, and if you knew what it was, you would be amazed, and it might even cheer you up." "What kind of secret do you have," said Luciana, "that could relieve us from all that we're suffering?"

"I have a fish," said Pietro, "that does whatever I command, and it would deny me nothing even if it risked losing its life. It was that fish that made you pregnant." "That's a good thing," said Luciana, "if it's true. But what's this fish called?" To which Pietro replied, "It's called tuna." "Make it give me the same power you have," said Luciana, "and order it to do whatever I say." "May your will be done," said Pietro.

And he called the tuna right over and ordered that whatever Luciana obliged it to do be done. Once she had the power to command the tuna, the young woman immediately ordered it to cast the barrel onto one of the loveliest and most secure cliffs that could be found in her father's kingdom. After this, she ordered it to make Pietro leave his filthy and crazy state and become the wisest and most handsome man in the world. And not yet content, she wished again that a sumptuous and rich palace be built on that cliff, with loggias and grand halls and splendid chambers, and that in back it have a delightful and elegant garden full of trees that produced gems and precious pearls, in the middle of which would be a fountain of icy cold water and a vault of precious wines. All of this was carried out completely and without further ado.

The king and queen, remembering how miserably they had deprived themselves of their daughter and the baby, and imagining that their flesh had already been devoured by fish, were filled with regret, and could not find a moment of happiness or cheer. And in this state of affliction and mourning, they decided to go off to Jerusalem and visit the Sacred Lands as a means to comfort their distraught hearts. When a ship had been prepared and equipped with everything that was needed, they got on the ship and left, and sailed with prosperous and favorable winds.

They were not yet a hundred miles from the island of Capraia, when from offshore they saw a rich and superb palace high above the sea, on a little island. And since it was quite lovely, as well as subject to their dominion, they resolved to go and see it. They sailed in close to the island, landed, and got off the ship. They had not yet reached the palace when they were recognized by Crazy Pietro and the king's daughter, Luciana, who descended the steps to meet them and cordially received them with the warmest of welcomes. The king and the queen did not recognize them, however, as they were completely transformed.

When they had entered the lovely palace, they looked it over closely and offered many compliments, and then they descended a secret ladder that led to the garden, which the king and queen found so pleasing that they swore that in all of their days they had never seen any other that they liked as much. In the middle of the beautiful garden there was a tree with three golden apples on one of its branches, and the caretaker, by Luciana's express command, watched over them so that they would not be stolen. But, and I'm not sure how, someone hid the most beautiful of the apples in the king's shirt without him noticing. And when the king was preparing to leave, the caretaker said to Luciana, "Madam, one of the three apples—the most beautiful—is missing, and I don't know who stole it."

Luciana then ordered the caretaker to thoroughly search each person present, since it was not a matter to be taken lightly. When the caretaker had carefully searched everyone not once but twice, he returned to Luciana and told her that he had not found the apple. Upon hearing this, Luciana pretended to be very upset, and turning to the king, she said, "Holy Majesty, you must forgive me if I have you searched again, for the golden apple that I am missing is of the highest value, and I esteem it over all else."

The king, unaware of the plot and certain that he was not at fault, loosened his robes, and the apple immediately fell to the ground. At the sight of this, the king was amazed and bewildered, as he did not know how it had come to be in his clothes. Luciana, observing this reaction, said, "My lord, we have treated you most warmly and honored you, offering you the welcome and tributes that you worthily deserve, and in exchange for such a welcome you steal the fruit of our garden behind our backs. It appears that you show us great ingratitude."

The king, who was innocent, went to great efforts to make her believe that he had not stolen the apple. Luciana saw that the appropriate time to reveal herself and prove her innocence to her father had arrived. With a tearful countenance she said, "My lord, you should know that I am that Luciana whom you unhappily begot, and whom you cruelly condemned to death, together with Crazy Pietro and the little boy. I am that Luciana, your only child, whom you found pregnant, although I had known no man. And this is the innocent child whom I conceived without the stain of sin," and she presented the boy to him.

"And this is Crazy Pietro, who thanks to a fish called tuna became the wisest of men, and built this great and magnificent palace. It was he who, unbeknownst to you, placed the apple under your clothes. It was he by whom

I became pregnant, not through carnal union but because of an enchantment. And just as you are innocent of having stolen the golden apple, I too am entirely innocent of the pregnancy."

Weeping with happiness, everyone then embraced, and great festivities ensued. After several days had gone by, they got on the ship and returned to Capraia, where there was a grand celebration and more festivities. The king wed Luciana to Pietro, and awarded his son-in-law such status that he lived honorably and in comfort for a long time. And when the king arrived at the end of his life, he named Pietro his successor.

Biancabella

This tale has elements of ATU 403, The Black and the White Bride, and ATU 706, The Maiden without Hands. The theme of the persecuted heroine who has her hands cut off is found in earlier miracle plays such as Santa Uliva *and* Stella; *some of these motifs also appear in Chaucer's "Man of Law's Tale," Giovanni Fiorentino's* Pecorone *(tale 10.1), and Basile's* Tale of Tales *("Penta with the Chopped-Off Hands"). The motif of combing pearls and jewels from hair is present in Basile's "The Two Little Pizzas," among others, and the conflicts of a "white beauty" with a stepmother recalls the Snow White tale type. There are also similarities with ATU 887, Griselda, and ATU 900, King Thrushbeard (see, e.g., Basile's "Pride Punished").*

Biancabella, the daughter of Lamberico, marquis of Monferrato, is sent by the stepmother of Fernandino, king of Naples, to be killed, but the stepmother's servants cut off her hands and take out her eyes instead. She is restored to her previous state by a snake, and she happily returns to Fernandino.

A long time ago there ruled in Monferrato a marquis named Lamberico, who was powerful in status and wealth, but without children. He had a great desire for them, but God had denied him His graces.

It came to pass that one day the marchioness was taking her pleasure in one of her gardens when she was overcome by drowsiness and fell asleep at the foot of a tree. As she was sweetly sleeping, a little snake approached her and slid under her clothing. Without her feeling a thing, it entered her private parts and, imperceptibly winding up her body, reached her womb, where it began to quietly live.

It hadn't been there long before the marchioness became pregnant, causing no small pleasure on her part and the joy of the entire city. When she reached the end of her term, she delivered a girl whose throat was encircled three times by a snake, which greatly frightened the midwives. But without harming anyone, the snake loosened itself from the baby's neck, slithered onto the ground, straightened itself out, and went off into the garden.

After the baby had been washed and tidied up in a clear bath and wrapped in lily-white swaddling cloths, a most exquisitely crafted golden necklace slowly began to reveal itself on her neck, and it was so beautiful and striking that it made her flesh and skin shine as only the most precious things, such as the finest crystal, are wont to do. And this necklace encircled her neck as many times as the snake had encircled it. The girl, who was named Biancabella because of her beauty, grew up to be so virtuous and kind that she appeared to be not human but divine.

Biancabella had reached the age of ten when one day, while sitting at a balcony, she saw the garden full of roses and lovely flowers. She turned to the nurse who took care of her and asked her what that place was, since she had never seen it before. In answer she heard that it was a place of her mother's, where she would sometimes go to take her pleasure. The girl said, "I've never seen a more beautiful thing, and I'd love to go there."

The nurse took her by the hand and led her to the garden, where she separated from the girl and went off to sleep under the shade of a leafy beech tree, leaving the girl to take her pleasure. Biancabella, who was enchanted by the delightful place, walked to and fro picking flowers, and when she grew tired she sat down under the shade of a tree. As soon as the girl had settled herself on the ground, she was approached by a snake, at which she grew very frightened and was about to cry out. But the snake said to her, "Come now, hush and be still, and don't be afraid, for I am your sister, born the same day and from the same womb as you, and my name is Samaritana. If you obey my orders, your life will be full of bliss; but if you do otherwise, you will become the most miserable and unhappy woman the world has ever seen. Go now, without fear of any sort, and tomorrow have two jars brought to the garden, one filled with pure milk and the other with the finest rosewater, and then come to me here, alone and unaccompanied."

The snake left, and the girl arose and went to her nurse, whom she found still resting; she woke her and went with her into the house, without saying anything about what had happened.

The next day, Biancabella was alone with her mother in her room, and had a very melancholy look on her face. Seeing this, her mother said, "What's the matter, Biancabella; why the long face? You were cheerful and gay before, and now you're all sad and sorrowful." To which her daughter replied, "All I want is to have two jars brought to the garden, one filled with milk and the other with rosewater." "And you're upset over such a little thing, my daughter?" said her mother. "You know that everything here is yours."

And she had two beautiful, large jars brought in, one filled with milk and the other with rosewater, and then she sent them down to the garden. When the time stipulated by the snake arrived, Biancabella went to the garden, unaccompanied by any of her maidservants; she opened the gate, closed it after her so that she was alone, and then sat down next to the jars.

No sooner had Biancabella settled down than the snake approached her, immediately had her undress, and then, naked, bade her get into the creamy-white milk. The snake bathed her from head to toes with the milk, and with its tongue licked and cleansed her wherever she seemed to have an imperfection. After taking her out of the milk, it placed her in the rosewater, which gave her a scent that was greatly refreshing. Then it dressed her again, expressly ordering that she be silent and not reveal what had happened to anyone, not even her father or mother. Then she told her that she intended that no woman who equaled her in beauty and kindness might ever be found. Finally, after endowing her with infinite other virtues, the snake departed.

Biancabella left the garden and returned to the house, and when her mother saw that she was so beautiful and full of grace that she surpassed all other women in beauty and grace, she was overwhelmed and did not know what to say. But then she asked her what she had done to attain this perfect beauty. And the girl replied that she did not know. Then her mother took a comb and began to comb and arrange her blond tresses, and from her head pearls and precious jewels fell; she washed her hands, and from her hands issued forth roses, violets, and delightful flowers of varied colors and such a sweet scent that they seemed to create an earthly paradise.

When her mother saw this, she ran to her husband, Lamberico, and with maternal joy said, "My lord, we have a daughter who is the kindest, most beautiful, and most gracious girl that nature has ever created. And in addition to the divine beauty and grace that one can clearly see, pearls, gems, and other precious jewels fall from her hair, and from her lily-white hands—what an astonishing thing!—come forth roses, violets, and every other sort of flower, which render to all who behold them the sweetest scent. I would never have believed any of this, but I saw it with my own eyes."

Her husband, who was by nature incredulous and didn't fully trust his wife's words so readily, laughed and made fun of her; then, when she stubbornly insisted, he decided to see what it was all about. And after he summoned his daughter to appear before him, he discovered even greater things than his wife had told him of. This put him in such a state of joy that he firmly esteemed that there was no man in the whole world worthy of uniting with her in marriage.

The glorious fame of the lovely and immortal beauty of Biancabella had already spread through the entire universe, and kings, princes, and marquises from all over competed for her hand, trying to acquire her love and take her for their wife. But none of them possessed sufficient virtues to win her, since each was lacking in something.

Finally, Ferrandino, king of Naples, arrived. His valor and name shone like the sun among the tiny stars; he went to the marquis and asked to take his daughter for his wife. The marquis saw that he was handsome, elegant, well-built, and very powerful in status and wealth, and after the wedding was arranged, his daughter was called, and, without further ado, they touched hands and kissed.[1]

No sooner had the nuptials been celebrated than Biancabella remembered the words that her sister, Samaritana, had lovingly said to her. She left her husband and, pretending that she had certain things to see to, went to her room, where she locked herself in and then secretly entered the garden alone through a little door. She began to call in a low voice for Samaritana, who did not present herself as she had before. At this, Biancabella greatly marveled, and when she could neither see nor find her sister in any part of the garden, she was distressed, since she knew this had happened because she had not obeyed the snake's commands. Feeling great sadness, she returned to her room, opened the door, and sat down next to her husband, who had been waiting for her for a long time.

When the wedding was over, Ferrandino moved his wife to Naples, where with grand pomp and glorious rejoicing and resounding trumpets they were honorably received. Ferrandino had a stepmother who had two ill-mannered and ugly daughters, one of whom she had wanted to unite in marriage with Ferrandino. But now that every hope of attaining her desire was taken from

1. Before the Council of Trent in the sixteenth century, Catholic marriages did not require the presence of a church official but merely the consent of the two parties.

her, she turned her anger and resentment against Biancabella, whom she refused to see or even to hear, though she pretended to love her and hold her dear.

Fortune willed that the king of Tunisia was making extensive preparations on land and at sea for declaring war on Ferrandino—I don't know whether because of the wife he had taken or for some other reason—and he had already penetrated the borders of his realm. For this reason, it was necessary for Ferrandino to take up arms to defend his kingdom and confront the enemy. And so, once he had put his affairs in order and entrusted Biancabella, who was pregnant, to his stepmother, he left with his army.

After a few days, the wicked and arrogant stepmother decided to put Biancabella to her death and, summoning several of her most trusted servants, told them that they were to go with her to some pleasant place and not leave before they had killed her; and as proof of her death they were to bring her some evidence. The servants, ready to do evil, obeyed the lady. Pretending to take her to a certain place of recreation, they led her to a wood and were already preparing to kill her when they saw how beautiful and gracious she was, and then they felt pity and no longer wanted to kill her. So instead they detached both her hands from her arms and extracted her eyes from her head, and brought them to the stepmother as manifest proof that they had killed her. When the cruel and evil stepmother saw this, she was satisfied and full of joy.

The nefarious stepmother, intent on seeing her evil resolution to its end, sowed the rumor throughout the whole kingdom that her two daughters had died, one from a high fever and the other from an abscess near her heart that had suffocated her, and that Biancabella had lost her child on account of her grief over the king's departure and that she had been overcome by a tertian fever that was devastating her, although the hope that she would live was greater than the fear that she would die. But in place of Biancabella, the wicked and villainous woman had put in the king's bed one of her own daughters, who was pretending to be the feverish Biancabella.

Ferrandino, who had already defeated and dispersed the enemy army, returned home in glorious triumph. Thinking that he would find his beloved Biancabella festive and cheerful, he found her lying in bed, thin, pale, and deformed. When he went over to her and stared at her face and saw how wasted she was, he was stunned, and could in no way imagine that she was Biancabella. He had her hair combed, and instead of the gems and precious jewels that had fallen from her blond locks before, there appeared huge lice, which were devouring her without pause; and from her hands, from which used to issue roses and fragrant flowers, now issued such filth and dirt that anyone who came near her felt sick to their stomach. But the nefarious woman comforted him and told him that this had happened because of the duration of her illness, which produced such effects.

Meanwhile, the miserable Biancabella, with two stumps for hands and blind in both eyes, dwelled in solitary affliction in that lonely and out-of-the-way place, calling again and again for her sister, Samaritana, to come and help her. But no one answered, except for the echo that resounded in the air. As the unhappy woman was living in this state of suffering, entirely lacking in any human assistance, an old and wizened man, benevolent in appearance and most compassionate, entered the woods. When he heard the melancholy lament of that voice, he approached it first with his ears and then, very slowly, on foot, and found the blind and handless young woman fiercely bemoaning her harsh fate.

When the kind old man saw her, he could not bear to leave her among the branches, thorns, and brambles, and, overcome by paternal compassion, he took her to his house and entrusted her to his wife, ordering her in the strictest manner to take care of the girl. And turning to his three daughters, who looked like three shining stars, he passionately commanded them to keep her company, to hold her dear, and to make sure that she wanted for nothing. At this, his wife, who was more cruel than merciful, was sparked by angry rage and turned furiously to her husband, saying, "So, husband, what do you intend for us to do with this blind and handless girl, who is doubtless in this state not because of her virtue but as recompense for her less than noble deeds?" To which the little old man replied indignantly, "Do what I ask you, and if you do otherwise, do not expect me to come home again."

While the afflicted Biancabella was living with the wife and three daughters, she would discuss various things with them, and, reflecting on her misfortune, one day she begged one of the daughters to please comb her hair a little. When the mother heard this, she became indignant, since under no circumstance did she want her daughter to become a servant to Biancabella. But the daughter was more charitable than the mother, and since she had in mind what her father had ordered her to do, and saw something in Biancabella's appearance that signaled her grandeur, she untied the freshly laundered apron that she was wearing and, after laying it on the ground, began to lovingly comb her hair. And she had barely started combing before pearls, rubies, diamonds, and other precious jewels spilled from the blond tresses. Upon seeing this, the mother was astonished and not a little afraid, and the great hatred that she had felt earlier for Biancabella now turned into true love.

When the little old man returned home, everyone ran to embrace him, rejoicing greatly with him over the fortune that had arrived after so much poverty. Biancabella asked that a pail of fresh water be brought and that her face and stumps be washed; as they all watched, roses, violets, and an abundance of other flowers spilled forth. And they all judged her to be not human but divine.

It came to pass that Biancabella decided to return to the place where she had been found earlier by the little old man. The little old man, his wife, and his daughters had, however, seen the great profit that she brought them, and they wheedled and begged her insistently not to leave, rattling off many arguments aimed at getting her to change her mind. But she remained firm in her will and wanted to leave at all costs, though she promised them that she would return. Upon hearing this, the old man took her without further delay to the place where he had found her. She ordered him to leave and come back that evening, when she would return home with him.

After the little old man left, the unfortunate Biancabella began to wander through the woods, calling for Samaritana, and her cries and laments rose all the way up to the heavens. But Samaritana, although she was nearby and had never abandoned the girl, did not wish to reply. When the poor thing saw that her words were being thrown to the wind, she said, "What is there left for me to do in this world if I am without eyes and hands, and I lack all human assistance?" And sparked by a frenzy that caused her to lose all hope of salvation, she grew desperate and decided to kill herself. Since she had no other way to end her life, she set off in the direction of some nearby water, so that she could throw herself in. When she got to the bank and was about to plunge in, she heard a thundering voice that said, "Alas, do not make of yourself a murderer, nor be a murderer of yourself! Put your life to a better purpose."

Biancabella was bewildered by the voice, and she felt every hair on her head stand on end. But then she seemed to recognize the voice, and, mustering up her courage, she said, "Who are you, who wander in these places and manifest yourself to me with a sweet and charitable voice?"

The voice replied, "I am Samaritana, your sister, the one you call so insistently."

When she heard this, Biancabella said, in a voice broken by fervent sobs, "Ah my sister, I beg you to help me; and if I ignored your advice, I now ask your forgiveness. I was wrong, and fully confess my error, but it was out of ignorance, not malice, for if it had been out of malice, divine providence would not have put up with it for long."

After Samaritana heard this pitiful lament and saw how ill-treated the girl was, she was quick to comfort her. She gathered some herbs that had marvelous powers and placed them on Biancabella's eyes, at the same time attaching two hands to her arms, and the girl was immediately restored to her previous state. Then Samaritana removed her own squalid snakeskin, and came forth as a magnificent young woman.

The sun was already hiding its brilliant rays and night's darkness was beginning to appear, when the little old man arrived in the woods with hurried step and found Biancabella sitting with another nymph. He looked into her bright face and was astonished, almost thinking that it wasn't she. But when he had recognized her, he said, "My daughter, this morning you were blind and without hands; how have you been cured so quickly?" Biancabella replied, "Not by any merit of my own, but because of the virtue and kindness of she who sits beside me, who is my sister." And they both arose and with the greatest happiness went home with the old man, where they were lovingly received by his wife and daughters.

Many, many days later Samaritana, Biancabella, and the little old man with his wife and three daughters went to the city of Naples to live. They saw an empty lot in front of the king's palace and sat down there. When night's darkness arrived, Samaritana took a little laurel branch in her hand and struck the ground three times as she said some words. And just as she had finished saying them, a palace sprang up, the most beautiful and magnificent palace that had ever been seen.

When King Ferrandino went to the window early the next morning, he saw the lavish, marvelous palace, and was stunned and astonished. He called his wife and his stepmother, and they came to see, but were displeased, since they suspected that something sinister had occurred. Ferrandino stood there contemplating the palace, and when he had inspected it from all angles, he lifted his eyes, and at the window of one of the rooms he saw two ladies whose beauty was the envy of the sun. And as soon as he saw them, he felt rage in his heart, since one of them seemed to have the countenance of Biancabella. He asked them who they were and where they came from, to which they replied that they were two women in exile, and that they had come from Persia with all their possessions to live in that glorious city. And when he asked them if they would welcome a visit from him and his ladies, they replied that they would like that very much, even if it was more appropriate and proper for them, as his subjects, to visit him and his ladies rather than for the ladies and queen to visit them.

Ferrandino called the queen and the other ladies, and although they tried to refuse, since they were in great fear of their impending ruin, they all set off for the palace of the two ladies, who received them with the greatest distinction, offering them a kind welcome and treating them with honorable manners. They showed them the ample loggias, the spacious halls, and the ornate chambers whose walls were of the finest alabaster and porphyry and were decorated with figures that seemed alive. When they had seen the sumptuous palace, the beautiful young lady went to the king and sweetly beseeched him to consent to dine with them one day together with his lady. The king, who did not have a heart of stone and was by nature magnanimous, graciously accepted the invitation. And after he thanked them for the honorable welcome that they had given him, he left with the queen and went back to his palace.

When the day of the scheduled invitation arrived, the king, the queen, and the stepmother, regally dressed and accompanied by various matrons, went to honor the magnificent dinner that had been lavishly prepared. After the king and queen rinsed their hands, the steward placed them at the most distinguished table, which was close to the other ones; then he seated everyone else according to their rank, and with great comfort and cheer they all dined. When the sumptuous dinner was over and the tables had been cleared, Samaritana rose to her feet, and, turning to the king and queen, she said, "My lord, may someone propose some activity that gives pleasure and joy, so that we do not sit here in idleness."

Everyone confirmed that this was a good idea, but there was no one bold enough to put forth a proposal. Seeing everyone silent, Samaritana said, "Since no one is making a move to say anything, with Your Majesty's permission I will call in one of our damsels, who will offer us no small delight." And she called in one of her ladies-in-waiting, whose name was Silveria, and ordered her to take up the zither and sing something worthy of praise for the king. Obeying her lady's every word, she took the zither, sat down before the king, and with a sweet and delectable voice began to pick the sonorous strings and to tell Biancabella's story in an orderly manner, without, however, mentioning her by name. And when the damsel arrived at the end of the story, Samaritana rose to her feet and asked the king what the appropriate penalty and fitting punishment would be for whomever committed these grave excesses. The stepmother, who thought that she could cover her guilt with a quick and ready response, did not wait for the king to reply, but boldly said, "The hottest of furnaces would be a small punishment compared to what they deserve."

Samaritana, her face aflame as if with burning embers, said, "You are that criminal and cruel woman who caused all of this misfortune. And now, wicked and accursed creature, you have condemned yourself with your own mouth." Then Samaritana turned to the king, and with a happy face said, "This is your Biancabella. This is your wife, whom you love so dearly. This is the woman without whom you could not live."

And to prove the truth of this, she ordered the three damsels, daughters of the little old man, to comb Biancabella's blond and wavy hair in the presence of the king; and as has already been said, this caused precious and exquisite jewels to come forth, and from her hands issued morning roses and scented flowers. And as an even greater assurance, she showed the king her snow-white neck, which was encircled by a little chain of the finest gold that shone like crystal between her flesh and her skin.

When the king recognized from these true signs and clear indications that she was his Biancabella, he began to cry with tenderness, and embraced her. And he did not leave until the furnace was lit and the stepmother and the daughters were placed inside; repenting for their sins too late, they thus ended their miserable lives. After this, the little old man's three daughters were honorably wed, and King Ferrandino lived with his Biancabella and Samaritana for a long time, leaving after him legitimate heirs to the kingdom.

Adamantina

This tale combines ATU 571, All Stick Together, and ATU 571C, The Biting Doll. Variants include Basile's "The Goose" (5.1) and the Grimms' "The Golden Goose" (64).

Adamantina, daughter of Bagolana Savonese, becomes the wife of Drusiano, king of Bohemia, due to the magic powers of a doll.

Not so long ago, in Bohemia, there was a little old woman who went by the name of Bagolana Savonese. Since she was quite poor and had two daughters, one of whom was named Cassandra and the other Adamantina, she decided to order her affairs by drawing up a will for what little property she had, so that she could then die happy. But seeing as she had nothing in her house or outside it to put in a will, except for a little chest full of tow, she made her will and left the little chest and the tow to her daughters, beseeching them to live peacefully together after her death. The two sisters, however lacking in fortune's goods, were nevertheless rich in spiritual goods, and their virtues and manners were no less than those of other women.

When the little old woman had died and been buried, Cassandra, the older of the two, took a pound of the tow and began to spin it with great care. After it was spun, she gave the thread to Adamantina, the younger sister, and ordered her to take it to the square and sell it, and with whatever she earned to buy as much bread as she could, so that both of them could be supported by her labor.

Adamantina took the thread, put it under her arm and, following Cassandra's order, went off to the square to sell it. But when she had reason and opportunity to sell it, she did the opposite of what she and her sister desired, for in the square she encountered a little old woman who was holding a doll in her lap, the most beautiful and finely crafted doll that had ever been seen.

After Adamantina caught sight of it she contemplated it for a while, and she took such a fancy to the doll that she started thinking more about how she could obtain it than about selling her thread. As Adamantina was deliberating over this, not knowing what she might do or say to get the doll, she finally decided to test her fortune by attempting an exchange. She went over to the old woman, and said, "Dear mother, if it pleases you, I'd like to exchange my thread for your doll."

The little old woman saw that the girl was beautiful and of pleasant manners, and that she desired the doll badly, and did not want to say no. So she took the thread and presented the girl with the doll. When Adamantina had the doll, she was the happiest girl in the world, and she returned home full of joy and delight.

Her sister, Cassandra, said, "Did you sell the thread?" "Yes," replied Adamantina. "And where's the bread that you bought?" said Cassandra. In response, Adamantina opened the freshly laundered apron that she always wore, and showed her the doll that she had exchanged. When Cassandra, who was dying of hunger, saw the doll, she blew up with such rage and indignation that she grabbed Adamantina by her braids and beat her so hard that the miserable girl could barely move. Adamantina received the beating patiently, without defending herself in any way, and then to the best of her ability she went off to her room with the doll.

When evening fell, Adamantina took the doll in her arms and went to sit at the hearth, as little girls do. Then she took some oil from the lamp, greased the doll's stomach and kidneys, wrapped it up in some rags she had, and put it in her bed. Shortly thereafter she went to bed herself, and lay down next to the doll.

Adamantina had barely entered her first sleep when the doll began to call, "Mommy, mommy, poop!" Adamantina woke up and said, "What's the matter, my daughter?" To which the doll replied, "I'd like to go poop, mommy." And Adamantina said, "Wait, my daughter." And she arose from bed, got the apron that she had been wearing the day before, and held it out to the doll, saying, "Do your poopy, my daughter," and the doll, pushing as hard as it could, filled the apron with a large quantity of coins. When Adamantina saw this, she woke up her sister, Cassandra, and showed her the coins that the doll had shit. When Cassandra saw the great number of coins, she was amazed. She thanked God for His goodness in not abandoning them in their poverty, and turning to her sister, she begged forgiveness for the beating that Adamantina had so unjustly received from her. Then she caressed the doll, kissing it tenderly and holding it tightly in her arms.

When morning came, the sisters supplied themselves with bread, wine, oil, firewood, and everything else that a well-equipped family has. And every evening they would grease the doll's stomach and kidneys, wrap it in fine cloth, and ask it often if it wanted to poop. And it would answer that it did, and then poop large quantities of coins.

It came about that a neighbor of theirs went to the two sisters' house and saw how well stocked the house was with everything they needed to live. She was most astonished, and couldn't explain to herself how they had become rich so quickly, since they had been so very poor until recently, especially because she knew they led an honorable life and were so upright in their ways. And since she continued to dwell on this, she decided to take action and try to discover the cause of all that good fortune. She went back to the two sisters' house, and said, "My dear girls, how have you been able to provide so richly for yourselves, seeing as in the past you've always been so poor?"

Cassandra, the older sister, replied, "We exchanged a pound of tow thread for a doll, which supplies us with endless coins." When the neighbor heard this, she became greatly agitated, and was so consumed by envy that she decided she had to steal it from them. When she returned home, she told her husband how the two sisters had a doll that day and night dispensed large amounts of silver and gold, and that she had made the decision to rob them of it. And although her husband made fun of his wife's words, she was finally able to make him believe her. But then he said to her, "How are you going to steal it from them?" To which his wife replied, "One evening you'll pretend to be drunk and you'll take your sword and chase me as if you wanted to kill me, striking the sword on the walls. I'll pretend to be frightened and flee into the street, and those two, who are full of compassion, will open their door and lock me up inside their house, and I'll stay with them for the night and see what I can do."

The next evening, the husband of the good woman took his rusty sword and, striking it against this wall and that wall, he chased after his wife, who, crying and screaming at the top of her lungs, fled from the house. When the two sisters heard this, they ran to their windows to see what had happened, and they recognized the voice of their neighbor, who was screaming very loudly. The two sisters abandoned the windows, went down to the door and opened it, and pulled her into the house. And when the good woman was asked why her husband was chasing her so angrily, she replied, "He came home so dizzy from wine that he didn't know what he was doing, and when I scolded him for always getting drunk, he took his sword and ran after me, trying to kill me. But I'm braver than he is, so I decided that the better solution was to escape, and I came here."

The sisters told her, "Dear mother, you did the right thing, and you'll stay with us tonight so that you don't endanger your life, and in the meantime your husband will sober up." They set the table and had dinner together, and afterward they greased the doll and went to get their rest. When the hour that the doll needed to poop arrived, it said, "Mommy, poop." And Adamantina, following the usual procedure, put the clean little cloth under it, and the doll pooped the coins, to the great marvel of them all. The good woman who had fled from home saw it all and was quite astounded, and each hour before she could steal it and try it out herself seemed like a thousand years.

At daybreak, while the two sisters were still sleeping, the good woman quietly got out of bed, and, without Adamantina noticing, she stole the doll that was lying next to her. Then she woke the sisters and took her leave to go back home, telling them that she thought that by then her husband had digested the wine that he had drunk in such excess. When she arrived home the good woman said to her husband, happily, "My husband, now we've found our good fortune: this doll here." And each passing hour before night fell and they could become rich seemed like a thousand years.

When the dark of night arrived, the woman took the doll, built a nice fire, and greased its stomach and kidneys; then she swaddled it in some fine white cloth and laid it in bed, after which she undressed and got into bed next to the doll. After its first sleep, the doll woke up and said, "My lady, poop." It didn't say, "Mommy, poop" because it didn't know who she was, and the good woman, who was vigilantly awaiting the fruit that was to follow, got out of bed, took a cloth of pure-white linen, and placed it under the doll, saying, "Poop, my daughter, poop."

The doll pushed as hard as it could, but instead of coins it filled the cloth with such a large quantity of stinky excrement that you could hardly get near it. Then the husband said, "You see, you crazy thing, how it's treating you; I was a fool to believe such craziness."

But the wife, countering her husband, insisted that she had seen the doll shit a large quantity of coins with her own eyes. And when the wife said that she wanted to reserve judgment and try the experiment again the next night, her husband, whose nose could no longer stand the stench that he was smelling, insulted his wife more violently than any guilty woman in the world had ever been insulted, and then took the doll and threw it out of the window, where it landed on top of a garbage heap in front of their house.

It so happened that the garbage heap was loaded onto a cart by some peasant laborers, and without anyone noticing, the doll was put into the cart as well, and the garbage was used to make a compost pile that would be used, when ready, to fertilize the soil.

One day it came to pass that King Drusiano was out amusing himself at the hunt and had an overwhelming desire to unload the excess weight of his belly. He got off his horse and did what nature required him to do, and since he had nothing to wipe with, he called for a servant to give him something with which he could clean himself. The servant went over to the compost pile, and looking around to see if there was anything that could serve this purpose, by chance he found the doll; and taking it in his hand, he brought it to the king. Without thinking twice, the king grabbed the doll, but when he put it to his backside to clean off mister butts, he let out the loudest scream that had ever been heard. And this was because the doll had latched on to one of his buttocks with its teeth, and was holding on so tightly that it was causing him to scream at the top of his lungs.

Everyone heard the unrestrained screaming and immediately ran over to the king. They saw him lying on the ground as if he were dead, and they were all stunned; and when they saw how he was being tormented by the doll, they all joined forces to get it off his buttocks. But they labored in vain, and the greater the efforts they made to remove it, the greater the pain and torment the doll gave him, nor was there anyone who could get the doll to ease up, let alone pull it off. And from time to time the doll would grab hold of his jingle bells with its hands, and squeeze them so hard that it made him see all the stars in the sky.

When the exhausted king had returned to his palace with the doll attached to his buttocks, and still couldn't find any way or means to remove it, he had a proclamation issued: if anyone, no matter what their rank or status, could be found who had the courage to detach the doll from his buttocks, he would give them a third of his kingdom, and if it were a young lady and it were pleasing to her, he would take her as his dear and cherished wife; and he swore on his own crown that he would respect all the terms of this proclamation.

When word got out about the proclamation, many people came to the palace with the highest hopes that they might obtain the promised reward. But no one was granted the favor of being able to remove it from the king; indeed, as soon as anyone approached the doll, it would become even more bothersome and zealous. And the torments of the afflicted king were so fierce, and his attempts to find a remedy for his incomprehensible pain so vain, that he lay there as if he were near death.

Cassandra and Adamantina, who had shed many tears for their lost doll, heard of the proclamation and came to the palace, where they presented themselves to the king. Cassandra, the older sister, was overjoyed to see the doll, and hugged her as tightly as she could. But the doll clenched its teeth and squeezed its hands, tormenting the disconsolate king even further. Then Adamantina, who had been standing at a distance, came forward and said, "Holy Majesty, let me try my fortune," and she presented herself to the doll, saying, "Come now, my daughter, leave my lord at peace, give him no more torment," and she took hold of the cloth it was wrapped in and began to caress it lovingly.

The doll, who recognized its mother, the one who took care of it and controlled its behavior, immediately detached itself from the buttocks; and, once it had abandoned the king, it jumped into her arms. When the king saw this, he was shocked and speechless; and then he lay down to rest, since he hadn't been able to find a way to rest for many, many nights and days due to the great suffering he had undergone and endured.

Once King Drusiano was restored back to health after the intense pain and terrible bites, he had Adamantina brought before him so as not to renege on his promise. When he saw that she was a lovely, charming young lady, he married her in the presence of all his people, and he had her older sister, Cassandra, married in the same honorable fashion. And after the solemn and lavish festivities and celebrations ended, they all lived for a long time happily and in the most tranquil peace.

When the doll witnessed the sumptuous weddings of both sisters, and saw that everything had reached a beneficial ending, it immediately disappeared. And nothing more was ever heard about what happened to it. But what I think is that it may have vanished into thin air, as ghosts always tend to do.

2

Giambattista Basile (1575–1632)

The Italian writer, poet, and courtier Giambattista Basile is today remembered for his groundbreaking book of fairy tales, *Lo cunto de li cunti overo lo trattenemiento de' peccerille* (*The Tale of Tales, or Entertainment for Little Ones*), also known as the *Pentamerone*. Written in Neapolitan dialect in the early years of the seventeenth century and published posthumously in 1634–36, it is the first integral compilation of authored, literary tales in Western Europe. Its tales of magic stand in marked contrast to the realism that was the heritage of Boccaccio and the novella tradition, still dominant at Basile's time; and the absolute originality of the fantastic world conjured forth by Basile remains striking even today.

Basile was a man of multiple literary personas. He was born to a middle-class family of courtiers and artists outside of Naples, at the time a major European metropolis and cultural center of the Baroque. For the most part, Basile's life was that of a typical man of letters. As he migrated from patron to patron, he composed verse on command; organized court festivities and spectacles in Naples, northern Italy, Venice, and Crete; was a member of several academies; and even briefly served as a soldier of fortune. He later held administrative positions in the Neapolitan provinces and ended his life with the title of count. His literary output, praised during his lifetime but little remembered since, included poetry, pastoral and musical dramas, religious works, and, as a scholar, philological and editorial projects, all penned in standard literary Italian in the prevailing style of the time. But in these same busy years Basile initiated a set of projects written in Neapolitan dialect that were radically different, in spirit and in letter, from his Italian production: *Le muse napoletane* (The Neapolitan Muses), a series of nine satiric poems celebrating the music, taverns, and other popular places and practices of Naples (1635), and his masterpiece, *The Tale of Tales*, both of which were probably read aloud at the "courtly conversations" that were an elite pastime of the period. In these works, Basile proved to be a sharp-eyed and inquisitive recorder of the popular and folkloric culture that he observed in his city and in the rural areas of southern Italy where he spent time (in one of his letters he facetiously complains that he's stuck in the wilds of Calabria, where the only pastime is "filling up scraps of paper with nursery rhymes"), and in Venice and Crete, both crossroads of international culture and hubs of commercial and narrative exchange.

The Tale of Tales is an expression of the interest in popular culture and folk traditions that culminated in the Renaissance, when single fairy tales began to be included in novella collections, such as Giovan Francesco Straparola's *The Pleasant Nights*. It also marked a generic crossroads, constituting one of the last great expressions of the waning Italian novella tradition just as it signaled the start of the new narrative paradigm of the literary fairy tale. Basile did not simply transcribe the oral materials he most likely heard in and around Naples and on his travels but re-elaborated them into singular versions, in many cases the first in literary form, of celebrated tale types such as Cinderella, Sleeping Beauty, Rapunzel, All-Fur, and Hansel and Gretel, all of which would be included in later collections like Charles Perrault's *Stories, or Tales of Past Times* (1697) or Wilhelm and Jacob Grimm's *Children's and Household Tales* (1812).

In many ways the structure of *The Tale of Tales* mirrors, in parodic fashion, that of earlier novella collections, in particular Boccaccio's *Decameron*, suggesting that Basile was well aware of the radically new course he was taking. It shares with the *Decameron* (and with the *Arabian Nights*) a framed structure in which the urgent circumstances of one tale—in this case, a fairy tale itself—generate the rest of the tales and lead to a resolution of the initial dilemma. The frame tale, also the fiftieth one, or "tale of tales," begins with the common motif of a princess who would not laugh: Princess Zoza is cheated out of her predestined prince, Tadeo, by a slave girl, Lucia, who marries Tadeo and becomes pregnant. Determined to win back her usurped husband with the help of magic objects obtained from fairies, Zoza makes her way into Tadeo and Lucia's life, ultimately casting a spell on Lucia that causes her to crave tales. Tadeo summons the ten best tale-tellers of his kingdom, a motley group of grotesque hags who are an explicit reversal of the elegant and aristocratic groups who commonly populated novella frame tales, but who also evoke the "old wives" archetype of oral tradition. The women each tell one tale apiece for five days; each day of telling is preceded by banquets, song and dance, and gaming and concludes with the recitation of verse "eclogues" that satirize social ills of the time. On the fifth and last day, Princess Zoza is asked to substitute for an ill teller, and she concludes the frame by telling her own story and revealing Lucia's deceit. Still pregnant, the slave is buried alive from the head down, Zoza takes her rightful place as Tadeo's wife, and *The Tale of Tales* ends.

The fifty stories of *The Tale of Tales* are both light-years distant from the Boccaccian model and, unlike other fairy tales, just as informed by elite literary culture as by folkloric traditions and the formulas of orality. They can be bawdy and irreverently comic but also tender and whimsical, acute in psychological characterization and at the same time encyclopedic in description. In a dazzling display of parodic intertextuality, Basile engages critically with dominant discourses by deformatively citing the most diverse authors and traditions and employing hyperbolic description and flamboyant metaphoric play. The humanity of the characters in *The Tale of Tales* is portrayed with a complexity that does not always meet our fairy-tale expectations: for example, we find simpleton heroes with no redeeming qualities, active heroines whose intelligence turns events to their advantage, kings unable to live up to the royal ideal of responsible management of subjects and reign, and conventional antagonists—such as ogres—who are often far from evil. All of their irregularities and loose ends manage, magically, to merge into a splendid portrait of creatures engaged in the laborious, complex, and sometimes joyful business of learning to live in their worlds.

Basile's journeys of initiation ultimately bear a certain familiarity to our own conflicted dialogues with the world around us. Indeed, the Italian film director Matteo Garrone, well-known for films like *Gomorra* (2008), an adaptation of Roberto Saviano's brutal exposé of the Neapolitan mafia, and *Reality* (2012), a reflection on the contemporary obsession with celebrity culture, chose for his 2015 film *The Tale of Tales* three tales that address uncannily modern concerns: the pursuit of youth and beauty ("The Old Woman Who

Was Skinned" [1.10]); the desperate longing for a child and the recourse to "artificial" means to have one ("The Enchanted Doe" [1.9]); and the conflict between paternal projections and filial needs ("The Flea" [1.4]). Just as many perceptive readers over the centuries, Garrone was struck by how "these tales describe a world which contains the opposites of life: the ordinary and the extraordinary, the magical and the mundane, the frightening and the pleasant, shreds of mythology and streams of popular wisdom."

Further Reading

Primary

Basile, Giambattista. *Lo cunto de li cunti overo lo trattenemiento de' peccerille*. Ed. Carolina Stromboli. 2 vols. Rome: Salerno, 2013. 1:2–25, 106–21, 122–37, 196–219, 294–303, 328–39; 2:534–51, 914–23. [source text]

Basile, Giambattista. *The Tale of Tales, or Entertainment for Little Ones*. Trans., introd., and notes by Nancy L. Canepa. Foreword by Jack Zipes. Illus. Carmelo Lettere. New York: Penguin, (2007) 2016.

De Simone Roberto. *Il Cunto de li cunti di Giambattista Basile nella riscrittura di Roberto de Simone*. Turin: Einaudi, 2002.

Garrone, Matteo, dir. *The Tale of Tales*. Rome: Archimede Film, 2015.

Secondary

Canepa, Nancy. *From Court to Forest: Giambattista Basile's "Lo cunto de li cunti" and the Birth of the Literary Fairy Tale*. Detroit: Wayne State University Press, 1999.

Croce, Bendetto. "Giambattista Basile e l'elaborazione delle fiabe popolari." In Giambattista Basile, *Il Pentamerone*, ed., intro., and trans. Benedetto Croce. Bari: Laterza, (1925) 1982.

Della Terza, Dante. "Il barocco e la fiaba: Il caso Basile." In *I capricci di Proteo: Percorsi e linguaggi del barocco, Atti Del Convegno Internazionale di Lecce, 23–26 Ottobre 2000*. Rome: Salerno, 2002.

Garrone, Matteo. "Director's Notes." 2015.

Getto, Giovanni. "La fiaba di Giambattista Basile." In *Barocco in prosa e in poesia*. Milan: Rizzoli, 1969. 379–401.

Maggi, Armando. *Preserving the Spell: Basile's "The Tale of Tales" and Its Afterlife in the Fairy-Tale Tradition*. Chicago: University of Chicago Press, 2015.

Magnanini, Suzanne. *Fairy-Tale Science: Monstrous Generation in the Tales of Straparola and Basile*. Toronto: University of Toronto Press, 2008.

Penzer, Norman. "Introduction." In *The "Pentamerone" of Giammbattista Basile*, ed., intro., and trans. Norman Penzer. 2 vols. London: John Lane and The Bodley Head, 1932.

Picone, Michelangelo, and Alfred Messerli, eds. *Giovan Battista Basile e l'invenzione della fiaba*. Ravenna: Longo Editore, 2004.

Rak, Michele. "Il racconto fiabesco." In Giambattista Basile, *Lo cunto de li cunti*, ed., intro., and trans. Michele Rak. Milan: Garzanti, 1986.

The Tale of the Ogre (Lo cunto dell'uerco)

Basile's tale is a version of ATU 563: The Table, the Ass, and the Stick, a very common tale type; see, for example, the Grimms' "The Magic Table, the Golden Donkey, and the Club in the Sack." As the opening tale, "The Tale of the Ogre" sets the stage for the structure that all of the tales share. First there is a descriptive rubric of the tale. A preamble follows, which may include discussion of topics that range from the classic Renaissance themes of fortuna *and* virtù, *to envy and ingratitude, to more concrete observations on the ills and virtues illustrated in the present or previous tale. Starting with the second tale (1.2), these preambles are generally divided into three "narrative moments": a description of the reactions of the textual audience (Prince Tadeo and his court) to the preceding tale, often with comments on the performative skill of the teller; Tadeo's call for silence; and the next teller's "moral introduction" to her tale. Each tale ends with a proverb, which in many cases is an inappropriate fit for the tale itself. In this translation of Basile's tales I do not include the comments on the previous tale.*

After Antuono of Marigliano is kicked out by his mother for being the ringleader of all fools, he enters into the service of an ogre, from whom he receives a gift whenever he wants to return to see his home. Antuono is tricked each time by an innkeeper, but finally the ogre gives him a club that punishes him for his ignorance, makes the innkeeper do penance for his ruses, and brings Antuono's family riches.

Whoever said that Fortune is blind knows a lot more than master Lanza,[1] stick it to him! For she certainly strikes blindly, raising people you wouldn't deign

1. A well-known Venetian ballad singer and oral storyteller of the time.

to kick out of a bean field to great heights and beating to the ground people who are the flower of mankind, as you shall now hear.

It is said that in the town of Marigliano[2] there once was a respectable woman named Masella. Besides her unmarried daughters, six little farts as thin as poles, she had a son who was such a birdbrain and muttonhead that he couldn't even throw a snowball. And so she sat around like a sow with a bit in her mouth, and there wasn't a day that she didn't say to him, "What are you doing in this house? Damn the bread you eat! Clear out, you big piece of you know what; make yourself scarce, Maccabee; go fall in a hole, troublemaker; get out of my sight, chestnut-guzzler! Someone must have switched you in the cradle; instead of an adorable dollikins and a pretty little baby I got a big lasagna-gobbling pig." But even with all this, Masella talked and he just whistled.

Seeing that there was no hope that Antuono (that was her son's name) would get it into his head to do any good, one day that was like any other she gave his head a good washing without soap, took a rolling pin in her hand, and began to measure him for a jacket. Antuono found himself fenced in, stockaded, and staked when he least expected it, and as soon as he could get out of her hands he threw up his heels and walked so far that around dusk—when the lamps began to be lit in Cynthia's[3] shop—he reached the foothills of a mountain so high that it butted horns with the clouds. Here, atop an enormous poplar root at the foot of a grotto decorated in pumice stone, there sat an ogre; and oh, dear mother, what an ugly one he was!

He was a little old midget; a bunch of dried twigs; his head was bigger than an Indian squash, his forehead all lumpy, his eyebrows joined; his eyes popped out of his head, his nose was dented by two horse's nostrils that looked like two sewer mains, his mouth was as big as a grape press, with two tusks that hung all the way down to the little bones of his feet; his chest was hairy, his arms like spinning reels, his legs vaulted like a cellar, and his feet as flat as a duck's. In short, he looked like a wicked spirit, an old demon, a filthy pauper, the spitting image of an evil shade, and he would have made Roland tremble with fright, Skanderbeg quake with terror, and the most skilled wrestler grow pale.[4]

2. A town in the province of Caserta, about fifteen miles from Naples.
3. The goddess of the moon, Diana.
4. Roland was the protagonist of the French epic (ca. 1100) *Chanson de Roland*; Skanderbeg or Iskanderbeg was the commonly used name of Giorgio Castriota (1403–68), the Albanian national hero.

But Antuono, whom even the crack of a slingshot couldn't ruffle, bowed and said to him, "Good day, sir, what's up? How are you? You want anything? How far is it from here to the place where I have to go?" The ogre, when he heard this speech straight out of the blue, began to laugh, and since he liked the beast's temperament, he said to him, "Do you want to work for me?" And Antuono replied, "How much do you want a month?" And the ogre came back with, "Take care to serve me honorably; we'll get along fine and you'll see good times." The deal was thus closed and Antuono stayed on to serve the ogre, where food was thrown in his face, and as far as working went he lived like a sheep at pasture. And in four days he grew as fat as a Turk, as big bellied as an ox, as bold as a rooster, as red as a lobster, as green as garlic, as round as a chestnut, and so massive and burly that he could barely see past his nose.

But before two years had gone by, he became bored by all the plenty and felt a craving and a great longing to go take a peek at Pascarola, and all that thinking about his home sweet home had almost reduced him to his original state. The ogre, who could see straight through to his innards and recognized by smell that his ass was itching like someone poorly attended to, called him over and said to him, "My dear Antuono, I know you're burning with desire to see your flesh and blood. And for this reason, since I love you like the pupils of my eyes I'll be happy if you go for a little visit and have this pleasure. So take this donkey, which will save you the fatigue of the journey, but mind you, never say, 'Giddy up, shit gold,' or you'll regret it, on the soul of my grandfather."

Antuono took the donkey and, without even saying, "Good evening," climbed onto its back and set out at a trot. But he hadn't gone a hundred yards before he got off the ass and started saying, "Giddy up, shit gold," and he had barely opened his mouth when the animal began to shit pearls, rubies, emeralds, sapphires, and diamonds, each as big as a walnut. With his mouth hanging wide open, Antuono stared at those lovely bowel movements, at the superb diarrhea and rich dysentery of the little ass, and with great joy he filled up a saddlebag with the jewels. Then he got back on and set off at a good pace, until he arrived at an inn where, after dismounting, the first thing he said to the innkeeper was, "Tie this donkey at the trough and feed it well, but see that you don't say, 'Giddy up, shit gold,' or you'll regret it. And store these little things of mine in a safe place."

When he heard that extravagant request and saw the jewels, which were worth hundreds, the innkeeper—an expert at his trade, a harbor fish, well experienced with acid and the crucible—became curious to see what the words meant. So after he fed Antuono well and gave him as much to drink as he could, he had him stuffed between a straw mattress and a thick blanket, and no sooner did he see that his eyes had grown heavy and that he was snoring at top speed than he ran to the stable and said to the donkey, "Giddy up, shit gold." With the medicine of those words the donkey performed the usual operation, tapping its bowels of streams of golden shit and bejeweled excrement. When the innkeeper saw the precious defecation, he decided to substitute the donkey and trick that moron Antuono, since he figured it would be a simple task to blind, swindle, bamboozle, trick, cheat, hoodwink, and embroil him, passing off baskets for lanterns in the eyes of a fat pig, bumpkin, macaroni head, booby, big sheep, and sucker like the one that had fallen into his hands.

And so, upon waking the next morning—when Aurora went to empty her old man's urinal, full of fine red sand, at the window of the Orient—Antuono rubbed his eyes with his hand, stretched for half an hour, and after a dialogue between sixty yawns and as many farts, he called the innkeeper and said, "Come here, pal: frequent bills make for long friendships; let us stay friends and our wallets do battle; draw up my bill and be paid." And so, after so much had been calculated for bread, so much for wine, this sum for soup, that one for meat, five for the stabling, ten for the bed, and fifteen to your health, he shelled out the beans. Then he retrieved the counterfeit donkey, together with a sack of pumice stones in place of the gemstones, and raced off in the direction of his village. And before he even set foot in the house he began to shout as if he had been stung by a nettle bush, "Hurry, Mommy, hurry; we're rich! Get out the tablecloths, unfold the sheets, spread the blankets: you're about to see some treasures."

With great joy, his mother opened a chest that held her marriageable daughters' trousseaus, and pulled out sheets so fine that if you blew on them they would float on air, freshly laundered tablecloths, and blankets of stunning beauty, arranging them in a nice display on the floor. Antuono placed the donkey on top of them and began to intone "giddy up, shit gold"; but with all the "giddy up, shit gold"s that you like, the donkey paid no more attention to those words than it would have to the sound of a lyre. Nonetheless, after repeating the words three or four times, which was the same as throwing them to the wind, he took hold of a nice club and began to pester the poor beast, planing it down, touching it up, and padding it so well with blows that the poor animal lost control down below and took a fine yellow crap on the white cloths. When she saw the animal's bowels thus tapped, poor Masella, who had founded her hopes on enriching her poverty and now found herself with such a liberal foundation that her whole house reeked, grabbed a stick and, not giving him time to show her the pumice stones, patched Antuono up so well that he immediately beat it back to the ogre's.

The ogre saw Antuono coming, more at a trot than a walk, and since he knew what had happened because he was enchanted, he gave him a juicy scolding for having let himself be fooled by an innkeeper, calling him a good-for-nothing, oh-dear-mother-drink-this-one-up, birdbrain, jackal, idiot, piece of junk, noodlehead, chestnut-guzzler, simpleton, boor, and nitwit, who in exchange for a donkey well lubricated with treasures had allowed himself to be given an animal lavish with makeshift mozzarellas. Antuono swallowed this pill and swore that never ever again would he allow himself to be conned and made fun of by a living man.

But before another year had gone by he got the same headache and was dying to go see his people. The ogre, who had an ugly face and a kind heart, gave him not only permission to go but a lovely tablecloth as well, telling him, "Take this to your mother, but be careful not to act like an ass as you did with the donkey, and until you're at home say neither 'open' nor 'close, tablecloth,' because if you get into any more trouble it'll be at your own expense. Now go with my best wishes, and come back soon."

So Antuono left, but not far from the grotto he put the tablecloth on the ground and quickly said "open" and "close, tablecloth." And when it opened up, lo and behold! There was such beauty, such magnificence and elegance, that it was an incredible thing. Seeing all of that, Antuono immediately said, "Close, tablecloth," and after everything was closed back up inside it, he hotfooted it in the direction of the same inn as the other time, where, upon entering, he said to the innkeeper, "Here, put away this tablecloth and see that you don't say 'open' and 'close, tablecloth.'" The innkeeper, a thrice-baked rogue, said, "Just leave it to this fellow," and after he stuffed Antuono and made sure he had grabbed the monkey by its tail,[5] he sent him off to bed, got the tablecloth, and said, "Open, tablecloth." And when it opened, the tablecloth brought forth so many precious things that it was stupendous to behold. Then the

5. I.e., got him drunk.

innkeeper found another tablecloth similar to the first, and after Antuono awoke he palmed it off on him. Antuono hoofed it out of there and arrived at his mother's house saying, "Now we'll really give our poverty a kick in the face; now we'll really find a remedy for our rags, tatters, and patches!"

That said, he spread the tablecloth on the ground and began to say, "Open, tablecloth." But he could have said it from today till tomorrow and he would have been wasting his time; it yielded neither a crumb nor a bit of straw. And so, seeing that his business was going against the nap, he said to his mother, "Bless the new year, the innkeeper has stuck it to me again! But watch out; there are two of us! Better if he had never been hatched! Better if he had fallen under the wheel of a cart! May I lose the best piece of furniture in my house if when I stop by that inn to get my refund for the jewels and the stolen donkey I don't make dust of his dishes!" Hearing this new donkey logic, Antuono's mother began to spit fire and said to him, "Go break your neck, you godless boy! Go dislocate your shoulder bone! Get out of my sight; I'm losing my guts over you, I can't stomach you anymore; my hernia is swelling and I get a goiter when you're underfoot! So cut it short, and may this house be like fire to you, for I'm going to shake you out of my clothes and pretend I never shat you!"

Poor Antuono saw the lightning and didn't want to wait for the thunder, and, as if he had stolen a load of fresh laundry, he lowered his head and threw up his heels and raced off toward the ogre's house. When the ogre saw him arrive at a listless pace and with a lackluster demeanor, he played him another prelude, saying, "I don't know what keeps me from tearing out one of your orbs, you fart-throat, gas-mouth, filthy gullet, hen's ass, *ta-ta-ta-ta*, trumpeter of the Vicaria:[6] you make a public proclamation about every private matter, you vomit whatever's in your stomach, you can't hold down even a chickpea! If you had kept your mouth shut at the inn, none of this would have happened to you, but since you used your tongue like the sail of a windmill, you've ground to dust the happiness that this hand gave you!"

Poor Antuono tucked his tail between his legs and sucked up the music. He stayed in the ogre's service without event for another three years, thinking about his home as much as he thought about becoming a count. And still,

6. "The public crier of the grand Court of the Vicaria of Naples, who issued proclamations to the sound of a trumpet" (Croce 21).

after all that time the fever returned, and once more he got the whim to take a spin back home. So he asked leave of the ogre, who was happy to let him go and thus rid himself of such a nuisance, and he gave him a lovely carved club, saying, "Take this with you in remembrance of me, but be careful not to say 'up, club' or 'down, club,' because I want nothing more to do with you." Antuono took it and replied, "Come on, I've cut my wisdom teeth; I know how many pair three oxen make! I'm not a little boy anymore, and whoever wants to cheat Antuono can kiss his own elbow first!" The ogre replied to this, "'The praise of masters lies in their works; words are female and deeds are male.' Let's wait and see. You heard me better than a deaf man: 'a man forewarned is a man half-saved!'"

As the ogre went on talking, Antuono slipped away in the direction of his house; before he was half a mile away he said, "Up, club!" This was no mere word, though, but a magical formula, for just as if it had a little imp in its core, the club began to burnish poor Antuono's shoulders so hard that the blows seemed to shower down from the open sky, each stroke waiting for the next. Finding himself pounded and dressed like a piece of Moroccan leather, the unfortunate fellow immediately said, "Down, club!" and the club ceased writing counterpoint on the staves of his back. And so, after he learned the lesson at his own expense, he said, "May he who flees become lame; on my word, this time I won't let it get away from me! He who's in for a bad evening hasn't gone to bed yet!" Thus saying, he arrived at the usual inn, where he was received with the warmest welcome in the world, since it was clear what that pork rind would render. As soon as he arrived, Antuono said to the innkeeper, "Here, store this club for me, but be sure not to say, 'Up, club!' or you'll be in danger! Listen to me carefully: don't you complain about Antuono again, for I won't put up with it, and I'm making my bed beforehand."

The innkeeper, full of joy over this third stroke of luck, made sure Antuono was filled to the gills and shown the bottom of the jug, and as soon as he had dumped him onto a little cot, he raced off to get the club. Calling his wife to the festivities, he said, "Up, club!" The club began to search out the hold of the innkeepers' bodies, and with a *boom!* here and a *crash!* there, it was like the round trip of a thunderbolt. Realizing that they were scantily and poorly protected, they ran off with that business following them and woke Antuono up, begging him for mercy. When he saw that the matter was going down just as it was supposed to, and that the macaroni was falling into the cheese and the broccoli into the lard, he said, "There's no cure: you're going to die from the blows of this club unless you give me back my things."

The innkeeper, who at this point was beaten to a pulp, shouted, "Take everything I have and get this backscratcher off me!" And to reassure Antuono, he brought out everything that he had pinched from him. Once it was all in hand, Antuono said, "Down, club!" and the club went and hunkered down in a corner of the room. Then he gathered up the donkey and the other things and left for his mother's house, where, after performing a royal trial on the donkey's ass and a thorough test on the tablecloth, he put together a good store of money, married off his sisters, and made his mother rich, proving the truth of the saying, *God helps madmen and children.*

The Flea (Lo pulece)

"The Flea" incorporates ATU 311, Rescue by the Sister; ATU 513A, Six Go through the Whole World; ATU 621/857, The Louse-Skin; and ATU 653, The Four Skillful Brothers. The tale consists of two distinct parts, each having many variants. The first, a riddle about a mysterious animal skin, can also be found in the Grimms (124 and 134) and Gonzenbach (22), among others. The second part features the very common folkloric motif of villains defeated by magical obstacles thrown in their path, often by a joint effort on the part of superheroes endowed with exceptional physical gifts.

A king who does not have much to think about raises a flea until it becomes as big as a sheep and then has it skinned and offers his daughter as a reward to anyone who is able to recognize its hide. An ogre identifies it by smell and takes the princess, but she is freed by the seven sons of an old woman after seven trials.

Resolutions made without judgment always lead to ruin without remedy; he who behaves like a madman suffers like a wise man, as happened to the king of High Mountain, who on account of a four-soled mistake committed a high-heeled folly and put his daughter and his honor in immeasurable danger.

The king of High Mountain was once bitten by a flea, and when he had picked it off with great dexterity and saw how beautiful and solidly built it was, it seemed a shame to him to execute it on the block of his fingernail. And so he placed it in a carafe, and, feeding it daily with blood from his own arm, it grew so quickly that at the end of seven months, when he had to change its quarters, it was bigger than a sheep. On seeing this, the king had it skinned, and when the hide had been dressed he issued a proclamation: whoever was able to recognize to which animal the pelt belonged would be given his daughter in marriage. After the notice was made public, flocks of people came running, arriving from the asshole of the earth to be present at this exam and try their luck. There was one who said it was a monster cat, another a lynx, one a crocodile, one some animal, and another a different one; but they were all a hundred miles off, and not one was on the mark.

Finally, an ogre presented himself at this anatomy exam, an ogre who was the most horrible thing in the world, the mere sight of whom would bring tremors, diarrhea, worms, and chills to the boldest young man in the world. Now, as soon as he arrived, the ogre started buzzing around the hide and sniffing at it, and he hit the bull's-eye straight on when he said, "This pelt belongs to the ringleader of all fleas."

The king saw that the ogre had grafted onto the right tree, and summoned his daughter Porziella, who looked like she was made of nothing but milk and blood. Oh, my dear! She was a little bobbin, so beautiful that you could just coddle her with your eyes. The king said to her, "Daughter, you know the proclamation I issued and you know who I am. All things considered, I can't go back on my promise. Either you're a king or you're poplar bark: I gave my word and now I have to keep it, even if it breaks my heart. Who could ever have imagined that an ogre would win this lottery? But since a leaf can't fall unless it's the will of the heavens, we have to believe that this marriage was arranged first of all up there and then down here. So be patient, and if you're a blessed daughter don't talk back to your daddy, for my heart tells me that you're going to be happy; a plain stone jar often houses treasures."

When Porziella heard this bitter decision, her eyes grew dark, her face became yellow, her lips drooped, her legs trembled, and she was on the verge of sending the falcon of her soul off to pursue the quail of her suffering. Finally, breaking out in tears and raising her voice, she said to her father, "Just what kind of bad service have I performed in this house to receive such punishment? What sort of bad manners have I used with you to be delivered into the hands of this bogeyman? O miserable Porziella! Here I am, about to be deliberately sent down the throat of this toad like a weasel; here I am, an unfortunate lamb about to be stolen away by a werewolf! This is the affection you have for your own blood? This is the love you show toward she whom you called the pupil of your soul? This is the way you tear one who shares your own blood from your heart? This is the way you remove the apple of your eye from your sight? O father, cruel father, you can't possibly have been born of human flesh! Orcas gave you your blood, wild cats your milk! But why do I speak of sea and land animals? Every animal loves its offspring; you alone treat your own seed with a contrary heart and nausea, you alone cannot stomach your own daughter! Oh, better if my mother had suffocated me, if my cradle had been my deathbed, my wetnurse's tit a bladder of poison, my swaddling clothes nooses, and the little whistle they tied round my neck a millstone, considering that this calamity was to befall me and that I was to find this accursed creature sitting right next to me, to find myself caressed by a harpy's hand, embraced by two bear's shins, and kissed by two pig's tusks!"

She was intending to say more, when the king, sending off fumes every which way, said to her, "Enough with the anger; sugar is expensive! Slow down there; your shields are made of poplar! Plug your mouth; it's spewing filth! Shut up, not a peep; you're a sharp-tongued, spiteful bigmouth! Whatever I do is done well! Don't try to teach a father how to have daughters! Cut it out; stick that tongue back in and take care the mustard doesn't reach my nose, since if I get my paws on you I won't leave a hair on your head, and I'll sow this earth with your teeth! Just look at this stink of my own ass who wants to play the man and lay down the law for her own father! Since when does a girl whose mouth still reeks of milk have the right to question my will? Hurry up, give him your hand, and get off to his house this instant; I don't want to see your impudent and presumptuous face in front of my eyes for even another quarter of an hour."

Finding herself in these straits, poor Porziella had the face of one sentenced to death, the eyes of one possessed by spirits, the mouth of one who has taken the Domini Agustini laxative, and the heart of one whose head is between the blade and the stone. She took the ogre's hand and was dragged by him, without company, into a wood—where the trees formed a palace for the meadow so that it wouldn't be discovered by the Sun, the rivers complained that when they flowed in the dark they tripped on stones, and the wild animals enjoyed their Benevento, not having to pay duty tax, and wandered safely through the thickets[1]—in which no one ever entered unless he had lost his way. In this place, dark as a clogged chimney and frightening as the facade of hell, stood the ogre's house, decorated and plastered all over with the bones of men he had eaten. Anyone who's a Christian can imagine the tremors, the horror, the tightening of the heart, the runs, the fright, the worms, and

1. "The right of *fida* [care] was paid by those who pastured their animals on land belonging to others, or on royal or communal land. Benevento was part of the pontifical state and was, therefore, a close and easy-to-reach 'land of exile' for Neapolitan outlaws" (Croce 55).

the diarrhea that the poor girl experienced: let's just say that there wasn't a drop of blood left in her veins.

But that was nothing, not even a dried fig, compared to the rest of the change, since she had chickpeas for antipasto and fava beans for dessert.[2] Indeed, the ogre returned home from hunting, laden down with quarters of slaughtered men, and said to her, "Now you can't complain, my dear wife, that I don't take care of you! Here's a nice supply of things to go with your bread; take them and enjoy them and love me, for even if the sky were to fall I wouldn't deprive you of your chow." Poor Porziella, retching like a pregnant woman, turned her face the other way. When the ogre saw this gesture, he said, "That's what happens when you give sweets to pigs! But never mind: just keep calm until tomorrow morning, for I've been invited to hunt some wild pigs. I'll bring a couple of them home for you, and then we can have a first-rate wedding celebration with all our relatives and in that way consume our relationship with even greater pleasure."

That said, he marched off into the woods. While Porziella was at the window lamenting her fate, an old woman chanced to pass by the house. Feeling faint with hunger, the woman asked for some refreshment, to which the miserable girl answered, "Oh, my good woman, only God knows my heart. I am under the power of an infernal creature who brings me nothing but quartered men and pieces of slaughtered bodies, and I don't know how I even have the stomach to look at such revolting things; indeed, my life is the most wretched one a baptized soul has ever lived. And yet, I'm a king's daughter, and yet, I was brought up on pappardelle, and yet, I've always lived in the midst of plenty!"

As she was saying this, she started crying like a little girl whose snack has been snatched away from her, so that the old woman's heart softened, and she said, "Cheer up, my pretty girl; don't consume your beauty crying, for you have found your fortune and I am here to help you mount any saddle I can. Now listen to me. I have seven sons who are seven jewels, seven oak trees, seven giants—Mase, Nardo, Cola, Micco, Petrullo, Ascadeo, and Ceccone—and they have more virtues than rosemary. In particular, each time Mase puts his ear to the ground he hears and eavesdrops on everything that's happening up to thirty miles away; each time Nardo spits he makes a huge sea of soap;

2. "Chickpeas and dried fava beans were given to prisoners and to those condemned to death" (Rak 123).

whenever Cola throws down a little piece of iron he makes a field of sharpened razors; every time Micco hurls a stick he makes a tangled wood; whenever Petrullo shakes a drop of water to the ground he makes a frightful river; each time Ascadeo throws a stone he makes a mighty tower spring up; and Ceccone shoots so straight with a crossbow that he can hit a chicken's eye from a mile away. Now, with the help of these seven, all of whom are courteous and kind and will have compassion for your condition, I want to see if I can get you out from under the claws of that ogre, for this lovely, tempting morsel is not fit for the gullet of that bogeyman." "There's never been a better time than now," answered Porziella. "That evil shadow of my husband has gone out and won't be back this evening, so we'll have time to throw up our heels and clear out of here." "It can't be this evening," replied the old woman, "because I live at some distance from here. But all right: tomorrow morning my sons and I will be here to put an end to your troubles."

That said, she left, and Porziella, with her heart completely at rest, slept through the night. And as soon as the birds shouted, "Long live the Sun!" there was the old woman with her seven sons, and when Porziella had joined them they set off for the city. But they had gone no farther than half a mile when Mase, putting his ear to the ground, shouted, "Look out! Hey! The fox is after us! The ogre is back home already, and since he didn't find this girl he's coming after us with his hat under his armpit." Upon hearing this, Nardo spit on the ground and made a sea of soap; when the ogre got there and saw the lather, he ran home, got a sack of bran, and rubbed such great amounts of it on his feet that, with great difficulty, he surpassed the obstacle.

But when Mase put his ear to the ground again he said, "Your turn, brother; here he comes." Cola threw down his piece of iron, and a field of razor blades shot up. Finding his way blocked, the ogre ran back home again, dressed from head to toe in iron and, upon his return, stepped clear over the ditch. But Mase, when he stuck his ear to the ground once more, shouted, "Come on, come on, grab your weapons; the ogre's going to fly in here at full speed any moment now!" And Micco quickly took his stick and summoned forth a terrifying wood, one that was most difficult to penetrate. As soon as the ogre got to this impasse he grabbed a cleaver that he carried at his side and began to fell a poplar tree over here, an oak over there; on one side he sent a dogwood crashing, on another a service tree, so that with four or five blows he had beaten the wood to the ground and freed himself from the entanglement.

Mase, who had the ears of a hare, started raising his voice again: "Let's not stand here as if we were shaving; the ogre has sprouted wings, and in a minute he'll be at our backs." When Petrullo heard this, he took a sip of water from a little fountain that was trickling one drop at a time from a stone shell, spit it on the ground, and lo and behold! a wide river suddenly appeared. When the ogre saw this new impediment and realized that for every hole he made the others found a plug, he stripped down stark naked and swam to the other side with his clothes on his head.

Mase, who put his ear to every hole, heard the trampling of the ogre's feet and said, "This business of ours is going badly, and the ogre is already beating his heels so hard that the heavens can tell you about it. So let's keep our wits about us and shelter ourselves from the storm; otherwise, we're done for." "Have no fear," said Ascadeo. "I'll show that ugly bum a thing or two now," and as he said this he threw down a stone and a tower appeared, into which they immediately crowded, bolting the door behind them. But when the ogre got there and saw that they had escaped to safety he ran home, found a grape harvester's ladder and loaded it onto his back, and then ran back to the tower.

Mase, whose ears were hanging, heard the ogre's arrival from afar, and said, "Our candle of hope is down to the quick, and our life's last refuge lies with Ceccone, since the ogre's coming back now. And is he ever furious! Oh, dear, my heart is beating and I predict it's going to be a bad day!" "What a pants-shitter you are!" answered Ceccone. "Leave it to Menechiello here, and you'll see if my pellets hit the bull's-eye." Just as he was saying this the ogre leaned the ladder against the tower and started to climb up; but Ceccone took aim and, after knocking out one of his orbs, he sent the ogre falling to the ground like a pear. Then he came down from the tower and, with the knife that the ogre himself had been carrying, slit his throat as if it were ricotta.

They carried the ogre off with great merriment to the king, who was overjoyed to get his daughter back, since he had repented a hundred times that he had given her to an ogre. And after a few days he found her a lovely husband, and bestowed riches on the seven sons and their mother who had freed his daughter from such an unhappy life. He never stopped declaring himself a thousand times guilty to Porziella for having placed her in such danger on account of a mere whim, without a thought to how big a mistake is made by those who go looking for *wolves' eggs and fifteen-teethed combs*.

The Cinderella Cat (La gatta cennerentola)

Basile's tale is the earliest literary version of the Cinderella tale type (ATU 510A) in Europe, preceding Perrault's "Cendrillon" (1697) by over sixty years. Basile's version contains various motifs that do not commonly appear in other versions. Perhaps the most striking is the episode where Cenerentola murders her first stepmother by letting the lid of a chest fall on her neck (recalling the Grimms' "The Juniper Tree," in which a wicked stepmother kills her stepson in a similar fashion). Another unique motif, "the stopping of the ship," appears in other folktales as well as in Basile's 2.8. In general, this Italian Cinderella is much more proactive in constructing her own destiny than her sisters in Perrault and the Grimms, making the final moral, "those who oppose the stars are crazy," seem curiously out of place.

Zezolla, incited by her teacher to kill her stepmother, believes that she will be held dear for helping the teacher to marry her father; instead she ends up in the kitchen. But due to the power of some fairies, after numerous adventures she wins a king for her husband.

In the sea of malice, envy always finds herself with a hernia[1] in place of a bladder, and where she expects to see another drown, she finds herself either underwater or dashed against a reef, just as happened to certain envious girls that I have in mind to tell you about.

You should know, then, that there once was a widowed prince who had a daughter so dear to him that he had eyes for no one but her. He had employed a first-rate sewing teacher for her, who taught her the chain stitch, point lace,

1. "It was popular belief that hernias, and especially strangulated hernias, were caused by envy, since one can 'die' from both" (Guarini and Burani 81).

fringes, and openwork hems, and he showed the girl more affection than words can express. But the father had just remarried; he had taken a fiery, wicked, and demonic thing for his wife, and her stepdaughter soon began to make this accursed woman's stomach turn. She gave the girl sour looks, made awful faces at her, and knitted her eyebrows in such a frightful manner that the poor little thing was always complaining to the sewing teacher of her stepmother's ill treatment, saying, "Oh God, couldn't you be my little mommy, since you're the one who's always giving me smooches and squeezes?"

She chanted this so incessantly that she planted a wasp in the teacher's ear, and one day, blinded by evil spirits, the teacher said to her, "If you follow the advice of this madcap, I'll become your mother and you'll be as dear to me as the pupils of these eyes." She was about to go on speaking when Zezolla (for that was the girl's name) said, "Forgive me if I take the words out of your mouth. I know you love me dearly, so mum's the word, and *sufficit*; teach me the trade, for I'm new in town; you write and I'll sign." "All right, then," replied the teacher, "listen carefully; keep your ears open and your bread will come out as white as flowers. As soon as your father leaves, tell your stepmother you want one of those old dresses in the big chest in the storeroom so that you can save the one you're wearing. Since she likes to see you all patched up in rags, she'll open the chest and say, 'Hold the lid up.' And as you're holding it while she rummages around inside, let it bang shut, and she'll break her neck. Once that's done, you know that your father would coin counterfeit money to make you happy, so when he caresses you, beg him to take me for his wife and, lucky you, you'll become the mistress of my life."

Once Zezolla heard this, every hour seemed like a thousand years to her. She followed her teacher's instructions to a tee, and when the mourning for the stepmother's accident was over, she began to play her father's keys to the tune of marrying the teacher. At first the prince thought it was a joke, but his daughter beat so hard that she finally broke the door down, and in the end he yielded to Zezolla's words. He took Carmosina, the teacher, for his wife, and held grand festivities.

Now, while the newlyweds were off carrying on and Zezolla was standing at one of the balconies of the palace, a little dove flew down onto the wall and said to her, "If ever you should wish for something, send your request to the dove of the fairies on the island of Sardinia, and you will be immediately satisfied."

The new stepmother smoked Zezolla with caresses for five or six days, seating her at the best place at the table, giving her the best morsels, dressing her in the best clothes. But in no time at all she annulled and completely forgot the service rendered (oh, sad is the soul housed in a wicked mistress!), and began to raise to all heights six daughters of her own whom she had kept secret up until then. And she worked her husband over so well that as his stepdaughters entered into his graces, his own daughter fell from his heart, and from one day to the next Zezolla ended up being demoted from the royal chamber to the kitchen and from a canopied bed to the hearth, from sumptuous silks and gold to rags, from the scepter to the spit. And not only did her status change, but her name as well, for she was no longer called Zezolla but Cinderella Cat.

It came to pass that the prince had to go to Sardinia for affairs of state, and, one by one, he asked Imperia, Calamita, Shiorella, Diamante, Colombina, and Pascarella, who were the six stepdaughters, what they wanted him to bring them on his return. One asked for luxurious clothing, one for ornaments for her hair, one for rouges for her face, one for toys to pass the time, one for one thing, and one for another. Finally he asked his daughter, almost as if he were taunting her, "And you, what would you like?" And she: "Nothing, except that you give my regards to the dove of the fairies and tell her to send me something; and if you forget, may you be unable to go forward or backward. Keep in mind what I say: your arm, your sleeve."

The prince departed, did his business in Sardinia, and bought what his stepdaughters had requested; Zezolla slipped his mind. But after he embarked on his vessel and it was about to set sail, the ship was unable to leave port, just as if it had been blocked by a sea lamprey.[2] The captain of the ship, close to desperation, fell asleep from fatigue and in his dreams saw a fairy, who said to him, "Do you know why you cannot remove the ship from port? Because the prince who is with you broke a promise he made to his daughter, remembering everyone except his own flesh and blood." The captain awoke and told his dream to the prince, who, confused about his failing, went to the fairies' grotto and, after giving them his daughter's regards, asked that they send her something.

2. The sea lamprey "attaches itself, by a sort of suction cup, to other fish or to ships; according to popular lore the lamprey could prevent or hinder navigation (Pliny, *Natural History* IX 25)" (Rak 138).

And lo and behold! a splendid young woman who was a banner to beauty came out of the cavern and told him that she thanked his daughter for remembering her so kindly, and that she hoped Zezolla would be happy, for the fairy's sake. With these words, she gave him a date tree, a hoe, a golden pail, and a silk cloth, and told him that the date tree was for planting and the other things for cultivating it. The prince, astonished by these gifts, took leave of the fairy and returned to his land, where, when he had given all of the stepdaughters what they had requested, he at last gave his daughter the gift sent by the fairy.

Nearly bursting out of her skin with joy, Zezolla planted the date in a fine pot and hoed it, watered it, and dried it with the silk cloth every morning and evening. And after four days, when the plant had grown as tall as a woman, a fairy came out and said to her, "What is your wish?" Zezolla answered that she wished to leave the house now and then but didn't want her sisters to know. The fairy replied, "Whenever you like, go to the pot and say,

Golden date of mine
I've weeded you with the little hoe of gold,
I've watered you with the little pail of gold,
I've dried you with the cloth of silk,
Now strip yourself and dress me!

And when you want to undress, change the last verse to 'Strip me and dress yourself!'"

Now, a feast day arrived and the teacher's daughters went out, all flowery, bedecked, and painted; all ribbons, little bells, and baubles; all flowers, scents, rosies, and posies. Zezolla immediately ran to the pot, uttered the words the fairy had taught her, and found herself fixed up like a queen, after which she was placed on a white thoroughbred with twelve trim and elegant pages in tow. Then she went to the place her sisters had gone, and they drooled over the beauty of that resplendent dove.

As fate willed it, the king showed up there, too, and when he saw Zezolla's matchless beauty, he immediately fell under her spell, and he asked his most trusted servant to find out how he could get more information about this phenomenon of beauty—who she was and where she lived. Without a moment's delay, the servant went after her; but having discovered the ambush, she threw out a handful of golden coins obtained from the date tree for this purpose. When he caught sight of those gleaming coins, the servant forgot about following the horse, preferring to fill his claws with small change, while Zezolla raced back and slipped into the house. Once she had undressed the way the fairy had instructed her to, those harpies of her sisters arrived and, just to make her boil, told her of all the fine things they had seen. In the meantime the servant went back to the king and told him about the coins, at which the king blew up in a great rage and told him that for four shitty beans he had sold off his pleasure, and that on the next feast day he was at all costs to make sure he found out who the beautiful girl was and where the lovely bird had its nest.

The next feast day arrived, and after the sisters went out, all decorated and elegant, and left the despised Zezolla at the hearth, she immediately ran to the date tree. Once she had said the usual words, a band of damsels came out: one held a mirror, one a little bottle of squash water, one a curling iron, one a rouge cloth, one a comb, one some brooches, one the clothes, and one pendants and necklaces. They made her as beautiful as a sun, and then put her in a coach drawn by six horses and accompanied by footmen and pages in livery, so that upon reaching the same place where the other festivities had been held, she only compounded the astonishment in her sisters' hearts and the fire in the king's breast.

But when she left again and the servant followed after her, she threw out a handful of pearls and jewels so that he would not catch up with her, and while that worthy fellow stopped to peck at them, since they were not to be wasted, she had time to tow herself home and undress in the usual fashion. With a face this long, the servant returned to the king, who said, "I vow on the soul of my ancestors that if you don't find her, you'll get a fine beating and a kick in the ass for every hair in your beard!"

The next feast day arrived, and after the sisters went out, Zezolla returned to the date tree and repeated the enchanted song, at which she was magnificently dressed and placed in a golden coach accompanied by so many servants that she looked like a whore arrested in the public promenade and surrounded by cops. She went, made her sisters' mouths water, and then left, with the king's servant tailing the coach as if he were stitched to it by a double thread. When she saw that he was still stuck to her side she said, "Use your whip, coachman!" and the coach rushed forth at breakneck speed. Indeed, it raced along so fast that she lost one of her pattens,[3] the prettiest little thing you ever did see. The servant, who wasn't able to reach the flying coach, picked the patten up from the ground and brought it to the king, telling him what had happened.

The king took the patten in his hand and said, "If the foundations are so beautiful, what must the house be like? O lovely candlestick that held the candle that consumes me! O tripod of the charming cauldron in which my life is boiling! O beautiful corks, attached to the fishing line of Love used to catch this soul! There: I'll embrace and squeeze you; if I cannot reach the plant, I will adore its roots, and if I cannot have the capitals, I will kiss its base! You were once the memorial stone for a white foot, and now you are a snare for this black heart. You made the lady who tyrannizes this life a span and a half taller, and you make this life grow just as much in sweetness, as I contemplate and possess you."

As he was saying this, the king called the scribe, summoned the trumpeter, and—*ta ta ta ta!*—issued a proclamation: all the women of the land were invited to come to the festivities and banquet that he had gotten the idea to hold. And when the appointed day came, oh, my goodness! What a spread, what merrymaking! Where did so many pastries and casseroles come from? And the stews and meatballs?[4] The macaroni and sweet ravioli? There was enough to feed an entire army!

Once the women had all arrived—noble and common, rich and ragged, old and young, beautiful and ugly—and polished off their due, the king made a toast and then tried the patten on each of his guests, one by one, to see whom it would fit like a glove and as neatly as a pin, in the hope that he might recognize the one he was seeking from the fit of the patten. But when he couldn't find a foot to match it, he began to despair. Nonetheless, after he had requested silence, he said, "Come back tomorrow to do penance with me again; but if I am dear to you, leave no woman at home, whoever she may be." The prince said,

3. "The *chianielli* were . . . overshoes whose soles and heels—often of exaggerated height—were made of cork. . . . They allowed their wearer to get out of a carriage and walk on the street without getting the hem of her dress dusty or muddy; during the sixteenth and seventeenth centuries in Naples, the use of *chianielli* also became popular among courtesans" (Guarini and Burani 87).

4. Here Basile refers to the *pastiera*, Naples's famous Easter cake; the *casatiello*, a ring-shaped bread also made for Easter; and a veal stew seasoned with fruits and spices.

"I have a daughter, but she looks after the hearth and is an unworthy wretch and does not deserve to sit at the same table at which you eat." The king said, "Let her be at the top of the list, for that is my wish." And they left, and then all came back the next day, and along with Carmosina's daughters came Zezolla. As soon as the king saw her, he had a feeling that she was the one he wanted, although he pretended not to notice.

After they finished working their jaws, it was time to try the patten on. And no sooner was it drawn close to Zezolla's foot than it hurled itself with no help at all onto the foot of that painted egg of Love, just like iron runs to a magnet. When the king saw this, he raced to clamp her in the press of his arms, and when he had seated her under the royal canopy, he put a crown on her head and commanded that all the women present curtsy and show her their veneration, for she was their new queen. At the sight of this, the sisters nearly died of envy, and, not having the stomach to stand this heartbreak, they quietly stole away to their mother's house, confessing in spite of themselves that *those who oppose the stars are crazy.*

The Old Woman Who Was Skinned (La vecchia scortecata)

The tale type ATU 877, The Old Woman Who Was Skinned, contains various motifs common to religious traditions, folklore, and the literary fairy tale tradition. These include a man marrying a hag who then turns into a beautiful lady ("The Weddynge of Syr Gawayne," the legend of Perceval); the "false sybarite" motif; and the flaying of the sister. With regard to the latter, Penzer notes that the "terrible end of the other sister is rather surprising when we remember that the lucky sister had been given gifts by the fairies to make her beautiful, noble, and virtuous. Yet as soon as she is married, she proceeds to treat her less lucky sister in the most heartless and cruel way imaginable" (1:104). Furthermore, the two sisters, who are virtually indistinguishable, meet their different ends in absolutely arbitrary fashion, suggesting that the final moral does not have to do so much with envy as with the impenetrable workings of fortune.

The king of Strong Fortress falls in love with the voice of an old woman, and after he is tricked with a sucked-on finger, he gets her to sleep with him. But when he discovers the deception, he has her thrown out the window, and she remains hanging on a tree. After she is enchanted by seven fairies, she becomes a splendid young woman whom the king takes for his wife. But because the other sister is envious of her fortune, she gets skinned to make herself more beautiful, and dies.

The accursed vice, embedded in us women, of wanting to look beautiful reduces us to the point where to gild the frame of our forehead we spoil the painting of our face, to whiten our old and wizened skin we ruin the bones of our teeth, and to put our limbs in a good light we darken our eyesight, so that before it is time to pay our tribute to time we procure ourselves rheumy eyes, wrinkled faces, and rotten molars. But if a young girl who in her vanity gives in to such empty-headedness deserves reproach, even more worthy of punishment is an old woman who out of her desire to compete with young ladies becomes a laughingstock for others and the ruin of her own self, as I am about to tell you, if you will lend me a bit of your ears.

Two old women had retired to a garden facing the king of Strong Fortress's quarters. They were the summary of all misfortunes, the register of all deformities, the ledger of all ugliness: their tufts of hair were disheveled and spiked, their foreheads lined and lumpy, their eyelashes shaggy and bristly, their eyelids swollen and heavy, their eyes wizened and seedy looking, their faces yellowed and wrinkled, their mouths drooly and crooked; in short, they had beards like a billy goat's, hairy chests, round-bellied shoulders, withered arms, lame and crippled legs, and hooked feet. And to prevent even the Sun from catching a glimpse of their hideous appearance, they stayed holed up in a few ground-level rooms under the windows of that lord.

The king was reduced to such a state that he couldn't even fart without causing those old pains in the neck to wrinkle their noses, for they grumbled and threw themselves about like squid over the smallest thing. First they said that a jasmine flower fallen from above had given one of them a lump on her head, then that a torn-up letter had dislocated one of their shoulders, and then that a pinch of dust had bruised one of their thighs.

Upon hearing of this monster of delicacy, the king concluded that underneath him lived the quintessence of softness, the prime cut of the most delectable of meats, and the flower of all tenderness, by reason of which he was overcome by a craving all the way down to the little bones in his feet and by a desire straight through to his bone marrow to see this marvel and to get a clearer idea of the matter. And so he began to send down sighs, to clear his throat when there was nothing to clear, and, finally, to speak more expeditiously and with greater boldness, exclaiming, "Where, oh where do you hide yourself, jewel, splendor, beautiful product of the world? 'Come out, come out, Sun, warm up the emperor!'[1] Uncover those lovely graces, show those lamps of the shop of Love, stick out that dainty head, O counting house heaped with beauty's money! Don't be so stingy about letting yourself be seen! 'Open your doors to the poor falcon!' 'Give me an offering if you want to give me one!' Let me see the instrument from which issues that sweet

1. A Neapolitan children's song.

voice! Allow me to see the bell where that tinkling is formed! Let me catch a glimpse of that bird! Do not make me graze on absinthe like a sheep from Ponto by refusing to allow me to look at and contemplate that beauty of all beauties!"

The king said this and other words, but he might as well have been playing the Gloria, for the old women had stopped up their ears. This, however, only added wood to the king's fire: he felt himself heated up like an iron in the furnace of desire, squeezed by the tongs of deliberation, and pounded by the hammer of amorous torment, and all to forge a key that could open the little chest of jewels that was making him die of longing. And still he did not pull back, instead continuing to send forth entreaties and to strengthen his assaults, never taking a rest.

The old women, who had begun to put on airs and grow cocky as a result of the king's offers and promises, resolved not to waste this opportunity to nab a bird that was about to fly into the snare all by himself. And so, one day when the king was ranting and raving above their window, they told him through the keyhole in a tiny little voice that the greatest favor they could do would be to show him, in eight days, just one finger of their hand. The king, who as a practiced soldier knew that fortresses are won span by span, did not refuse this solution, hoping to conquer finger by finger the stronghold that he was keeping under siege, since he also knew that "first take and then ask" was an ancient proverb. And thus, once he accepted this ultimatum of the eighth day by which to see the eighth wonder of the world, the old women's sole activity became that of sucking their fingers like a pharmacist who has spilled some syrup, with the plan that when they reached the established day whoever had the smoothest finger would show it to the king.

Meanwhile, the king was on tenterhooks as he waited for the agreed-upon hour to blunt his desire: he counted the days, he numbered the nights, he weighed the hours, he measured the moments, he made note of the seconds, and he probed the instants that had been meted out to him in anticipation of the desired good. Now he begged the Sun to take a shortcut through the celestial fields so that by gaining ground it would unhitch its fiery carriage and water its horses, tired after such a long trip, before the usual time; now he implored Night to sink the shadows so that he could see the light, which yet unseen was keeping him in the kiln of Love's flames; now he grew incensed with Time, who to spite him was wearing crutches and leaden shoes so as to delay the hour for liquidating the debt to the thing he loved and for respecting the contract stipulated between them.

But as the Sun in Leo would have it, the time came, and he went in person to the garden and knocked on the door, saying, "Come out, come out, wherever you are!" Then one of the two old women—the one most laden with years, since the touchstone had shown her finger to be of greater carats than her sister's—stuck her finger through the keyhole and showed it to the king.

Now, this was no mere finger, but a sharpened stick that pierced the king's heart. Or rather, it was no stick, but a cudgel that stunned him on the noggin. But what am I saying, stick and cudgel? It was a match struck on the tinder of his desires, a fuse lit from the powder magazine of his longings. But what am I saying, stick, cudgel, match, fuse? It was a thorn under the tail of his thoughts—indeed, a cure of laxative figs that made him eliminate the gas of amorous affect in a mess of sighs.

And as he held that hand and kissed that finger, which had been transformed from a shoemaker's rasp to a goldsmith's burnisher, he began to say, "O archive of sweetness, O rubric of joys, O register of Love's privileges, by reason of which I have become a store of troubles, a warehouse of anguish, and a customhouse of torment! Is it possible that you wish to appear so obstinate and hard that my laments cannot move you? I beg you, my fair heart, if you have shown me your tail through this hole, now show me your snout, and let us make a gelatin of happiness! If you have shown me your shell, O sea of beauty, now show me your sweet flesh, uncover those eyes of a peregrine falcon and let them feed on this heart! Who keeps the treasure of that beautiful face sequestered in a shithouse? Who quarantines that fair merchandise in a hovel? Who imprisons the forces of Love in that pigsty? Come out of that ditch, flee that stable, abandon that hole! 'Jump, little snail, and give Cola your hand';[2] spend me for what I'm worth! You know, after all, that I'm a king and not any old cucumber; you know that I can do and undo as I like. But that impostor of a blind boy, son of a cripple and a whore,[3] who has free rein over scepters, has willed that I be your subject and that I beg you for the grace of what I could seize however and whenever I please. And furthermore, I know, as a certain someone said, that caresses, and not bravado, sweeten up Venus."

---

2. The first verse of a Neapolitan *villanella*.
3. Love or Cupid, the son of Venus and Vulcan.

The old woman knew where the old devil kept his tail, since she was a master fox, a big old cat, a shrewd, astute, and wily one, and she reflected that it's precisely when a superior begs for something that he's actually issuing a command, and that a vassal's stubbornness gets the choleric humors of the master's intestines moving, which then burst forth in a dysentery of ruin. And so she decided to act accordingly, and with the little voice of a skinned cat she said, "My lord, since you are inclined to put yourself beneath one who is under you, having deigned to descend from the scepter to the distaff, from the royal halls to the stable, from lavish robes to rags, from greatness to misery, from the terrace to the cellar, and from a steed to an ass, I cannot, nor ought not, nor want not to contradict the will of so great a king. And since you desire this alliance between prince and servant, this mosaic of ivory and poplar, this inlay of diamonds and glass, here I am, ready and prepared to do your will. I beg of you only one favor, as a first sign of the love that you bear me: that I be received in your bed at night and without a candle, since my heart could not bear the burden of being seen naked." The king, gurgling with delight, swore to her with one hand on the other that he would willingly do this. And so, after he launched a kiss of sugar to that fetid mouth, he left, and could hardly wait for the Sun to stop plowing and for the fields of the heavens to be sown with stars, so that he in turn could sow the field where he intended to harvest bushels of joy and pecks of delight.

When Night arrived—and, finding itself surrounded by so many shop burglars and cloak thieves, squirted out black ink like a squid—the old woman smoothed back all the wrinkles on her body and gathered them behind her shoulders in a knot, which she tied tightly with a piece of twine. A servant then led her by the hand in the darkness to the king's bedroom, where, once she had taken off her rags, she flung herself onto the bed. The king was more than ready to light the fuse on his artillery, and as soon as he heard her come and lie down he smeared himself all over with musk and civet and sprayed himself from head to toe with cologne water, and then raced to bed like a Corsican hound. And it was lucky for the old woman that the king was wearing so much perfume, on account of which he wasn't able to smell the fumes coming from her mouth, the stink of her little tickly areas, and the stench of that ugly thing.

But no sooner had he lain down than, feeling around, he became aware of that business on the back of her neck and discovered the dried tripe and deflated bladders that the wretched old woman kept in the back of her shop. Keeping his composure, he decided not to say anything right then, since he needed to have a clearer idea on the matter. And so, pretending not to notice, he cast anchor at Mandracchio when he had believed he would be on the coast of Posillipo, and sailed forth on a barge when he had thought he would be charting his course on a Florentine galley.[4] But no sooner had the old woman dropped off into her first sleep than the king took a chamois bag containing a flint stone from his writing table of ebony and silver, and lit a little oil lamp. After conducting a search under the sheets and finding a harpy in the place of a nymph, a Fury in the place of a Grace, and a Gorgon in the place of a Cypriot, he flew into such a rage that he decided to cut the towrope that had moored this ship. Snorting with fury, he yelled for all his servants, who when they heard the call to arms threw on their shirts and came upstairs.

Flailing about like an octopus, the king said to them, "Look at the fine trick this old bogeyman's grandmother has played on me! I believed I was going to gobble up a milk-calf and instead I find myself with a buffalo placenta; I thought I had trapped a resplendent dove and I end up with this owl in my hand; I imagined I had a morsel fit for a king and I find myself with this disgusting thing in my claws: taste it and spit it out! But this and even worse happens when you buy a cat in the bag! It was she who arranged this affront, and it will be she who shits her penance! So go and get her right now, just as she is, and throw her out the window!"

When the old woman heard this, she began to defend herself with kicks and bites, saying that she appealed the sentence, since he was the one who had turned her like a winch until she came to his bed and that besides, she could call a hundred doctors to her defense, as well as citing the saying that goes, "An old chicken makes a good broth," and that other one, "Don't leave the old road for the new." But after all that, they picked her straight up and hurled her down into the garden, and she had the luck not to break her neck, for she was left hanging by her hair on the branch of a fig tree.

Early the next morning—before the Sun took possession of the territories it had been ceded by Night—some fairies came passing through that garden. Due to some irritation or other they had never spoken or laughed, and when

4. Mandracchio was an area of ill repute near the Dogana (Customs) in the port of Naples; the famous Neapolitan hill of Posillipo was, since ancient times, the site of aristocratic pastimes. Florentine galleys were renowned for their elegance.

they saw, hanging from the tree, the ugly shade who had caused the shadows to clear out before the usual time, they were overcome by such side-splitting laughter that they came close to getting a hernia, and once they set their tongues in motion they weren't able to close their mouths about that lovely spectacle for a good while. And such was their amusement and pleasure that in payment each of them cast a spell on her: one by one, they wished that she would become young, beautiful, rich, noble, virtuous, well loved, and blessed by good luck.

When the fairies had left, the old woman found herself on the ground, sitting on a chair of rich velvet fringed in gold, under the same tree as before, which had been transformed into a canopy of green velvet backed in gold. Her face had turned into that of a fifteen-year-old girl, and was so beautiful that by comparison all other beauties would have looked like worn-out house slippers alongside an elegant, perfect-fitting little pump; next to this enthroned grace all other graces would have been deemed worthy of Ferrivecchi or Lavinaro;[5] and where she played her chitchat and blandishments with a winning hand, all the others would have played a losing bank. And, furthermore, she was so primped up, fancified, and sumptuous that she looked like a royal majesty: her gold was blinding, her jewels dazzling, the bloom of her flowers stunning; and surrounding her were so many servants and ladies-in-waiting that it looked like the day of pardon.

In the meantime, the king, who had thrown a blanket over his shoulders and a pair of old slippers on his feet, went to the window to see what had happened to the old woman. When he saw what he never would had imagined, he stood there with his mouth hanging open and looked that fine piece of a girl up and down from head to toe for a good long while, as if he were enchanted. Now he admired her hair, in part spread out over her shoulders and in part harnessed with a golden tie, which gave the Sun cause for envy; now he stared at her eyelashes, crossbows that took hearts as their targets; now he gazed at her eyes, blind lanterns of Love's patrol; now he contemplated her mouth, amorous winepress where the Graces squeezed out delight and obtained sweet Greco and savory Mangiaguerra wines. He swayed from side to side like a loose rafter, and nearly went out of his mind when he saw the baubles and trinkets that were hanging at her neck and the magnificent clothes she was

5. Ferrivecchi and Lavinaro were among the poorest streets in Naples.

wearing. Talking to himself, he said, "Am I asleep or am I awake? Am I in my right mind or am I going crazy? Am I myself or am I not myself? What kind of move caused such a lovely ball to hit this king, so that I am sent to my ruin? I'll be done for, I'll be destroyed if I don't pull myself out of this! How has this sun risen? How has this flower blossomed? How was this bird hatched, so that she can pull my desires like a hook? What sort of boat brought her to these lands? What sort of cloud rained her down? What sort of torrents of beauty are carrying me straight to a sea of woes?"

As he was saying this, he flew down the stairs and ran into the garden, where he went before the renewed old woman and, nearly wiping the ground, said to her, "O my dear little pigeon-face, O little doll of the Graces, splendid dove of the carriage of Venus, triumphal cart of Love! If you have set your heart to soak in the Sarno River, if cane seeds have not gotten into your ears and sparrow shit has not fallen into your eyes, I am sure that you can see and hear the pain and torment that, directly and on the rebound, this beauty of yours has cast into my chest. And if you cannot surmise from the ash cloth of this face the lye that boils inside this chest, if you cannot imagine from the flames of these sighs the furnace that burns in these veins, then if you are sympathetic and of good judgment you can at least infer from that golden hair what sort of cord binds me, and from those black eyes what sort of coals roast me, and from the red arches of those lips what sort of arrow pierces me.[6] Do not, then, bar the door of pity, do not lift the bridge of mercy, do not stop the duct of compassion! If you do not deem me worthy of obtaining a pardon from this lovely face, at least give me a safeguard of good words, a pass of a promise or two, and a pledge card of fair hopes, for otherwise I shall take my slippers far from here and you shall never see their shape again."

These and a thousand other words issued forth from the depths of the king's heart and deeply moved the renewed old woman, who at the end accepted him as her husband. Then she rose from her seat and took him by the hand, and they went together to the royal palace, where in the blink of an eye a huge banquet was prepared. Since all the ladies of the land were invited, the old bride wanted her sister to be among them, but they had a lot to do

6. Anything immersed in the waters of the Sarno River, it was said, would turn to stone; cane seeds were thought to have dangerous properties; sparrow feces was believed to cause blindness; the "ash cloth" was used to cover laundry basins to contain the ash therein (which was used as a detergent); lye is also a common detergent.

and say before they were able to find her and drag her to the feast, since out of great fear she had gone and holed herself up and hidden away so that not a trace of her could be found. But God willed that she finally came, and once she was sitting next to her sister, whom it was no joke for her to recognize, they began the merrymaking.

The wretched old woman had another hunger that was gnawing at her, though, since she was consumed with envy to see her sister's coat shine, and every few minutes she would pull her by the sleeve and say, "What did you do, my sister, what did you do? Lucky you, you've got the chain!" And her sister would answer, "Just think about eating now, and we'll talk about it later." The king kept on asking what was going on, and to cover things up his bride answered that her sister wanted a little green sauce. And the king immediately ordered that garlic paste, mustard, pepper sauce, and a thousand other relishes that stimulate the appetite be brought out.

But the old woman, to whom the grape relish tasted like cow bile, went back to nagging her sister, and asked her again, "What did you do, my sister, what did you do? Tell me, or I'll make you the fig under my cloak."[7] And her sister answered, "Be quiet, for we have more time than money; eat now, and warm yourself up, and then we'll talk." The king, curious, asked what she wanted, and his bride, who felt as tangled up as a chick in a pile of tow and would have liked to do without that hammering at her temples, answered that she wanted something sweet. At that, there came a blizzard of pastries, a storm of wafers and little doughnuts, a flood of blancmange, and a downpour of honey brittle.

But the old woman, who was as agitated as a squid and had a bad case of the runs, started up with the same music again until the bride could no longer stand it, and to get her off her back she answered, "I skinned myself, sister." When the envious sister heard this she said, under her breath, "All right, then, your words don't fall on deaf ears! I want to try my luck, too, for every spirit has a stomach, and if I come away with my hands full you won't be the only one having a good time. I want my part, too, right up to the fennel."[8]

As she was thus speaking, the tables were cleared. Pretending to go and satisfy a bodily need, she ran straight off to a barber's shop, where she found

7. An insulting gesture on which the thumb is inserted between the index and middle fingers, evoking the female genitals.

8. Up to the very end; fennel is served at the end of the meal.

the master barber, took him aside in a back room, and told him, "Here are fifty ducats for you; skin me from head to toe." The barber, judging her to be crazy, answered, "Go on, sister; you're talking funny and you're surely in need of someone to accompany you." And the old woman replied, with a face of marble, "You're the one who's crazy, if you can't recognize your own good fortune. For if I win at a certain game, in addition to the fifty ducats I'll let you hold your basin under Fortune's beard. So, then, gather up your instruments and don't waste time; you're in for some good luck!"

After arguing, fighting with her, and protesting for a good while, the barber was finally led by the nose and behaved like the guy who "ties up the ass wherever his master wants." And when he had set her on a stool, he began to hack away at that black bark, which drizzled and piddled blood everywhere and which every now and then, as steady as if he were giving her a shave, said, "Ugh, she who beautiful wants to appear must pay with suffering and have no fear." And as he continued to send her to her ruin and she repeated the same refrain, they kept up a counterpoint on the lute of her body until he reached the rosette of her navel, at which point her blood abandoned her and with it her strength, and she fired a departing shot from below, proving at her own risk the truth of Sannazaro's verse: *Envy, my son, destroys itself.*[9]

9. The reference is to Iacopo Sannazaro's *Arcadia* (6.4–6).

Petrosinella

This tale combines types ATU 310, The Maiden in the Tower, and ATU 313, The Girl as Helper in the Hero's Flight. There are similar versions in Pitrè's Sicilian Fairy Tales *("The Old Woman in the Garden" [20], as well as 13 and 18); readers will also recognize the tale as a predecessor of Grimms' "Rapunzel" (12).*

A pregnant woman eats some parsley from an ogress's garden, is caught in the act, and promises the ogress the offspring she will bear. She gives birth to Petrosinella, and the ogress takes the child and locks her in a tower. A prince steals her away, and with the help of three acorns they are able to flee from the danger of the ogress, and after Petrosinella is brought to her lover's house she becomes a princess.

There once was a pregnant woman named Pascadozia who, while sitting at a window that overlooked an ogress's garden, noticed a lovely patch of parsley, for which she got such a craving that she felt she would faint. And so, not being able to resist, she kept close watch until the ogress went out, and then she picked a handful. But after the ogress came back home and wanted to make a sauce, she realized that a sickle had been at work and said, "May my neck snap if I don't collar this plunderer and make him repent, so that he may learn to eat from his own cutting board and not to dip his spoon into the pot of others."

But the poor pregnant woman continued to go down to the garden, until one morning she was caught by the ogress, who, full of anger and venom, said to her, "I've got you, you swindling thief! What, you think you pay rent on this garden, so that you can come with so little discretion and pinch my herbs? On my word, I'll send you to Rome for your penance!" The unfortunate Pascadozia started to apologize, explaining that it wasn't because she was a glutton or ravenous that the demon had blinded her and made her commit this sin, but because she was pregnant and afraid that the face of her newborn would be sown with parsley; in fact, the ogress should be grateful that Pascadozia hadn't sent her a sty or two.[1] "The bride wants more than just words!" answered the ogress. "This chatter is no bait for me! You're finished with the job of life if you don't promise to give me the baby you're going to have, and it matters not whether it's a boy or a girl." To escape the dangerous situation in which she found herself, poor Pascadozia swore to this with one hand on the other, and the ogress let her go free.

When it came time to give birth, Pascadozia bore a daughter so beautiful that she was a joy to behold, and she named her Petrosinella on account of a lovely little sprig of parsley that she had on her chest. Petrosinella grew a span every day, and when she was seven, her mother sent her to a teacher. Whenever she was on the road and ran into the ogress, the ogress would say to her, "Tell your mother to remember the promise!" And she bothered her about it so many times that one day the poor mother, who couldn't bear to listen to this music any longer, said to her daughter, "If you run into the old woman again and she asks you about that damned promise, you answer her, 'Take her!'"

When Petrosinella, who knew nothing about the matter, next encountered the ogress, she repeated the usual proposition, to which Petrosinella innocently answered what her mother had told her to say. At that, the ogress grabbed her by the hair, took her to a wood—where the Sun's horses never entered, so as not to pay rent on those pastures of shadow—and locked her in a tower that she had created with a spell. This tower was without doors or stairs; it had just one little window through which the ogress climbed up and down on Petrosinella's hair, which was very long, like a ship boy uses shrouds to climb the masts.

Now, it happened that one day while the ogress was away from the tower, Petrosinella stuck her head out of the hole and spread her braids in the sun. The son of a prince came passing by, and when he saw those two golden banners summoning souls to enlist in the ranks of Love, and gazed upon that heart-enchanting face of a Siren amid those precious waves, he became hopelessly infatuated with such beauty. And after sending her a memorial of

---

1. This is a reference to several popular beliefs: that refusing to fulfill a pregnant woman's cravings can lead to a sty and, even more widespread, that if a pregnant woman's craving is not satisfied and she touches a part of her body, the shape of what was craved will appear on the newborn's body in that same spot. Birthmarks are, in fact, called *voglie* in Italian: "longings" or "cravings."

sighs, it was decreed that the stronghold should be surrendered to his grace. The negotiations went so well that the prince received nods of the head in exchange for kisses sent on his hands, winks of the eye in exchange for bows, thanks in exchange for offers, hopes for promises, and kind words for salaams. When this had gone on for many days, they became so friendly that they made an appointment to meet, which had to take place at night—when the moon played "Mute Sparrow" with the stars—at which time Petrosinella would give the ogress a sleeping potion and then hoist the prince up on her hair.

And so they remained. The appointed hour came and the prince arrived at the tower. He gave a whistle and Petrosinella lowered her braids, which he grabbed with both hands, saying, "Heave ho!" And when he had been pulled up, he threw himself through the little window of the room and made himself a meal of that parsley of the sauce of Love, and then—before the Sun taught its horses to jump through the hoop of the zodiac—lowered himself down on the same golden ladder and went off to look after his affairs.

Since they continued to do this often, one of the ogress's neighbors caught on, and, troubling herself about it like Rosso,[2] she decided to stick her face in the shit. She told the ogress to take heed, for Petrosinella was making love with a certain young man and she suspected that things might have gone even further because she could see the buzz of activity and trafficking, and feared that once they had made a clean sweep, they would vacate the house before May.[3] The ogress thanked her neighbor for the helpful warning and told her that she would take care of blocking Petrosinella's way, and that besides, she couldn't possibly escape because she had put a spell on her. If she didn't have three acorns in her hand, which were hidden in one of the rafters in the kitchen, trying to slip out of there was a lost cause.

While they were engaged in this talk, Petrosinella, who had been keeping her ears to the ground since she was a bit suspicious of the neighbor, heard the whole conversation, and—as soon as Night shook out its black clothes so they wouldn't be eaten by moths—when the prince arrived in the usual manner, she got him to climb up into the rafters. They found the acorns, which Petrosinella knew how to use because she had been enchanted by the ogress, made a rope

2. "A proverbial thief who while being jolted along a potholed street on his way to the gallows, asked his guard to request that the street be repaired" (Croce 562).

3. In Naples, May 4 was the traditional day for evictions and changing residence.

ladder down which they both went, and then threw up their heels and took off in the direction of the city.

But as they were leaving, they were seen by the neighbor, who began to scream and call for the ogress, and her screams were so loud that she woke her up. When the ogress heard that Petrosinella had escaped, she went down that same ladder, which was still tied to the little window, and began to run after the lovers. They saw her coming after them faster than an unreined horse, and thought they were lost; but then Petrosinella remembered the three acorns and immediately threw one of them on the ground. Out sprang a Corsican hound; and oh dear mother, was it terrifying! It started barking, and with its mouth wide open it ran toward the ogress, intending to eat her right up. But since she was slyer than Old Nick himself, she reached into her little sack, pulled out a loaf of bread, and gave it to the dog, which caused its tail to lower and its fury to subside.

The ogress went back to running after the fleeing ones, and Petrosinella, seeing her draw close, threw down the second acorn. Out came a ferocious lion, which, beating its tail on the ground and shaking its mane, opened its gaping jaws two spans wide and prepared to crush the ogress between them. The ogress backed off, skinned a donkey that she found grazing in a field, put on its skin, and ran back to confront the lion, which thought she really was a donkey and was so scared that it's still running.

Having jumped this second ditch, the ogress returned to chasing after those poor youngsters. When they heard the footfalls and saw the cloud of dust that was rising up to the sky, they conjectured that the ogress was back again. Since she suspected that the lion might still be after her, the ogress had not taken off the donkey skin, and when Petrosinella threw down the third acorn, out came a wolf, which—without giving the ogress time to find another solution—gobbled her up as if she really were a donkey. Now that the lovers were freed from their predicament, they set off at a leisurely pace to the prince's kingdom, where, with the kind permission of his father, the prince took Petrosinella for his wife. And thus they proved, after so many tempests of travail, that *just one hour in a safe harbor, and a hundred years of bad fortune are forgotten.*

Cagliuso

This tale type, ATU 545B, Puss in Boots, became better known in Charles Perrault's version, "The Master Cat, or Puss in Boots." Basile had a predecessor in Straparola ("Costantino Fortunato"), and there are many other popular variants. A version of this tale (largely derived from Perrault) also appeared in the 1812 edition of the Grimms' tales, though was later removed. Penzer comments that "Perrault was troubled about the ending to the tale and affixes a moral that is quite inapplicable. It has been repeatedly pointed out that the cat is an unscrupulous adventurer who indulges in a series of mean frauds to benefit a worthless youth who usually plays a very passive part in the tale. . . . We are still ignorant whence Straparola and Basile derived their tale—a curious tale that never seemed to have a satisfactory end. . . . Thus in some cases the cat turns into a human being, in others he becomes prime minister" (1:158). The end of Basile's tale differs notably both from Straparola's "Costantino," in which the cat simply disappears from the tale once its important work as a helper is done, and from Perrault's and other later versions of the tale, in which the cat is rewarded for his help. Another notable difference between Straparola's and Basile's variants and later versions is that the cat in the first two is female.

Due to the industry of a cat left to him by his father, Cagliuso becomes a gentleman. But when he shows signs of being ungrateful to the cat, it reproaches him for his ingratitude.

Ingratitude, my lords and ladies, is a rusty nail that when driven into the tree of courtesy causes it to dry up; it is a broken sewer that rots the foundations of affection; it is a bit of soot that, falling into the pot of friendship, takes away its aroma and taste. And this can be formally seen and proved; you'll see a rough sketch of it in the tale that I am about to tell you.

There once was, in my city of Naples, an old, wretchedly poor man, who was so full of withouts, so destitute, hungry, miserable, gaunt, and lacking even the smallest wrinkle in his purse, that he went around as naked as a louse. When he was about to shake out the sacks of his life, he called Oraziello and Pippo, his sons, and said to them, "I have already been convened according to contract for the debt I owe Nature. And believe me, if you are Christians, that it would be my great pleasure to sail out of this Mandracchio of sorrows and escape from this pigsty of suffering, if it weren't for the fact that I'll be leaving you impoverished, as penniless as Saint Chiara, stranded on the five roads of Melito without a coin, as clean as a barber's basin, as light on your feet as a sergeant, and as dry as a prune pit.[1] For you own as much as a fly can carry on its foot, and if you run for a hundred miles you won't drop a cent, since my luck has driven me to where the three dogs shit; life is no longer mine to have, and what you see is what you can write about, because I have always, as you know, been one for yawns and little crosses,[2] and I've always gone to bed without a candle. But despite all of this, I still want to leave you a sign of my love when I die; so you, Oraziello, my firstborn, take that sifter that's hanging on the wall, with which you'll be able to earn your bread; and you, Pippo, the nest-shitter, take the cat. And remember your papa." As he was saying this, he burst into tears, and a short while later said, "Farewell, night has come!"

Oraziello had his father buried with the help of some charity, and then took his sifter and went running about this way and that trying to make a living, and the more he sifted the more he earned. But Pippo, after he took the cat, said, "Just look what a pathetic inheritance my father has left me! I don't know how to provide for myself and now I have to shop for two! Who ever heard of such a wretched legacy? Better if it had never been!" The cat, who heard this lament, said to him, "You complain too much! You've got more luck than brains, though you don't know your own luck, for I can make you rich if I try." When he heard this, Pippo thanked Her Royal Catness, petted her three or four times on the back, and warmly entrusted himself to her care. And then the cat, feeling sorry for poor Cagliuso,[3] began to show up every morning—when the Sun went fishing for Night's shadows with its golden hook and bait of light—at either the Chiaia beach or the Rock of Fish, and

1. Mandracchio was a neighborhood of ill repute in Naples; Saint Chiara (Claire) was the founder of the monastic order of the Clarisse, with its ideal of absolute poverty; the five roads of Melito was an area where beggars congregated.
2. After yawning (out of hunger), crosses were made to keep evil spirits out.
3. At this point in the tale Pippo's name changes to Cagliuso.

when she spotted a big mullet or a nice bream she would grab it and bring it to the king, saying, "Lord Cagliuso, slave to Your Highness from the ground floor up to the terrace, sends you this fish with his respect and says, 'Great lord, small gift.'" The king, with the happy face usually awarded to those who bring gifts, answered the cat, "Tell this lord whom I don't know that I send him infinite thanks."

Other times the cat would run off to the hunting grounds, either the swamps or the Astroni, and when the hunters shot down an oriole or a great tit or a blackcap, she collected them and presented them to the king with the same message. And she employed this stratagem so often that one morning the king said to her, "I feel so obliged to this Lord Cagliuso that I would like to meet him in order to reciprocate the affection that he has shown toward me." To which the cat answered, "Lord Cagliuso's desire is to give his life and blood for your crown; and tomorrow morning—when the Sun sets the stubble of the aerial fields on fire—he will, without a doubt, come to pay homage to you."

And so when morning came, the cat went to the king and said to him, "My lord, Lord Cagliuso sends his apologies, for he cannot come. Last night some servants of his ran off, and they didn't even leave him the shirt on his back." Upon hearing this, the king immediately had an armful of clothes and undergarments taken from his wardrobe, and sent them to Cagliuso. And before two hours had gone by, Cagliuso, led by the cat, came to the palace, where he received a thousand compliments from the king; and after sitting him at his side, the king gave orders that a magnificent banquet be prepared.

But as everyone was eating, every now and then Cagliuso would turn to the cat and say to her, "My little kitty, keep an eye on those rags of mine, for I wouldn't want anything bad to happen to them." And the cat answered, "Be quiet; shut your trap and don't talk about such trifles!" When the king wanted to know what Cagliuso needed, the cat answered that he had gotten a craving for a little lemon, and the king immediately sent someone to the garden to get a basket of them. And Cagliuso kept up with the same music about his tatters and shirttails, and the cat kept on telling him to plug his mouth, and the king asked him again what he needed, and the cat invented another excuse to make up for Cagliuso's pettiness.

Finally, after having eaten and chatted for a long time about this and that, Cagliuso took his leave. But that fox of a cat stayed with the king and described to him Cagliuso's valor, brains, good judgment, and above all his great riches in the countryside outside of Rome and in Lombardy, for which he would deserve to marry into the family of a crowned king. When the king asked what exactly there was, the cat answered that it was impossible to keep track of the furniture, buildings, and other furnishings of that moneybags, since even he did not know how much he had, and that if the king wanted to find out more about it, he could send his people out of the kingdom with her, and they could see with their own eyes that Cagliuso's riches were without equal in the world.

The king summoned some of his faithful men and ordered them to obtain detailed information on the matter, and they followed in the cat's footsteps. As soon as they had gotten beyond the borders of the kingdom, the cat, with the excuse that she had to find refreshment for them along the way, at every turn ran ahead, and for every flock of sheep, herd of cattle, stable of horses, and drift of pigs she came across, she said to the shepherds and guardians, "Hey there, take heed! A gang of bandits is planning to sack everything they find in this land! But if you want to escape their fury and make sure your possessions go unharmed, just say they belong to Lord Cagliuso, and no one will touch a hair on your head." She said the same thing at all the farms along the road, so that wherever the king's men arrived, they found a bagpipe tuned to the same key: everything they encountered was said to belong to Lord Cagliuso. And then, tired of asking, they returned to the king and praised Lord Cagliuso's riches from the sky to the sea. When the king heard this, he promised the cat a nice reward if she arranged the marriage between Cagliuso and his daughter, and the cat, shuttling back and forth, finally pulled off the deal.

When Cagliuso arrived, the king delivered him a great dowry and his daughter, and after a month of festivities, Cagliuso said that he wanted to take his bride to his estates. The king accompanied them to the border of his kingdom, and they set off for Lombardy, where, on the cat's recommendation, Cagliuso bought some properties and land, and became a baron.

Cagliuso now found himself rolling in wealth, and he thanked the cat over and over again, saying that he owed his life to her and his greatness to her good offices, that a cat's devices had done him more good than his father's wits, and that she should therefore feel free to do and undo his possessions and his life in whatever manner she pleased and thought fit. Finally, he gave her his word that as soon as she died—a hundred years from then!—he would have her stuffed and placed inside a golden cage in his own bedroom, so that he might always keep the memory of her before his eyes.

The cat listened to this show of braggadocio, and before three days had gone by, she pretended to be dead and lay herself out stiff in the garden. When Cagliuso's wife saw this, she shouted, "Oh, my husband, what a great tragedy! The cat is dead!" "And may every evil accompany her!" answered Cagliuso. "Better her than us." "What shall we do?" replied the wife. And he: "Take her by her foot and throw her out the window!"

Hearing of this fine reward when she would have least imagined it, the cat began to speak: "This is the great gratitude for the fleas that I picked off your neck? These are the thousand thanks for those rags I got you to throw away, so worn out that you could have hung them on spindles? This is what I get back, after having dressed you as elegantly as a spider and fed you when you were hungry, miserable, and threadbare? When you were in tatters, covered with shreds, all patched up and coming apart at the seams, you corpse-stripper? This is the fate of those who try to wash an ass's head! Get lost, and may everything I've done for you be damned; your throat doesn't deserve to be spit in! What a lovely golden cage you've prepared for me, what a fine burial you've planned for me! There you have it: you offer your services, you make sacrifices, you labor, you sweat, and all for this nice prize! Oh, miserable is he who fills up his pot with the hopes of someone else! That philosopher was right when he said, 'If you go to bed an ass, you'll wake up one!' In short, the more you do, the less you should expect. Good words and wicked actions deceive only the wise and the mad."

Speaking in this manner and shaking her head, she headed out of there, and however much Cagliuso tried to lick her down with the lung[4] of humility, nothing could get her to come back. And as she ran off without once turning her head, she said, *May God save you from the rich who become poor and from the beggar who has worked his way up.*

4. Street vendors would sell lung to the houses of Naples; "all the cats in the neighborhood would become agitated and meow as they heard their benefactor getting closer" (Croce 172).

The Cockroach, the Mouse, and the Cricket (Lo scarafone, lo sorece e lo grillo)

This tale combines types ATU 554, The Grateful Animals, and ATU 559, The Dungbeetle, and features another of the many foolish protagonists of The Tale of Tales *as well as another "princess who would not laugh." Here, the hero Nardiello distinguishes himself by his kindness toward small creatures: although this is a common enough folkloric motif, in this case the animals appear as consummately baroque artists, which is the reason for Nardiello's initial interest in them.*

Nardiello is sent three times to market by his father, each time with a hundred ducats. The first time he buys a mouse, and then a cockroach and a cricket. When this leads to his father kicking him out of the house, he ends up in a place where he cures the daughter of a king by means of the animals, and after various other adventures he becomes her husband.

Fortune is a stubborn woman who avoids the faces of learned men, because they pay more attention to the turning of pages than to the rotation of a wheel. For this reason she more willingly associates with ignorant and paltry people and—in order to receive plebeian glory—does not worry about dividing her goods among the big birds, as I will tell you about in the tale that follows.

There once was, on the Vomero hill,[1] a very rich farmer named Miccone, who had a son named Nardiello, the most wretched blockhead you could ever find on any ship of fools. The poor father was embittered and miserable, for he knew of no way or means of inducing his son to lead a level-headed and useful life. If Nardiello went to the tavern to guzzle with his buddies he was

1. A hilltop neighborhood of Naples, home to country villas in Basile's time.

cheated by crooks; if he associated with women of ill repute he was given the worst meat for the top price; if he played in gambling dens they kneaded him like a pizza and took him out when he was nice and hot. And so, in one way or another, he had dissipated half of his father's wealth.

For this reason Miccone was always armed and ready to defend his castle, and would shout and threaten, saying, "What do you think you're doing, spendthrift? Can't you see that my wealth is trickling away like water at low tide? Leave, leave those damned taverns, which start with the name of the enemy and end up signifying evil![2] Leave them, for they're migraines to your head, dropsy to your throat, and diarrhea to your wallet! Leave, leave that godless gambling, which puts your life at risk and gnaws away at my fortune, which repels happiness and eats up cash, where the dice reduce you to zero and the words whittle you down to a peg! Leave, leave your bordello commerce with that evil race of the daughters of ugly sin, where you squander and spend! You consume pouches of money for a perch and you suffer agonies and reduce yourself to picking at a bone for a piece of rotten meat; they are not meretrices, but a Thracian sea[3] where you are captured by the Turks! Keep away from the occasion, and you'll give up the vice; if the cause is remote, said that fellow, the effect will be removed. So here are a hundred ducats: go to the Salerno fair and buy as many steer, so that in three or four years we'll have as many oxen. Once we've got the oxen, we'll work the fields; once we've worked the fields, we'll start dealing in wheat; and if we meet up with a good famine, we'll weigh our coins by the bushel, and at the very least I'll buy the title on some friend's land and then you'll be titled, too, like so many others. So be careful, my son, everything has a head; he who does not begin cannot continue."

"Leave it to this fellow," answered Nardiello. "I know how to do my calculations now, and I've learned the rules for every situation!" "That's what I want to hear," answered his father, and when he had forked out the money, Nardiello started off to the fair. But he had not yet reached the waters of the Sarno when he came upon a lovely little elm wood where, at the foot of a rock that had surrounded itself with fronds of ivy so as to cure its perpetual wound of cool water, he saw a fairy frolicking with a cockroach, and the cockroach

2. *Ostarie* (Neap.): a burlesque etymology; the origin of *oste* is posed as *ostis* (Latin; enemy) and that of *rie*, *rio* (wicked).

3. Another facetious etymology, which plays on the phonetic similarity between *meretrice* (meretrix) and *mare trace* (Thracian sea).

was playing a tiny guitar so beautifully that a Spaniard would have said that it was a superb and grandiose thing. When Nardiello saw this, he stopped to listen as if enchanted, and said that he would give one of his eyes to have such a talented animal. The fairy told him that if he paid her a hundred ducats, she would give it to him. "There's never been a better time than this," Nardiello answered, "since I have the money ready and waiting!" Saying this, he threw the hundred ducats in her lap, then took the cockroach away in a little box and ran back to his father with a joy that went all the way from the little bones of his feet on up, and said, "Now you'll really get to see, my sir, if I'm a man of ingenuity and know how to go about my business, for without tiring myself by going all the way to the fair, I found my fortune when I was halfway there, and for a hundred ducats I got this jewel!"

Upon hearing these words and seeing the little box, his father was certain that his son had bought a diamond necklace or something of the sort, but when he opened it and saw the cockroach, the humiliation of being tricked and the pain of losing his money were a set of bellows that made him swell up like a toad. And while Nardiello would have liked to tell him about the virtues of the cockroach, he wasn't allowed to say a word, for his father went on and on, saying, "Shut up, plug it, close that mouth, cork it; not a peep, you mule, you horse-brain, you ass-head! Take the cockroach back this very instant to whoever sold it to you, and with these other hundred ducats that I'm giving you buy just as many steer. And come right back, and take care the Wicked One doesn't blind you, or I'll make you eat your hands with your own teeth!"

Nardiello took the money, and set off toward the Tower of Sarno, and when he had reached the same place as before he came upon another fairy, who was playing with a mouse that was executing the loveliest dance steps you ever did see. For some time Nardiello watched with amazement the fawn steps, twirls, caprioles, point dancing, and leaps of this animal, until he was beside himself with wonder. Then he told the fairy that if she was willing to sell it to him he would give her a hundred ducats. The fairy accepted these terms, and after taking his coins she gave him the mouse in a box. When Nardiello went back home and showed poor Miccone the fine purchase he had made, Miccone made an awful scene, slamming himself around like a beaten octopus and snorting like a skittish horse. Indeed, if it hadn't been for a neighbor of his who happened to appear in the midst of all this uproar, he would truly have taken the measure of Nardiello's shoulders. Finally Miccone, boiling with anger, took a hundred more ducats and said to Nardiello, "I'm warning you, don't try another one of your tricks, because the third time it won't work. Go to Salerno and buy the steer, and I swear on the souls of my ancestors that if you slip up this time, woe to the mother who gave birth to you!"

With his head hanging, Nardiello made off in the direction of Salerno. When he arrived at the same place as before, he came upon another fairy, who was amusing herself with a cricket that sang so sweetly that it lulled people to sleep. Upon hearing this new breed of nightingale, Nardiello immediately felt the desire to do business, and once they had agreed on a hundred ducats, he put it in a tiny cage made of a long hollowed squash covered with sticks, and went back to his father. When he saw the third bad service his son had performed for him, Miccone lost his patience, and, grabbing a club, fixed Nardiello up so well that even Rodomonte[4] couldn't have done better.

Nardiello escaped from Miccone's clutches as soon as he could; he took all three animals, cleared out of town, and set off in the direction of Lombardy, where there lived a great lord named Cenzone who had an only daughter whose name was Milla. On account of a certain illness Milla had become so melancholy that no one had seen her laugh for seven years straight, so that her father, after having attempted a thousand remedies and spent money high and low, issued a proclamation announcing that he would give her in marriage to whomever made her laugh.

Nardiello heard of this proclamation and fancied that he would try his fortune, and he went before Cenzone and offered to make Milla laugh. To which the lord responded, "Be mindful, my friend, that if you don't succeed your hood will lose its shape!" "Both my hood and my shoe can lose their shape, for all I care," replied Nardiello, "for I want to try my luck, and whatever happens will happen!" The king summoned his daughter to come sit with him under a canopy, and Nardiello took the three animals out of the box. They played, danced, and sang with such grace and such charm that the princess burst into laughter, whereas the king's heart wept, for according to the terms of the proclamation he was now forced to give a jewel of a woman to a scum of a man. But since he was not able to go back on his promise, he said to Nardiello, "I will give you my daughter, and my state as dowry, but with the agreement that if

4. The Saracen warrior of the two best-known Italian chivalric epics, M. M. Boairdo's *Orlando innamorato* and L. Ariosto's *Orlando furioso*; a symbol of superhuman strength.

you do not consummate the marriage in three days I will feed you to the lions." "I have no fear," said Nardiello, "since in that time I'm man enough not only to consummate the marriage but to consume your daughter and your whole house as well!" And the king: "Slow down, we'll get to that; as Carcariello said, you can't know a good watermelon until you've seen its flesh."

After the festivities were held and evening fell—when the Sun, like a thief, was taken off to the prison of the West with a cape over its head—the bride and bridegroom went to bed. But since the malicious king had arranged for a sleeping draught to be given to Nardiello, he did nothing but snore all night. After the same thing happened on the second and the third days, the king had him thrown into the lion pit, where Nardiello, realizing he was nearing his end, opened the animals' box and said, "Since my fate has dragged me with a bitter towline to this wretched impasse, and since I have nothing else to leave to you, O lovely animals of mine, I will free you, so that you may go where best you please." As soon as they were let out, the animals began to exhibit themselves in so many little capers and games that the lions became as still as statues. In the meantime, the mouse addressed Nardiello, whose spirit was already in his mouth, saying, "Cheer up, master, for even if you've given us our freedom, we want more than ever to be your slaves, seeing that you've nourished us with so much love and cured us with so much affection, and that at the end you gave us a sign of your great devotion by setting us free. Have no doubts: he who does good may expect good; do good, and then forget about it. But you should know that we are enchanted, and if you want to see what we are capable and worthy of, follow us, and you'll free yourself of this danger."

With Nardiello behind them, the mouse soon made a hole in the wall big enough for a man, through which, after going up a staircase, they led him to the top, where it was safe. There they put him in a hut and told him to order them to do whatever he wished, for they would leave nothing undone that might bring him pleasure. "My desire would be," responded Nardiello, "that if the king has given Milla another husband, you do me the favor of not allowing the marriage to be consummated, because it would bring about the consummation of my own miserable life." "That and nothing are but the same," answered the animals. "Keep your spirits up and wait for us in this shack; we'll clean up the mess without delay!"

They set off for the court, and found that the king had married his daughter to a great German lord, and that that very evening the cask was to be uncorked.

Once the animals had skillfully entered the chamber of the newlyweds, they waited until the banquet was over and evening came—when the Moon came out to feed the Pleiades with dew—and the couple went to bed. And since the bridegroom had loaded his crossbow and taken one too many cards,[5] as soon as he had holed himself up under the sheets he immediately fell asleep, and lay there as if his throat had just been cut. When the cockroach heard the bridegroom's snoring, it crawled very quietly up the foot of the bed, made its way under the covers, and nimbly slipped into the bridegroom's asshole, serving him a suppository that uncorked his body in such a way that one might have said, with Petrarch: "Love drew from him a subtle liquid." The bride, who heard the rumbling of this dysentery—"the breeze and the fragrance and the coolness and the shade"[6]—woke her husband up. When he saw the sort of perfume he had incensed his idol with, he nearly died of shame and croaked with rage, and once he had gotten out of bed and had sent his whole body to the laundry, he called for the doctors, who attributed the cause for this disgrace to the excesses of the banquet the day before.

When the next evening arrived, and he asked his servants' advice, they were all of the opinion that he should swathe himself with sturdy cloths so as to avoid another mishap; he did this and then went to bed. But after he fell asleep again and the cockroach returned to play a second trick on him, it found the passageway blocked. And so it went back unhappily to its companions, and told them how the bridegroom had prepared shields of bandages, dikes of diapers, and trenches of rags. Upon hearing this, the mouse said, "Come with me, and you'll see whether I'm a good enough sapper to clear you a way!" When the mouse arrived in sight of the place in question, it started to gnaw at the cloth, and made a hole that communicated with that other one; the cockroach then went in and administered another one of its medicinal cures, so that a sea of liquid topaz flowed forth and the Arabian fumes infected the palace. This caused the befouled bride to awaken, and when, by the light of the lamp, she saw the citron-colored flood that had turned the Dutch bed linens into yellow-rippled Venetian moiré, she plugged her nose and flew into her damsels' room. The wretched bridegroom called his valets, and complained at

5. I.e., had too much to drink.

6. Petrarch's *Canzoniere*, or *Rerum vulgarium fragmenta* was one of the most important models for the Italian lyric tradition.

length of the disgrace of having begun to construct the grandeur of his house on such a slippery foundation.

His servants comforted him, and advised him to keep his wits about him the third night, telling him the tale of the gassy patient and the sharp-tongued doctor who, when his patient let loose a fart, put on erudite airs and said to him, "Sanitatibus!" When another fart followed he added, "Ventositatibus!" But when a third proceeded, he opened his mouth wide and said, "Asinitatibus!" Consequently, if the first mosaic work that had decorated the nuptial bed could be blamed on excessive eating, and the second on the bad state of his stomach, which had upset his whole body, the third would be imputed to a shitty nature and he would be driven away in stink and shame. "Have no doubt," said the bridegroom, "because tonight, even if I have to die for it, I intend to stay awake the whole time and not let sleep win me over. And furthermore, we'll think of some remedy for plugging the main pipe, so that no one can say to me, 'Three times he fell and the third time he lay still!'"[7]

That agreed, when the next night arrived and the bridegroom moved to a different room and bed, he summoned his friends and asked them for advice on how to stop up his body so that it wouldn't play a third trick on him; as for staying awake, all the poppies in the world couldn't have put him to sleep. Among his servants there was a young man who dabbled in the bombardier's art; and, since everyone is most interested in his own trade, he advised the bridegroom to have himself a wooden stopper made, like the ones used for firecrackers. It was prepared without delay, and after the German had positioned it in the right manner, he went to bed—neither touching the bride, for fear that his exertions might ruin the creation, nor closing his eyes, so that he could be ready for any movement that his intestines might make.

The cockroach, who saw that the bridegroom wasn't falling asleep, said to its companions, "Alas! This time they've shown us; our skills aren't of any use to us, since the bridegroom isn't sleeping and won't give me a chance to carry on my business!" "Just a minute," said the cricket, "I'll take care of this for you now!" and, starting to sing sweetly, it put the bridegroom to sleep. When the cockroach saw this, it raced forth to apply its usual syringe, but upon finding the door closed and the road barricaded, it went back to its companions in desperation and confusion and told them what had happened. The mouse,

7. This verse from Virgil's *Aeneid* is found at the end of book 4.

who had no other goal than to serve and to please Nardiello, went off to the larder that very instant, and after sniffing in jar after jar, came across a pot of mustard. It rubbed his tail in it and then ran to the bridegroom's bed and lubricated the nostrils of the wretched German, who began to sneeze so hard that the stopper flew out with such fury that it hit the bride, to whom he had his back turned, in the chest so violently that it almost killed her.

The king came running when he heard the bride's shrieks, and when he asked what the matter was, she told him that a firecracker had been shot at her chest. The king marveled at this absurdity, and at the fact that she could even speak with a firecracker in her chest. But then he lifted the covers and the sheets and found the explosion of bran and the stopper to the firecracker, which had given the bride a nice eggplant-colored bruise, although I'm not sure if the stink of the fire powder or the blow of the cannonball caused her more harm. Upon seeing this revolting scene and hearing that it was the bridegroom's third attempt at liquidating the contract, the king threw him out of his kingdom, and when he considered that this whole misfortune had been caused by the cruelty shown toward poor Nardiello, he began to beat his fists on his chest. And while, repentant for what he had done, he was wailing, the cockroach appeared before him and said, "Do not despair: Nardiello is alive, and for his fine qualities deserves to be the son-in-law of Your Highness, and if it pleases you that he come, we will send for him immediately." "Oh, be welcome, you who bring me this news worthy of a reward, my dear animal! You have given me life, you have rescued me from a sea of woes, since I felt such pain in my heart for the way I did that poor young man wrong! And so let him come, for I want to embrace him like a son and give him my daughter for his wife."

When it heard this, the cricket went hopping away to the shack where Nardiello was and told him of everything that had happened. Then it brought him to the royal palace, where, once the king had met and embraced him, he was given Milla's hand. The animals cast a spell on Nardiello so that he became a handsome young man, after which he sent for his father from the Vomero. And they all lived together, happy and content, proving after a thousand hardships and a thousand woes that *more happens in one hour than in a hundred years.*

Sun, Moon, and Talia (Sole, Luna e Talia)

This tale is a fascinating example of the chain of influence in literary versions of ATU 410, Sleeping Beauty. It is apparent that Charles Perrault was familiar with Basile's early version when he published "The Sleeping Beauty in the Wood" (1697), with which it bears close resemblance. Later, in the Grimms' version, called "Brier Rose" (1812), the entire second part of the tale is eliminated, and the tale ends with the heroine waking up to her prince. Basile's tale offers a singular assortment of dysfunction and violence: rape, necrophilia, adultery, intended cannibalism, and death at the stake.

Talia dies due to a splinter of flax and is left in a palace, where a king chances to pass by and causes her to have two children. The children fall into the hands of the king's jealous wife, who orders that they be cooked and served to their father and that Talia be burned. The cook saves the children, and Talia is freed by the king, who has his wife thrown into the same fire that had been prepared for Talia.

There once was a great lord who at the birth of a daughter named Talia summoned all the wise men and fortune-tellers of his kingdom to predict her future. After conferring a number of times, they concluded that she would find herself in great danger because of a splinter of flax. And so the king issued a prohibition aimed at avoiding that baleful encounter: in his house neither flax nor hemp nor anything of the sort was to enter.

But when Talia came to be a big girl and was looking out the window one day, she saw an old woman who was spinning pass by. Since she had never seen a distaff or a spindle and was greatly pleased by all that winding, she became so curious that she had the woman come up, and, taking the distaff in her hand, she began to draw the thread. But then, by accident, a splinter of flax got under her fingernail, and she fell dead to the ground.

At the sight of this, the old woman started running, and she's still jumping down those stairs. And when the hapless father heard of the accident that had occurred, he paid for that pail of bitter wine with a barrel of tears, and had her placed inside that same palace, which was in the countryside, seated on a velvet chair under a brocade canopy. Then he closed the doors and abandoned forever the palace that had been the cause of such great sorrow, so as to thoroughly erase every memory of this misfortune.

But some time later, a king who was out hunting lost his falcon, which after escaping flew into a window of that house. When it didn't respond to his call the king knocked at the door, since he thought people lived there. After knocking for a long time, he had a harvester's ladder brought, intending to scale the house himself to see what was inside. He climbed up and looked all over the place and, not finding a living soul, he just stood there awhile like a mummy. Finally, he arrived at the room where Talia was sitting, as if enchanted, and when he saw her he thought she was asleep. He called to her, but no matter what he did or how loudly he yelled she did not wake up, and since her beauty had enflamed him, he carried her in his arms to a bed and picked the fruits of love. Then he left her in the bed and returned to his kingdom, where he did not remember what had happened for a long time.

After nine months, Talia unloaded a pair of babies, one a boy and the other a girl, who looked like a pair of jewels. They were cared for by two fairies that had appeared in the palace, who would place them at their mother's teats; one day, when they were trying to suck but couldn't find the nipple, they grabbed her finger and sucked so long that the piece of flax came out. Talia felt like she was awakening from a long sleep, and when she saw those jewels beside her she offered them her tit and held them as dear as her own life.

And while she did not know what had happened to her and how it was that she was alone in that palace with two children by her side and people who brought her things to eat without her being able to see them, the king, who now remembered Talia, found an occasion to go hunting and came to see her. Finding her awake and in the company of two painted eggs of beauty, he was stunned with joy and told Talia who he was and what had happened. They made friends and a strong bond was established, and after staying several days with her, he departed with the promise that he would return and take her away with him.

He then went back to his kingdom, where he mentioned Talia and the children at every chance he got, so that when he was eating he had Talia in his mouth as well as Sun and Moon, for those were the names he had given the children, and when he went to bed he called for the one and the other.

The king's wife had already become a little suspicious after her husband's delay in returning from the hunt, and when she heard all this talk of Talia, Sun, and Moon, she felt burned by something other than the sun. And so she called her secretary and said to him, "Listen here, my boy: you're between Scylla and Charybdis, the jamb and the door, the club and the prison bars. If you tell me who my husband is in love with, I'll make you rich, and if you hide it from me I'll make sure you're found neither dead nor alive." Her buddy was on the one hand shaken up by fear, but on the other fleeced by interest, which is a blindfold on honor's eyes, a veil on the face of justice, and a crowbar on words given. He thus gave her bread for bread and wine for wine, at which the queen sent the secretary to visit Talia on the king's behalf and tell her that he wanted to see the children. Talia sent them to him with great joy, and that heart of Medea ordered the cook to slit their throats, make various little dishes and delicacies out of them, and then serve them to her poor husband. The cook, however, was of tender lung, and when he saw those two beautiful golden apples, he took pity on them and gave them to his wife to hide, instead preparing two goat kids in a hundred different sauces.

The king came home, and the queen had the food served with great gusto. While the king was eating with great gusto, too, and exclaiming, "Oh, on the life of Lanfusa, this dish is so good! Oh, on the soul of my grandpa, this other one is so tasty!" she kept on saying, "Eat up, for you're eating what is yours." The king paid no attention to this refrain the first two or three times, but finally, when he heard the music still playing, he answered, "I know that what I'm eating is mine, since you didn't bring a thing with you to this house!" and he got up angrily and went out to a nearby town to unleash his anger.

In the meantime, the queen, not yet satisfied with what she had done, called the secretary back and had him summon Talia with the excuse that the king was waiting to see her. Talia came the instant she heard this, eager to find her light without realizing that only fire awaited her. She appeared before the queen, who with a face like Nero's, livid with rage, said to her, "May you be welcome, madam slut! So you're that fancy piece of trash, that weed with whom my husband takes his pleasure! So you're that bitch who makes my head spin like a top! Go on, you've reached purgatory, and I'm going to make you pay for the pain you've caused me!"

When Talia heard this she began to apologize, saying that it wasn't her fault and that the king had taken possession of her territory when she was under a sleeping spell. But the queen, who had no intention of listening to excuses, had a huge fire lit right there in the courtyard of the palace, and ordered that Talia be thrown onto it. Seeing that things had taken a bad turn, Talia fell down on her knees before the queen and begged her to at least give her the time to take off the clothes she was wearing. Not so much out of pity for the poor girl as to retrieve those gold-and pearl-embroidered clothes, the queen said, "Get undressed; that I will allow you to do." Talia began to undress, letting out a shriek with every piece of clothing she took off. And when she had taken off her dress, her skirt, and her jacket, and was about to take off her petticoat, she let out the last shriek as they were dragging her off to supply the ashes for the laundry tub where Charon washed his breeches.

At that very moment the king ran in and, finding this spectacle, demanded to know the whole story. He then asked about his children and heard his own wife, who reproached him with betraying her, tell him of how she had gotten him to gobble them down. When the hapless king heard this, he fell prey to desperation and began to cry, "So I was the werewolf that attacked my own little sheep! Alas, why didn't my veins recognize the springs of their own blood? O renegade Turk, what kind of a ferocious thing did you do? But just wait; you're going to end up as compost in a broccoli patch, and I won't be sending this face of a tyrant to the Colosseum for her penance!" And as he was saying this, he ordered that she be thrown onto the same fire that had been lit for Talia, together with the secretary who had been an instrument in the bitter game and a weaver of the wicked plot. He was intending to do the same with the cook who he thought had chopped up his children, but the cook threw himself at the king's feet and said, "Actually, my lord, the service I performed for you would deserve a pension other than a furnace full of coals, a subsidy other than a pole in the ass, an entertainment other than to blacken and shrivel in a fire, and a profit other than to mix the ashes of a cook with those of a queen! This is certainly not the great thanks that I expect for having saved your children in spite of that sack of dog bile, who wanted to kill them so that what was part of your body would return to that same body."

When he heard those words, the king was beside himself and thought he was dreaming; he couldn't believe his own ears. He finally turned to the cook and said, "If it is true that you saved my children, you may rest assured that I will free you from turning the spit and that I will place you in the kitchen of this heart, where you can turn my desires as you please and claim for yourself a prize so great that you will consider yourself happy to be in the world!" While the king was speaking these words, the cook's wife, who saw the state of need her husband was in, brought Sun and Moon before their father. And, playing the game of three with Talia and the children, he sent out a whirlwind of kisses first to the one and then to the other, and when he had given the cook a large reward and named him his gentleman-in-waiting, he took Talia for his wife. She enjoyed a long life with her husband and children, and recognized after all her ordeals that for those who are lucky, *good rains down even when they are sleeping.*

PART III

Sleeping Beauty

The Italian Fairy Tale after Basile

1

Pompeo Sarnelli (1649–1724)

The writer and bishop Pompeo Sarnelli was born in Bari, Italy; at the age of around fourteen, he moved to Naples, where he would remain for the rest of his life. A man of great erudition and curiosity, Sarnelli produced editions of well-known Neapolitan authors of his time, as well as the tour guide *Guida de' forestieri curiosi di vedere e di riconoscere le cose più memoriabili di Napoli* (Guide for Those Foreigners Curious to See and to Become Acquainted with the Most Memorable Things of Naples). In 1674 he edited the first edition of Giambattista Basile's *Tale of Tales* to bear the alternate name of *Pentamerone* on the frontispiece, and in 1684 he published his own *Posilecheata* (An Outing to Posillipo) under the pseudonym of Masillo Reppone de Gnanopoli. The *Posilecheata* comprises five fairy tales told in Neapolitan dialect and is the only other seventeenth-century Italian collection of fairy tales after *The Tale of Tales*. The tales are embedded in a realistic frame in which peasant women entertain guests at the end of a country banquet with their stories. Both the overall structure and the style owe much to Basile's model; Sarnelli fuses, for example, elements from learned and folk cultures and employs an abundance of metaphor.

The tales themselves—"La piatà remmonerata" (Mercy Recompensed), "La vajassa fedele" (The Faithful Servant), "La 'ngannatrice 'ngannata" (The Deceiver Deceived), "La gallenella" (The Young Hen), and "La capo e la coda" (The Head and the Tale)—include many common folkloric motifs, such as kindness rewarded, magical resurrection from death, fairies' curses, a cruel mother-in-law, false messages, and helping animals. They also contain abundant description of Neapolitan monuments and landmarks, along with information on their origins. Unlike Basile's opus, the *Posilecheata* has met with little critical attention.

Further Reading

Primary

Sarnelli, Pompeo. *Posilecheata*. Ed. Enrico Malato. Rome: Gabriele e Mariateresa Benincasa, 1986. 141–75. [source text]

Sarnelli, Pompeo. "Foreword to Giambattista Basile's *Pentamerone* (1674) and Foreword to *An Outing to Posillipo* (1684)." In *Fairy Tales Framed: Early Forewords, Afterwords, and Critical Words*. Ed. Ruth B. Bottigheimer. Albany, NY: SUNY Press, 2012.

Secondary

Allasia, Clara. "La Posilecheata, una still life fiabesca." In *I novellieri italiani e la loro presenza nella cultura europea: rizomi e palinsesti rinascimentali*. Ed. Guillermo Carrascón and Chiara Simbolotti. Turin: Accademia University Press, 2016. 255–67.

D'Eugenio, Daniela. "Pompeo Sarnelli's *Posilecheata*: Paremias and the Multifacted Neapolitan Baroque." *Paromia: Brusantino, Florio, Sarnelli, and Italian Proverbs from the Sixteenth and Seventeenth Centuries*. West Lafayette, IN: Purdue University Press, 2021.

Malato, Enrico. "Introduction." In *Posilecheata*, by Pompeo Sarnelli. Rome: Gabriele e Mariateresa Benincasa, 1986.

The Little Hen (La Gallenella)

"The Little Hen" offers a version of the familiar scenario of a wronged underdog who overcomes obstacles to regain what is rightfully hers. As such, it is more of a "restoration" narrative than a tale of social betterment. It contains many motifs diffuse in folk traditions, such as animal helpers (here, a lizard), treacherous in-laws, and transformation as a result of eating a serpent's egg. In his 1885 edition, Vittorio Imbriani mentions similar Greek, Syrian, and Portuguese folktales. Particularly noteworthy are Sarnelli's description of the devastating effects of the plague (most likely that of 1656) on Naples and his attention to the topography of the city.

It must have been a great doctor who said that as a man is born, so he comes up. And if a bumpkin was ever known to act like a gentleman, he must have been either a Janissary or a white crow, since eagles are not born to owls, nor doves to magpies. And so the saying goes—"Keep company with those better than you and help them in their affairs"—because those who are born to better stations proceed through life at a better clip, and those who sleep with the dogs don't get up without fleas. Just as you'll see for yourselves if you listen to this tale that I am about to tell you.

That good soul Pascarella, who was the grandma of my grandma, told us a tale one evening, as we were roasting a few chestnuts in the hot ashes (I remember it as if it were now, because as one of the chestnuts crackled in the fire, a bunch of sparks flew into my eye and burned half my eyelid off). This is how it went:

Once upon a time in Naples there was a merchant by the name of Peppone, who with his wife, whose name was Zezolla, had a son and a daughter, fruit of the same birth. And they were the most beautiful creations ever produced by Nature's paintbrush, so beautiful that the father decided to call them Sun and Moon. And since Zezolla's milk was scarce, or perhaps because she thought (as certain women do) that she would become ugly if she nursed her children—a notion that can turn good stock into bad or even worse—she gave them to a wet nurse named Cenza, who lived in the village of Grumo, which is where she brought the children.

It happened that in the span of a few months that terrible disease called the plague—and may it keep far from us and sink to the bottom of the sea!—arrived in Naples for the first time. And lo and behold! You saw the city become as clean as a barber's basin, since men were evicted from the houses of their bodies by the thousands without even waiting until the fourth of May.[1] And just as in the case of people who are forcibly kicked out of their homes, all of their stuff was thrown from the windows. Death, who always travels with his executors, instead of bringing along those fire-mouthed thugs who go "bow-wow,"[2] this time had his victims tied up in their boils[3] and thrown into the prison at the bottom of their bed, where a sign read: "It is hereby proclaimed that no one shall come near this bed, at the risk of their life." And even if there were a lot of people who didn't want to listen to this talk, they all ended up falling for it. If the doctor touched his patient's wrist to take his pulse, then Death's thugs tied up the doctor's wrists, and he was taken prisoner to a grave; if a father embraced his son, then Death, who was always close by, with a blow of his sickle killed two birds with one stone, striking them both down at once. Do you want to hear about the mother, too? If she nursed her children, she poisoned them, and if she didn't, she saw them waste away and die of hunger before her eyes. And good luck finding gravediggers and a place to dig the graves! Everyone tried to keep away from the dead, for Death, like another Caesar, had written on the forehead of his subjects, "Noli me tangere," and the gravediggers would grab hold of the poor souls with their hooks and throw them, half-dead and half-alive, on top of the carts that Death led in his triumphal march not to the Capitol but to the Grotto of the Bats.[4] The city had become a field of nettles, and where elegant carriages used to promenade, now all you could see were carts overflowing with dead bodies. And just as the senses had once reveled in those streets, they now suffered: eyes saw nothing

1. In Naples, the traditional day for evictions and relocations.
2. A reference to Cerberus, the multiheaded dog that guards the entrance to the Underworld.
3. Here Sarnelli plays on the sound of dogs barking—*bú-bú*—And the word for the buboes, or boils, caused by the plague—*bubune (Neap.).*
4. A grotto in Naples where many of the dead in the 1656 plague were buried.

but human flesh dragged through the streets and torn apart by pigs and dogs; noses went about with their nostrils plugged with cotton wool soaked in vinegar, so as not to smell the infectious stench; ears heard nothing but the moans of those poor souls in the throes of death; mouths were constantly spitting, as if they had eaten unripe grapes and their stomachs were revolting; and people were afraid to feed on air because of the danger that it might take away their breath for good. To sum it all up, those who were still alive appeared deader than the dead, as a result of their suffering and fear.

Now, Peppone and Zezolla, too, ran into the same fate as the many who were passing on to the other world. The city without people looked like a sacked village, and the houses, no longer inhabited, began to fall to pieces. The few city folk who remained—I don't know whether it was to lament the dead or to be able to tell what happened to generations to come—had the houses that were still standing boarded up, so that their heirs, if any existed in the leftovers of the plague, would not find themselves without both family and possessions. But Sun and Moon, who had been with the wet nurse in Grumo, escaped this unfortunate fate, and were raised as best they could be. The poor wet nurse received no more help from the city, and because there was little to live on since no one was doing business, and those who had escaped the plague took many years to come back, she decided that when they were a little older she would send them away.

And in fact, once the children had reached a certain age, when they might be of use to someone as servants and learn how to earn their bread, Cenza went off to the city with them. She took them to the house where their father had lived, which she found nailed shut, with all of its doors and windows walled up. She left them in a half-destroyed room on the ground floor next to the house, and said to them, "I don't know, my children, how I can take care of you any longer, since just as you've been growing like shoots, may God bless you, my provisions have been losing their roots. I'm a poor wretch who's dying of hunger, and God only knows how I was able to raise you; to each his own and God for all; may the heavens send you down the right path." As she was saying this, Sun and Moon put on a grand show of weeping, and Cenza, crying herself, bathed them with a sea of tears and then dumped them like rotten cucumbers and went back to her village.

Now, a certain lady who lived across the street from that room happened to hear the children crying all night, and it seemed like a thousand years to her before it was morning and she could go see who they were. And when dawn came out with the brushes of its rays to paint the flowers, which had all been turned a single color by the night's soot, she got up and saw those two little flowers that were wilting from all they had suffered. She invited them up to her palace, and when she asked them who they were, those poor things were able to explain neither who they were nor whence they came, since that upstanding wet nurse of theirs had not had the good judgment to tell them who their mother and father were. The good lady, who lived a comfortable life, would have treated them like her own children if she hadn't herself had a handful of brats who stuck to her like leeches, sucking her blood from morning till night. Even so, she fed them well, and had a mattress put in their room; they would stay there at night, and during the day she would always give them something, so that she wouldn't have to see them die of hunger. It also helped that Moon knew how to spin; the lady would always give her some work, and the girl, who had the wisdom of an old woman, helped out night and day. Her brother, too, would do odd jobs, and he was as quick paced as a sergeant. And thus the lady developed a great affection for them, and let them suffer for nothing. And she gave them names—Cecca for the girl and Mineco for the boy—so that she would have something to call them.

One day this good lady said to Cecca, "Now, my little Cecca, I want to put the hen to brood, and since I'm fond of you, one of her eggs will be yours, and whatever is hatched, whether it's a boy or a girl chick, I want to give to you, since you're such a good girl." Cecca thanked her for her kind thought, and prayed to the heavens that she would get back all that she was giving. And so, after twenty-two days the chicks came out and Cecca's egg hatched a pretty baby hen, with a tuft on her head that made her look like a little miss. Then the lady called Cecca over, and said to her, "Here is your little hen, my dear Cecca, this is what hatched. Take good care of it, and be careful not to lose it, my pet!" And the girl replied, "A thousand thanks!" and took the hen to her room, where she raised it on breadcrumbs and held it in her lap all day.

A few months later, after it had rained for a number of days, a little lizard happened to slip in through a hole in the wall of the room that communicated with the palace next door, and began to sun itself. This lizard was more beautiful than words can describe: its head was speckled all over with gold, its little feet looked like miniature silver hands, and its tiny eyes were just like two rubies. When the little hen saw the lizard, she ran after it, intending to tear it to pieces and eat it up, but Cecca felt sorry for it—apart from the fact that she had never let her hen eat the junk that other hens eat—and she chased her away, saying, "Shoo shoo, beat it!" And she clapped her hands and stomped her feet so hard that the lizard went back into its little hole, and the little hen flew up to a window of the room that communicated with the palace, one that Cecca had never been aware of because it was so sooty that it looked like it was walled up.

Now, once the little hen had penetrated those cobwebs, she was able to hop through the window to another room on the ground floor of the palace. Little Cecca borrowed a ladder and climbed up to the window, and, after clearing away the soot, she saw a room that was so well appointed that it looked like a museum. And so she pulled up the ladder, lowered it back down into that elegant room, and went in. Then she retrieved the little hen, which was all tangled up in cobwebs, and began to take a look at the chamber. There was a group of statues, and among them a bronze horse that was larger than ordinary-sized horses, from whose neck a set of keys was hanging; and while she was observing all of this she noticed that the lizard she had saved from the hen was on the horse's forehead. The lizard started talking, because it was enchanted, and this is what it said: "Moon, my dear girl, you should know that you did not gain entrance to this room without the heavens willing it, because this is the palace that belonged to your father, who died at the time of the plague and whose name was Peppone Stipa; your mother was Zezolla Guadagna, and she, too, died at that time. This father of yours was the richest merchant in all of the Armiere district. I am enchanted, and due to the fact that I received many services at your home, I have watched over this palace, and I have saved the cloth in the warehouse from moths. I have always been, though, a little anxious, knowing that because of a hen my life would be at mortal risk, and that if something bad happened to me I wouldn't be able to help you. Now, bless the heavens, not only has this mortal danger passed, but I have been saved by your own little hands. And because I remain obliged to you, I want to give some advice that will serve you well in times of need. Keep this written in your heart, and don't forget it: 'Do not let Sun into this house unless he has acquired good judgment. Do not give Sun a wife unless she is a poor girl, and keep track of her rags, for they will be of use to you. And when you find yourself in trouble, make use of milk.' Now, take this set of keys, which are for all the rooms and chests in the palace and the warehouse, and be aware that this horse is filled with money, and that it opens between the neck and the shoulders. The front of its belly is full of silver coins, and the rest with gold *zecchini* and doubloons. Make sure to use it well, and to take care of yourself."

The good Cecca, who was of honey-sweet spirit and quick wits, first stored away these suggestions in the closet of her memory, and then wanted to see how she could open up the horse. But her own strength was not enough, since the horse was so big, and so she took the ladder and propped it under its throat, and as she was thus prying it open, a handful of silver ducats fell out, maybe a hundred of them. When she saw that they were more than enough for the time being, she immediately removed the ladder, and the heavy weight of the horse's neck once again closed the gap between head and shoulders. After this, she began to try the keys in all the doors and chests, marking each of them so that she wouldn't have to make the effort again. The rooms that she discovered were all richly decorated, with magnificent paintings and silver objects on every surface. All of the chests were stuffed to bursting, crammed full, bulging over, and jam-packed with linens, tapestries, and an astounding quantity of other goods. When she had seen and made note of all of this, she locked everything up and went back out through the little hen's window, silent and soundless, without saying a word to anyone, and with her pockets full of ducats, with which she ably made ends meet, buying a few things here and there for herself and her brother.

But when nearly a year had gone by, during which she hadn't told Mineco anything, even if she never let a week go by without going to clean the palace, the rooms, and everything in them, she started wondering whether she should let her brother know about those riches. But then she remembered the words of the lizard, who had told her not to let Sun into the room unless he had acquired good judgment, and she thought that by Sun the lizard had meant her brother, since it had called her Moon, too. And so she began to test what sort of good judgment little Mineco had acquired now that he had become big Mineco. One evening when they were at the table, she said to him, "My dear Mineco, what should we do with this little hen? I'd like to hear your opinion."

He replied, "Let's eat it up!"

"What do you mean?" said his sister. "We had to make so many sacrifices to raise it, and now we want to chop its head off just like that? Wouldn't it be better to buy some eggs for her to brood? That way we'd have chicks, and when they become hens we'd have a henhouse fit for a prince."

"Who wants to wait that long?" said Mineco. "We'll be ashes before we ever see this henhouse. Don't you know that they say 'Better a chicken today than an egg tomorrow'?" And little Cecca said to herself, "It's a good thing I didn't say anything to him; this Sun here would have melted away all the money like snow, since he has less good judgment than a horse."

When another year had gone by, she asked him, "Tell me, my dear little Mineco, if we found a sack of doubloons, what would you do?"

"What would I do?" he answered. "I'd go out into the streets with a sword at my side and have myself some fun, just like so many who are less than me."

"Fortune did well to make you a pauper," said little Cecca, "because if she hadn't you would have yourself, the way you squander right and left." And then she thought to herself, "Alright, then, Sun hasn't found good judgment yet."

When another year had gone by, she asked her brother again, "What do you say, Mineco, if you had some money, what would you do with it?"

"What would I do?" answered Mineco. "I would buy myself a shopping bag and work as a delivery boy to earn a few coins, since I've become a man now, but I'm still all raw and naked, there's not a wrinkle in my purse, I'm light as a feather and dry as a prune pit, and I could run for a hundred miles and I wouldn't shed a cent."

"And if you found a treasure," replied his sister, "what would you do?"

"I would parcel it out carefully," said her brother, "and we would get by honorably, and I would have you live like a lady."

"There we go," said Cecca, "the treasure won't be long in coming, as long as you're really serious about all this."

"I sure am, and in a big way!" answered Mineco. "Let's not waste any more time; we need to get the top spinning, and I intend to show you what this fellow is capable of!" And when they had come to this understanding, Cecca began to think about how she could open the palace without complications, since a permit issued by the court was necessary.

Now, one day when she went into the palace to tidy up, taking the little hen, who followed her around like a puppy, with her, the hen flew up onto a table where there was a writing chest, and began to pull a piece of paper out from a little slit in the chest. Cecca shooed the hen away so that it wouldn't tear the paper, and then she pulled it the rest of the way out in one piece. Once she had tidied up the house, she tucked the piece of paper into her blouse and went to show it to a student she knew so that he could read it to her, not wanting to let anyone else see it for fear that if there was some good news they might try to cheat her. The student read it through, and found that it was a will written for her father by Solicitor Wheeler Dealer, which stated that he left as principal heir his son, who was in Grumo in the care of the wet nurse Goitered Cenza of the same village, who also had in her care his twin sister, to whom he ordered be given as her share ten thousand ducats if she did not marry, but fifteen thousand if she married, as a dowry.

After she found the will, she sent to Grumo for the wet nurse Cenza, and with the help of a charity lawyer she appealed to the court of the Vicaria. The will spoke clearly, and when the witnesses from Grumo were examined, it was evident that these were the children of Peppone Stipa and Zezolla Guadagna, merchants of Naples, and they received permission to open their palace and enjoy their father's inheritance. And so they got the warehouse up and running again, and made chests of money, no less than what was in the bronze horse, because business had increased in the city and the merchandise they sold rendered them great riches.

The time came for the brother to marry, and he began to fill his head with high-flown ideas about ennobling his stock and becoming a seated knight.[5] "Since, God help me," he would say, "I have the money—and that's all it takes—I have in mind that I should try out higher quarters. There have been many worse off than me who have made their way up with less money than I have; so I should stay behind? We won't allow that! Whoever has a horse like mine, bronze on the outside but inside full of ducats, *zecchini*, and doubloons, would already have been a knight for a hundred years. There has to be a noble title waiting for me on some piece of land, and more besides: I know my business!"

But his sister, who remembered the lizard's warning, was of a different opinion, and stopped him at mid-sentence, saying, "Cut the crap, brother! And save that mouth for eating figs, for I don't want to see anyone but an honorable poor girl in this house. And although I know that with respect to the money that I've allowed you to earn you could marry into the best lineage of this city, you would in any case be putting fire in your chest, a foot on your throat, and an ax to your legs; you would be acquiring a proprietress, not a wife, and right

5. In Naples at this time there were six "seats" of nobility, which corresponded to different districts of the city. Belonging to one of these was a guarantee that one came from a family of old nobility.

away you would start up with carriages, pages, footmen, and this and that, and before you know it you would find yourself with an empty shovel, lying flat on the ground. Besides that, marriage is like a yoke, and under the yoke oxen need to be equal, since if one of them is big and the other one little, they'll always be scraping against each other. And so, my brother, let's keep to our rank and not go buying expensive cheeses for our table. Take a poor girl, the daughter of a good woman, and you'll be doing what the heavens will. She'll be a servant, a companion, and a wife to you, and we'll both live in peace. And I'm saying this more for you than for me, since I could get married and take my dowry with me, but I prefer to stay here and serve you."

Cecca's brother saw that her advice would bear good fruit and treasured these words, and to the great pleasure of Cecca he married a poor woman's daughter, honorable without a doubt but without anyone to care for her. She left the house rarely or not at all because her clothes were in such poor shape that they were falling off her, and you couldn't tell what color they had once been, they were so old.

Little Cecca treated her better than a sister. She dressed her up from head to toe, and took the tattered rags that Belluccia (that was the girl's name) had been wearing and laundered them well, then bundled them up and put them at the bottom of a chest, remembering the words of the lizard, "Keep track of her rags, for they will be of use to you." Then she filled up the rest of the chest with linens.

And in this way they lived together happily for a time. But the ancient proverbs always prove right, since a motto is never told, unless it's half or whole. That is to say: there's nothing worse than a pauper grown rich, for the fat goes right to her heart, and the horse that has barley and straw in excess throws a good kick. And so Belluccia began to regard Cecca with hatred and disgust, because Cecca acted like the mistress of the house, as in fact she was, and she had to obey her orders. And for this reason she decided to get her out of the picture, and she spent all day at the touchstone of her evil brain doing nothing but testing various plans, to see which had the most carats. And one day, while she was in this pensive and anxious state, a woman who would come to sell her rouge and powder stopped by. (You have to watch out for certain old women who frequent houses, since for the most part they are like stew pots: I mean that as long as they're in good shape, they cook their meat at their own hearth, but when they're cracked or broken, they take their fire to the homes of others and cook up all sorts of tricks and scams, and more than one home has gone up in smoke because of it.) Now, this old woman said to her, "What's the matter? You look so anxious. Your home, heaven help you, is overflowing with riches; your warehouse looks like a sea into which all the rivers of merchants, with their silvery waters and golden sands, flow; and you're acting like the newlywed who got hit by bad luck? What's the matter? How can I be of help? Spend me for whatever I'm worth, and let me handle this."

"What do you think the matter is?" replied Belluccia. "Does it seem like nothing to you to be a wife who's treated like a servant girl? My husband's sister is the mistress here, and I can't get my way even over a few coins!"

"Is that all there is?" said the old woman. "Let me handle this, and I'll make her disappear from your sight. You know what you need to do? I'm going to bring you some serpent eggs. Give them to her to eat, and little serpents will be born inside of her and her belly will swell as if she were pregnant. Then you say to your husband, 'There's something fishy going on here,' and he'll bounce her out of there like a balloon, and then it'll be party time for you."

"Thank you, auntie," said Belluccia, and she gave her a bag of flour and a slice of lard, hiding all of this from her sister-in-law. "Take this for now," she said, "and if the plan goes as scheduled I intend to take you on as my lady-in-waiting."

At this promise, the old woman set upon her task with even greater enthusiasm, and the next day, as soon as dawn, pecking away like a hen, had eaten up all the stars, she presented herself to Belluccia with the diabolical eggs. After she gave them to Cecca to eat, that poor little thing found that in just a few days her belly had grown as big as a bale of hay, and she didn't know what had happened to her. When her brother saw her like that, looking big and pregnant, he began to grow suspicious, and all night he did nothing but consult with his wife about what they should do. His wife, who was a malicious tongue-wag and a rumormonger capable of setting green grass on fire, began to stir up discontent, saying to him, "What do you mean? Is all this deliberation really necessary? You're too much of a simpleton, my husband! Can't you see that your sister's belly is growing, and with it the horns on the moon of your honor?[6] Don't give those who intend to write the story of your

6. A man had "horns" when he was betrayed by a woman close to him, who could be his wife but also a female relative, as in this case. Cuckoldry was a favorite topic and a source of endless sayings and proverbs at this time, as this whole paragraph attests.

shame the opportunity to empty their inkwells; she wants to give you a horn to carry your gunpowder in when you go hunting for goats, but you use it to load your shotgun and cut her down. It's better that you get a sow out of your house than to be singled out as a deer; better that you tie a noose around her gullet than for it to be said about you, 'Men are bound by horns, and oxen by words.' She's growing your horns, and you make sure you butcher her flesh; she wants to supply you with the material to make combs, and you comb her up so good that she doesn't live to tell it; she wants to teach you how to be field master, so that you can conduct the horns in the army of the shameless. Stab her in the chest with a knife, all the way to the hilt; and make sure the knife is made of horn!"

This was the good advice of that ungrateful pauper turned social climber. In part pulled by his suspicion, in part pushed by his wife, who was always ready to help a dog go to stud, one day her husband called over his sister and said to her, "Come with me, we have something important to do." And they set off, one step after another, until they ended up forty miles from the city in a remote village where there was a gulley that looked like a horse cemetery, because people would go there to unload all of their dead donkeys and horses, and so many of them had been thrown down there that the ground was paved with white bones in a horrifying fashion. Cecca's brother left her at the bottom of the gulley, saying, "Wait here a little while, and I'll be back." Then he turned keel and ditched her right there, like an unwanted zucchini. He beat it back to the city, where he was received by Belluccia with great pleasure, since when she didn't see Cecca return, she thought that her husband had thrown her off a cliff or killed her in some other way; and she began to act like the mistress of the house. She made the old woman who had given her the egg, whose name was Colospizia Papara, her lady-in-waiting, and she began to splurge and squander, turning the whole house upside down and making the palace into a stable. And she filled the room that housed the bronze horse, which stood there with its head hanging at its feet since by then it had been delivered of all of its money—placed in banks and invested—with firewood and other sorts of junk, just to spite Cecca, who had always kept it so clean.

But let's return to poor Cecca, so that we don't leave her as her brother left her. The unfortunate soul waited for Mineco to return, but she could have waited forever and he wouldn't have come back, for that was the sort of man he was. Now, the miserable little thing knew that she hadn't tangled any yarn, and so did not despair, but waited for the heavens to provide her with the thread that would lead her out of that labyrinth of deception, because it was more or less clear to her that she was in a tangle due to her sister-in-law. In any case, she had quite a time of it, since she had to spend the whole night among all those bones, and she was worse off than a dead mare; thank goodness it was summertime. But in the morning—when dawn, like a chimneysweep, takes her broom of light and starts sweeping away the soot from the chimney of the sky, at whose hearth the coals of stars had been glowing all night—a merchant from Foggia who had lost his way came by on the road above; and even if he seemed to be just passing through, he had been sent by the heavens. When he saw the miserable girl in that gulley, he helped her get out, and asked her what had happened. She told him the whole story, swearing with one hand on the other that she had never had carnal relations with a living man and that she suspected she had dropsy. The merchant took a good look at her and said, "Alright, I can tell from the yellow cast of your face that you've eaten a serpent's egg, and by now you must have a bunch of baby serpents in your belly, which I'm afraid are going to gnaw away your innards until you, like a viper, will die giving life to others."

When Cecca saw what a tight spot she was in, she thought that this had to be the big trouble that the lizard had announced to her, for which she would need some milk. She said to the merchant, "My dear gentleman, may heaven help you if you take me to a sheep farm, for I remember a certain secret that someone who cared for me dearly shared with me, and that is that I need to have a drink of milk."

"I get what you're talking about," answered the merchant, "but you don't want to drink the milk. I know what you have to do: come with me, and let's pray to the heavens that we can figure it out." He took her to a farm that was a short distance from the gulley, which he had noticed on his way there, and he very politely asked the shepherd's wife, "Do me a favor, and ask whatever you like for it: fill me up a big cauldron of milk, and place this young lady upside down directly over it, and we'll see what happens." The good shepherdess, anxious to do the job well, hung the girl by her feet, causing her gut to slide down to her throat. The baby serpents smelled the milk, and immediately came out of her mouth and slithered into the cauldron, so that not a single one was left in her body. The shepherdess was amazed and terrified, and went out to tell the merchant what had happened. He gave the shepherdess a nice gift, and he found that poor little Cecca's state had improved so much from before that she looked like a different person. And when he saw that she was quite beautiful, even if a bit worn-down, his compassion turned into love, and he asked her if she would like to marry him, telling her that he would take her with no other dowry than her fine qualities. She answered that she was pleased to, since she owed him her life, and that as far as the dowry went they would have occasion to speak about it later, because with time she would help him to recover her fifteen thousand ducats. The merchant, who was a respectable man, was so happy with this encounter that he decided not to go to Naples this time. He took Cecca to Foggia, where he treated her like a queen, since he was rich and wanted for nothing. And at the end of a year they had a daughter who was as pretty as a picture, whom they named Liviella.

Now, it happened that Rienzo (that was the name of Cecca's husband, the merchant) had to go to Naples, and since he needed to stay there for several months, he said to Cecca, "My dear, blessed wife, I have to go to Naples, and I need to stay there for more than a month, as I have to manage various business interests of mine with a number of merchants from that city, and especially with Mineco Stipa, who is the richest of all of them. Going without you would be the same thing as going without my eyes or my heart, for your goodness has taken possession of all my affection. And so I would like to know if it pleases you to come with me, since I don't want to do anything that displeases you. And we could also bring our Liviella, for, as you know, we are blessed by the heavens and can afford every comfort."

When Cecca heard the name of her brother, she was pleased at this news, and answered, "My dear husband, I will never argue with your commands, and I will always be at your side, whether I have to walk barefoot to Naples, which is my town, or even all the way to India, so grateful I am to you for your kindness." After they agreed on this, they made their preparations, and then set off in a rented carriage at an early hour. They journeyed for three days, and were growing close to Naples; before they arrived Cecca told Liviella that when they were at Mineco's table she should say, "Oh, mommy dearest, tell me a tale!" and that she shouldn't stop chanting this until she told her a tale. Once this bagpipe had been tuned, they arrived safe and sound at Mineco Stipa's house, where they were invited to stay for the first days.

Mineco received them with great pleasure, and neither he nor Belluccia realized that Rienzo's wife was Cecca, because they thought that she had been eaten by wolves, or else that the little serpents had gnawed away her intestines. Now, on the evening that they arrived the table had been set by Colospizia Papara, who had become Belluccia's lady-in-waiting, although she was just as wretched as she had always been. The company heard a commotion coming from the kitchen, which was due to the fact that at that very moment Colospizia was trying to catch the curly-feathered hen so that she could kill it and roast it. But the hen was flying all over the kitchen, and refused to be caught; in fact, it escaped and flew, squawking, into the dining hall, where it saw Cecca and went straight to her lap (for it was the first to recognize its real mistress), almost as if it were looking for help and defense against those harpies. Colospizia ran over and tried to tear the hen from Cecca's lap, but Cecca, defending it, said, "What kind of manners are these, trying to tear the hen from my lap? Leave it alone! By now it's too late to prepare it anyway; this morning we'll eat something else in its place." And so she kept the hen on her lap, petting it. In the meantime the food arrived, and when Mineco and Rienzo, Cecca, Liviella, and Belluccia were seated at the table, they began to get their jaws moving, and while they were eating Liviella began saying, "O mommy dearest, tell me a tale!"

"What do you mean, a tale?" said her mother. "What kind of request is that? Eat up, if you want to eat."

"And why can't you grant her this wish?" said Belluccia.

And Cecca said, "It's better not to do everything these little girls ask for, or else they get too sassy."

But as Liviella continued to eat, she kept on repeating the same tune: "O mommy dearest, tell me a tale!"

"Will you stop, now?" said Cecca. "You're really sassy! So full of yourself!"

When they got to the end of the meal and Liviella was still repeating, "O mommy dearest, tell me a tale!" Belluccia said, "For the life of you, tell her a tale, for my sake."

"What sort of tale should I tell her?" Cecca replied, "The only tale I know is the one about the little hen" (she was still holding the little hen on her lap).

"It can be about a duck, for all I care!" said Belluccia, laughing in Colospizia's face as she came in to hear the tale. And Cecca began:

"They say that there once were a brother and a sister, named Sun and Moon, though one had no rays and the other was eclipsed, since they were dying of hunger. But one day a little hen just like this one was scratching and digging with its feet, and found a treasure that made them rich, and Sun turned into gold and Moon into silver. Now, the brother got married, and he took a threadbare wretch for his wife and made her into a lady. But this wife was ungrateful and unappreciative, crueler than a dark bitch, and she tried to banish her husband's sister from the world by destroying her reputation and with that her life, so that she could be the sole mistress of the house once she had everything that had once belonged to the sister. But what happened? She was like a dog barking at the moon: all of her scheming went up in smoke. Now let me be even clearer, and make a long story short: you, Mineco, are that Sun, if you remember, and I am that Moon; this is the little hen, and Belluccia is the dark-haired one who tried to get rid of me by feeding me the serpent's egg given to her by Colospizia Papara, here present, which made my belly swell till it was as big as a half bushel, and I would have died if this kind gentleman had not saved me. And these are the thousand thank-yous that you, madam Belluccia, owe me for having picked the lice off your head and turned your rags into vestments fit for a queen? Well, if you can't remember, I remember quite well!" Cecca got up from the table and opened the chest where she had put Belluccia's rags, and as she pulled them out, she said, "This is the estate that you brought to my house; and when I raised you to the station in which you now find yourself, you treated me worse than you would treat your fiercest enemy. You're an ingrate, a thankless wretch, a ragbag, a beggar-woman! That's how you look after my brother's things? In all these years you hadn't even opened this chest and realized that it was full of your shame?" And as she was saying this she threw the rags in Belluccia's face.

When Cecca's husband saw this and Mineco understood what was going on, they stood there like mummies, and the wicked Belluccia started turning one color after another, until she had an attack of gout, which she suffered from, and as her body fell to the ground she hit her head on the marble of the windowsill, where she left her brains. The brother, shocked and regretful of his mistake, went to his sister and embraced her, asking for her forgiveness and telling her that he intended to hold her even dearer than he had in the past, for his accursed wife had been the cause of his mistake. In the meantime Renzo, using his kind words to bring them to an agreement, said that he wanted to give Mineco his sister for a wife, that she was a close friend of Cecca's, and that he wanted to move to Naples with his whole family, so that everyone could live happily together.

Mineco accepted the proposal, especially since Belluccia had kicked the bucket without ever having produced children and had half-ruined their household. And to give Cecca some satisfaction he told his servants to go get hold of Colospizia Papara. But she had heard the outburst, seen her mistress die, and, realizing that she had been exposed and imagining the bad day to come (even if it was still night), she went and hid in the bronze horse, thinking that no one would look there. And since everyone was searching all over the house for her, they went down to the ground floor, where the bronze horse was standing without a head. The lizard, which was sitting on the horse's shoulders, opened its little mouth and said, "Search no further, because that witch Colospizia Papara, who was responsible for all of Cecca's suffering, is right in here. Take that sack over there on the floor, fill it with straw, stuff it in the horse, and then set it on fire: that's the way this whore, witch, baby-drowner, blood-sucker, mother of the devil must die." That's what the lizard said, and that's what Rienzo and Mineco did, and that pig was smothered by the smoke and flames, and gave up the ghost like a blister when it bursts. Then they had the corpse taken out and thrown in a latrine, which they walled up.

Now, Mineco didn't want to keep that witch's instrument of death in his house, so he sold the blackened bronze horse to a merchant who lived in Vicolo delle Campane, who made cannons and other devices out of it. One day a knight was passing by that street, and when he saw a horse's leg, he asked if the rest of the body was there. The merchant said that he had melted it down, but that if he had come by a week earlier he would have found it in one piece, except for the head and the neck, which were at the home of Mineco Stipa, in the Armieri district. The knight went there out of curiosity, and when he saw that fine head he asked Mineco if he wanted to sell it, and what its price was. Mineco had business dealings with the knight's house, which he supplied with cloth, and since he had made a few thousand ducats off of him, he gave it to him as a present. And nowadays it's in the courtyard of a lovely palace right beyond the Seggio di Nido, in the street that goes to Foro Nistriano, and the palace itself has taken the name of Bronze Horse.

And now, to get to the end of the tale, Cecca witnessed the revenge that the heavens had waged on Belluccia, and received her dowry of fifteen thousand ducats, which she enjoyed with Rienzo. Mineco took Rienzo's sister as his wife, and a lovely lady she was. Colospizia Papara obtained nothing but poisonous venom from the serpents' eggs, and died in fire, fumes, and fetor. The wretched Belluccia, although she had never had much of a brain, was able to sow just enough of it to reap her death, and being the wife of a rich merchant served her no purpose beyond having a plaque on her tomb that guaranteed perpetual dishonor, since on it was written in massive letters:

There's nothing worse than a peasant who becomes a lady.

2

Carlo Gozzi (1720–1806)

Born to an aristocratic family in Venice, the playwright and memorialist Carlo Gozzi was a lively participant in literary debates of his time, holding the position of political conservative and literary traditionalist. In particular, he was an outspoken critic of the theatrical reforms of his fellow Venetian, Carlo Goldoni, who was at this time moving in the direction of bourgeois realism and comedy of character. Today Gozzi is best known for his ten *Fiabe teatrali* (Fairy Tales for the Theater). Performed between 1761 and 1770 and first published in the 1772 edition of Gozzi's *Opere*, the *Fairy Tales* set forth the hybrid model of the fairy-tale play, in which fairy-tale plots and characters encounter the stock masks and slapstick humor of the commedia dell'arte tradition, a form of improvised comedy that had its origins in the late Renaissance.

The first of the *Fiabe* was *L'amore delle tre arance* (*The Love of the Three Oranges*), based on the last tale of Giambattista Basile's *The Tale of Tales*; it was soon followed by *Turandot*, *Il corvo* (*The Raven*), based on Basile's "The Crow," *Il re cervo* (*The King Stag*), and the others. Besides Basile, sources for Gozzi's material included the commedia dell'arte; Eastern collections such as the *Arabian Nights*, together with their French orientalist derivatives; and the oral tradition.

The somewhat melodramatic plots of these plays are moved forward, on the one hand, by serious fairy-tale characters who speak in Italian and sometimes in verse and offer heavy-handed ideological pronouncements; the stock characters of the commedia (Arlecchino, Pantalone, Pulcinella et al.), on the other hand, tend to jest lightheartedly, interact occasionally with the audience, and speak in a mix of Italian and dialect. As in his opus overall, Gozzi uses his *Fiabe* as a mouthpiece for his criticism of Goldoni and contemporary theatrical reforms and, more generally, to comment on the world he lived in and the role that literature should have in it.

Gozzi's attempt to recover the marvelous that had so dominated the poetics of the seventeenth century and to revitalize older comic forms often yields curiously cerebral results, far from the effervescence of either Basile's tales or the early commedia scenarios. Likewise, the common fairy-tale progression toward social betterment is often substituted by the reinforcement of rigidly hierarchical social structures and values such as resignation to the work of Providence and submission to the powerful. At the same time, however, the ever-present dialectic in these plays between order and disorder creates a dramatic dynamic that in many cases undermines overt ideological certainties.

Gozzi received less critical acclaim at home than he did outside of Italy, where still today the *Fiabe* continue to garner interest for both their ideological content and the eclectic style expressed therein. The consummate theatricality of his work, with its spectacular combination of styles, traditions, and messages, has influenced numerous other artists, in particular in the field of opera, where Gozzi's influence is present in the magic plays and singspiels that climaxed with Wolfgang Mozart's *Die Zauberflöte* (*The Magic Flute*, 1791) and even more directly in Sergei Prokofiev's *L'amour des trois oranges* (*The Love of the Three Oranges*, 1919) and both Ferruccio Busoni's and Giacomo Puccini's versions of *Turandot* (1917 and 1926, respectively). Closer to our times, Gozzi's suggestive mix of fairy-tale marvelous and theatrical magic has appealed to directors of musical theater such as Andrei Serban (*The King Stag*) and Julie Taymor (*The Green Bird*) and has been enthusiastically received by their audiences.

Further Reading

Primary

Gozzi, Carlo. *Fiabe teatrali*. Introd. Alberto Beniscelli. Milan: Garzanti, 1994. 3–38. [source text]

Secondary

Beniscelli, Alberto. "Carlo Gozzi." In *A History of Italian Theatre*, ed. Joseph Farrell and Paolo Puppa. New York: Cambridge University Press, 2006. 177–85.

Bosisio, Paolo. "Introduzione." In *Fiabe teatrali*, by Carlo Gozzi. Rome: Bulzoni, 1984. 11–71.

Emery, Ted. "Carlo Gozzi in Context." In *Five Tales for the Theatre*, by Carlo Gozzi. Chicago: University of Chicago Press, 1989. 1–19.

The Love of the Three Oranges (L'Amore delle tre melarance)

The plot of the tale The Love of the Three Oranges *is based on Giambattista Basile's "The Three Citrons" though probably mediated by folkloric versions of ATU 408, The Three Oranges, in circulation at Gozzi's time.* The Love of the Three Oranges *was first performed in Venice in 1761.*

In the preface, Gozzi refers to the genesis of this piece, which from its origins as a "children's fairy tale" morphed into the hybrid form of a play that resuscitates the structure and techniques of the commedia dell'arte, with its emphasis on physical gags, slapstick humor, and improvisation. Gozzi explains that he chose this form to explicitly parody the dramatic works of his contemporaries Pietro Chiari and, especially, Carlo Goldoni, the latter of whom was a groundbreaking dramatist of his time. In his plays Goldoni experimented with forms of bourgeois realism whose characters and situations Gozzi felt were too insignificant or coarse to be seen on stage.

I have abridged the play somewhat, eliminating a number of minor plot turns and some of the long sections in verse, as well as Gozzi's comments and polemical asides to Goldoni and Chiari, who are explicitly allegorized in the figures of the bumbling sorcerer Celio and the evil Fata Morgana, respectively. The plot of the play is described in the past tense in the original. In my translation, I have preferred to use the present tense, as I feel it better captures the dynamic sense of theatrical action.

Although uncommon in the world of erudite theater, the form of the play mimics to some degree the older forms of the commedia or, to use the words that Gozzi adopts in the secondary title of the play, "reflective analysis." The play is structured in three acts but has almost no dialogue, adopting the form of the canovaccio, *the scenario or set of stage directions that guided commedia performances, which had no rigid textual tradition. The* canovaccio *included a list of acts and scenes, as well as* lazzi *(comic interludes and gags), which were all fleshed out onstage by professional actors who would improvise, drawing on their storehouse of stock characters, episodes, jokes, and lines.*

Act 1

Silvio, the King of Hearts, is the monarch of an imaginary kingdom; his clothing, as his name suggests, imitates that of kings on playing cards. One day he is complaining to Pantalone[1] about the misfortune that has befallen his only son, the hereditary Prince Tartaglia, who for ten years has suffered from an incurable illness. According to the doctors, it is an insurmountable effect of hypochondria, and they abandoned all hope some time ago. King Silvio cries loudly. Pantalone, enacting a satire of doctors, suggests instead the miraculous secrets of certain charlatans. The king protests, saying that they have tried everything, to no avail. Pantalone loses himself in a reverie about the origin of the illness, and asks the king in secret, so as not to be heard by the guards surrounding the king, if His Majesty acquired some disease in his youth that he may have transmitted to the hereditary prince, thus reducing him to his miserable state, and also asks if some mercury might help.[2] With the utmost seriousness the king protests that he has always remained faithful to the queen. Pantalone adds that perhaps the prince is concealing a contagious condition that he has contracted, out of shame. The king, again serious, assures him imperiously that he should rest assured: after all the paternal exams that have been conducted, this is not the case, and his son's infirmity is nothing more than the deadly effect of hypochondria, which the doctors predict will put him underground shortly if he does not laugh, for only laughter will be a clear sign of recovery. And this is impossible. He adds that the fact that he is already decrepit, with his only son on his deathbed, and his niece, Princess Clarice, a bizarre, odd, and cruel young lady, next in line for his kingdom, is of great distress to him. He pities his subjects and cries his heart out, forgetting his royal duties. Pantalone consoles him; he reflects that if Prince Tartaglia's recovery depends on him laughing, then the royal court should not be kept in a state of

1. Pantalone is one of the main characters in traditional commedia. He is a wealthy and greedy Venetian merchant who is frequently hoodwinked by the other characters, in particular servants. Many commedia plots focus on Pantalone being cuckolded by younger men.
2. Mercury was a common cure for syphilis.

melancholy. Festivities, games, masquerades, and spectacles should be ordered. Truffaldino,[3] a person with great abilities for eliciting laughter and thus a true prescription against the effects of hypochondria, should be given free rein to associate with the prince. Indeed, he has discovered that the prince has an inclination to confide in Truffaldino. The prince might laugh and recover. The king is persuaded, and prepares to give all the necessary orders.

Enter Leandro, Jack of Hearts and prime minister. This character is also dressed like its figure in playing cards. In an aside, Pantalone signals his suspicions about Leandro's traitorous behavior. The king orders Leandro to organize festivities, games, and revelry of every sort. He says that whoever is able to make the prince laugh will win a great prize. Leandro advises the king against this resolution, deeming it of greater harm to the ill prince. Pantalone insists in his advice. The king reconfirms his orders and leaves. Pantalone is exultant. In an aside, he says that he has discovered Leandro's desire for the prince's death. He follows the king. Leandro continues with his feeble-minded objections, saying that he perceives some opposition to his desired plan but isn't sure where it's coming from. He exits the stage.

Enter Princess Clarice, the king's niece. A princess of such a strange, bizarre, and resolute character as Clarice has never been seen on the stage. Having agreed to marry Leandro and raise him to the throne if she remains heiress to the kingdom after the death of Tartaglia, her cousin, she yells at Leandro for the excessive calm that he is exhibiting while waiting for her cousin to die of such a slow disease as hypochondria. Leandro justifies himself by saying that they have to be cautious and that the Fata Morgana, his protectress, gave him some magical briefs in alexandrine verse[4] to administer to Tartaglia in the form of a large number of suppositories, which will make him slowly die from the effects of hypochondria. The Fata Morgana is the enemy of the King of Hearts because she lost a good part of her treasure betting on his card. She is friendly with the Jack of Hearts because he was able to recover some of her money. She lives in a lake near the city. The Moorish Smeraldina, who is the maid in this dramatic parody, is the messenger for Leandro and Morgana. Clarice is furious when she hears how Tartaglia's death is so slow in coming. Leandro

3. One of the many commedia servant figures, the best-known of whom is Arlecchino. Truffaldino, like Arlecchino, is from the northern city of Bergamo.

4. Alexandrine is a heroic verse line most famously used in classic French poetry of the seventeenth century but also adopted by Gozzi's archrival Goldoni in some of his comedies.

adds his own worries about the usefulness of the briefs in alexandrines. A certain Truffaldino has been sent to the court, but no one knows by whom; he is a very funny character, and if Tartaglia laughs at him, he will be cured of his ailment. Clarice is frantic; she has seen Truffaldino, and at the mere sight of him she split her sides laughing. Conclusion: the briefs in alexandrine verses would be useless. From these conversations the reader may note a defense of the masked commedia dell'arte as a remedy for the effects of hypochondria, when compared to the verse writings of melancholy poets. Leandro sends off Brighella,[5] his messenger, to Smeraldina to find out what the mysterious appearance of Truffaldino might imply and to ask for assistance.

Enter Brighella. He reports, in all secrecy, that Truffaldino has been sent to the court by a certain sorcerer, Celio, enemy of Morgana and great friend of the King of Hearts, for the reasons cited above. And that Truffaldino is a prescription for the effects of the hypochondria caused by the briefs in alexandrine verses, and that he has arrived in court to save the king, the king's son, and all of their people from the contagious disease of the aforementioned briefs.

The news delivered by Brighella about the mystery of Truffaldino plunges Clarice and Leandro into a state of great confusion. They confer over various methods for secretly implementing a death, so that they can eliminate Truffaldino. Clarice suggests arsenic, or else a few shots from a musket. Leandro suggests briefs in alexandrine verses in suppository form, or else opium. Clarice maintains that alexandrine verses and opium are very similar, and that Truffaldino appears to have a very strong stomach that could easily digest those ingredients. Brighella adds that when Morgana learned of the entertainments ordered to amuse the prince and make him laugh, she promised to make an appearance and to counter his life-giving laughter with a curse that will result in his death. Clarice enters to begin preparations for the entertainments that have been ordered. Leandro and Brighella also enter to assist.

The next scene opens in the chambers of the hypochondriac prince. This funny Prince Tartaglia is dressed in the most comic sort of invalid's clothing, and is sitting in a large armchair. Next to him there is a small table on which he is leaning, which is full of vials, unguents, spitting cups, and other equipment appropriate for his state. He moans in a weak voice about his miserable

5. Another servant, also from Bergamo but usually sharper than Arlecchino; he is sometimes more of a middle-class figure.

situation. He tells of the medical treatments that he has uselessly endured; he proclaims the strange effects of his incurable disease. He is the only one onstage, and this valiant character could not play his role with greater inventiveness. His buffoonish discourses spontaneously cause continual bursts of universal laughter in the audience. Then the equally funny Truffaldino enters, and tries to make the invalid laugh. The improvised scene that these two excellent comedians engage in is of the most rollicking order. The prince is favorably disposed toward Truffaldino, but no matter how hard he tries, he isn't able to laugh. He wants to talk about his ailment; he wants to solicit Truffaldino's opinion. Truffaldino engages in confusing satirical argumentations on physical topics, which are the most delightful ever heard. Truffaldino sniffs at the prince's breath and smells an odor of overripe, indigestible alexandrine verses. The prince coughs and wants to spit something out. Truffaldino holds out the cup, collects the spit, and examines it; he discovers rotting and malodorous verses. This scene lasts for twenty minutes, with continuous laughter on the part of the audience. Musical instruments can be heard, which signal the merry festivities that are taking place in the great courtyard of the royal palace. Truffaldino is supposed to take the prince onto the balcony to see them. The prince protests, saying that that is impossible. They have a ridiculous argument. Angered, Truffaldino throws vials, cups, and all of the equipment used for Tartaglia's illness out the window. Tartaglia shrieks and weeps as if demented. Finally, Truffaldino loads the prince on his back and carries him off to see the entertainment; the prince shouts as if someone were ripping out his entrails.

The next scene opens in the great courtyard of the royal palace. Leandro mentions that he has executed the orders for the entertainment; that the dejected members of the populace, eager to laugh, have all donned masks; that they intend to come to the courtyard for the festivities; that he has taken the precaution of masking a large number of people in gloomy costumes, so that as the prince watches them his melancholy will grow; and that it is time to open the courtyard to allow access to the populace.

Enter Morgana, transformed into the caricature of a little old woman. Leandro is amazed that she was able to come in through the closed doors. Morgana reveals herself, and says that she has arrived in that form to more easily exterminate the prince, as will be seen; and that the festivities should begin. Leandro thanks her, and calls her the queen of hypochondria. Morgana withdraws. The doors to the courtyard are opened wide.

On a balcony on the facade of the palace the king, the hypochondriac prince wrapped in furs, Clarice, Pantalone, the guards, and then Leandro make their appearance. The entertainments and festivities are none other than the ones children hear about when they're told the fairy tale of the three oranges. The people enter. A joust on horseback begins, with Truffaldino, the captain, ordering the jousting knights to perform comic movements. After each move he turns to the balcony, asking His Majesty if the prince is laughing. The prince is crying, moaning that the air is bothering him and that the noise is deafening; he begs His Paternal Majesty to allow him to be put into a nice warm bed.

The members of the populace are competing for their share of the oil and wine that gush from two fountains: they engage in quarrels of the most trivial and plebeian sort. Nothing makes the prince laugh.

Enter Morgana as a little old woman, with a jar to collect oil from the fountain. Truffaldino addresses various insults to the little old woman; she falls to the ground with her legs in the air. At the sight of the little old woman falling the prince bursts into loud and long peals of laughter.[6] He is suddenly cured of all of his ailments. Truffaldino wins the prize, and when they hear the merry prince laughing, the audience is relieved of the oppression caused by the infirmities of that unhappy man and begins to laugh uproariously.

The whole court is lighthearted at this outcome; Leandro and Clarice are miserable.

Morgana gets up from the ground, furious, and begins to yell at the prince emphatically, casting upon him the terrible, evil spell that follows:

I pray to you, dark Pluto, and Pindar, with your poetic flights,
that of the three oranges this prince acquire lover's rights.
May threats, prayers, and tears be empty specters and idle prate;
now hurry to your horrid search for the oranges, before it is too late.

Morgana disappears. The prince enters into a state of robust enthusiasm due to the love of the three oranges. He is led out amid great confusion on the part of the court.

6. This whole scene of the prince who could not laugh, the fountains that spew precious substances, and the exposure of female private parts, which finally elicits the desired laughter, directly recalls the frame tale of Basile's *Tale of Tales*.

Act 2

In one of the prince's rooms, Pantalone despairs. Beside himself, he tells of how the prince is raving because of the curse cast on him, and how it is impossible to placate him. He wants from his father a pair of iron shoes that will allow him to walk through the world until he finds the fated oranges, the object of his love. Pantalone has received the order to ask the king for these shoes, under pain of causing the prince great misfortune. It is a most serious case, and a topic fit for the theater. Pantalone speaks satirically, joking about the various topics that are popular onstage these days. He runs off to find the king.

Enter the prince, as if possessed, and Truffaldino. The prince is impatient because of the delay on the iron shoes. Truffaldino starts making ridiculous requests. Tartaglia declares that he intends to go off in search of the three oranges, which, on the basis of what his grandmother used to tell him, are two thousand miles away and under the power of Creonta, a giant sorceress.[7] He asks for his armor and orders Truffaldino to arm himself, since he wants him for his squire. A buffoonish scene between these two characters, always hugely amusing, ensues. They equip themselves with suits of armor, helmets, and huge swords in the most farcical manner.

Enter the king, Pantalone, guards. One guard carries a pair of iron shoes on a tray.

In performing this scene the four characters treat the situation so solemnly that they render it doubly ridiculous. With a tragic and dramatic majesty the father tries to dissuade his son from the perilous enterprise. He begs, threatens, sentimentalizes. The prince, out of his senses, insists. He will fall back into his state of hypochondria if he is not allowed to go. He resorts to brutal threats against his father. The king is astonished and aggrieved. He reflects that the scarce respect his son has for him must derive from examples gleaned from the new comic theater.

The prince shows no sign of calming down. Truffaldino puts the iron shoes on his feet. The scene ends with a quartet of dramatic verses made up

7. Creonta is a character in Luigi Pulci's comic epic *Morgante*; there, too, she is a giantess who guards an enchanted castle.

of whining, farewells, and sighs. The prince and Truffaldino leave. The king falls to a chair in a swoon. Pantalone calls for some first aid in the form of vinegar.

Clarice, Leandro, and Brighella come rushing in; they scold Pantalone for all the noise he is making. Pantalone replies that they are dealing with a swooning king and a prince who has gone off to perish in the arduous search for the oranges. Brighella replies that these situations are jokes. The king comes to his senses and begins a tragic dramatization. He grieves for his son, as if he were dead. He orders the whole court to dress in mourning, and goes off to lock himself in his study and end his days under the weight of his affliction. Pantalone, professing that he will join his weeping with the king's, mixes their respective tears in one handkerchief . . . and follows the monarch.

Clarice, Leandro, and Brighella are merry, and praise Morgana. The bizarre Clarice wants to draw up an agreement regarding the division of power in the kingdom before Leandro ascends to the throne. During wartime she wants to be the head of the armies. Even if she were vanquished, she would use her charms to make the enemy captain fall in love with her. Once she lured him into love and trust, as soon as he drew close she would plant a knife in his belly. Clarice also wants the authority to distribute the positions in court as she sees fit. Brighella asks to have, on the basis of his merits, the post of superintendent of royal performances.

The scene opens on a desert. The sorcerer Celio, protector of prince Tartaglia, can be seen tracing magic circles. He demands that the demon Farfarello appear.[8] Farfarello comes out and in a terrifying voice speaks in alexandrine verses in this manner:

Ho! Who calls me from the dark and horrid infernal cavity?
Are you a real sorcerer or a theatrical depravity?

Celio replies, in prose, that he is a real sorcerer.

Celio asks if Truffaldino, whom he magically sent to the court of the King of Hearts, has produced any effect; if Tartaglia has been induced to laugh, and has been cured of the effects of his hypochondria. The demon replies:

8. Farfarello is a demon in both Dante's *Inferno* and Pulci's *Morgante*.

He laughed, he was cured; but then, Morgana your foe
by means of a curse all our labors let go.
Raving, panting, with his cheeks aflame,
to find the love of the three oranges is now his sole aim.

The demon disappears. Celio cries out against his enemy Morgana. He explains the great peril that Tartaglia and Truffaldino face, since they have been sent to Creonta's castle, not far from there, where the three fatal oranges are kept. He withdraws to prepare the things necessary to save two worthy people who are of great use to society. But the sorcerer Celio should not have protected Tartaglia and Truffaldino.

Enter Tartaglia and Truffaldino, armed as previously described, and running at top speed. Behind them is a demon with a bellows in his hand who, blowing on them from behind, forces them into a headlong run. The demon stops blowing, and disappears. When the wind is suspended, the two travelers fall to the ground due to the momentum with which they were running.

Tartaglia and Truffaldino have to travel two thousand miles before they arrive at Creonta's castle. When these two characters, who are always amusing, are lifted from the ground, they are astonished by the situation and marvel at the wind that has propelled them. They embark on an exaggerated geographical description of the countries, mountains, rivers, and seas that they are passing over. When the wind stops, Tartaglia concludes that the three oranges are nearby. Truffaldino is panting, he is hungry, and he asks the prince if he has brought a supply of money or promissory notes with him. Tartaglia treats all of these vulgar and useless requests with disdain; he notices a castle on a mountain, a short distance away. Thinking that it is the castle of Creonta, guard of the oranges, he sets off; Truffaldino follows him, hoping to find some food.

Celio the sorcerer comes out, frightening the other two characters; he attempts, in vain, to dissuade the prince from the dangerous enterprise. He describes the insuperable perils, those that children hear about when the fairy tale is told to them; but Celio describes them with his eyes a-goggle, in a terrifying voice, and as if they were huge obstacles. The dangers consist in an iron gate, which time has covered with rust; a hungry dog; a well rope, rotted out from dampness; and a baker woman who, not owning a broom, sweeps the oven with her breasts. The prince, not at all frightened by those terrifying objects, wants to go into the castle. Celio sees that he is resolved to go, and gives him some magic lard to oil the lock on the door; some bread to throw to the hungry dog; and a bunch of brushes to give to the baker woman who sweeps the oven with her breasts. He reminds them to lay the rope out in the sun to get rid of the dampness. And he adds that if by some happy circumstance they are able to carry off the three guarded oranges, they should immediately flee the castle, and remember not to open any of the oranges unless there is a fountain nearby. He promises that if they are able to escape this danger unharmed and carry out the theft, he will send the same demon with the bellows to blow on them from behind and push them back to their country in just a few moments. He entrusts them to the heavens, and leaves. Tartaglia and Truffaldino set off toward the castle with the objects they have been given.

The next scene opens in the courtyard of Creonta's castle.

An iron gate at the back, a hungry dog howling, a well with a tangle of rope next to it, and a baker woman sweeping her oven with two enormously long breasts put the theater in a state of silence and attention.

Prince Tartaglia and Truffaldino can be seen outside the gate, working hard to oil the lock of said gate with the magic lard. The gate opens wide. Marvel of marvels! They enter. Barking, the dog starts to attack them. They throw the bread to him; he quiets down. Miracle of miracles! While Truffaldino, filled with fear, lays the rope in the sun and gives the brushes to the baker woman, the prince enters the castle and shortly after comes happily back out with the three huge oranges that he has stolen.

But momentous events do not end like this. The sun darkens, an earthquake is felt, great rumbles of thunder echo. The prince hands over the oranges to Truffaldino, who is shaking violently; they prepare to flee. A dreadful voice resounds from the castle; it is Creonta herself, who shouts out, using exactly the same words as in the children's tale, in this manner:

O baker, O baker, how can you bear my disgrace?
Throw them by the feet into the oven's embrace!

The baker woman, faithful custodian of the text of the fairy tale, replies:

Not I; for so many years, and so many months, again and again,
I have consumed my white breasts in suffering and pain.

You, cruel one, did for me not once a broom supply;
These men brought many: may they go in peace, as you I defy!

Creonta shouts, following the text:

O rope, O rope, hang them!

And the rope replies, following the text:

O cruel one, can't you recollect
the many years, the many months that dirty and in neglect
you left me there in the damp, in a cruel, forgotten hell?
These men lay me in the sun: may they go in peace, and to you, farewell!

Creonta, still faithful to the text, yells:

Dog, my faithful guard, tear apart those wretched ones!

The dog, diligent guard of the text, replies,

How can I, Creonta, tear apart these unfortunate sons?
For so many years and so many months I served you without bread.
These men fed me my fill. Your shouting holds no dread.

Creonta shouts:

Gate of iron, close; and crush the heinous thieves without fail.

The gate replies:

Cruel Creonta, you summon my help to no avail.
For so many years and so many months in rust and in pain
You left me. These men oiled me; from being ungrateful I now abstain.

It is a nice sight to see, Tartaglia and Truffaldino marveling at the richness of this poetry. They are amazed to hear even baker women, ropes, dogs, and gates hold forth in alexandrine verses. They thank those objects for their compassion.

The audience was delighted with this marvelous juvenile novelty, and I confess that I laughed at myself, as I necessarily felt my spirit a bit humiliated by my enjoyment of those childlike images, which brought me back to the time of my youth.

The giantess Creonta comes out again, towering over everyone else and dressed in a long evening gown. At this horrifying sight, Tartaglia and Truffaldino flee.

Gesticulating desperately, Creonta recites these desperate alexandrine verses:

O unfaithful ministers: rope, dog, gate,
Wicked baker, traitors, all of you I berate!
O sweet oranges! Who from me has taken you away?
My dear oranges, my soul, my life, my mainstay!
O Jove the Fulminator, send me my defeat,
With thunder from the heavens, shatter me from my head to my feet.

A lightning bolt hits, and burns the giantess to ashes.

At this point the second act ends, to even greater applause from the audience than the first act.

Act 3

The scene opens onto the place where the Fata Morgana's lake is located. There is a large tree, and under it a large rock in the form of a seat. Some boulders dot the countryside.

Smeraldina, whose language is an Italianized Turkish, stands on the shore of the lake awaiting orders from the fairy. She grows impatient and begins to call out.

The fairy comes out of the lake. She tells of how she has been to hell, where she learned that Tartaglia and Truffaldino, with the help of Celio and propelled by the bellows of a demon, were victorious in their quest for the three oranges. Smeraldina scolds her for her incompetence in magic; she is angry. Morgana tells her not to tire herself worrying about it. Because of an accident she has arranged, Truffaldino will arrive there separately from the prince. A magical hunger and thirst will torment him. Since he will have the three oranges with him, great misfortunes will occur. She gives the Moorish Smeraldina two demonic hairpins. She tells her that she will see a beautiful girl seated on the rock under the tree. This will be Tartaglia's chosen bride. She shall, with great care, stick one of the hairpins into the girl's head. The girl will then transform into a dove. Then she shall sit down on the rock in the girl's place. Tartaglia will marry her; she will become queen. That night, as she sleeps with her husband, she shall drive the other hairpin into his head; he will become an animal, and the throne will thus be free for Leandro and Clarice. The Moor sees some problems with this plan, in particular with regard to being recognized in court. But she has to believe that Morgana's magic arts will smooth over all these impossibilities. Morgana leads the girl away so that she can give her more precise instructions, but also because she sees Truffaldino arriving, pushed along by the infernal wind.

Enter Truffaldino, running alongside the demon, who is blowing on him, and with the three oranges in his bag. The demon disappears. Truffaldino tells of how the prince fell down a short distance from there, due to the momentum of their running; he will wait for him. He sits down. An extraordinary hunger and thirst assail him. He decides to eat one of the three oranges. He feels remorse, and plays a tragic scene. Finally, greatly bothered and blinded by his extraordinary hunger, he determines to make the great sacrifice. He reflects that he can compensate for the damage with a few coins. He cuts an orange. A miracle! Out comes a young lady dressed in white, who promptly says:

Woe is me; give me something to drink! I'm going to die, my beau:
I'm dying of thirst, O wretched me! Hurry, cruel one! My god! Oh!

She falls to the ground, in the grips of a mortal lethargy. Truffaldino hasn't remembered Celio's orders not to open the oranges unless they were near a fountain. Foolish by nature, and desperate over this incredible situation, he doesn't see the lake nearby; the only expedient he can think of is to cut open another of the oranges, and to assist the girl who is dying of thirst with the juice of the other orange. He quickly performs the irrational action of cutting open another orange, and out comes another beautiful girl who speaks in this manner:

Woe is me; I'm dying of thirst. Come on, something to drink, you brute.
I'm going to croak with thirst, O God! And I'm about to faint, to boot!

She falls to the ground, like the other one. Truffaldino expresses his great agitation. He is beside himself, desperate. One of the girls speaks again, with a feeble voice:

Savage fate! Must I die of thirst? I'm dying . . . I'm dead.

She expires. The other one adds:

I'm dying, cruel stars: woe is me, I see no comfort ahead!

She too expires. Truffaldino is crying; he speaks to them tenderly. He decides that he will cut open the third orange to help them. He is about to cut it, when:

Enter Tartaglia. He is furious, and threatens him. Truffaldino, frightened, flees, abandoning the orange. After a long and ridiculous soliloquy, Tartaglia sees two peasants passing by, and commissions an honorable burial for the two young ladies. The peasants carry them off.

The prince turns to the third orange. It has, to his surprise, grown extraordinarily, to the size of a large squash.

He sees the lake nearby, and, remembering the words of Celio, thinks that it is an appropriate place to open it; he opens it with his sword, and out comes a big, beautiful maiden wearing a fine white dress, who exclaims, respecting the solemn content of the text:

Who will free me from my bonds? Oh God! Of thirst I am dying!
Quick, give me something to drink, or in vain you will be crying!

She falls to the ground. The prince understands the reason for Celio's order, but is confused by the fact that he has nothing to collect the water in. It is not a situation that acknowledges any regard for refined manners. He takes off one of his iron shoes, fills it up with water, and begging her pardon for the impropriety of the glass, he gives the young lady refreshment. Having regained her strength, she stands up, thanking him for his assistance.

She tells him that she is the daughter of Concul, king of the Antipodes, and that together with her two sisters she has been condemned by a spell cast by the cruel Creonta to reside inside the skin of an orange, for reasons as plausible as the whole situation is plausible. A comic love scene follows. The prince swears that he will marry her. The city is close, but the princess has no decent clothing. The prince obligates her to sit on a rock in the shade of the tree and wait for him. He will return with a lavish selection of clothes and his entire court, to remove her from there. After this is arranged, they separate with sighs.

Moorish Smeraldina, stunned by what she has seen, comes out. She sees the shadow of the beautiful girl in the water of the lake. There is no risk that she will not diligently carry out what the fairy tale says this Moorish girl did. She no longer speaks Italianized Turkish; Morgana had sent a Tuscan demon onto her tongue,[9] and she can match any poet for correctness of speech. She discovers the young princess, whose name is Ninetta. She flatters her, she shows off her hairdressing skills, she draws her closer, she betrays her. She plants one of the two magical hairpins into her head. Ninetta becomes a dove, and begins flying through the air. Smeraldina sits in her place, waiting for the court; she prepares to betray Tartaglia with the other hairpin, that night.

To the sound of a march the King of Hearts, the prince, Leandro, Clarice, Pantalone, Brighella, and the rest of the court arrive to solemnly carry off the princess. The new figure of the Moor that they find, whom they do not recognize due to Morgana's witchcraft, angers the prince. The Moor swears that she is the princess who was left there. The prince does not fail to provoke laughter, with his desperate behavior. Leandro, Clarice, and Brighella are lighthearted. They know where the mystery is coming from. The King of Hearts assumes a serious demeanor, and obligates his son to keep his princely word and marry the Moor. He threatens. With buffoonish mannerisms the prince consents, full of sadness. Instruments play. The group proceeds to court to celebrate the marriage.

Truffaldino hasn't come with the rest of the court. He has obtained a pardon from the prince for his mistakes. He has received the position of royal cook, and has stayed behind in the kitchen to prepare the wedding banquet.

9. "Tuscan" is standard Italian, so called because it was based on the Tuscan dialect of Dante, Petrarch, Boccaccio, and others that eventually was adopted as the literary lingua franca.

The scene that follows the departure of the court is the boldest of this playful parody.

CELIO: *Princess Ninetta, who was changed into a dove*
Will soon be restored, that is my opinion thereof;
And in second place, as a consequence of this deed,
Clarice and your Leandro will fall into a state of great need.
And Smeraldina the Moor, that regrettable hack,
Will as her just desert feel the flames on her back.

MORGANA: *May Clarice rise to the throne and of your haughty pain brag,*
And may Tartaglia be transformed, just like Acteon, into a stag.

CELIO: *I will let nothing remain unanswered, and at my behest,*
I will respond to your mendacity with an official protest.

MORGANA: *Of the monarchs of Hearts may this land be free.* (exit)

CELIO (shouts after her): *And I will re-protest, protected by the law and free of all fees.* (exit)

The following scene opens in the royal kitchen. Never has there been a more pitiful royal kitchen.

Truffaldino can be seen busy skewering a roast. He is recounting, in a great state of agitation, that while he was turning the spit himself, since there is no rotisserie in that kitchen, a dove appeared on one of the windowsills, and the following dialogue took place between the dove and him. The dove said to him, "Good day, cook in the kitchen." He replied, "Good day, little white dove." The dove added, "I beseech the heavens that you may fall asleep and that the roast may burn, so that the Moor, that ugly mug, won't be able to eat any of it." He was overcome by a miraculous sleepiness, and he fell into a slumber; the roast was burned to ashes. The same thing happened again twice. Two roasts were burned. Now he is hurriedly putting the third roast on the fire. The dove appears again, and the dialogue is repeated. The miraculous sleep overpowers Truffaldino. This charming character makes every effort possible to ward off sleep; his gags are most amusing. He falls asleep. The flames incinerate the third roast.

Pantalone arrives, shouting. He detests Truffaldino. He says that the king is in a rage because they have already eaten the soup, the boiled meat, and the liver, and there's no sign of the roast. Truffaldino tells the story of the dove. Pantalone can't believe such an amazing thing. The dove appears, and repeats the miraculous words. Truffaldino is about to fall asleep on his feet. These two characters start chasing the dove, which flutters around the kitchen. They finally catch the dove, place it on the table, and start petting it. They can feel something sticking out of its head; it is the magic hairpin. Truffaldino pulls it out, and the dove transforms back into Princess Ninetta.

There is great astonishment. His Majesty the King of Hearts appears, with royal gravitas and scepter in hand, and threatens Truffaldino because of the delay in the roast, and the shame that this has conferred on someone of his status in front of his guests. Prince Tartaglia comes in, and recognizes his Ninetta. He is crazy with joy. Ninetta briefly recounts what happened to her; the king is stunned. The Moor and the rest of the court appear, having followed His Majesty into the kitchen. With a supremely imperious manner the king orders the prince and princess to withdraw into the broom closet. He designates the hearth as his throne, and sits down with royal bearing. The Moor comes before him, with the rest of the court. The king, faithful custodian of the fairy tale, presents the case and then asks what sort of punishment the criminals involved in this case deserve. All are in a state of amazement, and offer their opinions. In a fury, the king condemns Smeraldina the Moor to death at the stake. Celio appears. He declares the secret crimes of Clarice, Leandro, and Brighella. They are condemned to a cruel banishment. The prince and princess are called from the broom closet. Everything ends in great happiness.

Celio urges Truffaldino to keep the diabolical alexandrine verses far from the royal cooking pots, and to make his sovereigns laugh. The fairy tale doesn't fail to end with the usual finale, which every child knows by heart: marriage, a turnip casserole, hairless mice, skinned cats, etc.

PART IV

The Golden Age of the Italian Fairy Tale

1

Laura Gonzenbach (1842–78)

Laura Gonzenbach is best known for the Sicilian fairy tales that she collected around Messina and Catania, predominantly from female tellers, most of them probably peasants or artisans. The tales were translated into High German and published in 1870 as *Sicilianische Märchen* (*Sicilian Fairy Tales*). We know little about the original versions of the tales collected by Gonzenbach and thus about her transcription and translation strategies, as all of her papers were destroyed in the Messina earthquake of 1908. Yet even though they were translated into High German, the tales still retain, stylistically, an oral flavor. Like Giuseppe Pitrè's collection, which appeared five years after hers, the tales were not heavily edited or "sanitized" and were not intended for children. Gonzenbach's tales constitute a uniquely female take on many common tale types and are distinguished by their uncompromising representation of bleak social conditions, even in the context of the marvelous.

Gonzenbach's father, Peter Viktor, a Swiss German textile merchant, had arrived in Messina as a young man. He ended up remaining the rest of his life in Sicily, raising his family of eight children there and later in life also becoming the Swiss consul of Messina. Although Gonzenbach was not a scholar of folklore to the degree that her contemporary Pitrè was, she received a good private education and continued throughout her life to educate herself, at a time when this was still unusual for women, as did her sister, Magdalena, who was an activist for women's causes and founded a school for girls in Messina. In the 1860s the minister and historian Otto Hardwig spent five years in Messina as the head of its Protestant community, and shortly after his departure he asked Gonzenbach to collect a few folktales for inclusion in a work of his on Sicily. The "few" tales then became the ninety-two that were published in two volumes of their own in 1870. Although *Sicilian Fairy Tales* was the first comprehensive volume of Sicilian tales, and as such gave the island's rich storytelling traditions their first international exposure, Gonzenbach remained relatively unknown to nonspecialists until quite recently, when the tales were translated into Italian by Luisa Rubini (1999) and into English by Jack Zipes in two volumes (2004).

In the words of Rubini, "The female element is the true protagonist of this collection." She and others have noted the concentration of characters and themes relating to women's real experiences, such as beastly husbands, child brides, housebound daughters, acts of extreme sadism, and revenge. And yet, notwithstanding the restrictions imposed on them, Gonzenbach's enterprising heroines also frequently offer stunning displays of boldness and intelligence in their determination to get the upper hand.

Further Reading

Primary

Gonzenbach, Laura. *Fiabe italiane.* Ed. Lusia Rubini. Trans. Vincenzo Consolo. Rome: Donzelli, 1999. 3–5, 1126–19, 204–10, 261–62, 408–12. [source text]

Gonzenbach, Laura. *Beautiful Angiola: The Great Treasury of Sicilian Folk and Fairy Tales Collected by Laura Gonzenbach.* Ed. and trans. Jack Zipes. New York: Routledge, 2004.

Gonzenbach, Laura. *The Robber with a Witch's Head: More Stories from the Great Treasury of Sicilian Folk and Fairy Tales Collected by Laura Gonzenbach.* Ed. and trans. Jack Zipes. New York: Routledge, 2004.

Gonzenbach, Laura. *Sicilianische Märchen.* 2 vols. Lepizig: W. Emgelmann, 1870.

Secondary

Noyes, Dorothy, and Jack Zipes. "Buried Treasure or Fairy-Tale Verismo." *Marvels & Tales* 19, no. 2 (2005): 331–49.

Rubini, Luisa. *Fiabe e mercanti in Sicilia: La raccolta di Laura Gonzenbach, la comunità di lingua tedesca a Messina nell'Ottocento.* Florence: Olschki, 1998.

Rubini, Luisa. "Introduzione." In *Fiabe italiane*, by Laura Gonzenbach. Ed. Lusia Rubini. Trans. Vincenzo Consolo. Rome: Donzelli, 1999. xv–xxix.

Zipes, Jack. "Laura Gonzenbach's Buried Treasure." In *The Robber with a Witch's Head: More Stories from the Great Treasury of Sicilian Folk and Fairy Tales Collected by Laura Gonzenbach*, by Laura Gonzenbach. New York: Routledge, 2004. xi–xxviii.

The Clever Farmer's Daughter (Die kluge Bauerntochter)

This tale combines tale types ATU 1533, The Wise Carving of the Fowl; ATU 875, The Clever Farmgirl; and ATU 875A, Girls' Riddling Answer Betrays a Thief. Early versions appears in the exempla collection Scala coeli *by Giovanni Gobi and in Franco Sacchetti's* Trecentonovelle *(123). It is the first tale in Gonzenbach's collection and as such sets the tone, with its strong female protagonist, for the many stories of winning heroines that follow. Significantly, there is no magic in this tale apart from the heroine's ingenuity, for which she is richly rewarded.*

I have translated from Luisa Rubini and Vincenzo Consolo's Italian translation from the German, while consulting the German for titles and any details I was unsure of.

Once upon a time there was a king who had gone hunting. When evening came, he suddenly realized that he had gotten separated from the rest of his company, and that only his groom was following him. Night fell, and in the thick woods the two of them were not able to find their way back. They wandered for hours and hours, and finally caught sight of a light in the distance. They galloped toward the light, and found themselves in front of a little house. The servant knocked, and right away a farmer appeared at the window. He asked, "Who's knocking at this hour of the night?" And the servant replied, "His Majesty the king is out here and he can't find the road back to the castle. Would you give him food and shelter for the night?" The farmer rushed down to open the door, woke up his wife and daughter, and told them to kill a chicken and cook it. When the table was set, they apologized to the king for the meager fare that they were able to offer him.

The king took the chicken and divided it up. He gave the head to the father, the breast to the mother, and the wings to the daughter; he took the thighs, and he gave the legs to his servant.

Then they all went to bed.

When they were alone, the mother asked her daughter, "Why did the king divide up the chicken in such a strange way?" And the daughter said, "That's obvious! He gave father the head because he's the head of the family; you the breast because you're getting up there in years; me the wings because one day I'm going to take flight; he kept the thighs for himself because he's a horseman, and he gave his groom the legs so that he can ride faster."

The next morning they served the king breakfast and showed him the way. When he arrived at the castle, the king gave his groom a nice roast chicken, a big round focaccia, a little barrel of wine, and twelve *tarì*,[1] ordering him to take all those things to the peasant's family, along with an assurance of his goodwill.

The road was long, and the servant was assailed by hunger and fatigue. He could no longer resist: he cut off half the chicken and ate it. Then he was thirsty, and he guzzled down half of the wine. Back on the road, he looked at the focaccia and thought, "That's got to be good." And he devoured half of the focaccia. Then he thought, "I have to do the whole job!" and he put six of the twelve *tarì* in his pocket.

When he finally reached the farmer's house, he handed over half the chicken, half the focaccia, half the barrel of wine, and six *tarì*. The peasant and his family were delighted with the honor the king had bestowed upon them, and begged the servant to thank him very much.

But the daughter, who had noticed that everything was half of what it was supposed to be, told the servant that she wanted to entrust him with a special message for the king, which he was to repeat word for word. The servant said he would, and she began,

The one that sings at night,
Oh, God, why only half?

"Will you be able to remember that?" "Oh, yes!" answered the man. "Alright, then, you also have to say":

1. A *tarì* was a gold and then silver coin used in Sicily, of small value.

The moon at five tenths,
Oh, God, why only half?

"Will you be able to remember that, too?" "Sure!" answered the servant. "Then you need to say this as well":

With a plug above and below,
Oh, God, why only half?

"You won't forget that, will you?" "Of course not!" "And the last thing you need to tell him is":

The twelve months of the year,
Oh, God, why only half?

The servant promised to report all of this to the king in exactly those words, and then set off, continuously repeating the rhyme to himself so that he wouldn't forget it. When he reached the castle, the king asked him, "So, did you deliver everything?" "Yes, Your Majesty. I also have a message for you from the farmer's daughter. It starts like this":

The one that sings at night,
Oh, God, why only half?

"What?!" yelled the king. "You ate half the chicken!" "Ah, Your Majesty!" implored the servant, "First listen to the rest of the message":

The moon at five tenths,
Oh, God, why only half?

"What?!" shouted the king. "You ate half the focaccia, too!" "Ah, Your Majesty! First let me finish. Here's the third verse":

With a plug above and below,
Oh, God, why only half?

"What?!" yelled the king. "You drank half the barrel of wine, too!" "Your Majesty, let me finish the message!" answered the servant. "The last thing the girl said was":

The twelve months of the year,
Oh, God, why only half?

"So you stole six *tarì*, too!" yelled the king. The servant threw himself at the king's feet and begged for forgiveness. And the king was so pleased at the girl's cleverness that he forgave him. He sent the farm girl a beautiful carriage, some magnificent clothes, and then he married her.

They lived forever, happy and content
And here are we, with not even a cent.

The Bandit Who Had a Witch's Head (Von Räuber, der einen Hexenkopf hatte)

The tale begins in the manner of ATU 857, The Louse-Skin (see Basile, "The Flea," pp. 102–7), and later continues like ATU 311, Rescue by the Sister, related to the Bluebeard tale type. Pitrè's collection also contains several versions of this tale.

Once upon a time there was a king who had three beautiful daughters, but the youngest was the most beautiful and the most clever. One day he called her over and said, "Come and pick some lice off of me." And when she did, she found a louse. Then the king put the louse in a big jar with some lard and left it there for many years. When one day he ordered the jar to be broken, the louse had grown and had become a monster that frightened everyone. The king had it killed. Then he had it skinned and had the skin nailed to a door, and said, "Whoever guesses which animal this skin belongs to will marry my eldest daughter. Whoever does not guess right, on the other hand, will have his head cut off."

Princes and lords came from far and wide to ask for the beautiful princess's hand in marriage, but no one was able to resolve the riddle, and they all were forced to meet a miserable death.

There was, however, a bandit who lived by himself in a wild place. He kept a witch's head in a small basket, of which he would always ask advice before any undertaking. This bandit learned of the princess's many contenders who had lost their lives, and how no one had been able to resolve the difficult riddle. He went to the witch's head and asked, "Tell me, head, to which animal does the skin that the king has nailed to the door belong?" "To a louse," answered the head. Delighted, the bandit set off for the city. People in the road asked him where he was going. "I'm going to the city to ask for the princess's hand in marriage." "Then you're going to your death," said the people.

When he arrived in the city, he announced to the king that he wanted to guess, too. The king had him brought in, showed him the skin, and asked, "Can you tell me which animal this skin belongs to?" "A hare?" said the bandit. "Wrong!" "Perhaps a dog?" "Wrong." "Is it perhaps the skin of a louse?" He had guessed it right, and the king gave him his eldest daughter in marriage. Once the wedding festivities were over, the bandit said to the king, "Now I want to return home with my wife." And so the girl hugged her father and sisters and left with her husband.

After walking for a long, long time, they arrived at a wild, solitary place. "Ah," said the princess, "where are you taking me?" "Come with me!" answered the bandit. They finally reached his house, which was so dark and horrible that the princess immediately said, "This is where you live? Oh, what an ugly place!" "Enter!" replied the bandit.

The princess now had to live in that wild place and work hard. The second day they were there, the bandit said, "I have to tend to my business. In the meantime, you look after the house." But he whispered to the witch's head, "Pay attention to what she says about me." When the bandit left, the princess could no longer restrain herself, and she began to curse her husband, because she had married him against her will and she really couldn't stand him. "That wicked man!" she said, "I hope he breaks his neck! May misfortune follow him wherever he goes!" and other things as well. The witch's head heard it all and relayed it to the bandit upon his return. He grabbed the princess, cut off her head, and threw her in a little room where there were many other dead bodies of girls that he had killed in the same way.

The next day he returned to the king's court. When he arrived, the king asked him, "How is my daughter?" "Very well," answered the bandit, "although she's bored and would like her sister, the middle one, to keep her company." And so the king gave him his second daughter, and he took her to that wild place. "Ah, brother-in-law," she said, "what a strange place! Where are you taking me?" "Come!" said the bandit. When they reached his house, the princess asked again, "Ah, brother-in-law, this is your house? It's horrible!" "Enter!" said the bandit. "Where is my sister?" she asked. "Don't worry about her, just do your work." And so the princess had to toil away while in her heart the rage and hatred she felt for her brother-in-law grew ever greater.

One day he said to her, "I have to go handle some business. I'll be back this evening." Then he went to the witch's head and said, "Pay attention to what she says about me." And he left. The princess began to vent her hatred; she cursed him, she called him evil, and she wished upon him all the misfortune possible. When the bandit returned home, the witch's head told him everything, and the poor princess fared no better than the first one.

Then the bandit returned once again to the king, who asked him how his daughters were. "Oh, very well," answered the bandit, "but they would like to have the youngest sister there, to keep them company." So the king gave him the youngest sister as well. She, however, was very clever, and once they had reached that wild place, she said, "Brother-in-law, what a beautiful place this is! Is this where you live?" And at the sight of the house, she once again said, "Oh, what a beautiful house!" When they went in, though, she was very careful not to ask about her sisters, and she cheerfully went straight to work. Then the bandit left again on business, and the witch's head had to pay attention to what the princess said about him.

When the princess had finished her work, she knelt down and prayed out loud for the bandit, whom she wished all the best, even if deep in her heart she wanted something terrible to happen to him. That evening, the bandit returned and immediately asked the witch's head, "So, what did she say about me?" "Ah, we've never had one like her before! She prayed all day, wishing you the best of everything." The bandit was very happy, and said to the princess, "Since you've been more reasonable than your sisters, you will fare well here, and I'll show you where your sisters are." He led her into the little room and showed her the dead sisters. "You did well to kill them, brother-in-law," said the clever girl. And from then on she lived well at the bandit's, and was the mistress of the house.

One day, though, the bandit left home for a long time. The princess just happened to go into his room, and when she raised her eyes, she saw the witch's head. It was in a little basket above the window, hanging from two nails. Since she was a clever one, she asked the head, "What are you doing up there? Come down here to me, where you'll be much more comfortable." "No," answered the head, "I'm really fine up here, and I have no desire to come down." Then the girl gave the head so many compliments that it finally succumbed to her spell, and came down. "What messy hair you have!" said the princess. "Come with me, I want to make you pretty." The witch's head followed her into the kitchen, and the princess got a comb and began to comb the head. She had just heated up the oven to bake the bread, and as she was combing the head, she wrapped the long braid around her arm and quickly flung the head into the oven, shut the door, and left it there to safely burn.

The bandit's life was tied to the witch's head, and so as the head burned, the bandit felt his own life fading away, until he died. Then the princess climbed up to the window, where the basket that had held the head was hanging. She found a little pot filled with some ointment, which she smeared on her sisters, and they came back to life. Then she used it on all the other girls in there, and each of them took as many of the bandit's treasures as she could carry. Finally, they all returned to their parents.

The three sisters returned to their father and lived with him happily ever after, until they married three handsome princes.

The Story of Sorfarina (Die Geschichte von Sorfarina)

The oldest known literary version of this common tale, ATU 891, The Man Who Deserted His Wife, is from eleventh-century India. It is found in Boccaccio's Decameron *3.9 ("Giletta of Nerbona"), Straparola's* Pleasant Nights *7.1, and Basile's* Tale of Tales *3.4 and 5.6. Rubini notes how, with respect to Pitrè's version, "Caterina la Sapienti," this tale "appears less censored: Sorfarina becomes, disguised, the prince's lover, with explicit allusions to the practice of prostitution in Rome, Naples, and Genoa" (*Fiabe italiane *511).*

Once upon a time there were a king and a queen who had an only child. To ensure that the boy learned everything necessary for someone of his rank, they sent him to a teacher at a school. Many other children also went to that school, and among them was a merchant's daughter who was more beautiful than the sun, named Sorfarina. Sorfarina learned more than any of the other children, and much more than the king's son. The teacher was proud of her and loved her very much.

Now, one day it came to pass that the teacher was forced to leave on a journey, and he was at a loss as to who he could leave in charge of the school during his absence. Seeing him so worried, Sorfarina asked him, "Teacher, sir, what's the matter?" "Ah, Sorfarina, I find myself in a difficult situation, because I have to take a journey and I don't know who to leave in charge of the school." "Leave me in charge," said Sorfarina. "I'll teach the pupils during your absence." The teacher agreed and left, and Sorfarina kept the school running. One day she was holding a class for the king's son, and he wouldn't pay attention to her, so she got angry and slapped him. The king's son didn't react, but this insult remained in his heart.

Many years went by. The king's son no longer went to school, and Sorfarina had become a magnificent young woman, so beautiful that he fell hopelessly in love with her.

One day he went to his father and said, "My dear father, I've found a woman to my liking. Beautiful Sorfarina must become my wife." The king would actually have preferred the daughter of a king for his son, but since he was incapable of saying no to him, he said, "Alright, my son, if you want her, take her." And so a lavish wedding was held with endless festivities, and the king's son married Sorfarina.

As they were going to their room on their wedding night to prepare for bed, he said, "Sorfarina, do you remember how back then you gave me a smack? Tell me, are you sorry?" "No," she replied,

I don't regret it, nor will I ever,
And if need be, I'll repeat the endeavor.

"What?" screamed the king, flying into a blinding rage. "You dare to say those things to me? In that case, I don't want you in my bed!" He pushed her out of the bed, and Sorfarina had to sleep on the ground. But since he loved her and his heart ached to see her lying there on the cold floor, he said to her, "Dear Sorfarina, tell me, then, are you sorry?" "No," she said,

I don't regret it, nor will I ever,
And if need be, I'll repeat the endeavor.

However much he begged and tried to convince her with gentle manners, she always answered in the same way, so that he finally became infuriated and said, "Alright, stay where you are!" The next day he rushed off to his mother, the queen, told her everything, and said, "Just imagine; after spending the whole night on the cold floor, she still refuses to say she's sorry." "But my son," answered the queen, "forget about it, those are things of the past." "No, mother, I want her to say it just once." Then he rushed back to Sorfarina. "Sorfarina, Sorfarina, tell me, are you sorry?"

I don't regret it, nor will I ever,
And if need be, I'll repeat the endeavor.

"Ah, Sorfarina," he grumbled, "you're so stubborn! You know that I'll have you thrown in the water cistern, if you don't say it?" "Have me thrown in the water cistern, then!" In short, although he was running off to her many times a day, and would try this strategy one time and that strategy the next, it was impossible to get any other answer from her. Finally the king's son got angry and had her thrown in the water cistern in the courtyard. But then he would be running off to the cistern every minute. "Sorfarina, I'm begging you, tell me right now that you're sorry." "No," she answered,

I don't regret it, nor will I ever,
And if need be, I'll repeat the endeavor.

"You know that I'm leaving on a long journey, and you're going to stay here in the cistern?" "Go wherever you like," she answered. "Just do me the favor of telling me whether you're going by land or by sea." They spent several more days like this, and Sorfarina could be persuaded by neither pleas nor threats to say she was sorry. When the king's son saw how stubborn she was, he finally yelled at her, "Goodbye! I'm going to Rome!" "Have a nice trip! Are you going by land or by sea?" "By sea." "Good," thought Sorfarina to herself, "I'll go by land." The king's son left, and she immediately got out of the cistern and went to Rome by land. There she rented a nice house right in front of the inn where the king's son was staying.

One morning, when he was at the window, he saw her on the balcony across the way. He gazed at her in wonder and thought, "Oh, what a marvelous woman! If I hadn't left my wife, Sorfarina, in the cistern, I would say that it's her." He waved and then said a few words to her. She answered politely. After a few days, he went to her house, and in short, they embarked on such an intimate friendship that after a year they welcomed a lovely baby boy into the world, whom they named Romano. The king's son, though, had told the woman that he had a wonderful wife at home, but that she was so stubborn that she couldn't deign to say she was sorry for the slap. "Ah," said Sorfarina, "forgive that poor woman and get her out of the cistern." "No, I want her to do what I say at least once."

When the baby was a few months old, one day Sorfarina said to the king's son, "Why don't you go home and see if your poor wife is still in the cistern, and if she perhaps has changed her mind by now?" The king's son left by sea, and returned home. Sorfarina, for her part, left the baby with the fairies that served her—for she possessed magical gifts—and returned home. At the arrival of the king's son, she was already sitting in the cistern. "Well, Sorfarina," he said, "do you still want to keep up with your stubbornness? I beg you, tell me that you're sorry." "No," she said,

I don't regret it, nor will I ever,
And if need be, I'll repeat the endeavor.

The king's son was desperate, because he loved his Sorfarina so much and she wouldn't do what he wanted her to. So he said to her, "Sorfarina, if you don't say you're sorry, tomorrow I'm leaving for Naples." "Have a good trip! Are you going by land or by sea?" "By sea." "I'll go by land, then," she thought. The king's son had barely left when Sorfarina got out of the cistern and left for Naples. There she rented a house across the street from the inn where her husband was lodged, and when he looked out of the window, he saw her sitting on the balcony, and he observed her in wonder. "What's happening here? If I hadn't left my wife in the cistern and the Roman woman in Rome, I would think that this woman is one of the two." He waved and then said a few words to her. She answered him politely, and, to make a long story short, after a year the king's son and Sorfarina had a baby boy, whom they named Napoletano.

When the baby was a few months old, Sorfarina said, "Don't you want to go home to see if your wife has changed her mind?" The king's son returned home, but Sorfarina was quicker than he was; and even though he rushed to the cistern, she was already inside it, and asked him, "Well, then, did you have a good time?" "Ah, Sorfarina, if you would only do what I want you to, how happy I would be to stay here with you! Please, dear Sorfarina, tell me that you're sorry!" But no matter how much he begged or threatened, Sorfarina would always give the same answer, until one day he got angry and said, "Sorfarina, say it! Otherwise I'm leaving for Genoa today!" "Have a good trip!" she yelled, making fun of him. And as soon as he had left, she got out of the cistern and arrived in Genoa at the same time he did. There she rented a house across the street from the inn where her husband was living, and the first thing he saw when he looked out the window was, once again, the beautiful woman sitting on the balcony across the way. "There's something going on here!" he exclaimed. "Here's another beautiful woman who looks like my dear Sorfarina. If I hadn't left my wife in the cistern, the Roman woman in Rome, and the

Neapolitan woman in Naples, I might think that she's one of them." And so he waved to her and she thanked him; soon they became friends, and before a year had gone by a baby girl named Genova was brought into the world.

When the baby was just a few months old, Sorfarina said to the man, "Don't you want to go home a little to see how your poor wife is doing? Who knows, maybe she's feeling sorry." The king's son returned home, but Sorfarina hadn't been sitting around idle, either, and when he got to the cistern, she was already right there inside it. "Dear Sorfarina," he pleaded, "after all this you can't possibly still be so stubborn. I beg you, tell me that you're sorry."

I don't regret it, nor will I ever,
And if need be, I'll repeat the endeavor.

No matter how often the king's son ran over to the cistern, Sorfarina would always answer him in the same way. "Sorfarina!" he finally said, "If you don't do what I want you to, I'm going to find another woman!" "Go find her, then!" she answered. And so he had a beautiful princess brought in, and they prepared to celebrate a magnificent wedding. But the king's son wasn't able to forget his beautiful Sorfarina. He rushed back to her and pleaded, "Sorfarina, do it out of love for me. Look, I'm seriously about to marry another woman, and this evening there will be a grand ball at the castle." "I hope you have a good time," she answered, "do whatever you want." That evening, though, she ordered that her three children be present. They immediately appeared before her, dressed in royal clothing, and more delicate and beautiful children could nowhere be found. Then she ordered the most beautiful of dresses and the richest of jewels for herself, together with a train of maidservants who washed her with orange-blossom water and dressed her up elegantly. Finally, she ordered a golden carriage pulled by four horses and equipped with all the necessary accessories. Then she got into the carriage with the three children, and went to the castle.

When she arrived, she entered the hall with the children, and everyone stared at her, full of admiration, since she was the most beautiful one there, and no one was dressed as splendidly as she was. The king's son rushed over to her and asked her to dance. Then she said in a loud, ringing voice, "Romano, Napoletano, take your sister Genova by the hand and dance with her." When the king's son heard these names, he stood there speechless. Then he had a better look at her, suddenly recognized who she was, and yelled, "Ah, Sorfarina!

It's you! And you were also the Roman woman, the Neapolitan woman, and the Genoese woman!" "Well, yes, it was I," answered Sorfarina, "and that's how you spent your time, while your wife was in the cistern!" and in front of everyone present she slapped him.

You can imagine what an indignity it was for the king to be treated like that in front of everyone, and yet he was unable to do anything but ask for her forgiveness. Then, looking at the children, he joyfully embraced them, and said to Sorfarina, "Well, then, you will remain my dear wife." And so the foreign princess had to return home and the king's son once again accepted Sorfarina as his honorable wife. But she was smart, and continued to think, "There's no telling if he has really forgiven me!"

Sorfarina went into their bedroom before he got there, and prepared a pretty doll made of sugar and honey that was exactly as tall as she was; the doll had a little cord attached to its neck, which when pulled made the doll move her head. She put the doll in the bed and she hid underneath it with the cord in her hand. After a little while, the king's son came into the room, went over to the bed, and asked, "Well, then, Sorfarina, are you sorry now?" Sorfarina pulled on the cord, so that the doll shook its head to signal denial. "What?" he yelled, "You're still being stubborn like this?" And he got so angry that he pulled out his sword and cut the doll's head off. But when he licked the sword to clean it off, the blood had such a sweet taste that he became very sad and cried, "Ah, how sweet your blood is, my beloved Sorfarina, and now I've killed you! I want to die, too!" And he was about to run himself through with the sword. Then Sorfarina came out from under the bed and fell into his arms, shouting, "Stop! I'm still alive,"

And this dove with sugar and honey made sweet
Together as husband and wife we shall now eat.

The king's son was full of joy and embraced his wife, saying, "You've made fun of me until now, but I forgive you everything." "And I want to tell you that I'm sorry that I slapped you," Sorfarina said. And then their joy was truly great, and together with their children,

They lived forever, happy and content,
And here we are, with not even a cent.

The Serpent That Testified in Favor of a Girl (Von der Schlange, die für ein Mädchen sengte)

This remarkable tale loosely belongs to tale type ATU 672, The Serpent's Crown. Here, though, we find the unique version of a poor girl who is raped and then is vindicated when she marries her rapist, a prince. This plot reflects the centuries-long reality, until fairly recently codified in Article 544 of Italy's Criminal Code, of the matrimonio riparatore *(rehabilitating marriage, aka "marry your rapist" law) that established that if a rapist married his victim, he could not be subject to criminal prosecution, and she would not have to live the rest of her life as a "dishonored woman." (Only in 1981 was this article repealed.) In most cases, of course, the rapist could not promise as radically different a tenor of life for his victim as in this tale, which offers a momentary, and questionable, compensatory release from a reality that is not only harsh but quite dangerous, especially for women: an unsettling happy ending, but perhaps the only one possible in this not so fairy-tale Sicily.*

Once upon a time there was a poor woman, so poor that she lived in a wild and completely remote place with her only child, a daughter who was more beautiful than the sun. The mother would go to gather greens, and then sell them in town, while the daughter would stay home, washing clothes and cooking.

One day the mother had gone to town with her greens and the daughter was by herself. A prince who had gone hunting and lost his way found himself in the area, and when he saw the little hut he got off his horse, knocked on the door, and asked for a glass of water, since he was very thirsty. The girl did not open the door, however, but handed him the glass through the window. The prince saw how beautiful she was, and was overcome by a wicked desire; in a frenzy, he demanded that she open the door. But she refused. Then, in his savage lust, he broke down the door, forced his way into the house, and violated her. She shouted and cried out, but no one heard her; she looked around for help, but the only thing she saw was a serpent slithering around in front of the house. "If no one hears me in my moment of anguish," said the girl, "I call this serpent to bear witness: may you, prince, never marry anyone but me." After pronouncing these words, the girl abandoned herself to the desire of the prince. Then he left the hut. The girl, however, told her mother nothing.

It wasn't long before word spread of the upcoming wedding between the prince and a beautiful princess. And one day when the mother had been to town again, her daughter asked her, that evening, "Well, dear mother, what's new in town?" "My daughter," answered the mother, "they're telling a story that's so extraordinary that it's almost impossible to believe. Just imagine: the prince has a serpent around his neck, and no one is able to pull it off. And when they try to, the serpent squeezes even harder, until it nearly strangles him." When she heard this, the girl immediately understood which serpent she was talking about. Early the next morning she set off, without her mother's knowledge, and went to the castle.

The sentry asked her what she wanted, and the girl answered, "Announce me to the king, because I know of a way to free the prince of the serpent that's wrapped around his neck." The guards began laughing and said, "So many physicians and wise men have tried without success, and now you want to try?" She insisted, "Announce me to the king!" The king heard all the clamor, and asked what was going on. His servants told him, "There's a girl down there who claims that she knows of a way to free the prince of the serpent." "Well, then," ordered the king, "have her come up! There's no harm in trying."

And so the beautiful girl was brought before the king, who immediately accompanied her to his son's room, where he left her alone with him. She planted herself in front of him and said, "Look at me: do you recognize me?" "No," replied the prince, and the serpent wrapped itself even more tightly around his neck. "How is that possible?" continued the girl. "Have you forgotten how you entered my house with violence and forced me to submit to your lust? Don't you remember that I called on the serpent to bear witness to my promise that you would never be able to marry anyone but me?" He intended to answer no again, but the serpent squeezed his neck so hard that at the end he said, "Yes." Then the serpent relaxed its grip a little. "And now you want to marry a princess and abandon me?" asked the girl. "Yes," he replied, but the serpent immediately squeezed his neck tighter, so that at the end he promised not to marry the princess. "Swear that you'll marry me," said the girl. The prince swore. The serpent immediately fell from his neck and disappeared. The prince went straight to the king and said, "Dear father, send my fiancée home, for this girl has freed me from the wicked serpent and now she must become my wife."

And so the prince married the beautiful girl, and brought her mother to the castle, too.

They lived forever, happy and content,
And here we are, with not even a cent.

The Story of the Courageous Girl (Die Geschichte von dem mutigen Mädchen)

This tale of female solidarity belongs to type ATU 545A, The Magic Castle, with some elements of ATU 326, The Youth Who Wanted to Learn What Fear Is. Gonzenbach collected another similar tale, in Sicilian, "Lu cuntu de li tri soru" (The Tale of the Three Sisters); and Pitrè's "Lu Sangunazzu" shares some details with her versions, though not the surprising main episode of the noblewoman who by the hand of the "courageous girl" finally exacts her revenge on the violent lover who had killed her.*

Once upon a time there were three sisters who had neither a father nor a mother and who earned their meager daily bread by spinning. Every day the three of them would spin a spool of flax and bring it to their employers, who would give them two coins, with which they had to survive.

One day they had a great desire to eat some liver. "You know something?" said the eldest sister to the others. "Today it's my turn to take the spinning to the mistress. With the money she gives me I'll buy a little liver, a little bread, and some wine, and for once we too can spend a pleasant evening." "Good," answered her sisters. That evening the eldest sister went to town with the spinning, and after their mistress had paid her, she bought a little liver, a little bread, and some wine. She put everything carefully into her basket and set out toward home.

As she was passing along a solitary lane, the basket fell from her hand. A dog suddenly leaped out, snatched the basket, and dashed off. She ran after the dog, but couldn't catch up with it, and at the end she returned home without her basket and without the food. "Don't you have anything for us?" her sisters asked. "Ah, dear sisters," she replied, "What can I do? That's how things went."

The next evening it was the second sister's turn to go to their mistress, and she said, "Today I'll bring the liver." After she received the money, she bought liver, bread, and wine, put them in the basket, and left for home. In a solitary lane the basket fell from her hand, too, and the dog leaped out and dashed off with it, so quickly that she wasn't able to catch up with it.

When she arrived home and told her sisters all of this, the youngest said, "Tomorrow I'll go; the dog won't get away from me." And so the next evening she went to their mistress with the spinning and received the money, with which she bought liver, bread, and wine. When she got to the lane, the basket fell from her hand. The dog immediately raced out, snatched it, and dashed off. But she was quicker than her sisters, and even though the dog was running very fast, she followed it and kept sight of it at all times. The dog ran down many roads, and finally went into a house, with the girl behind. She climbed the stairs and called out, but no one answered. She walked through all the rooms and saw marvelous things: in one room a beautiful table was set, in another there were fine beds, and in a third there were all sorts of treasures and precious things. But she didn't see anyone. Then she got to a little room, where she found the dog lying on the floor with the three baskets in front of it, although after she had seen all those riches she wasn't concerned about that anymore.

She continued, finally arriving at a large room where there were piles of treasures and chests and boxes full of precious jewels and, on the ground, sacks overflowing with gold coins. She took one of the sacks of gold, left the castle, and returned home. "My dear sisters," she said, with great delight, "abundance now reigns among us: look what I've brought you!" When the sisters saw the sack full of gold coins, they were very happy, but the youngest said, "My dear sisters, let's give everything we own to the poor, and leave our little house. We'll bury the gold here, though, and then we'll all go to the castle and see what happens. If things don't go well for us, there will always be the gold that we left here."

And that's what they did. They gave everything they owned to the poor, buried the gold in the empty house, and all three of them went to the mysterious castle. In the first room they found the beautiful table, which was still set, and they sat down, ate and drank to their heart's content, and then had a look at all the treasures and marvelous things housed in the castle. In the evening, the youngest sister said to the eldest, "We can't all go to sleep, because something bad might happen. It's best if you stay awake tonight while the two of us sleep." And so the two younger sisters went off to sleep, while the eldest kept vigil.

At midnight she suddenly heard a loud cry that resounded through the whole house. "Wait, I'm coming down!" shouted a menacing voice. She was so frightened that she ran straight to her bed and pulled the covers up over her ears. Right away it was silent again. The next morning the other sisters asked, "Did you hear or see anything last night?" "Nothing at all, everything was quiet."

The next night the second sister had to keep vigil, and the other two went to bed. At midnight, though, a menacing voice shouted, "Wait, I'm coming down!" She was frightened, ran to her bed, and pulled the covers up over her ears. And then it was silent again. The next morning the other two sisters asked if she had heard or seen anything. She answered, "No, absolutely not, everything was quiet." But she said to the eldest sister in secret, "Did you hear that terrible scream?" "Yes, of course I did, but keep quiet about it. We've had our fright, now let our younger sister have hers."

That evening the two older sisters went off to bed and the youngest kept vigil. At midnight the same voice was heard: "Wait, I'm coming down!" "As you like!" she replied. Then the door opened and a beautiful, tall lady in a long black dress that trailed behind her entered the room. She went up to the girl and said, "I see that you're a courageous girl; if in the future you show this same courage and do exactly what I tell you to do, this palace and everything in it will be yours, and you will be a princess, just as I once was." "Noble lady," replied the girl, "tell me what I have to do, and I will do it all to the best of my ability." "You see," said the lady, "I am a princess and I cannot find peace in my tomb because the one who killed me has not been punished. Over there in that wardrobe there are many beautiful dresses; you must put one of them on and go out onto the balcony. At around noon a nobleman will pass by and he will address you, mistaking you for me since you're wearing my dress. Answer him politely, and invite him to come up. When he is with you, keep him there with polite conversation until evening comes, and then invite him to eat with you. Take these two bottles: in one there is wine, and in the other there is a sleeping potion. When you are eating dinner, you are to pour him from the second bottle, and as soon as he falls asleep, cut the vein in his neck with this little knife, and may he die for his sins. For just as I have no peace, he must not enjoy the beatitude of life beyond, either." After saying this, the black figure disappeared and the girl remained alone.

The next morning she put on a lavish and magnificent dress and went out onto the balcony. At around noon a distinguished gentleman passed by, and seeing her at the window, said to her, "Hello, noble lady, are you better now? You were ill for a long time." "Well, yes, noble lord, I was, but I am well now. Won't you do me the honor of coming up?" And so the nobleman went up, and when he saw the other two sisters, he asked who they were. "My maids," she replied, and with the greatest graciousness she kept the nobleman there until evening. "May I also have the honor of dining with you?" she asked, and the nobleman stayed. During dinner she offered him the bottle with the sleeping potion, and when the gentleman had drunk barely a sip, he fell into a deep sleep. Then she took the little knife and cut the vein in his neck, so that he died for his sins, with neither confession nor absolution. After that, she called her sisters, and the three of them dragged him to a deep well and threw him in. At midnight the door suddenly flew open again, the black lady entered, and she said to the youngest sister, "Your courage has saved me, and now all these treasures are yours. Farewell; today is the last time I will come, because I have now found peace." As she was saying this she disappeared, and she never returned again. The three sisters stayed in the marvelous palace, and they each married a distinguished lord. And so they lived happily ever after, while here we are, just looking on.

2

Giuseppe Pitrè (1841–1916)

Giuseppe Pitrè was a physician; scholar of literature, history, and philology; and above all a towering figure in nineteenth-century folkloristics and the study of popular traditions, which he had a major role in establishing as a serious and independent discipline in Italy. He opposed a strictly aesthetic approach to folklore, maintaining that folk traditions offered precious historical and anthropological information on national heritages and the life of the people, which revealed submerged realities no less important than the master narratives of the official history of, in his words, the "dominators." His homeland of Sicily offered him an especially rich corpus of folkloric materials, which he studied and collected throughout his life. Pitrè had rigorous standards of transcription, attempting to reproduce as closely as possible his informants' language; in fact, he published the tales and other materials in the language he heard them, Sicilian dialect. At the same time as he sought to explore and make better known the riches of Sicilian culture, he also investigated the commonalities among folk cultures from around the world.

Son of a sailor from Palermo, Pitrè spent his youth in a vibrant lower-class district of the city, Borgo, where already as a young man he became interested in studying popular traditions of every sort. Later in life he held the first chair in folklore (in his terminology, "demopsychology," or "folk psychology") at the University of Palermo (1910), founded the Museo di etnografia siciliana (1909, today named for Pitrè), and became an Italian senator (1915). Pitrè was a practicing physician all of his life, which may have limited his time but also gave him the opportunity to be in close contact on a daily basis with people from every walk of life, especially from the lower classes. The horse-drawn buggy he used to make his rounds in and outside of Palermo was outfitted as a "travelling study," and it was there that he would transcribe and organize the material he collected.

The fruits of Pitrè's research are concentrated in the vast *Biblioteca delle tradizioni popolari siciliane* (Library of Popular Sicilian Traditions), published in twenty-five volumes between 1871 and 1913; the various sections comprehend traditional songs and poetry, proverbs, festivities and theatrical spectacle, children's games, customs and beliefs, legends, popular medicine, riddles, and rituals of daily life regarding the home and family. Folktales and fairy tales occupy a place of honor as volumes 4–7, published in 1875 with the title *Fiabe, novelle e racconti popolari siciliani* (Sicilian Fairy Tales, Novellas, and Popular Tales); Pitrè also compiled another important volume of Tuscan fairy tales, *Novelle popolari toscane* (Popular Tuscan Tales, 1885). He directed the sixteen-volume series *Curiosità popolari tradizionali* (Curiosities of Popular Tradition, 1885–99), whose sphere of investigation extends to all of Italy, and the *Bibliografia delle tradizioni popolari d'Italia* (Bibliography of Italian Popular Traditions, 1894); together with another important Sicilian scholar, Salvatore Salomone-Marino, Pitrè founded the journal *Archivio per lo studio delle tradizioni popolari* (Archive for the Study of Popular Traditions, 1880–1906). Pitrè was also very interested in comparative folklore. Although he rarely left Sicily, he acquired a huge storehouse of knowledge about the folkloric traditions of other nations and corresponded with many of the leading folklorists of his time, among whom he was respected and consulted.

Sicilian Fairy Tales is one of Italy's most important reservoirs of folktales and would become a precious document for later anthologists of Italian fairy tales like Italo Calvino. The collection includes three hundred folktales, divided into five sections: "common popular fairy tales" (the largest group); "jokes and anecdotes"; "historical and fantastic traditions about people and places" (legends); "proverbs and proverbial expressions, with anecdotes"; and "fables and animal tales." Pitré's principal sources for *Fairy Tales* included the lower-class oral storytellers Agatuzza Messia, Rosa Brusca, and others; approximately 60 percent of his informants were women. He transcribed the tales with relative precision (opposing his method to that of the Grimms, for instance) and for many of them offered extensive annotations, commentary, and variants.

But even if Pitrè may have doctored the tales to some extent to present Sicilian culture in a better light (for which he has sometimes been criticized), these tales, like those of Laura Gonzenbach and other collectors of the nineteenth century, depict a universe of poverty and oppression whose lower-class heroes model marvelous, and sometimes not so marvelous, strategies for survival.

Further Reading

Primary

Pitrè, Giuseppe. *Fiabe novelle e racconti popolari siciliani.* Trans. Bianca Lazzaro. Ed. and introd. Jack Zipes. 4 vols. Rome: Donzelli, 2013. 1:154–69, 398–407, 554–63, 648–58; 2:132–39; 3:590–621. [source text]

Pitrè, Giuseppe. *Catarina the Wise and other Wondrous Sicilian Folk Tales.* Ed. and trans. Jack Zipes. Chicago: University of Chicago Press, 2017.

Pitrè, Giuseppe. *The Collected Sicilian Folk and Fairy Tales of Giuseppe Pitrè.* 2 vols. Trans. and ed. Jack Zipes and Joseph Russo. New York: Routledge, 2009.

Secondary

Cocchiara, Giuseppe. "The Lesson of Pitrè." *The History of Folklore in Europe.* Trans. John N. McDaniel. Philadelphia, PA: Institute for the Study of Human Issues, 1981. 351–71.

Cocchiara, Giuseppe. *Pitré, la Sicilia e il folklore.* Messina: D'Alma, 1951.

Russo, Joseph. "The Sicilian Folk Tales of Giuseppe Pitrè." In *The Collected Sicilian Folk and Fairy Tales of Giuseppe Pitrè*, trans. and ed. Jack Zipes and Joseph Russo. 2 vols. New York: Routledge, 2009. 21–32.

Zipes, Jack. "Giuseppe Pitrè and the Great Collectors of Folk Tales in the Nineteenth Century." *The Irresistible Fairy Tale: The Cultural and Social History of a Genre.* Princeton: Princeton University Press, 2012. 109–34.

Zipes, Jack. "The Indomitable Giuseppe Pitrè." In *The Collected Sicilian Folk and Fairy Tales of Giuseppe Pitrè*, trans. and ed. Jack Zipes and Joseph Russo. 2 vols. New York: Routledge, 2009. 1–20.

The Story of "It Is Told" (Lu cunto di "Si raccunta")

This tale opens the section of Sicilian Fairy Tales, Novellas, and Popular Tales *dedicated to fairy tales and is, in a sense, a mission statement. Although the little girl of the tale (perhaps a double of Pitrè's informant, who was an eight-year-old girl) is of modest means, she has a sharp and ready wit and, most importantly, is a creative storyteller who is aware that stories need to change in order to stay alive. Her strong "revision" of tradition and refusal of the formula "It is told" lead, in fact, to her triumphant ending.*

It is told time and again that there once was a mother who lived with her daughter. The mother had a lot of chicks, and when she went to mass she would leave them in her daughter's care. One day she said to her, "Sarina, Sarina, I'm leaving you the chicks; see to it that you also sweep the house and make the bed before I return." Sarina made the bed and swept the house, and then she picked up one of the little chicks and started to look for lice and nits; underneath one of its little feathers she found a scrap of paper, which she kept for herself.

Now, there was also a merchant, and this merchant sold cloth, and since he sold cloth he was filthy rich, one of those guys who's just rolling in it, and yet he was ready to pack up his shop and give it to anyone who could tell a tale without saying, "It is told." Many people presented themselves, but they all said, "It is told," and he would win the deal. Then the little girl with the scrap of paper presented herself and said, "Sir merchant, I've come to tell you a story without saying, 'It is told.'" As soon as he heard this, the merchant said to her, "Get out of here, you snot-nosed brat! What do you know about stories that can be told without saying, 'It is told'!" And then she said,

Once upon a time there was this scrap of paper.
This scrap of paper could talk, and it said:
"Clear out, merchant; the shop is mine."

And thus the little girl became the owner of the shop, and the merchant had to leave.

She ended up happy and content
And the rest of us are here without a cent.

And that was the end of the tale.

(*Erice*)[1]

1. For each tale, Pitrè indicates the town in which he collected it.

The Slave (Lu Scavu)

This is a version of ATU 311, Rescue by the Sister, connected to the Bluebeard tale type.

Once upon a time there was a man who foraged greens for a living, and he had three daughters. The poor soul would go look for a few greens, but he couldn't even find a blade of grass, so one day he said to his daughter Rosina, "Would you like to come with me to pick some greens? Maybe if you come along I'll find some." "Yessir, I'll come along!"

When they got to the countryside, they weren't able to find a single leaf. Now, at a certain point Rosina noticed a nice mushroom, and began to tug at it. But it was impossible to dig up, since its roots went down so deep, and she had to call her father. They pulled and pulled, and after the two of them had labored for an hour, the mushroom came loose, and a slave appeared.

"What are you two doing here?" said the slave. "Ha! We've been struggling for an hour to pull this mushroom up; it just wasn't coming." "And you," said the slave to the father, "how about you leave me this beautiful daughter of yours? What would you say if she were to stay here with me and become a queen? I've got a beautiful palace down there that's a marvel to behold." The poor father said, "You're asking me? She's the one who has to decide. You, my daughter: do you want to stay with this gentleman?" "Yessir."

The slave gave her father a bag of coins, and after her father said good-bye to Rosina, she said to him, "Give my best to my sisters." "What?" said the slave to Rosina, "So you have other sisters? How many do you have?" "Two," replied Rosina. "Well, then," said the slave to the girl's father, "send those little sisters to this hole every now and then so that they can see Rosina."

The forager returned back home, and told his wife every last thing that had happened.

As soon as Rosina disappeared with the slave, she found herself in an underground palace, where there were rooms full of gold, silver, and diamonds. The slave said to her, "Listen to me carefully. If you're faithful to me, and do what I tell you, these riches will all be yours." "I'll do everything you wish," answered Rosina.

They ate and drank, and after three days the slave said, "I'm leaving now, and I'll be gone a month. I'm giving you this hand of living flesh, which you are to eat while I'm away. If you don't, you'll be in trouble!"

Unfortunate girl! She took the hand and promised that she would eat it. The slave left.

After his departure, Rosina began to look at the hand, and she grew horrified and said, "Oh boy! How am I supposed to eat this hand of living flesh?" So what did she do? She took the hand, crushed it up into tiny pieces in a mortar, and then threw it in the commode.

The slave returned. "Rosina, did you eat the hand?" "Of course I ate it!" At that, the slave said, "Hand, my little hand, where are you?" "In the commode," answered the hand. "Ah!" he said to Rosina, "So you didn't eat the hand? Take this!" And in the blink of an eye he tore her head off her neck and threw it on top of a pile of other women's heads in another room.

After some time, the father was out foraging greens when the slave appeared and said to him, "Your daughter is enjoying the best of health, and lives in a palace of gold and silver, but she would like to have one of her sisters to keep her company." "Yessir, tomorrow I'll bring my daughter Caterina." "Here, take this," said the slave, and held out a bag of coins to him.

The father returned home, told his wife everything, gave her Rosina's news, and then took Caterina and went off to do the same business.

After they arrived in the countryside and Caterina had been lowered into the enchanted hole, the slave gave her the hand and played the same tune. Caterina, poor little thing, didn't know what to do, and she gave up the ghost just like her sister had.

The forager went back to the same place, and the slave, who was worse than the Evil Tempter himself, told him that Rosina and Caterina would like the other sister, whose name was Antonia, with them. "Yessir!" replied the father, and the next day he brought Antonia. But the fact of the matter is that Antonia was as sly as a fox. When, as usual, the slave mentioned the business about the hand, and that he needed to leave, she began to plot a way to get herself out of that big mess.

So what did she do? She took the hand, crushed it up in a mortar, and put it on her stomach, like a poultice. The slave came home. "Where's the hand?" "Inside my stomach." The slave went to have a look in the commode, but he didn't see it. Then he was convinced that Antonia had eaten the hand, and he opened all the secrets of his heart to her. He gave her the keys to all of the rooms in the palace, and showed her huge quantities of treasures and riches, a marvel to behold.

When she was alone, she began to open door after door. She went into one room, and what did she see?! She saw freshly killed cadavers of rulers, emperors, princes, princesses, and many other people strewn on the ground; some were missing their heads, others their feet or their arms.

And that was nothing. In the midst of the other people, who did Antonia see? Rosina and Caterina, with their heads chopped off. "Ah, my dear little sisters, I've lost you!" But there on the ground was a little pot with something in it. Antonia took a brush, dipped it in that stuff, and smeared it on Caterina's neck. Caterina revived, and hugged Antonia; Antonia did the same thing with Rosina, and Rosina revived. And with all the hugging and kissing, it was a tender sight to see. Antonia mustered up some more courage, and revived all of the dead people, one after the other. Those dead people had lost their lives at the hand of the slave, just like the two daughters of the forager; and the incredible thing was that they never decomposed but were preserved as if they had died a moment before.

No words can describe the celebration they had once everyone was revived. People over here and over there were hugging Antonia; one of them wanted to adopt her as his daughter, another as her mother, and yet another wanted to take her for his wife; one even wanted to give her his kingdom. But meanwhile time was passing, and they all agreed that Antonia should become the wife of the prince of Portugal, and that's what happened.

Let's leave these people and go back to the slave, who when he returned to the palace and found all the rooms open, the dead people revived, and the gold coins almost completely gone, just stood there in a daze. He wanted to do something, but what could he do? There was no possible solution . . . At the end of the day, though, he was a sorcerer, and so he decided to attempt this trick. He had himself locked up in a chest, and taken off to Portugal. The man carrying the chest brought it under the windows of the royal palace, and began to shout, "Look what a nice slave! Who wants to buy him?"

The prince and princess happened to look out right at that moment. The prince said, "Antonia, shall we buy this nice slave?" It was as if Antonia's heart had spoken, but she said neither yes nor no. The prince bought the slave, and as an act of gallantry had him brought into the palace.

Night fell. The slave had locked himself in the chest from the inside, and as soon as he found himself in the princess's chamber, he opened the lock so that he could get out and cast his curse. Antonia, who was nodding off, yelled, "Hey there! Hey there!" The servants rushed in, but they didn't see anyone. After a while, there was another sound, and, "Hey there! Hey there!" But the servants didn't see anyone, because the slave wasn't moving, and he looked like a statue. The third time, Antonia took notice of the tiniest movements that the slave was making, and as soon as she yelled, "Hey there! Hey there!" she had him tied up by his hands and his feet and put in an iron cage. They sent news of this to all of the royals, who came running to Portugal so that they could torture the slave and make him pay for what that wicked dog had caused them to suffer. And they tortured the slave in acts and in words until he died. And then there were great festivities.

They lived happily ever after, as content as can be,
While here we are, still sucking on our teeth.

(*Palermo*)

Tridicinu

This is a version of ATU 328, The Boy Kills the Giant, a tale type related to Jack and the Beanstalk, which here and in many versions features a trickster hero and fickle royalty.

It is told time and again that there once was a father who had thirteen children, and the youngest was named Tridicinu—Little Thirteen. This father didn't have the means to support his children, and he tried to make ends meet by gathering soup greens. The mother would say, to get them to hurry, "Whoever gets to the table first eats their soup hot." Tridicinu was always the first to come in and always got the hot soup, and for this reason his brothers couldn't stand him, and they started looking for a way to get rid of him.

One day, the king issued a proclamation: whoever dared to go steal the quilt of Patri-Drau[1] the ogre would receive a bushel of gold pieces. Tridicinu's brothers presented themselves to the king, and said, "Your Majesty, we have a brother named Tridicinu who can do this and more." "Have him come here at once," said the king. They brought Tridicinu, and he said, "Your Majesty, how am I supposed to take the quilt from the ogre? If he sees me, he'll eat me." "No arguments; you will go!" said the king. "I know that you're courageous, and you must undertake this challenge."

Tridicinu left, and went to the house of Patri-Drau. He wasn't there, but Mamma-Dràa the ogress was in the kitchen. Tridicinu crept in, quiet as a mouse, and crawled under the bed. That evening, Patri-Drau returned. He ate and then went to bed; as he was getting into bed, he said,

I smell the flesh of a human soul;
As soon as I see him, I'll gobble him down whole!

1. Literally, "Father Dragon," but in Sicilian folklore an ogre figure.

The ogress answered, "Calm down! No one's been here!" The ogre began to snore, and Tridicinu pulled on the quilt a little. The ogre woke up: "Who's there?" And Tridicinu began to go, "Meow! Meow!" as if he were the cat. Mamma-Dràa said, "Shoo! Shoo!" and clapped her hands, and then fell asleep again, as did the ogre. Then Tridicinu gave a nice hard tug, grabbed the quilt, and ran off. The ogre heard him running, recognized him in the dark, and said, "I see you! You're Tridicinu, I'm sure of it!"

Some time went by, and the king issued another proclamation: whoever was able to steal the ogre's horse and bring it to the king would receive a bushel of gold pieces. Tridicinu presented himself again, and asked to be given a silk ladder and a bag of honey cookies. Tridicinu left with those things, and arrived at the ogre's house when it was night; he entered without making a sound, and went down to the stables. The horse whinnied when it saw him, but Tridicinu gave it a cookie and said, "See how sweet it is? If you come with me, my master will feed you these every day." Then he gave the horse another one and said, "Let me ride you, and I'll show you the way." And so he mounted the horse, fed it the cookies, and brought it to the king's stables.

Then the king issued another proclamation: he would give two bushels of gold coins to whomever could bring him the bolster from the ogre's bed. Tridicinu said, "Your Majesty, how is that supposed to happen? The bolster is covered with bells, and you know that you can't even breathe without waking up the ogre." "I know nothing of the sort," said the king. "All I know is that I want that bolster at all costs."

Tridicinu left, and crawled under the ogre's bed. At midnight he extended his hand very slowly . . . but all the bells started ringing. "Who's there?" said the ogre. "Oh, it's nothing," said Mamma-Dràa. "It's probably the wind that's making them ring." But Patri-Drau, who was suspicious, pretended to sleep and kept his ears open.

Tridicinu started to extend his hand again and . . . *bam*! The ogre extended his own arm and grabbed Tridicinu. "You're trapped now! Give me a minute and I'll make you regret the first, the second, and the third time you came here!" Then he took Tridicinu and put him in a barrel, and started to feed him raisins and figs. One day he said to him, "Tridicinu, show me a little finger so that I can see if you're fattening up." Tridicinu found a mouse tail in there, and showed that to him. "Oh, how thin you are!" said the ogre. "And stinky, too!" "Eat, my boy; take these raisins and figs, and hurry up and get fat!"

After a few days, the ogre called to him again and asked to see a little finger, and Tridicinu showed him the end of a spindle. "Ah, you wretch! Still so skinny! Eat, eat, and hurry up and get fat!"

At the end of a month, Tridicinu had nothing left to show him, and he was forced to stick out his own finger. The ogre began to shout with joy, "He's fat now! He's fat now!" Then the ogress came running, and the ogre said to her, "Hurry, my ogress, heat up the oven for three days and three nights; in the meantime I'll go invite our relations, and we'll have a fine banquet with Tridicinu!"

The ogress heated up the oven for three days and three nights, and when the three days and three nights had gone by, she let Tridicinu out of the barrel and said to him, "Come over here, Tridicinu; we have to put the lamb in the oven." But Tridicinu got a whiff of what was cooking, and as soon as he was close to the oven, he said, "Eww, Mamma-Dràa, there's something black in the corner of the oven! What is it?" The ogress put her head into the oven a little, but she didn't see anything. "Put your head in farther," said Tridicinu, "and you'll be able to see it." As soon as put her head in farther, Tridicinu pushed her by her feet and shoved her all the way into the oven, which he bolted with a plate of iron. When she was cooked, he took her out all neat and clean, cut her in half at the waist, carved up her legs into small pieces, and set them on the table. Then he arranged her torso and arms on the bed, under the sheets, and tied one string to her chin and another to the back of her head.

When the ogre arrived with his guests, they found the plates on the table. They went over to the bed and asked, "Mamma-Dràa, would you like to eat?" Tridicinu pulled one of the strings, and Mamma-Dràa raised her head to say no. "What's the matter, are you tired?" And from under the bed where he was crouching, Tridicinu pulled the other string, making her drop her head to say yes. But by chance one of the relatives happened to move the covers, and discovered that Mamma-Dràa was dead and only half there. He began to shout, "Treason! Treason!" and everyone rushed to the bed. In the midst of all the racket and confusion, Tridicinu slipped out from under the bed and took off for the king's, bringing with him the bolster and other choice riches of the ogre's.

At the sight of this, the king said to Tridicinu, "Listen, Tridicinu, as your crowning feat I want Patri-Drau to be brought here in person, alive and kicking." "How am I supposed to do that, Your Majesty?" replied Tridicinu, but then he cheered up and said, "I'll take care of this!" He had a nice strong crate built, and then dressed up like a monk with a fake beard that went almost down to his feet and climbed the hill until he was right next to the ogre's house. When he arrived, he began to shout, calling out to the ogre, "Do you know Tridicinu? That scoundrel! He killed our Father Guardian, but if I get my hands on him . . . If I get my hands on him, I'm going to lock him up in this crate!"

When he heard that, the ogre went over and said, "And I'm going to help you find that scoundrel, that murderer; if you only knew the joke he pulled on me." And he started telling him the story. "But what should we do?" said the fake monk, "I don't know what Tridicinu looks like. Do you?" "You bet I do." "Well, then, Patri-Drau, tell me, how tall is he?" "As tall as I am." "If that's the case, then let's see if you fit into this crate," said Tridicinu, the fake monk, "because if you fit, then he will, too." "That's right!" said the ogre, and he got into the crate. Then Tridicinu shut the crate and said, "Make sure, Patri-Drau, that there aren't any holes." "No, there aren't any." "Wait a minute, let's see if it closes up tight, and how heavy it is to carry."

And meanwhile, Tridicinu nailed the crate shut, loaded it onto his back, and ran back to the city. And when the ogre said, "Enough; that's enough now!" Tridicinu began to run even faster, and, laughing, he sang this song, to spite the ogre:

It's me, Tridicinu—and don't give me flak—
The one and only, carrying you on my back;
Yes, once again I've got you on a string,
And now it's time to turn you over to the king!

When they reached the king's, the king had the ogre shackled, hand and foot, in iron chains, and left him to waste his bones away for the rest of his miserable life. Then he gave Tridicinu all the riches and treasures that he could possibly give him, and for the rest of his life he wanted him at his side, seeing as he was a brave fellow of the very first rank.

They lived happily ever after, as content as can be,
While here we are, still sucking on our teeth.

(*Borgetto*)

The Little Mouse with the Stinky Tail (Lu surciteddu cu la coda fitusa)

This is another example of the 425 tale group, here including ATU 425D, The Vanished Husband, and ATU 425A, The Animal as Bridegroom.

It has been told that there once was a king, and this king had a beautiful daughter, more beautiful than words could describe. The daughter received many attractive marriage proposals from rulers and emperors, but her father didn't want to give her away to anyone, because every night he heard a voice that said, "Don't allow your daughter to marry!" The poor girl would look in the mirror and say, "How is this possible? I'm so very beautiful, and I can't get married!" She couldn't resign herself to this fate.

One day while they were all at the table, the daughter said to the king, "Father, how is it possible that I'm so beautiful and I can't get married? Let me be very clear: I want to get married!" "My daughter," replied the king, "I can't very well force people to marry you!" "No matter, father; I'll give you two days' time: if in these two days you don't find me a match, I'll kill myself." "If that's how it is," said the king to her, "this is what you need to do: today you'll put on your finest clothes, and the first one who passes by and looks at you, you'll take for your husband."

That's what the daughter did, and as she was at the window a little mouse with a long stinky tail passed by. And as it passed by it looked at her. When the king's daughter realized it was looking at her, she ran inside screaming and crying, "Father, if only you knew! A mouse just ran by and looked at me. Does that mean that I have to take him as my husband?" "Yes, my daughter. What did I tell you? That you'd have to take the first one that passed by for your husband."

Between the daughter saying no and her father saying yes, the next day arrived. The king wrote to all the princes and court dignitaries and invited them to a banquet in celebration of his daughter's impending marriage. All of the guests arrived, and sat down at the table. In the middle of the meal they heard someone knocking at the door, and who was it? The little mouse with the stinky tail. A waiter went to open the door, and when he saw the mouse he said, "What do you want?"

"Tell the king that the mouse who is to marry the princess has arrived." The waiters laughed and made fun of him, and went to tell the king, who ordered that the mouse be shown in. As soon as he came in, the little mouse ran over and sat down next to the princess.

When the poor girl saw him next to her, she moved away in disgust, but the little mouse came even closer, as if her gesture had nothing to do with him. The king told his guests the whole story, and the guests said, laughing, "Perfect! That's just perfect! The little mouse is going to be the princess's husband!"

The next day there was another great feast, and in the middle of the meal, knock, knock: it was the little mouse, who went and sat down next to the princess. All the guests started to snicker, but the little mouse noticed; he called the king aside and told him to warn everyone at the table not to laugh, or else there would be a big stink. The mouse was little and couldn't eat sitting on a chair, so he had to sit in the middle of the table, and no one was to utter a word.

Among the guests at the banquet there was a very fussy lady. When the first course arrived, the mouse began to go from plate to plate; the lady was suffering, but didn't say anything. The second course arrived, and the same thing happened; when they got to the third course, she lashed out at the mouse and began to hurl abuse. When the mouse saw that he was being mistreated in this way, he flew into a rage, and began to jump from one guest's face to another; and in the midst of all the commotion, the table, the guests, the palace, and everything else suddenly disappeared, and found themselves dispersed, some here and some there, across a great plain.

Let's leave the others, now, and return to the princess. When she found herself alone on that plain she began to cry and said, "Ah, my little mouse! Even if I didn't want you then, I desire you now!" And she kept on repeating this same thing. As she was walking, in the hands of God and fortune, she met a hermit, who asked her, "What are you doing here, my dear girl, all by yourself among all these animals? Be careful; if you run into an ogress or a lion, you'll fare poorly!"

She replied, "None of that matters to me. I have to find my little mouse. I drove him away before, but now I desire him . . . Ah! My little mouse, where are you?" The hermit said, "You know what I say? Turn back and go home; otherwise you're going to get yourself killed." "What do I care about that? Whether I end up dead or alive, I've got to find my little mouse." "Ah, my girl, you have a long way to go if you want to find him! But I'll tell you what you have to do: keep on walking, and you'll meet another hermit older than me, and he'll tell you where to go."

Then the girl said goodbye and moved on, always repeating the same tune: "Ah, my little mouse, where are you?" While she was walking, she met an old geezer with a white beard that was so long it went all the way down to his feet. She was scared, but he said to her, "Don't be scared. I'm of Christian blood, same as you. Where are you going?" "I'm looking for the little mouse with the stinky tail." The hermit said to her, "Listen; this is what you have to do: dig a hole underground the same size as you are, then crawl into it and see what happens."

The poor thing didn't have anything to make the hole with, so she took out her hairpin and began to dig. She dug and dug until she made a nice big hole; then she crawled into the hole and disappeared. As soon as she was in there, she saw a huge underground vault. "Let's hope for good luck and fortune!" she said, finding herself in the dark, and she started walking.

All the spiderwebs that fell onto her face! For each one that she brushed away, a hundred more covered her; once so beautiful, she now turned as black as smoke.

After walking nonstop for a day, she heard the sound of water. She went over and saw a sort of pool, full of water. She wanted to see if she could cross it, but the pool was too deep, and she began to cry, saying over and over again, "Ah, my little mouse! I so desire you!" She couldn't move forward. Nor could she go back, because the hole had closed up, and so she cried and cried.

Then she saw some water spigots above her. "What do I do now? If I'm not dead yet, I'm surely going to die now!" And as soon as she said this, she heard a voice that said, "Why are you whining like that? You're breaking my ears. Throw yourself into that pool, and we'll see what happens when you get out." Since there was nothing else she could do, she threw herself in, and as soon as she was in the water she found herself in a huge palace, a true wonder to behold. She entered the first room and found it full of crystal; she entered the second room and found it full of velvet; she entered the third room and it was made of solid gold, with sofas and lamps such as she had never seen. She walked on and on; she forgot where she had entered, and lost her way: the palace was so big! When she saw that she was lost, she said, "Ah, my little mouse! What should I do?" Then she heard a voice that said, "Your wish is my command!" "I'd like to eat!" And there in front of her was a beautifully set table, with a big plate of pasta and other dishes that would have enticed even someone with no appetite. The poor girl, ravenous with hunger, threw herself on the food. But the funny thing was that she couldn't see anyone, and yet the dishes came and went without anyone carrying them.

After this she found herself inside a carriage, in a garden, and all around her there were so many beautiful things, but she couldn't understand where they had come from. In the evening she found a nice bed, and lay down. At midnight she heard a noise, and saw a little mouse approaching the bed. The poor girl was frightened and was shaking like a leaf because she didn't know who it was, and she prayed for the Lord's help, reciting Hail Marys and Our Fathers.

The next day she didn't see anyone. "Boy, a lot of strange things happened last night!" she said to herself, and carried on. The next night while she was sleeping she heard a noise. Who was it? There was no way to know. The third night, at the stroke of midnight, a mouse appeared—*pitter-patter, pitter-patter*—and began to dance. "Ah, Mother of God, this racket again! Come on, who is it that's making all this racket?" "Who is it? Light the lamp and you'll see." The poor girl got out of bed, lit the candle, and who did she see? A handsome young man! "I am the little mouse with the stinky tail. Because of a spell cast on me by some fairies, I was turned into a little mouse, and needed a girl to fall in love with me and endure the suffering that you have endured for the spell to be broken. Now that you have come all the way here, without disgust for me, I can return to my human form."

Just imagine how happy she was! Then they came up from underground and were immediately engaged and then married.

They lived happily ever after, as content as can be,
While here we are, still sucking on our teeth.

(*Palermo*)

The Ogress (La Mammadràa)

This is an example of ATU 480, The Kind and the Unkind Girls, in its simplest form, a tale that due to its clear moral message has been widely present since the medieval period. In this and other tales by Pitrè, the most marvelous realms lie in close contact with mundane village landscape and bleak everyday routines. In the wish-fulfillment fantasy of this tale, dumping garbage down a well leads to a radical change in fortune; in others (such as "The Slave"), the promise of fantastically lavish realms lies under a foraged vegetable.

Once upon a time there was a mother who had a daughter named Rosina. One day she said to her, "Rosina, Rosina, take the pail and go throw out the garbage." The little girl took the garbage pail and went to throw it out. There was a well nearby, and she went to throw the garbage in this well. But as she was throwing the garbage in, she dropped the pail.

The little girl had heard that Mammadràa the ogress lived in that well, and so she said, "Mammadràa, give me the garbage pail." Mammadràa answered, "Come down; come down and get it for yourself." "No; you'll eat me," said the little girl. "No I won't; I swear on the little soul of my son Cola that I won't eat you." "How am I supposed to get down there?" "Put one foot here, one foot there, and come down."

The little girl went down, since she was afraid that her mother would beat her if she didn't bring the garbage pail back. When she appeared in front of Mammadràa, the ogress gave her a big hug. "Oh, what a pretty girl you are, my dear Rosina, so pretty! Sweep my house." The little girl set to work sweeping. "What do you see in this house?" "A little bit of dirt, a little bit of trash, just like in other people's houses." "Take a look at my head. What do you see on this head?" The little girl began to look, and said, "A few little lice, a few little nits, just like on other people's heads." "Take a look at this bed. What do you see in this bed?" "A few little bedbugs, a few little fleas, just like in other people's beds." "What a lovely girl you are, Rosina! May a star sprout on your forehead, a star so splendid that it makes all who look at you lower their eyes. What a lovely head you have! May your head sprout hair like golden thread, and when you comb your hair, may diamonds and pearls fall from one side of your hair, and grains of wheat and gold from the other!"

Then she took her into a room where there were old clothes and new clothes. She started with the stockings, one pair that was pretty and one that was ugly. "Which of these would you like?" Rosina said that she wanted the ugly pair. "And I want to give you the nice pair," said the ogress. Then on to a blouse; and she chose the most ragged one. Then the dress; she wanted the oldest one, and the ogress gave her the newest one. Then other things, until she was dressed in so many beautiful, brand-new clothes that she looked like a German doll. Last, she gave her a nice bundle of money, and they said goodbye.

When Rosina's mother saw her, she said, "Oh, how wonderful! How did you get like that?" And Rosina told her all about what had happened. Now, you know how it is with neighbors! One of the women began to ask her about all those things, and Rosina's mother recited the whole story, chapter and verse.

This neighbor had a daughter who was as ugly as a knife slash, and she said to her, "You listen to your mother, now: do you see how many things Mammadràa gave to Rosina? Go throw away the garbage like she did, then throw the pail in the well and try to get Mammadràa to give it back to you."

And that's what she did. She took the garbage pail and threw it straight into the well along with the garbage. "Mammadràa, Mammadràa, give me back my pail!" "Come down; come down and get it for yourself." Without needing to be asked twice, she went down into the well. Mammadràa asked her to sweep, and then asked her, "What do you see in this house?" The girl replied, "Foul trash, foul dirt, just like in other people's houses." "Take a look at my head. What do you see on this head?" "Disgusting lice, disgusting nits, just like on other people's heads." "Make this bed; tell me, what do you see in this bed?" "Nasty bedbugs and nasty fleas, just like in other people's beds." "How awful you are!" said Mammadràa to her. "May your forehead sprout a stinking horn; may cow dung fall from one side of your hair, and stinking excrement from the other!" Imagine how this cheered the girl up!

Then Mammadràa led her into a room where there were old clothes and new clothes; she showed her the stockings, and said, "Which of these two do you want?" "Which do I want? The nice ones!" "And I want to give you the ugly ones!" Then she showed her the blouses: the same thing; then the dresses: again the same, until she had dressed the girl like a kitchen wench. Last, she slapped her and said, "Get out of here," and the girl climbed out of the well.

As soon as her mother saw her come to the surface, she said, "Oh, boy, oh boy! How did this happen?" "It was Mammadràa." Then the two neighbors had a falling out, but Rosina's mother ended up rich, and the other one, ugly and dirt poor. And that's how the Lord punishes malicious envy.

(*Palermo*)

Giufà Tales

The figure of Giufà, who has his own cycle of tales, is found in many regions of Italy, often under slightly different names; in Tuscany, for example, he is Giucca. He is thought to have Arab origins in the Turkish folk character of Nasrudin (or Nasreddin) and to have put down roots in Sicily during the centuries when it was under Arab occupation. Giufà interprets reality in a childlike, absolutely literal way, which often leads to the difficult predicaments he finds himself in. Because of his lack of the ability to dissimulate, though, he is also able to illuminate the foibles and hypocrisies of human behavior, as, for example, in "Eat, Little Clothes of Mine." "Giufà and the Plaster Statue" is a version of ATU 1643, Money Inside the Statue, and is also found in Basile ("Vardiello").

Giufà and the Plaster Statue
(Giufà e la statua di ghissu)

It is told that there was once a mother who had a son named Giufà; the mother was poor and Giufà was an idiot, a lazybones, and a troublemaker. The mother had a little piece of cloth that she had set aside, and she said to Giufà, "Let's get that piece of cloth; you'll go and sell it in a far-off town to one of those people who doesn't talk too much." Giufà put the cloth on his back and went off to sell it.

When he arrived in a town, he would start shouting, "Who wants some cloth?" People called out to him, and had all sorts of things to talk about: one said the cloth seemed heavy, another that it seemed expensive. Giufà thought that they were all talking too much, and so he decided not to sell it to anyone. And so he walked here and there until he slipped into a courtyard where there was nothing but a plaster statue. Giufà said to it, "Do you want to buy this cloth?" and the statue didn't answer. When Giufà saw that it wasn't doing much talking, he said, "You sure don't talk much, which means I should sell the cloth to you." And he took the cloth and put it on top of the statue. "I'll be back tomorrow to get the money," he said, and left.

At the break of day, Giufà went back to get the money, but the cloth wasn't there. He said to the statue, "Give me the money for the cloth," but the statue didn't say anything. "Well, if you won't give me the money, I'll show you who I am." Giufà borrowed a nice big hoe and came back and began to strike the statue, until he knocked it to the ground and it broke open. Then he found a jug full of coins in its belly. He put the coins in his pouch, and went back to his mother. As soon as he arrived home, he said, "I sold the cloth to someone who didn't talk, but last night he wouldn't pay me for it. Then this morning I went back with a hoe, and knocked him to the ground and killed him; and he gave me this money." His mother, who was a clever woman, said, "Don't you breathe a word about this, and we'll just spend the money a little bit at a time."

(*Casteltermini*)

Giufà and the Judge (Giufà e lu Judici)

It is told that one morning Giufà went to pick some fennel, and ended up getting back to the village late that night. Along the road he ran into Moon, who was clouded over, and would appear and disappear. Giufà sat on a rock and watched the Moon appear and disappear, and when it appeared he would say, "Come out, come out," and when it disappeared he would say, "Get out of here, get out of here," and he just kept on repeating, "Come out, come out! Get out of here, get out of here!"

Meanwhile, at the end of the road there were two thieves who were quartering a calf they had just stolen, and when they heard the words "Come out! Get out of here!" they were afraid the cops were coming, and they ran off, leaving the meat there. When Giufà saw the two thieves running away, he went over to see what was going on, and found the quartered calf; he took his knife, began to cut up the meat, and then filled his sack and left.

When he got home, he called out, "Mama, open up!" "Why are you coming back so late at night?" his mother asked. "I'm coming back at night because I've brought you some meat, and tomorrow you can go and sell it all, since I could use the money." His mother said, "Tomorrow you go back to the fields and I'll go sell the meat." When morning came, Giufà went off to the fields and his mother went to sell the meat.

That evening Giufà came back, and said, "Mama, did you sell the meat?" "Yes, I gave it to some flies on credit." "And when are they going to give you the money?" "As soon as they have it." Eight days went by, but the flies weren't bringing any money. Giufà went off to see the judge and said to him, "Lord judge, I want justice. I gave the meat to some flies on credit and they haven't paid me yet." The judge said, "My ruling is: when you see them, you may kill them." At that very moment a fly landed on the judge's own head, and Giufà gave him a punch and broke the judge's head.

(*Casteltermini*)

Eat, Little Clothes of Mine! (Manciati, rubbiceddi mei!)

Because Giufà was a real half-wit, no one was very friendly toward him or thought of inviting him to their homes or offering him food. Once Giufà went to a farm, in the hopes that they would give him something. But when the people there saw what a ragamuffin he was, they came close to siccing their dogs on him, and in any case they sent him back more crooked than straight. When his mother realized what had happened, she got him a nice jacket, a pair of trousers, and a velvet waistcoat. Then Giufà, dressed like a prosperous farmer, returned to the same farm, and you should have seen what a big fuss they made! They invited him to have dinner with them, and at the table, they all treated him like the guest of honor. And even if Giufà could neither read nor write, every time they passed him a full dish he would fill his belly with one hand, and with the other hand put what was left into his pockets, his cap, and his jacket. And with each thing he stowed away, he would say, "Eat, my little clothes, since you're the real guests!"

(*Palermo*)

Giufà, Pull the Door! (Giufà, tìrati la porta!)

Once Giufà's mother went to mass and said, "Giufà, I'm going to mass; pull the door behind me!" After his mother went out, Giufà took hold of the door and started pulling. He pulled and pulled and pulled so hard that the door came off its hinges. Then Giufà loaded it onto his back and went to the church, where he put it down in front of his mother. "Here's the door!" What a thing to do!

(*Palermo*)

Giufà and the Thieves (Giufà e li latri)

Once, while he was walking through the deserted countryside, Giufà had to pass water. As soon as he was done—you know how it is when you piss, it trickles down and makes lots of little streams—Giufà looked at those little streams and said, "You go this way, you go that way, you go this way (he was talking to the pee), and I'll go that way," and then set off again.

There was a grotto right down below, where a band of thieves was splitting up some loot. When they heard that talk, they said, "Ah, may Saint Dismas, the Good Thief, help us! The cops are coming to get us, they're surrounding us!" and they ran away, leaving the money behind. Giufà went down there, saw the large quantity of money, and without a word, took it for himself.

(*Palermo*)

3

Carlo Collodi (1826–90)

The Italian writer and journalist Carlo Collodi authored the children's novel *Le avventure di Pinocchio* (*The Adventures of Pinocchio*, 1881–83), one of the most widely read and beloved books in the world.

Collodi was born Carlo Lorenzini in Florence to a family of modest means. His parents hailed from a small town in Tuscany called Collodi, which provided Lorenzini with his pseudonym. Collodi was educated in a seminary but as a young man left the religious life to work at an important bookstore in Florence, where he immersed himself in the cultural humus of the city. Soon after he became active in the Risorgimento, the movement for Italian unification, and fought in the First and Second Wars of Independence in 1848 and 1859. After 1848 Collodi took a job as a civil servant and embarked on his career as journalist and writer, founding newspapers such as *Il Lampione*, dedicated to political satire, and producing novels and comedies.

Collodi's first official encounter with fairy tales came in 1875, when the Florentine publisher Paggi commissioned him to translate a small collection of early French tales by Charles Perrault and others, issued as *I racconti delle fate* (Tales of Fairies). In 1877 Collodi reworked a children's book character created several decades earlier in *Giannettino*, whose exuberant and mischievous hero in some way previews Pinocchio, and in 1878 continued his adventures in *Minuzzolo*. From 1880 to 1890 these characters appeared in nine more books for use in elementary schools. Collodi returned to experimentation with fairy-tale and fantastic material after *Pinocchio* as well, in

1887, with *Pipì o lo scimmiottino color di rosa* (*The Adventures of Pipi, the Pink Monkey*).

In 1881 the children's weekly *Giornale per i bambini* asked Collodi for a story to be published in installments. Featuring a wily wooden puppet and originally called *La storia di un burattino (The Story of a Puppet)*, it ran from July to October 1881 and ended after what is now chapter 15 of the complete work. But Collodi was persuaded to take up his tale again in a series of new chapters, with the title *Le avventure di Pinocchio*, from February 1882 to January 1883. Later in 1883 the complete *Pinocchio* was published in a single volume, with pen-and-ink illustrations by Enrico Mazzanti. Before Collodi's death, four more editions followed.

The late nineteenth century was a pivotal moment in the history of children's literature and in the history of Italy. Drawing on the emergence of the study of folk traditions earlier in the century and the editions and collections of folktales and fairy tales that resulted, much children's writing of the time, like *Pinocchio*, incorporated fairy-tale themes and motifs in highly innovative ways. Moreover, *Pinocchio* arrived shortly after Italian Unification (1860), and in light of Collodi's earlier experiences as a patriot and experiments with pedagogical literature, *Pinocchio* can be read as a somewhat ironic bildungsroman for the new Italian subject—what he must undergo, the lessons he must learn, and, ultimately, the sacrifices he must make in order to become a "proper" member of society.

Collodi's original chapters begin with Pinocchio's "birth" from a piece of wood to the wood-carver Geppetto and are structured as a cautionary tale along the lines of Little Red Riding Hood. The puppet immediately engages in every sort of mischief and is ultimately paid for these wrongdoings at the end of chapter 15, when he is hanged and left for dead, victim of his own unruly ingenuousness. It was on this dark note that Collodi had intended to end Pinocchio's story before he was convinced by his enthusiastic young readers to continue it for another twenty chapters.

In chapter 16 Pinocchio is revived, and his cycles of transgression and redemption resume. The Blue Fairy, a fairy godmother figure who also takes on the role of sister and mother, assumes an ever larger part in Pinocchio's reform, in which he is put to various tests as he traverses landscapes both fantastic and real. When Pinocchio finally realizes the advantages of changing his ways and in chapter 36 becomes a boy, his transformation has less the flavor of a utopian happily ever after than that of a coming of age in a harsh and all too familiar world.

The interplay between the everyday and the marvelous, fairy-tale expectations and brutal reality, emerges in the very first lines of *Pinocchio* and persists as Pinocchio encounters impoverished Tuscan peasants and thinly veiled representatives of contemporary institutions but also talking animals and magical helpers, all in a story that shares a basic structure not only with fairy stories but also with the nineteenth-century novel. Physical hardships like hunger, cold, and the threat of death punctuate Pinocchio's adventures, in a world where indifference and injustice reign; even his adoptive family of Geppetto and the Blue Fairy cannot always guarantee him a safe haven.

Collodi's vision is thus ambivalent. Pinocchio's struggles between transgression and conformity, anarchic vitality and respect of the social compact, reflect the instinctive anxiety that all of us feel about maturing in an imperfect world and the uncertainty, at the end, about determining who the puppets really are. As the great critic Benedetto Croce once commented, "The wood from which Pinocchio is carved is humanity itself."

Pinocchio has enjoyed phenomenal success. It has been translated into over a hundred languages, seen many theatrical and cinematic incarnations (such as Walt Disney's animated film of 1940, Roberto Benigni's live-action version of 2002, and another live-action film by Matteo Garrone in 2019), and been rewritten, extended, and otherwise reworked in countless ways. There is a veritable industry of Pinocchio gadgets and toys and even a sculpture theme park dedicated to him in the town of Collodi. Over the past half century, studies and conferences on Pinocchio have proliferated, as have critical interpretations ranging from the theological to the psychoanalytic to the politico-historical, further proof of the irresistible appeal that Pinocchio continues to wield, for young and old alike.

Further Reading

Primary

Collodi, Carlo (Carlo Lorenzini). *Le avventure di Pinocchio.* Ed. Ornella Castellani Pollidori. Pescia: Fondazione Nazionale Carlo Collodi, 1983. [source text]

Collodi, Carlo. *The Adventures of Pinocchio.* Bilingual edition. Ed. and trans. Nicolas Perella. Berkeley: University of California Press, 1986.

Collodi, Carlo. *The Adventures of Pinocchio: Story of a Puppet*. Intro. and trans. Nancy Canepa. South Royalton, VT: Steerforth Press, 2002.

Secondary

Asor Rosa, Alberto. "Le avventure di Pinocchio. Storia di un burattino." In *Letteratura italiana. Le opere III: Dall'Ottocento al Novecento*, ed. Alberto Asor Rosa. Turin: Einaudi, 1995. 879–950.

Cro, Stelio. "Collodi: When Children's Literature Becomes Adult." *Merveilles et Contes* 7, no. 1 (1993): 87–112.

Perella, Nicolas J. "An Essay on *Pinocchio*." *Italica* 63, no. 1 (1986): 1–47.

Sherberg, Michael, ed. *Approaches to Teaching Collodi's Pinocchio and Its Adaptations*. New York: Modern Language Association of America, 2006.

Wunderlich, Richard, and Thomas J. Morrissey. *Pinocchio Goes Postmodern: Perils of a Puppet in the United States*. New York: Routledge, 2002.

From *Le avventure di Pinocchio* (*The Adventures of Pinocchio*)

1. How it came about that Master Cherry, a carpenter, found a piece of wood that cried and laughed like a little child.

Once upon a time there was . . .

"A king!" my little readers will immediately say.

No, children, you're wrong. Once upon a time there was a piece of wood.

It wasn't anything valuable, just a simple piece of wood that you might find on a woodpile, like what you put in stoves and fireplaces in the winter to light a fire and heat your rooms.

I don't know how it happened, but the fact of the matter is that one fine day this piece of wood turned up in the workshop of an old carpenter whose name was Master Antonio, although everyone called him Master Cherry on account of the tip of his nose, which was always shiny and purple, like a ripe cherry.

As soon as Master Cherry saw that piece of wood he cheered right up, and, rubbing his hands together out of happiness, he muttered under his breath,

"This wood has turned up at the right moment; I'm going to use it to make a table leg."

No sooner said than done: he got his sharpened hatchet and prepared to remove the bark and whittle down the wood. But just as he was about to strike the first blow he stopped himself with his arm suspended in the air, because he heard a tiny little voice that was pleading,

"Don't hit me so hard!"

Imagine how surprised good old Master Cherry was!

His confused eyes roamed the room, trying to figure out where that little voice might have come from, but he saw no one. He looked under his workbench—no one; he looked in a cupboard that was always kept closed—no one; he looked in the basket of wood shavings and sawdust—no one; he opened the door of his workshop and had a look at the street, too—no one. Well, then?

"I see," he said, laughing and scratching his wig. "I guess I must have imagined that little voice. Let's get back to work now."

He picked the hatchet back up and struck the wood with an almighty blow.

"Ouch! You hurt me!" yelled the same little voice, in an afflicted tone.

This time Master Cherry was left speechless. His eyes bulged with fear, his mouth hung wide open, and his tongue dangled down to his chin; he looked like a gargoyle on a fountain.

As soon as he was able to form words again, he began to speak, shaking and stuttering with fright:

"Where did that little voice that said *ouch!* come from? There's not a living soul in here. Could it be that this piece of wood has learned to cry and whine like a little child? I can't believe that. Here it is: a piece of firewood, the same as any other; throw it on the fire and it'll boil a pot of beans. . . . Well, then? Could there be someone hiding inside? If there's someone's hiding in there, all the worse for him. I'll straighten him out!"

And as he was saying this he grabbed that poor piece of wood with both hands and began to slam it against the walls of the room without mercy.

Then he stopped to listen, to hear if there was any little voice whining. He waited two minutes—nothing; five minutes—nothing; ten minutes—nothing!

"I see," he said, then, forcing himself to laugh and ruffling his wig. "I guess I must have imagined that little voice that said *ouch!* Let's get back to work now."

And because he had had such a great fright, he tried singing under his breath, to muster up some courage.

In the meantime he put his hatchet to one side and took up his plane, intending to plane and polish the piece of wood; but while he was planing it up and down he heard the same little voice say, laughing,

"Stop! You're tickling my stomach!"

This time poor Master Cherry fell down as if struck by lightning. When he opened his eyes again, he found himself sitting on the ground.

His face appeared disfigured, and even the tip of his nose, which was almost always purple, had become blue from the great fright that he had had.

2. Master Cherry gives the piece of wood to his friend Geppetto, who takes it with the intention of making a marvelous puppet who can dance, fence, and do flips.

At that very moment there was a knock at the door.

"Come on in," said the carpenter, without having the strength to get to his feet.

Then into the workshop came a sprightly little old man by the name of Geppetto, although when the neighborhood boys wanted to make him really mad they would call him by the nickname of Polendina, because of his yellow wig that looked very much like corn polenta.

Geppetto was quite a cantankerous fellow. God forbid you call him Polendina! He would become a brute, just like that, and then there was no restraining him.

"Good day, Master Antonio," said Geppetto. "What are you doing there on the ground?"

"I'm teaching the ants some arithmetic."

"Much good may it do you!"

"What has brought you here, Geppetto, my friend?"

"My legs. You should know, Master Antonio, that I've come to ask you a favor."

"Well here I am, ready to serve you," replied the carpenter, getting up on his knees.

"This morning I came up with an idea."

"Let's hear."

"I thought I'd make myself a nice wooden puppet—a marvelous puppet, though, one who can dance, fence, and do flips. I plan to travel the world with this puppet and earn my crust of bread and glass of wine by him. What do you think?"

"Bravo, Polendina!" yelled the same little voice, which was coming from who knows where.

When he heard himself called Polendina, Master Geppetto had a fit of rage and grew red as a pepper. Turning to the carpenter, he said to him, furiously,

"Why are you insulting me?"

"Who's insulting you?"

"You called me Polendina!"

"That wasn't me."

"Don't tell me that it was me, then! I say it was you."

"No!"

"Yes!"

"No!"

"Yes!"

And as they got more and more fired up, they went from words to actions, and then they started to fight, scratching, biting, and roughing each other up.

When the combat was over, Master Antonio found Geppetto's yellow wig in his hand, and Geppetto realized that he had the carpenter's salt-and-pepper wig in his mouth.

"Give me back my wig!" yelled Master Antonio.

"You give me back mine, and then we'll make up."

Once each of them had gotten back his own wig, the two little old men shook hands and swore they'd stay good friends for the rest of their lives.

"So, Geppetto, my friend," said the carpenter as a token of the peace they had made, "what's the favor you want to ask me?"

"I'd like a bit of wood to make my puppet. Can you give me some?"

Master Antonio was very happy to do so, and went straight to his workbench to get the piece of wood that had given him such a fright. But just as he was about to hand it over to his friend, the piece of wood gave a sudden jerk, wriggled violently out of his hands, and went banging against poor Geppetto's scrawny shins.

"Ah! So these are the manners you use when you give your things away, Master Antonio? You almost crippled me!"

"I swear it wasn't me!"

"Don't tell me that it was me!"

"It's all the fault of this piece of wood . . ."

"I know that it's the wood, but you're the one who threw it at my legs!"

"It wasn't me who threw it!"

"Liar!"

"Don't insult me, Geppetto, or I'll call you Polendina!"

"Ass!"

"Polendina!"

"Donkey!"

"Polendina!"

"Ugly old ape!"

"Polendina!"

When he heard himself called Polendina for the third time, Geppetto lost his wits and rushed at the carpenter, and then they gave each other a sound beating.

When the battle was over, Master Antonio discovered two new scratches on his nose, and the other fellow two fewer buttons on his jacket. Once they had thus squared their accounts, they shook hands and swore they'd stay good friends for the rest of their lives.

And finally, Geppetto took his precious piece of wood, thanked Master Antonio, and limped back home.

3. After returning home, Geppetto immediately starts making the puppet, and gives him the name of Pinocchio. The puppet's first mischief.

Geppetto's house was a little room on the ground floor that got its light from a stairwell. The furnishings couldn't have been simpler: a battered chair, a dilapidated bed, and a broken-down little table. On the back wall you could see a fireplace with a fire burning; but the fire was painted, and near the fire there was a pot, also painted, that boiled cheerfully and sent forth a cloud of steam that looked just like real steam.

As soon as he entered the house, Geppetto picked his tools right up and began to carve and shape his puppet.

"What name shall I give him?" he said to himself. "I'll call him Pinocchio; that's a name that will bring him good luck. Once I knew a whole family of Pinocchios: the father was a Pinocchio, the mother was a Pinocchia, and the children were Pinocchios, and they all managed pretty well. The richest of them was a beggar."

When he had found a name for his puppet, he got down to work, and he quickly made the hair, then the forehead, and then the eyes.

Once the eyes were done, imagine his astonishment when he realized that they were moving and staring at him intently.

When he saw those two wooden eyes staring at him, Geppetto felt a bit offended and said in a resentful tone,

"Naughty wooden eyes, why are you looking at me?"

No one answered.

Then, after the eyes, he made the puppet a nose, but as soon as the nose was done it started to grow. And it grew and grew until in a few minutes it became so long that you could barely see the end of it.

Poor Geppetto wore himself out trying to cut it back, but the more he chopped at it and tried to cut it back, the longer that impertinent nose became.

After the nose, he made the puppet a mouth.

Before the mouth was even finished, it started right up laughing and making fun of Geppetto.

"Cut out that laughing!" said Geppetto, in a huff, but it was like talking to the wall.

"Cut out that laughing, I said!" he shouted in a threatening voice.

At that the voice stopped laughing, but it stuck out its entire tongue.

Geppetto pretended not to notice so that he wouldn't ruin what he was doing, and continued to work. After the mouth, he made the chin, then the neck, then the shoulders, the stomach, the arms, and the hands.

As soon as he had finished the hands, Geppetto felt his wig being removed from his head. He looked up, and what did he see? He saw his yellow wig in the hands of the puppet.

"Pinocchio! Give me back my wig this minute!"

But instead of giving him back the wig, Pinocchio put it on his own head and was nearly smothered by it.

That insolent and derisory conduct made Geppetto more sad and melancholy than he had ever been in his life, and, turning to Pinocchio, he said:

"You scoundrel of a son! You're not even finished, and you're already starting to be disrespectful to your father! That's bad, my boy, bad!"

And he dried off a tear.

The legs and the feet still remained to be made.

When Geppetto had finished making the feet, he felt a kick land on the tip of his nose.

"I deserve it!" he said to himself. "I should have thought of this before! But it's too late now!"

Then he took the puppet under the arms and placed him on the ground, on the floor of the room, so that he could start walking.

Pinocchio's legs were stiff and he didn't know how to move, so Geppetto led him by the hand and taught him how to take one step after another.

Once he had stretched his legs, Pinocchio began to walk by himself and then to race around the room, until finally he slipped out the door, jumped into the street, and started to run away.

Poor Geppetto chased after him, but he wasn't able to reach him because that rascal Pinocchio was leaping along like a hare; and the beating of his wooden feet on the pavement of the street made as much racket as twenty pairs of peasants' clogs.

"Grab him! Grab him!" shouted Geppetto; but when the people in the street saw that wooden puppet running along like a racehorse, they stopped in amazement to stare at him, and they laughed and laughed and laughed so hard that it was beyond all imagination.

At last—and lucky it was—a carabiniere happened to pass by. Hearing all the uproar, he thought that perhaps a colt had broken away from its master, and he planted himself courageously in the middle of the street with his legs wide apart, his mind set on stopping it and preventing any greater mishaps.

But when, at a certain distance, Pinocchio caught sight of the carabiniere barricading the whole street, he came up with the bright idea of surprising him by slipping between his legs. The idea was, however, a fiasco.

Without budging an inch, the carabiniere caught him cleanly by the nose (and it was an exorbitantly large nose, which seemed to have been made for the express purpose of being grabbed by carabinieri), and delivered him back into the very hands of Geppetto, who, as punishment, wanted to give his ears a good boxing as soon as he could. But imagine how he felt when he went to look for the ears and couldn't find them. And do you know why? Because in his great hurry to carve Pinocchio he had forgotten to make them.

So he grabbed him by the scruff of his neck, and as he was taking him back home he said, shaking his head menacingly:

"We're going straight home. And when we're home, you can be sure that we'll settle our scores!"

When he heard this sad tune, Pinocchio threw himself on the ground and refused to walk any farther. In the meantime, a crowd of busybodies and loafers had started to gather.

There were those who said one thing, and those who said another.

"Poor puppet!" some of them said. "He's right not to want to go home! Who knows what sort of beating that brute Geppetto is going to give him!"

The others added maliciously:

"That Geppetto seems like a respectable fellow, but he's a real tyrant with children. If they leave that poor puppet in his hands, he's more than capable of smashing it to pieces."

In short, they made such a commotion that the carabiniere set Pinocchio free and led poor Geppetto off to prison. And Geppetto, not coming up then and there with the right words to defend himself, started crying like a little calf, and as he went off toward the jail he stuttered through his sobs:

"Wretched son! And to think of all that I suffered to make him into a respectable puppet! But it serves me right! I should have thought of this before!"

What happened next is a story so strange that it's almost impossible to believe, and I'll tell you about it in the following chapters.

4. The story of Pinocchio and the Talking Cricket, where it can be seen how bad boys resent being corrected by those who know more than they do.

I'll tell you then, children, that while poor Geppetto was being taken off to prison through no fault of his own, that scamp Pinocchio, once he had escaped the clutches of the carabiniere, took to his heels, running through the fields so he could get home faster. And as he raced along, he jumped over huge embankments, briar hedges, and ditches full of water, as a young goat or hare might do if chased by hunters.

When he arrived at his house he found the street door ajar. He pushed it open, went inside, and as soon as he had bolted the door shut, threw himself on the ground and just sat there, letting out a huge sigh of contentment.

But that contentment didn't last very long, because he heard someone in the room go:

"*Chirp-chirp-chirp*!"

"Who's calling me?" said Pinocchio, terrified.

"It is I!"

Pinocchio turned around and saw a large cricket climbing slowly up the wall.

"Tell me, Cricket, who are you?"

"I am the Talking Cricket, and I have lived in this room for more than a hundred years."

"But from today on this room is mine," said the puppet, "and if you want to do me a favor, get out of here right now, and without a backward glance."

"I will not leave here," answered the Cricket, "if I do not first tell you a great truth."

"Tell me and be quick about it."

"Woe to those children who rebel against their parents and who abandon their homes to indulge their whims. They will never come to any good in this world, and sooner or later they will have to face a bitter repentance."

"Go ahead and sing as you will and wish, my dear Cricket. All I know is that tomorrow at dawn I'll be leaving, since if I stay around here the same thing will happen to me that happens to every other kid. I mean that they'll send me to school, and by hook or by crook I'll be forced to study; and—this is strictly confidential—I don't have the slightest desire to; I have more fun running after butterflies and climbing trees to snatch baby birds from their nest."

"Poor little fool! Don't you know that if you do that you'll become a fine jackass when you grow up, and everyone will make fun of you?"

"Shut up, you nasty, bad-luck Cricket!" shouted Pinocchio.

But instead of taking offense at this impertinence, the Cricket, who was both patient and a philosopher, continued in the same tone of voice:

"And if you don't like the idea of going to school, why don't you at least learn a trade so that you can earn your bread honestly?"

"You want me to tell you why?" replied Pinocchio, who was starting to lose his patience. "Of all the trades in the world there's only one that really appeals to me."

"And what trade would that be?"

"Eating, drinking, sleeping, having fun, and leading an idle life from morning till night."

"For your information," said the Talking Cricket with his usual aplomb, "those who practice that trade almost always end up either in the hospital or in jail."

"Watch out, you nasty, bad-luck Cricket! If I lose my temper, you're going to be in trouble!"

"Poor Pinocchio! I really pity you!"

"Why do you pity me?"

"Because you're a puppet, and even worse, because you have a wooden head."

At these last words Pinocchio flew into a rage. He jumped up, grabbed a wooden hammer from the workbench, and hurled it at the Talking Cricket.

Perhaps he didn't even think it would hit him; but, unfortunately, it got him right on the head, so that the poor Cricket hardly had the breath to say *chirp-chirp-chirp* before he ended up stone dead and stuck to the wall.

5. Pinocchio is hungry and looks for an egg so that he can make an omelet, but just as he's about to eat it the omelet flies out the window.

In the meantime night began to fall, and Pinocchio, remembering that he hadn't eaten a thing, felt a little pang in his stomach that quite closely resembled an appetite.

But a boy's appetite makes quick progress, and in fact, after a few minutes his appetite became hunger, and in the bat of an eye his hunger was transformed into a wolfish craving, into hunger so thick you could cut it with a knife.

Poor Pinocchio ran immediately to the hearth, where there was a pot boiling, and he went to uncover it so that he could see what was inside; but the pot was painted on the wall. Imagine how he felt. His nose, which was already long, grew at least a palm's-length.

At that point he began to run around the room, rummaging in all the drawers and cupboards in search of a bit of bread, even a bit of dry bread, a mere crust, a bone the dog had discarded, a bit of moldy polenta, a fish bone, a cherry pit: in short, something to chew on. But he found nothing, one big nothing, absolutely nothing.

And in the meantime his hunger was growing, and it kept on growing, and poor Pinocchio's only relief came from yawning; he yawned so wide and long that a few times his mouth stretched all the way to his ears. And after he yawned, he would spit, and it felt like he was spitting his stomach out.

And then, crying and despairing, he said,

"The Talking Cricket was right. I was wrong to rebel against my papa and run away from home . . . If my papa was here, I wouldn't be yawning to death now! Oh, what an awful disease hunger is!"

Then suddenly he thought he saw something round and white on top of the garbage heap, something that resembled a hen's egg. In less than a flash he took a leap and tackled it. It really was an egg.

It's impossible to describe the puppet's joy; you'll just have to imagine it. Almost believing it was a dream, he turned the egg over and over again in his hands, touching it and kissing it, and as he kissed it he said,

"And now how shall I cook it? I'll make an omelet! No, better to cook it right in a plate! Or maybe it would be tastier if I fried it in a skillet? Or if I soft-boiled it? No, the quickest way of all is to cook it in a plate or in a pan; I'm too eager to eat it!"

No sooner said than done. He put a little pan on top of a brazier full of hot embers; he put a little water in the pan, instead of oil or butter; and when the water started steaming, crack! He broke the egg open and prepared to drop it into the pan.

But instead of the white and the yolk, out jumped a perfectly cheerful and polite little chick who bowed low and said,

"Thanks a million, mister Pinocchio, for having saved me the effort of breaking the shell! Goodbye, stay well, and best regards to everyone at home."

Having said this, he spread his wings, slipped out the window, which was open, and flew off until he was out of sight.

The poor puppet stood there as if he were under a spell, his eyes staring, his mouth hanging open, and the pieces of eggshell in his hand. But when he had recovered from his initial shock, he began to cry, shriek, and stamp his feet on the ground in desperation, and as he was crying he said, "The Talking Cricket was right after all! If I hadn't run away from home and if my papa were here, I wouldn't be dying of hunger now! Oh, what an awful disease hunger is!"

And since his stomach continued to rumble more loudly than ever and he didn't know what to do to quiet it down, he decided to go out and take a quick visit to the nearby village, where he hoped to find some charitable person who might give him a bit of bread.

6. Pinocchio falls asleep with his feet on the brazier, and the next morning he wakes up with his feet completely burned off.

It happened to be a horrible, hellish night. Thunder crashed, lightening flashed as if the sky were on fire, and a terribly cold and violent wind whistled angrily and raised an immense cloud of dust that made all of the trees in the countryside creak and hiss.

Pinocchio was awfully afraid of thunder and lightning; it was just that his hunger was stronger than his fear. That was the reason why he pulled open the front door, set out at full speed, and in a hundred or so leaps arrived at the village, panting and with his tongue hanging out like a hunting dog.

But he found everything dark and deserted. The shops were closed, the doors to the houses closed, the windows closed, and there wasn't even a dog in the street. It looked like the land of the dead.

Then Pinocchio, overcome by desperation and hunger, latched onto the doorbell of a house and began to ring it without pause, saying to himself,

"Someone will look out the window."

In fact, a little old man with a nightcap on his head did look out the window, and yelled in a very cross voice,

"What do you want at this hour?"

"Would you do me a favor and give me a little bread?"

"Wait right there; I'll be back in a minute," answered the little old man, thinking he was dealing with one of those wild young toughs who amuse themselves at night by ringing doorbells just to harass respectable people who are sleeping peacefully.

After half a minute the window opened again, and the voice of the same little old man yelled to Pinocchio,

"Come closer and hold out your hat."

Pinocchio took off his pathetic little hat, but as he went to hold it out he felt an enormous bucketful of water rain down on him, which drenched him from head to toe as if he were a pot of withered geraniums.

He returned home, wet as a chick and nearly finished off by exhaustion and hunger. And since he no longer had the strength to remain standing, he sat down, resting his soaked and mud-splashed feet on a brazier full of hot embers.

And there he fell asleep; and as he was sleeping, his feet, which were made of wood, caught fire and burned down very slowly until all that was left of them was ash.

Pinocchio continued to sleep and to snore, as if his feet belonged to someone else. Finally, at daybreak, he woke up because someone had knocked at the door.

"Who is it?" he asked, yawning and rubbing his eyes.

"It's me!" answered a voice.

The voice was Geppetto's.

7. Geppetto returns home and gives the puppet the breakfast the poor man had brought for himself.

Poor Pinocchio, whose eyes were still filled with sleep, hadn't yet realized that his feet were completely burned off, and as soon as he heard his father's voice he sprang off the stool with the intention of running to unbolt the door. But instead, after staggering along for two or three steps, he fell flat on the floor.

And when he hit the ground he made the same sound that a sack of wooden soup ladles would have made falling from the sixth floor.

Meanwhile, Geppetto was yelling, "Open up!" from the street.

"Dear papa, I can't," answered the puppet, crying and rolling around on the ground.

"Why can't you?"

"Because they've eaten my feet."

"Who has eaten them?"

"The cat," said Pinocchio, looking at the cat, which was amusing itself by batting around some wood shavings with its front paws.

"Open up, I'm telling you!" repeated Geppetto. "Or else when I get inside, I'll give you the cat, I will!"

"I can't stand up straight, you've got to believe me. Oh, poor me, poor me! I'll have to walk on my knees for the rest of my life!"

Believing that all this blubbering was more of the puppet's mischief, Geppetto decided to put an end to it, and after climbing up the wall he entered the house through the window.

At first he knew exactly what he was going to say and do, but then, when he saw his Pinocchio stretched out on the ground with his feet truly missing, he was overcome by tenderness, and after he gathered him up in his arms, he began to kiss and caress and cuddle him a thousand times over. And with tears streaming down his cheeks, he said to Pinocchio, sobbing:

"My dear little Pinocchio! How is it that you burned your feet?"

"I don't know, papa, but believe me, it's been a hellish night and I'll remember it as long as I live. There was thunder and lightning and I was very hungry, and then the Talking Cricket said to me: 'It serves you right: you've been a bad boy, and you deserve it,' and I said to him, 'Watch out, Cricket!' and he said to me: 'You're a puppet and you've got a wooden head,' and I threw the handle of a hammer at him, and he died, but it was his fault because I didn't mean to kill him, and the proof is that I put a little pan on the hot embers in the brazier, but the chick jumped out and said: 'Goodbye . . . and best regards to everyone at home.' And I was getting hungrier and hungrier, which is why that little old man with the nightcap looked out the window and said to me: 'Come closer and hold out your hat,' and after that bucketful of water on my head—since asking for a little bread is nothing to be ashamed of, is it?—I came right back home, and seeing as I was still very hungry I put my feet up on the brazier to get dry, and you came back, and I saw that they were all burned off, and in any case I'm still very hungry and I don't have my feet anymore! *Boo-hoo!* . . . *Boo-hoo!* . . . *Boo-hoo!*"

And poor Pinocchio started to cry and bawl so loudly that they could hear him from three miles away.

Geppetto, who had only understood one thing in that whole muddled account, namely, that the puppet felt like he was dying of hunger, pulled three pears out of his pocket and, holding them out to him, said:

"These three pears were supposed to be for my breakfast, but I'm glad to give them to you. Eat them, and may they do you good."

"If you want me to eat them, do me a favor and peel them."

"Peel them?" replied Geppetto, amazed. "I would never have thought, my dear boy, that you were so picky and such a finicky eater. That's bad! In this world, from the time you're a child, you need to get used to tasting anything and eating everything, because you never know how things might turn out for you. Anything is possible!"

"You're probably right," interrupted Pinocchio, "but I'll never eat a piece of fruit unless it's peeled. I can't stand peels."

Then that good man Geppetto pulled out a little knife and, armed with saintly patience, he peeled the three pears, and put all the peels on a corner of the table.

After Pinocchio had eaten the first pear in two mouthfuls, he was about to throw away the core; but Geppetto caught hold of his arm and said to him:

"Don't throw that away; in this world everything can come in handy."

"But I really don't intend to eat the core!" shouted the puppet, snapping his head back like a viper.

"Who knows? Anything is possible!" repeated Geppetto, remaining calm.

The fact of the matter is that instead of being thrown out the window, the three cores were placed on the corner of the table, in the company of the peels.

After Pinocchio had eaten or, more precisely, devoured the three pears, he gave a very long yawn and whined,

"I'm still hungry!"

"But my dear boy, I have nothing left to give you."

"Nothing, nothing at all?"

"All I have are these pear peels and cores."

"Oh well!" said Pinocchio, "if there's nothing else, I'll eat a peel."

And he started chewing. At first he twisted up his mouth a little; but then in one breath he gobbled down all the peels, one after the other, and after the peels the cores, too. And when he had finished eating every last thing, he patted his stomach contentedly and said, quite pleased with himself,

"I sure feel good now!"

"So you see," observed Geppetto, "that I was right when I told you that you shouldn't make a habit out of having either too discriminating or too delicate a palate. My dear boy, you never know what may happen to you in this world. Anything is possible!!"

8. Geppetto makes new feet for Pinocchio and sells his own jacket to buy him a spelling book.

As soon as he had gotten rid of his hunger, the puppet immediately started grumbling and crying, because he wanted a new pair of feet.

But to punish him for his mischief, Geppetto let him cry and despair for half a day. Then he said to him:

"Why should I make you new feet? Just to see you run away from home again?"

"I promise you," said the puppet, sobbing, "that from today on I'll be a good boy . . ."

"All children say that," replied Geppetto, "when they want something."

"I promise you that I'll go to school, that I'll study, and that I'll make you proud of me . . ."

"That's the same old story that all children repeat when they want something."

"But I'm not like other children! I'm better than all the rest, and I always tell the truth. I promise you, papa, that I'll learn a trade and that I'll be the consolation and the staff of your old age."

Even if Geppetto put on a tyrant's face, his eyes were full of tears and his heart swollen with compassion when he saw his poor Pinocchio in that pitiful state. He uttered not another word in reply, but took hold of his tools and two small pieces of seasoned wood, and set to work with the utmost diligence.

In less than an hour the feet were finished: two nimble, lean, and sinewy little feet that looked like they had been carved by a great master.

Then Geppetto said to the puppet:

"Close your eyes and sleep."

And Pinocchio closed his eyes and pretended to sleep. While he was pretending to be asleep, Geppetto stuck the two feet in place with a little glue that he had dissolved in an eggshell. And he did such a good job of sticking them on that you couldn't even see where they were attached.

As soon as the puppet realized he had feet, he jumped down off the table where he had been lying and began to execute a thousand little leaps and capers, as if he had gone crazy with happiness.

"To pay you back for everything that you've done for me," said Pinocchio to his papa, "I want to go to school right away."

"That's a good boy."

"But if I go to school I'll be needing some clothes."

So Geppetto, who was poor and didn't have a cent in his pocket, made him a simple little suit of flowered paper, a pair of shoes of tree bark, and a little cap of breadcrumbs.

Pinocchio ran right off to look at himself in a basin of water, and he was so happy with what he saw that he said, as he strutted to and fro,

"I certainly do look like a gentleman!"

"And so you do," replied Geppetto, "because, and always keep this in mind, it's not nice clothes that make a gentleman, but rather clean clothes."

"By the way," added the puppet, "I'm still missing something that I'll need if I go to school: in fact, the most important and necessary thing of all."

"And what's that?"

"I'm missing a spelling book."

"You're right, but how do we get one?"

"That's easy enough: you go to a bookstore and buy one."

"And the money to pay for it?"

"I don't have any."

"Nor do I," added the good old man, becoming sad.

And although he was a very lighthearted boy, Pinocchio became sad, too: because poverty, when it's real poverty, can be understood by everyone, even children.

"Never mind!" Geppetto suddenly cried, standing up. And after he slipped on his old twill jacket full of patches and darning, he raced out of the house.

Before long he returned; and when he returned he had a spelling book for his son in his hand, but he no longer had his jacket. The poor man was in his shirtsleeves, and it was snowing outside.

"What happened to your jacket, papa?"

"I sold it."

"Why did you sell it?"

"Because I was too hot."

Pinocchio grasped the meaning of that answer at once, and, unable to rein in the surge of his heart, he flung his arms around Geppetto's neck and began to kiss him all over his face.

9. Pinocchio sells his spelling book so that he can go and see the puppet theater.

When it had stopped snowing, Pinocchio set off down the road that led to the school with his nice new spelling book under his arm, and as he was walking his little brain dreamed up a thousand thoughts and built a thousand castles in the air, each more lovely than the other.

And as he conversed with himself, he said:

"Today at school I want to learn to read, right away; then tomorrow I'll learn to write, and the day after tomorrow I'll learn my numbers. Then with all these abilities I'll earn lots of money, and with the first money that enters my pocket I want to immediately buy my papa a nice cloth jacket. But what am I saying, cloth? I'll get him one made of silver and gold, with diamond buttons. The poor man sure deserves it, since after all, if he's in shirtsleeves now it's because he wanted to buy me books and educate me . . . and in this freezing weather! No one but fathers are capable of certain sacrifices!"

As he was saying this he became very emotional; but then he seemed to hear, in the distance, the sound of fifes and the beating of a bass drum: *pi-pi-pi, pi-pi-pi, boom, boom, boom boom.*

He stopped and listened carefully. The sounds were coming from the end of a very long crossroad that led to a little village by the edge of the sea.

"I wonder what that music is? It's too bad I have to go to school; otherwise . . ."

And he stood there, confused. In any case, he needed to come to a decision: either he went to school or he went to hear the fifes.

"Today I'll go hear the fifes, and tomorrow to school; there's always time to go to school," that little rascal finally said, shrugging his shoulders.

No sooner said than done. He turned down the crossroad and raced off, kicking up his heels. The more he ran, the more distinctly he heard the sound of the fifes and the thuds of the bass drum: *pi-pi-pi, pi-pi-pi, pi-pi-pi, boom, boom, boom, boom.*

And then suddenly he found himself in the middle of a square full of people crowded around a large tent made of wood and canvas and painted a thousand different colors.

"What's that tent?" asked Pinocchio, turning to a little boy from the village.

"Read the sign and you'll find out; it's written right there."

"I'd be more than happy to read it, but it just so happens that I don't know how to read today."

"A fine ox you are! Then I'll read it to you. For your information, what's written on that sign in letters as red as fire is: GRAND PUPPET THEATER."

"How long ago did the show start?"

"It's starting now."

"And how much does it cost to get in?"

"Four pennies."

Pinocchio, who was burning with the fever of curiosity, lost all reserve and said, without the least shame, to the little boy with whom he was speaking:

"Would you give me four pennies until tomorrow?"

"I'd be more than happy to give them to you," answered the other boy, mocking him, "but it just so happens that I can't give them to you today."

Then the puppet said to him, "I'll sell you my jacket for four pennies."

"What would I do with a jacket made out of flowered paper? If it gets rained on, there's no way of getting it off."

"Do you want to buy my shoes?"

"All they're good for is lighting a fire."

"How much will you give me for my cap?"

"That would really be a fine purchase! A cap made out of breadcrumbs! The mice would probably come and eat it off my head."

Pinocchio was on tenterhooks. He was just about to make a final offer, but he didn't have the courage to; he hesitated, he wavered, he suffered. Finally, he said:

"Will you give me four pennies for this new spelling book?"

"I'm a boy, and I don't buy things from other boys," answered his little interlocutor, who was more sensible than he was.

"I'll take the spelling book for four pennies," yelled a rag seller who had been present during the conversation.

And so the book was sold right there, on the spot. And to think that poor Geppetto was at home shivering with cold in his shirtsleeves, because he had bought a spelling book for his son!

10. The puppets recognize their brother Pinocchio and give him a grand welcome, but at the height of all the excitement the puppet master Fire-Eater comes out, and Pinocchio risks coming to a bad end.

When Pinocchio entered the marionette theater, something occurred that caused a near revolution.

You should know that the curtain was up and the show had already begun.

On the stage you could see Harlequin and Punch bickering with each other and, as usual, threatening to exchange a charge of slaps and blows at any moment.

The very attentive audience was nearly dying of laughter as it listened to the squabbling between the two puppets, who were gesticulating and insulting each other in every way possible, and doing it so realistically that they might have been two rational creatures, two people of this world.

Suddenly, out of the blue, Harlequin stopped acting and, turning toward the audience and pointing to someone at the back of the orchestra section, began to declaim dramatically:

"Celestial deities! Am I dreaming or awake? And yet, that *is* Pinocchio down there!"

"It really is Pinocchio!" yelled Punch.

"It's truly him!" shrieked Madam Rosaura, peeking out from the back of the stage.

"It's Pinocchio! It's Pinocchio!" all the puppets cried out in chorus, jumping from the wings. "It's Pinocchio! It's our brother Pinocchio! Long live Pinocchio!"

"Pinocchio, come up here to me!" yelled Harlequin. "Come throw yourself into the arms of your wooden brothers!"

At this affectionate invitation, Pinocchio took a flying leap, and from the back of the orchestra ended up in the front section; then with another jump, from the front section he landed on the orchestra conductor's head, and from there darted up onto the stage.

It's impossible to imagine the hugs, the neck squeezing, the friendly pinches, and the head-butting, all signs of true and sincere brotherhood, that in the midst of all the commotion Pinocchio received from the actors and actresses of that dramatico-vegetal troupe.

It goes without saying that this was a touching spectacle, but when the members of the audience saw that the show had come to a halt, they grew impatient and began to yell,

"We want the show, we want the show!"

It was all wasted breath, since instead of carrying on with the performance, the puppets doubled the racket and their shouting, and after they hoisted Pinocchio onto their shoulders, they paraded him in triumph under the spotlights.

At that point the puppet master came out. He was a huge man, so ugly that the mere sight of him was enough to give you a fright. He had an awful beard as black as an inkblot, and so long that it reached from his chin all the way down to the ground; it's sufficient to say that with each step he took, he trampled on it. His mouth was as wide as an oven, his eyes looked like two lanterns of red glass with a flame burning inside, and his hands cracked a large whip made of twisted snakes and foxtails.

At the unexpected appearance of the puppet master, everyone was struck dumb, and no one dared to breathe. You could have heard a pin drop. Those poor puppets, both male and female, were shaking like leaves on a tree.

"Why have you come to wreak havoc in my theater?" the puppet master asked Pinocchio, with the deep voice of an ogre with a terrible head cold.

"Please believe me, most illustrious sir, it wasn't my fault!"

"That's enough! We'll settle our scores this evening."

In fact, after the performance was over, the puppet master went into the kitchen, where a fine mutton he had prepared for his dinner was slowly turning on the spit. And since he didn't have enough wood to finish roasting and browning it, he called Harlequin and Punch over and said to them,

"Bring me that puppet hanging on the nail over there. It appears to be a puppet made of very dry wood, and I'm sure that when I throw it on the fire it will give me a lovely flame for my roast."

At first Harlequin and Punch hesitated. But then, frightened by the terrible look their master was giving them, they obeyed, and soon after they returned to the kitchen carrying poor Pinocchio, who, wriggling like an eel out of water, shrieked desperately,

"Papa, save me! I don't want to die; no, I don't want to die!"

11. Fire-Eater sneezes and pardons Pinocchio, who then saves his friend Harlequin from death.

I can't deny that the puppet master Fire-Eater (for that was his name) appeared to be a frightful man, especially with that awful black beard that covered his whole chest and the length of his legs like an apron, but deep down he wasn't a bad man. And the proof is that when he saw poor Pinocchio brought before him, thrashing about every which way and screaming, "I don't want to die, I don't want to die!" he was immediately moved and began to feel sorry for him. And after resisting for a good while, he could no longer stand it, and he let out a resounding sneeze.

At that sneeze Harlequin, who up until then had been as despondent and downcast as a weeping willow, put on a cheerful face and, leaning toward Pinocchio, whispered to him under his breath,

"Good news, brother! The puppet master has sneezed, and that's a sign that he pities you; you're safe now."

Because you should know that whereas all other men either cry or at least pretend to dry their eyes when they feel sorry for someone, Fire-Eater had, instead, the bad habit of sneezing every time he was truly touched. It was just a different way of letting other people know that he had a sensitive heart.

After he sneezed, the puppet master kept up his gruff manner and yelled at Pinocchio,

"Stop crying! Your moaning and groaning have given me a funny feeling in the bottom of my stomach . . . I feel a pang that's almost, that's almost . . . Atchoo! Atchoo!" and he sneezed two more times.

"Bless you!" said Pinocchio.

"Thank you. And are your papa and mama still alive?" Fire-Eater asked him.

"My papa is; I never knew my mama."

"I bet your old father would be very sad if I had you thrown onto those burning coals now! Poor old man! I sympathize with him! . . . Atchoo, atchoo, atchoo!" and he sneezed three more times.

"Bless you!" said Pinocchio.

"Thank you! On the other hand, I'm to be sympathized with, too, since as you can see, I don't have enough firewood to finish roasting that piece of mutton, and to be truthful, in this situation you would have come in very handy. But at this point I'm feeling sorry for you, so never mind. Instead of you I'll put one of the puppets from my troupe to burn under the spit. Hey there, gendarmes!"

At this command, two wooden gendarmes immediately appeared. They were quite tall, very thin, wore bicorn hats on their heads, and carried unsheathed sabers in their hands.

Then the puppet master said to them in a raspy voice,

"Go get me that Harlequin over there, tie him up tightly, and then throw him on the fire to burn. I want my mutton to be well roasted!"

Imagine poor Harlequin! He was so frightened that his legs folded under him and he fell flat on the floor.

At the sight of that heartrending spectacle, Pinocchio went and threw himself down at the puppet master's feet, and as he wept his eyes out and watered every hair of the puppet master's terribly long beard with his tears, he began to say in a pleading voice,

"Have pity, Sir Fire-Eater!"

"There are no sirs here!" the puppet master harshly replied.

"Have pity, Sir Knight!"

"There are no knights here!"

"Have pity, Sir Commendatore!"

"There are no commendatores here!"

"Have pity, Excellency!"

When he heard himself called Excellency, the puppet master immediately pursed his lips and, suddenly becoming more human and reasonable, said to Pinocchio:

"All right, then, what do you want from me?"

"I beg you to grant poor Harlequin a pardon!"

"There's no granting pardons here. If I spare you, then I've got to put him on the fire, because I want my mutton to be well roasted."

"In that case," cried Pinocchio boldly, getting up and throwing off his cap of breadcrumbs, "in that case I know what my duty is. Come forward, gendarmes! Tie me up and throw me into those flames. No, it's not right that poor Harlequin, my true friend, should have to die for me!"

Those words, pronounced in a loud voice and with heroic diction, made all the puppets who witnessed the scene cry. The gendarmes themselves, although they were made of wood, wept like two little suckling lambs.

At first Fire-Eater remained hard-hearted and as immovable as a piece of ice; but then, little by little, he too began to soften up, and to sneeze. And after he had sneezed four or five times, he opened his arms affectionately and said to Pinocchio:

"You're one terrific boy! Come over here and give me a kiss."

Pinocchio ran right over and, scrambling up the puppet master's beard like a squirrel, went and planted a nice kiss on the tip of his nose.

"So is the pardon granted?" asked poor Harlequin, in a wispy voice that could barely be heard.

"The pardon is granted," answered Fire-Eater. Then he added, sighing and shaking his head,

"Oh well! For this evening I'll resign myself to eating my mutton half-raw; but too bad for whoever happens to be around next time!"

At the news that the pardon had been granted, all the puppets ran up onto the stage, and after they had lit the lamps and chandeliers as if for a gala performance, they began to jump around and dance. Dawn came and they were still dancing.

12. The puppet master Fire-Eater presents Pinocchio with a gift of five gold coins to take to his papa Geppetto; but instead Pinocchio lets himself be duped by the Fox and the Cat and then goes off with them.

The next day Fire-Eater called Pinocchio aside and asked him:

"What's your father's name?"

"Geppetto."

"And what's his trade?"

"Being a poor man."

"Does he earn a lot?"

"He earns just enough never to have a cent in his pocket. Just imagine, he had to sell the only jacket he owned to buy me a spelling book for school. A jacket that had so many patches and darns that it looked like an open wound."

"Poor devil! I almost pity him. Here are five gold coins. Go take them to him right away, and send him my regards."

As can be easily imagined, Pinocchio thanked the puppet master a thousand times. He embraced all the puppets in the troupe one by one, even the gendarmes, and then, beside himself with happiness, he set off, intending to return home.

But he hadn't yet gone half a kilometer when he met a Fox who was lame in one foot and a Cat who was blind in both eyes. They were making their way down the road, each helping the other like good companions in misfortune. The Fox, who was lame, leaned on the Cat as he walked; and the Cat, who was blind, let himself be guided by the Fox.

"Good day, Pinocchio," said the Fox, greeting him politely.

"How is it that you know my name?" asked the puppet.

"I know your papa well."

"Where have you seen him?"

"I saw him yesterday on his doorstep."

"And what was he doing?"

"He was in his shirtsleeves, and he was shivering with cold."

"Poor papa! But God willing, from today on he'll shiver no more."

"Why is that?"

"Because I've become a grand gentleman."

"You, a grand gentleman?" said the Fox, and he began to laugh in a vulgar, mocking manner. The Cat laughed, too, but he combed his whiskers with his front paws so that you couldn't see it.

"There's nothing to laugh about," yelled Pinocchio, in a huff. "I'm really sorry to make your mouths water, but these here are five splendid gold coins, if you know anything about such things."

And he pulled out the coins that Fire-Eater had given him.

At the pleasant sound of those coins the Fox, with an involuntary movement, extended the leg that appeared to be twisted, and the Cat opened both of his eyes so wide that they looked like two green lanterns; but then he closed them again immediately and, in fact, Pinocchio didn't notice a thing.

"And now," the Fox asked him, "what do you want to do with those coins?"

"First of all," answered the puppet, "I want to buy my father a fine new jacket made of silver and gold, with diamond buttons; and then I want to buy a spelling book for myself."

"For yourself?"

"That's right, because I want to go to school and start studying seriously."

"Look at me!" said the Fox. "Because of my silly passion for studying I lost a leg."

"Look at me!" said the Cat. "Because of my silly passion for studying I lost my sight in both eyes."

Just then a white Blackbird, who was perched on a hedge at the side of the road, gave his usual call and said:

"Pinocchio, don't listen to the advice of bad companions, or you'll be sorry!"

Poor Blackbird, he should never have said that! The Cat took a big leap, pounced on him, and without giving him the time to say *oh!* ate him up in one bite, feathers and all.

When he had finished eating and had wiped his mouth, the Cat closed his eyes again, and began once more to act like he was blind, just as before.

"Poor Blackbird!" said Pinocchio to the Cat. "Why did you treat him so badly?"

"I did it to teach him a lesson. That way the next time he'll know not to stick his beak into other people's conversations."

They were more than halfway there when the Fox, stopping unexpectedly, said to the puppet:

"Do you want to double your gold coins?"

"What do you mean?"

"Do you want to turn your five miserable gold pieces into a hundred, a thousand, two thousand?"

"I wish! But how?"

"How? It's very easy. Instead of going on home, you'd have to come with us."

"And where do you intend to take me?"

"To the land of the Featherbrains."

Pinocchio thought about it for a while, and then said firmly:

"No, I don't want to come. I'm close to home now, and I want to return home, where my papa is waiting for me. Goodness knows how the poor old man suffered yesterday when he saw that I wasn't coming back. I'm afraid I've been a bad son, and the Talking Cricket was right when he said: 'Disobedient children can't come to any good in this world.' And I've learned that at my own expense, because I've had a lot of hard luck, and just last night at Fire-Eater's house, I was in danger of . . . Brrr! I'm getting goose bumps just thinking about it!"

"So," said the Fox, "you really want to go home? Well, go ahead then, and too bad for you."

"Too bad for you!" repeated the Cat.

"Think it over carefully, Pinocchio, because you're kicking fortune in the pants."

"Fortune in the pants!" repeated the Cat.

"Between today and tomorrow your five gold pieces would have become two thousand."

"Two thousand!" repeated the Cat.

"But how is it ever possible for them to become so many?" asked Pinocchio, his mouth hanging open in amazement.

"I'll explain it to you right away," said the Fox. "You should know that in the land of the Featherbrains there's a blessed field, which everyone calls the Field of Miracles. You dig a little hole in this field and you put, for example, a gold piece in it. Then you cover up the hole with a bit of earth, you water it with two pails of fountain water, you sprinkle a pinch of salt over it, and in the evening you go calmly to bed. In the meantime, during the night the gold piece germinates and blooms, and the next morning as soon as you get up you go back to the field, and what do you find? You find a lovely tree laden with as many gold pieces as a fine stalk of wheat has grains in the month of June."

"So then," said Pinocchio, growing more and more astonished, "if I buried my five gold pieces in that field, how many would I find there the next morning?"

"That's easy enough to calculate," answered the Fox. "You can do it on your fingers. Suppose each gold piece yields a bunch of five hundred pieces. Multiply five hundred by five, and the next morning you'll find two thousand five hundred shiny gold pieces jangling in your pocket."

"Oh, that's really fine!" shouted Pinocchio, dancing with joy. "As soon as I pick those gold pieces, I'll keep two thousand for myself and I'll give the two of you the other five hundred as a gift."

"A gift for us?" yelled the Fox, growing indignant and acting insulted. "God forbid!"

"Forbid!" repeated the Cat.

"We," the Fox went on, "do not work out of vile self-interest; we work exclusively for the purpose of making others rich."

"Others rich!" repeated the cat.

"What good people!" thought Pinocchio to himself. And suddenly forgetting completely about his papa, the new jacket, the spelling book, and all the fine resolutions he had made, he said to the Fox and the Cat:

"Let's go right now; I'm coming with you."

13. The Red Lobster Inn.

On and on and on they walked, and finally, as evening was falling, they reached the Red Lobster Inn, dead tired.

"Let's stop here for a while," said the Fox. "Just long enough to get a bite to eat and rest a few hours. At midnight we'll start out again, so that tomorrow at dawn we can be at the Field of Miracles."

After they entered the inn, all three of them sat down at a table, although none of them had much of an appetite.

The poor Cat, who was feeling seriously sick to his stomach, was able to eat nothing more than thirty-five red mullets in tomato sauce and four portions of tripe Parmesan. And since he didn't find the tripe to be very well seasoned, he made up for it by asking three times for more butter and grated cheese.

The Fox would gladly have nibbled on something, too, but since the doctor had ordered him to follow a very strict diet, he had to be content with a simple hare in sweet-and-sour sauce, accompanied by a very light side dish of plump spring chickens and young cockerels. After the hare he ordered, as an appetite teaser, a little fricassee of grouse, partridge, rabbit, frog, lizard, and paradise grapes, and that was all he wanted. He felt such nausea at the sight of food, he said, that it was impossible to get anything near his mouth.

The one who ate least of all was Pinocchio. He asked for a slice of walnut and a crust of bread, and he left everything on his plate. With that fixation of the Field of Miracles in his head, the poor boy had got an advance case of indigestion from the gold coins.

When they had finished their dinner, the Fox said to the innkeeper:

"Give me two good rooms, one for Mister Pinocchio and the other for me and my companion. Before we leave we'll be taking a little snooze. But remember that we want to be awakened at midnight so that we can continue our journey."

"Yessirs," answered the innkeeper, and gave the Fox and the Cat a wink, as if to say, "I get the drift; it's a deal!"

As soon as Pinocchio got into bed he fell right to sleep and began to dream. And in his dream he saw himself in the middle of a field, and this field was full of little trees laden with bunches of gold pieces, which as they swung in the wind went *clink, clink, clink*, almost as if they were trying to say, "Whoever wants us, come and get us." But right at the best part—when, that is, Pinocchio stretched out his arms and started to grab those beautiful coins by the handful and put them in his pocket—he was suddenly awakened by three violent blows on the door of his room.

It was the innkeeper coming to tell him that it had struck midnight.

"Are my companions ready?" the puppet asked him.

"They certainly are! They left two hours ago."

"Why all the hurry?"

"The Cat got word that his eldest kitten, who's suffering from frostbite of the paws, was in danger of losing his life."

"And did they pay for the dinner?"

"You've got to be kidding! Those two are too well bred to slight your lordship like that."

"Too bad! I would have been very glad to receive such a slight!" said Pinocchio, scratching his head. Then he asked:

"And where did those good friends of mine say they would wait for me?"

"At the Field of Miracles, tomorrow morning at the break of dawn."

Pinocchio paid one gold piece for his dinner and that of his companions, and set off.

But you could say that he groped his way off, since outside the tavern it was dark, so very dark that it was impossible to see from here to there. You couldn't hear a leaf move in the surrounding countryside. There were only a few ghastly night birds, and as they flew occasionally across the road from one hedge to another, they flapped their wings against Pinocchio's nose, causing him to jump backward in fright and yell, "Who goes there?" And the echo off the surrounding hills repeated from afar, "Who goes there? Who goes there? Who goes there?"

In the meantime, as Pinocchio was walking along he saw, sitting on a tree trunk, a tiny little animal that glowed with a pale and opaque light, like a small night-light inside a transparent porcelain lamp.

"Who are you?" asked Pinocchio.

"I am the shade of the Talking Cricket," answered the little animal in a barely audible voice that seemed to come from the world beyond.

"What do you want from me?" said the puppet.

"I want to give you some advice. Go back and take the four gold pieces you still have to your poor papa, who has been crying and despairing because he hasn't seen you for a while."

"Tomorrow my papa will become a fine gentleman, because these four gold pieces are going to turn into two thousand."

"Don't trust people who promise to make you rich from morning to night, my boy. They're usually either madmen or swindlers! Listen to me; go back."

"But I want to go ahead."

"The hour is late!"

"I want to go ahead."

"The night is dark . . ."

"I want to go ahead."

"The road is dangerous . . ."

"I want to go ahead."

"Remember that children who follow their whims and want to do things their way regret it sooner or later."

"The same old story. Good night, Cricket."

"Good night, Pinocchio, and may the heavens save you from dampness and assassins."

As soon as he had said these last words, the Talking Cricket suddenly went out, like a candle goes out when you blow on it, and the road was left darker than before.

14. Because he didn't listen to the good advice of the Talking Cricket, Pinocchio runs into the assassins.

"Really," the puppet said to himself as he set off on his journey once again, "we poor kids are a miserable lot! Everyone is always yelling at us, warning us, giving us advice. If they had their way, they would take it into their heads to become our fathers and our teachers: all of them, even the Talking Crickets. And there you have it: just because I wouldn't listen to that tiresome Cricket, there's no telling what sort of disasters I'm in for, according to him! I'm even supposed to run into assassins! It's good that I don't believe in assassins, nor have I ever believed in them. In my opinion assassins were invented on purpose by fathers, to frighten children who want to go out at night. Even if I did run into them here on the road, you think they would intimidate me? Not a chance. I'd yell right in their faces: 'Mister assassins, what do you want with me? Remember that I'm not one to fool around with! So you can leave right now and go about your business, and not a word more!' If I really did speak like that to those poor assassins, they would run like the wind; I can see them right now. And in case they were so rude as to refuse to run away, then I would run away, and I'd put an end to it just like that . . ."

But Pinocchio wasn't able to finish this line of argument, because at that very moment he seemed to hear a faint rustling of leaves behind him.

He turned around to look, and there in the dark he saw two awful black figures. They were wrapped from head to toe in coal sacks, and were running after him on their tiptoes in little leaps, as if they were two ghosts.

"Here they are for real!" he said to himself; and not knowing where to hide the four gold pieces, he hid them in his mouth: more precisely, under his tongue.

Then he tried to run away. But he hadn't yet taken the first step when he felt his arms being grabbed and heard two horrible, cavernous voices that said:

"Your money or your life!"

Pinocchio couldn't answer with words, on account of the coins that he had in his mouth, and so he bowed and scraped a thousand times and mimed a thousand different gestures to make it clear to those two cloaked figures—of whom all you could see were their eyes, through the holes in the sacks—that he was a poor puppet and that he didn't have even a counterfeit penny in his pocket.

"Come on, come on! Less chitchat, and out with the money!" the two bandits yelled threateningly.

The puppet signaled with his head and hands, as if to say, "I don't have any."

"Out with the money or you're dead," said the taller of the assassins.

"Dead!" repeated the other one.

"And after we've killed you, we'll kill your father, too!"

"Your father, too!"

"No, no, no, not my poor papa!" shouted Pinocchio in a desperate voice; but when he shouted, you could hear the gold pieces clinking in his mouth.

"Ah, you scoundrel! So you've got the coins hidden under your tongue? Spit them out right now!"

But Pinocchio was tough.

"Ah! So you're playing deaf? Wait a little longer and we'll make sure you spit them out!"

In fact, one of them grabbed the puppet by the tip of his nose, and the other one took hold of him by the end of his chin, and they began to pull him roughly, one this way and the other that way, so that he would be forced to open his mouth. But it was no use. It was as if the puppet's mouth had been nailed and riveted shut.

Then the shorter assassin pulled out a nasty-looking knife and tried to wedge it like a lever or a chisel between the puppet's lips; but Pinocchio, as quick as lightning, sank his teeth into the assassin's hand, and after he had bitten it clean off, he spit it out. Imagine his astonishment when he saw that instead of a hand he had spit a cat's paw onto the ground!

Encouraged by this first victory, he freed himself by sheer force from the assassins' claws, leaped over the hedge at the side of the road, and began to flee through the countryside. The assassins ran after him like two dogs after a hare; and the one who had lost a paw ran on just one leg, and it's never been discovered how he did it.

After running for nearly ten miles, Pinocchio couldn't take it anymore. Realizing that he was done for, he climbed up the trunk of a very tall pine tree and sat himself down among the uppermost branches. The assassins tried to climb up, too, but when they were halfway up the trunk they slipped and fell back down to the ground, skinning their hands and feet.

Yet they refused to give up. On the contrary: after they arranged a bundle of dry kindling at the foot of the pine tree, they set it on fire, and in less than no time the pine tree began to burn and blaze like a candle in the wind. Seeing that the flames were climbing higher and higher and not wanting to end up like a roast pigeon, Pinocchio took a huge leap from the top of the tree and set off again, running through the fields and vineyards. And the assassins were there behind him, always behind him, never getting tired.

In the meantime daylight began to glimmer and they were still pursuing each other, when Pinocchio suddenly found his way blocked by a wide and very deep ditch, full of dirty stagnant water that was the color of coffee with milk. What to do? "One, two, three!" shouted the puppet, and after a strong running start, he soared over to the other side. The assassins jumped, too, but since they hadn't calculated the distance correctly, *plop!* . . . they fell right into the ditch. When Pinocchio heard the thud and the splash of the water, he shouted, laughing and continuing to run:

"Have a nice bath, Mister Assassins!"

He was already imagining that they were good and drowned when he turned to look, and instead realized that they were both running after him, still wrapped in their sacks and streaming water like two bottomless baskets.

15. The assassins chase Pinocchio, and after catching up with him they hang him from a branch of the Great Oak.

At this point the puppet had lost heart and was just about to throw himself on the ground and give up when, casting his eyes around, he saw a little snow-white house glowing palely in the distance against the dark green of the trees.

"If I had enough breath to get to that house, maybe I'd be safe!" he said to himself.

Without waiting a minute longer, he set off running through the forest again at full speed. And the assassins were still there behind him.

After a desperate race of almost two hours he finally arrived, gasping for breath, at the door of the little house, and knocked.

No one answered.

He knocked again, harder this time, because he heard the sound of his persecutors' footsteps and their heavy and labored breathing getting closer. More silence.

When it became clear that knocking served no purpose, out of desperation he began to kick the door and bang his head against it. At that, a beautiful little girl appeared at the window. She had blue hair and a face as white as a waxen image; her eyes were closed and her hands crossed on her chest. Without the slightest movement of her lips she said, in a faint voice that seemed to come from the world beyond:

"There is no one in this house. They are all dead."

"You open up, then!" shouted Pinocchio, crying and pleading with her.

"I am dead, too."

"Dead? Then what are you doing up there at the window?"

"I am waiting to be taken away in a casket."

As soon as she said this, the Little Girl disappeared, and the window closed again without making a sound.

"Oh beautiful little girl with the blue hair," shouted Pinocchio, "open up, for goodness sake. Have pity on a poor boy who's being chased by assass—"

But he wasn't able to finish the last word, because he felt himself being grabbed by the neck, and the same two dreadful voices growled menacingly:

"You won't get away from us now!"

When the puppet saw death flash before his eyes, he got such a bad case of the shakes that as he was shaking, the joints of his wooden legs and the four gold pieces hidden under his tongue started chattering.

"So?" the assassins asked, "are you going to open that mouth of yours or not? Ah! You're not answering? Never mind, this time we'll make sure you open it!"

And they took out two terribly long, horrible-looking knives that were as sharp as razor blades, and then *zap!* and *zap!* . . . they dealt him two blows in the middle of his back.

But luckily for him, the puppet was made of very hard wood, which is why the blades shattered into a thousand fragments and the assassins were left with the knife handles in their hands, looking at each other.

"I see," one of them said then, "we'll have to hang him! Let's hang him!"

"Hang him!" repeated the other one.

No sooner said than done. They tied his hands behind his back, and after passing a slipknot around his neck, they left him hanging on a branch of a large tree called the Great Oak.

Then they sat down on the grass and waited for the puppet to give his last kick, but after three hours the puppet still had his eyes open, his mouth closed, and was kicking harder than ever.

When they finally grew bored of waiting, they turned to Pinocchio and said to him, sneering:

"Farewell until tomorrow. When we come back here tomorrow, let's hope that you'll do us the courtesy of being nice and dead, with your mouth wide open."

And they left.

In the meantime a blustery north wind had risen, and blowing and howling furiously, it slammed the poor hanged puppet back and forth, and made him swing violently, like the clapper of a bell ringing at full peal. And all that swinging caused him to have severe spasms, and the slipknot, which was growing tighter and tighter around his neck, began to choke him.

Little by little his eyes misted over, and although he felt death approaching he nevertheless still hoped that some merciful soul might show up at any moment to help him. But as he continued to wait and saw that no one was coming, no one at all, then his poor papa came to mind again and he stammered, on the verge of dying:

"Oh, my dear papa! If only you were here!"

He didn't have the breath to say anything more. He closed his eyes, opened his mouth, stretched his legs, and, after giving a great shudder, hung there as if he were frozen stiff.

[It is at this point, after chapter 15, that the original Story of a Puppet, published in magazine installments, ended.]

4

Luigi Capuana (1839–1925)

Luigi Capuana was born in Catania, Sicily; after abandoning law studies, he embarked upon a career as writer, journalist, and playwright. Together with his fellow Sicilian Giovanni Verga, he was one of the protagonists of the *verismo*, or regional realism, movement, and as such embraced the expressive value of folkloric material, recognizing the similarities between the "impersonal" voice that was an essential element of *verismo* style and the narrative techniques of folktales. As novelist, he is remembered for *Profumo* (Perfume, 1890) and *Il Marchese di Roccaverdina* (*The Marquis of Roccaverdina*, 1901); he also published nearly twenty volumes of short prose.

Capuana was a prolific author of children's works, especially fairy tales. His tales draw on motifs and types commonly found in Sicilian folklore but also integrate literary materials and inject humor and graphic detail to create unique tales. The most important of Capuana's collections of fairy tales are *C'era una volta* (*Once Upon a Time*, 1882, enlarged in 1889), *Il regno delle fate* (The Kingdom of Fairies, 1883), *La reginotta* (The Princess, 1883), *Il Raccontafiabe* (The Fairy Tale-Teller, 1894), *Chi vuole fiabe, chi vuole?* (Who Wants Fairy Tales, Who Wants Them?, 1908), and *Le ultime fiabe* (The Last Fairy Tales, 1919); he also wrote fairy-tale plays such as *Spera di sole: Commedia per burattini* (Sunbeam: A Comedy for Marionettes, 1898).

The bipolar oppositions characteristic of the fairy tale can be extreme in Capuana's tales, where kings and queens rule tyrannically and the ruled—artisans, farmers, beggars, and other members of the lower classes—are often a meal away from destitution. The tales abound in realistic detail; kings and queens are depicted in their everyday rituals, and even magic helpers tend to be of humble and familiar appearance, seeming more like benevolent grandparents than fairies and wizards.

The tales of *Once Upon a Time*, of which three appear here, include "Le arance d'oro" (The Golden Oranges), "Ranocchino" (Little Froggy), "Cecina" (Little Chickpea), "I tre anelli" (The Three Rings), "La Fontana della bellezza" (The Fountain of Beauty), "L'uovo nero" (The Black Egg), "Serpentina" (Little Snake Girl), "Testa di Rospo" (Toad-Head), and eleven others. The last tale of the collection, "Il racconta-fiabe" (The Fairy Tale-Teller), suggestively illustrates Capuana's personal approach to his primary materials. It features a storyteller who, tired of telling the same old Cinderellas and Sleeping Beauties, meets up with some fairies in a wood as he is searching for new material. They send him to the wizard Tre-pi (an anagram of the folklorist Giuseppe Pitrè's name), but Tre-pi refuses to impart any of his narrative riches, instead directing him to Fairy Fantasy, who in turn offers him magical gifts that cause him to spew tales whenever he opens his mouth. His young audience tires of these tales, however, and he offers them to Tre-pi for his collection, but as they are changing hands the tales turn into "a handful of flies," and the teller concludes that his search for new tales is futile. The entire tale thus sums up the dialectic, common at the end of the nineteenth century, between folklorists concerned with collecting and recording traditional tales before they disappeared and innovative authors like Capuana, who affirm, through their original works, the potential for the creative regeneration of tradition.

Further Reading

Primary

Capuana, Luigi. *C'era una volta*. Ed. Stefano Rolando. Palermo: Sellerio, 1988. 32–42, 65–75, 125–35. [source text]

Capuana, Lugi. *Stretta la foglia, larga la via: Tutte le fiabe*. Ed. Rosaria Sardo. Rome: Donzelli, 2015.

Secondary

Cocchiara, Giuseppe. *Popolo e letteratura in Italia.* Turin: Einaudi, 1959.

Miele, G. M. "Luigi Capuana: Unlikely Spinner of Fairy Tales?" *Marvels & Tales* 23, no. 2 (2009): 300–324.

Zipes, Jack. "Luigi Capuana's Search for the New Fairy Tale." *Marvels & Tales* 23, no. 2 (2009): 367–90.

Ranocchino

This is a unique version of ATU 440, The Frog King, which is widespread in Northern Europe but much less common in Italy.

This is the nice story of Ranocchino Porgi il Ditino—Little Froggy Hold-Out-Your-Finger—and you'll soon hear why he's called that.

It is told that once upon a time there was a poor devil. He had seven children, and they were eating him up alive. The oldest was ten years old, and the youngest only two.

One evening their papa asked all of them to come before him.

"Children," he said, "it's been two days since we tasted even a drop of water, and I'm so desperate that I don't know where to turn. You know what I was thinking? Tomorrow I'll get our neighbor to lend us his donkey, I'll put the saddlebags on it, and I'll take you around and try to sell you. Let's see if you can meet up with a bit of luck."

The children started screaming; they didn't want to be sold, no sir! Only the youngest, who was two, wasn't screaming.

"How about you, Ranocchino, my Little Froggy?" asked his papa, who had given him that nickname because he was as small as a frog.

"I'm happy with that," he said.

And in the morning the poor devil put him on his back, and began going around the city. "Who wants to buy Ranocchino? Who wants to buy Ranocchino?"

But no one wanted him, a little thing like that!

The king's daughter appeared at her window. "What are you selling, my good man?"

"I'm selling this little boy to whoever wants to buy him." The princess looked at him, made a face, and slammed the window shutters in his face.

"Nice manners!" said the poor devil. And he started yelling again, "Who wants to buy Ranocchino? Who wants to buy Ranocchino?"

But no one wanted him, a little thing like that!

The poor devil didn't have the courage to return home, where the other children were waiting for him like so many souls in purgatory, dying of hunger.

In the meantime, Ranocchino had fallen asleep on his back.

At that point he decided that it was better to kill the boy than to see him suffer. He would kill of them, all of his children, one by one, starting with this one!

It was already evening by then, and after leaving the city he went into a cave, where no one could see him. He laid the little boy, who was calmly sleeping, on the ground, and before killing him he began to mourn for him:

"Ah, my dear heart!

"Now I have to kill you with these hands, my very own hands!

"Ah, my Ranocchino!

"I won't see you around the house any more, never again!

"Ah, my dear heart!

"And who was the witch that came to visit you in the cradle, who was she?

"Ah, my Ranocchino!

"Now I have to kill you with these hands, my very own hands!"

It was enough to break a heart of stone.

"What's the matter, why are you crying like that?"

The poor devil turned around and saw an old woman sitting at the mouth of the cave, with a little rod in her hand.

"What's the matter? I have seven small children, and we're all dying of hunger. I've decided to kill them so I won't have to see them suffer, and I'm starting with this one."

"What's his name?"

"His name's Beppe, but we call him Ranocchino, Little Froggy."

"And may he become a Little Froggy!"

The old woman had barely touched the little boy with her rod when he became a frog, and started jumping here and there.

His poor father was frightened.

"Come on, cheer up, now!" said the old woman. "Take a look in that corner; there's some bread and cheese that will be your meal for this evening. Tomorrow at noon, be waiting for me under the windows of the royal palace, and you will find your good fortune!"

When the children saw him return without their little brother, they started screaming.

"Hush! Here's some bread and cheese."

"But where's Ranocchino?"

"He's dead!"

He said that so they wouldn't bother him about it.

The next day, before the appointed time, he went and took his place under the windows of the royal palace. He waited and waited, but the old woman didn't show up. The king's daughter was at one of the windows, combing her hair. She recognized him and asked him, teasingly:

"Hey, you there, did anyone buy Ranocchino?"

But before he could reply, the old woman appeared, at the head of a line of people. The people gathered around her, and the old woman, in the middle, said,

"Ranocchino, hold out your finger!"

And Little Froggy extended his little hand, and held out his finger for the old woman. Then the others wanted to try: "Ranocchino, stick out your finger!" They couldn't get enough of it! They'd never seen anything so marvelous. And they all paid a coin each to see it.

The princess called the old woman over to the window; she wanted to see, too.

"Ranocchino, hold out your finger!"

She was captivated. And she immediately ran to the king.

"Papa, if you love me, you have to buy me that Ranocchino."

"What do you want to do with him?"

"I want to take care of him in my room; it'll be fun!"

The king agreed to this.

"My good woman, how much do you want for that Ranocchino?"

"Your Majesty, I'm selling him for his weight in gold. That's what he's worth."

"You're making fun of me, old girl."

"I mean it. Tomorrow the price will double. Ranocchino, hold out your finger!"

And Ranocchino extended his little hand, and held out his finger for the old woman. Then the others wanted to try: "Ranocchino, hold out your finger!"; they couldn't get enough of it!

"You see?" said the king to the princess. "The old woman needs to be there."

The princess wouldn't give up.

"Ranocchino, hold out your finger!"

Ranocchino took a jump, gave her a little bow, and held out his finger.

The king had to buy him; it was the only way to get the princess to quiet down.

They put Ranocchino on one pan of the scale, and a little piece of gold on the other, but it wasn't enough to lift Ranocchino. Could he possibly weigh that much? They piled more gold onto the scale, but it still wasn't enough to lift Ranocchino. The princess and the queen took off their earrings, rings, and bracelets, and threw them onto the scale. Nothing! The king took off his belt, which was made of solid gold, and threw it on the scale. Nothing!

"The crown, too! Let's see what happens now!"

At that point the scale balanced perfectly; there wasn't a hair of difference between the two sides.

The old woman emptied the pile of gold into her apron, and left.

The poor devil was waiting for her at the exit to the palace.

"Here you go!"

And she filled his pockets.

"But be careful! Spend it all any way you like; but if you sell or lose the royal crown, you'll be sorry!"

The princess entertained herself all day long with Ranocchino.

"Ranocchino, hold out your finger!"

It was a sight to see. She always had him in her hand; she took him with her everywhere. At the table, she even let him eat from her plate.

"That's disgusting!" said the queen.

But she was an only child, and they indulged all her whims.

The time came for the princess to take a husband. The prince of Portugal had asked for her hand, and the king and queen were overjoyed. But she said no, because . . .

She wanted to marry Ranocchino!

How could that be? But it was impossible to persuade her otherwise.

"Either Ranocchino, or no one!"

"I'll give you your Ranocchino!"

And the king grabbed him by one of his little legs and was about to slam him onto the ground when an eagle flew in through the window, tore Ranocchino from his hands, and disappeared.

The princess cried day and night. Poor child, she was a pitiful sight! The whole court was in mourning.

In the meantime, at Ranocchino's house every day was like Carnival. They squandered their riches on this and on that; half the neighborhood attended their banquets, and the money flowed in torrents. At last there wasn't a single cent left.

"Papa, let's sell the royal crown."

"We're not going to touch the royal crown!"

"So we're supposed to die of hunger? Let's sell it!"

"We're not going to touch the royal crown!"

The poor devil went back to the cave in search of the old woman, and began to cry.

"What happened?"

"My dear little mother, the money's all gone and those kids of mine wanted to sell the royal crown, but I wouldn't let them."

"Take a look in that corner; there's some bread and cheese that will be your meal for this evening. Tomorrow at noon, be waiting for me under the windows of the royal palace, and you will find your good fortune!"

He returned home and found a tragedy! Five of his children were lying dead on the ground in a pool of blood; the sixth was still barely breathing.

"Oh, papa! A big eagle landed at the window and started banging on it. 'Children, let me see the royal crown.' 'Papa keeps it locked up.' 'And where did he put it?' 'In this chest.' Then the eagle started to break it open with his beak, and when we tried to stand up to him, he killed us all."

After saying this, the boy expired.

The poor devil felt his hair stand on end. His children dead and the crown missing!

The next day, when he saw the old woman, he told her everything.

"Just leave it to me!" she said.

The princess was very ill. The doctors had run out of remedies.

"Your Majesty," they finally said, "we need Ranocchino back, or else the princess is done for."

The king was desperate. Where was he supposed to find that damned Ranocchino? The eagle had probably already digested him long ago.

The old woman presented herself. "Your Majesty, I would be able to help you find Ranocchino, but it's going to take a lot of courage."

"I would cut myself to pieces for her," replied the king.

"Find a diamond knife, the best ox in your herd, a mile-long piece of rope, and come with me."

The king found the diamond knife, the best ox in his herd, and a mile-long piece of rope; then he left with the old woman. No one was to follow them.

They walked for two days, and on the third day, toward dusk, they came to a plain, where there stood an enchanted tower a mile high with neither doors nor windows.

"That's where Ranocchino is!" said the old woman. "Those birds of prey that are circling around the top of the tower are his jailors. We have to climb up there."

"And how do we do that?"

"Kill the ox, Your Majesty, and you'll see."

The king killed the ox.

"Skin it, Your Majesty, but leave a lot of the flesh attached to the hide."

The king skinned it and left a lot of the flesh on the hide.

"Now, let's turn the hide inside out," said the old woman. "I'll sew you up inside it, and the birds will come down and carry you up there. Tonight you'll cut through the hide with the diamond knife, and tomorrow morning, when the eagle and the other birds have gone off hunting, you'll attach the rope to the top of the tower, get Ranocchino and the royal crown, put the knife between your teeth, and then lower yourselves down."

The king hesitated. "And what if the rope breaks?"

"If you keep the knife between your teeth it won't break."

Out of love for his daughter, the king let himself be sewn up inside the hide. And then right away, the birds of prey appeared: they seized him with their talons and took him up to the tower.

That night, he cut through the hide with the diamond knife and hid himself in a corner of a storeroom. When it was day, he waited for the eagle and the birds of prey to go hunting, then attached the rope to the top of the tower, got Ranocchino and the royal crown, and lowered himself down.

And the knife? He had forgotten it.

The rope started to moan, "Ouch! I'm breaking! Give me something to drink."

How to fix this? The king bit a vein in his arm, and squeezed until blood squirted out. He kept on sliding down.

But soon the rope started up again: "Ouch! I'm breaking! Give me something to drink."

The king bit a vein in his other arm, and squeezed until blood squirted out. He kept on sliding down.

But the rope started up again: "Ouch! I'm breaking! Give me something to drink."

Since they could almost touch the ground, the king replied, "Go ahead and break!"

And so it broke, but fortunately the king came out of it with only a few bruises. The old woman went looking for an herb for his broken veins, and when she had treated him, his wounds disappeared immediately.

As soon as she saw Ranocchino, the princess began to recover.

"Ranocchino, hold out your finger!"

Ranocchino held out his finger, and only to her.

To bring an end to this story, the king wanted to have the marriage immediately. But the old woman said to him, "You need to wait one more month. Meanwhile, prepare a cauldron of boiling oil."

"To do what with?"

"You'll find out later."

On the appointed day, the oil was boiling in the cauldron. The old woman arrived, followed by the poor devil with a cart on which were lying the corpses of his six children.

"Princess," said the old woman, "do you want to marry Ranocchino? Then you'll have to hold him by the foot and dunk him three times into that oil."

The princess hesitated.

"Dunk me, dunk me!" said Ranocchino.

And so she dunked him. One, two! But the third time he slipped out of her hand and fell to the bottom of the cauldron. The princess fainted.

The king wanted to have the old woman killed. But she quickly grabbed the dead children and threw them into the boiling oil, and then started stirring with her rod, as she sang,

Oh my fine lye, oh my fine lye,
They'll all jump out, by and by.

And in fact, out jumped the first of them, the oldest son, and he was alive and well.

Oh my fine lye, oh my fine lye,
They'll all jump out, by and by.

And she continued to stir. Out jumped the second. The same thing happened with all six of the children.

Oh my fine lye, oh my fine lye,
They'll all jump out, by and by.

And she continued to stir. Ranocchino floated up to the surface, but didn't jump out.

As soon as she saw him, the princess tried to grab him, but the old woman restrained her.

Did she want to burn herself? She had to do as she usually did.

"Ranocchino, hold out your finger!"

Ranocchino held out his finger to the princess and . . . guess who appeared? A young man as handsome as the sun.

The princess recognized him as the little boy the poor devil had wanted to sell, and she apologized for having slammed the shutters in his face. Obviously, Ranocchino had already forgiven her.

The wedding was celebrated with magnificent festivities, and in due course the royal crown passed to Ranocchino.

Some want it raw, some want to bake it,
If it's not to your liking, bring it back and I'll take it.

Cecina

Cecina is of the family of tiny and enterprising fairy-tale characters belonging to type ATU 700, Thumbling. Uther notes, "In variants from southern and south-eastern Europe many very small children originate from peas because of a curse or a wish; most are killed, but one survives" (1:375). In this tale and others, Capuana seems to delight in placing his royal characters—here the king—in ridiculous and grotesque situations; and as in this case, royals are often made to pay for judging others purely on the basis of their physical appearances. The marvelous quantities of wine and food that are freed from the king's stomach and provide an unexpected feast for his subjects recall Rabelaisian excesses as well as the Land of Cockaigne, a mythical land of plenty that had been present in literature and popular lore since the medieval period.

Once upon a time there was a king who was crazy about hunting, and since he wished to be as free as possible to go out every day, he had never wanted to take a wife.

His ministers would tell him, "Your Majesty, the people desire a queen."

And he would answer, "I'll take a wife next year."

A year would pass, and his minsters would start up again, "Your Majesty, the people desire a queen."

And he, again, "I'll take a wife next year."

But that year never arrived.

Each morning as soon as dawn broke, he would strap on his game bag, and with his rifle on his shoulder and his dogs by his side, out he would go into the woods and through the thickets. Anyone who needed to talk with the king had to go find him out there in the middle of the woods and thickets.

The ministers began to play the same tune, "Your Majesty, the people desire a queen."

Until finally the king made up his mind, and he sent his men to ask for the hand of the daughter of the king of Spain.

But when he went to marry her, he discovered that she was a bit hunchbacked. "Marry a little hunchback? No, never!"

"But she's beautiful, and full of virtues!" his ministers said to him.

"She's a little hunchback, and that's all there is to it: no, never!" And he went back to his hunting, to the woods and the thickets.

The best friend of that little hunchbacked princess was a fairy. When the fairy saw her crying because of the king's refusal, she said, "Don't worry, he'll marry you: and he'll have to come begging to do so. Leave it to me."

In fact, one day when the king was hunting he met a thin and spindly little woman, so slight that a breath of air could have blown her away.

"Your Majesty, have a good hunt!"

When he saw that face that looked like an ill omen, the king grew irritated, made a coarse gesture at her, and didn't answer. And that day he killed not even a wren.

Another morning, that thin, spindly little woman appeared again, the one that a breath of air could have blown away.

"Your Majesty, have a good hunt!"

"Listen to me, witch," the king said, "if I ever find you on this road again, I'll show you what's up!" And that day he killed not even a wren.

But the next morning, there she was again, that woman of ill omen.

"Your Majesty, have a good hunt!"

"I'll give you a good hunt!"

The king had brought his guards with him, and he ordered that the woman of ill omen be locked in prison.

From that day on, every time the king went hunting, he wasn't able to get a single shot out. The game had all disappeared, as if by magic, from the woods and thickets. There wasn't a rabbit or a hare to be had at any price, even its weight in gold.

Then something worse happened to him.

Since he wasn't able to get his usual exercise hunting, the king began to put on weight, and more weight, and then even more, and in a short time he became so big and fat that he weighed more than four hundred pounds, and he had a huge belly that looked like a barrel. When he took two steps in the rooms of the royal palace, it was as if he had gone a hundred miles. He would huff and puff worse than a bellows, sweat enough to flood the floor, and then he had to rest immediately and eat something substantial before he could get back his strength.

Depressed, he consulted the best doctors:

"I'd like to lose weight."

The doctors wrote prescription after prescription. A day wouldn't go by without the apothecary sending to the palace tall glasses full of concoctions that were as bitter as bile; these were supposed to cure His Majesty.

But the more concoctions His Majesty drank, the fatter he became.

In the royal palace they had already widened all the doorways so that the king could get through them; at one point the architects said that if the floors had not been so sturdily underpinned, with his tremendous weight His Majesty would have broken through them.

The poor king was desperate:

"Can't there possibly be a remedy?"

And he summoned more doctors, but it was useless. The more concoctions he drank, the fatter he became.

One day an old woman presented herself to the king and said, "Your Majesty, you're under a bad spell. I could break it; but in compensation you would have to marry my daughter, whose name is Cecina—Little Chickpea—because she's as tiny as a chickpea."

"I'll marry your Cecina!"

The king would have done just about anything to get rid of some of that fat and that big belly.

"Bring her here."

The old woman stuck a hand in her apron pocket and pulled out Cecina, who, although she was pint-sized, was pretty and well proportioned.

When she saw that huge belly, Cecina burst into laughter, and as the old woman was holding her on the palm of her hand to show her to the king, she leaped off and began to climb up the big belly, running from side to side as if it were a hill.

Those little feet tickled the king, and he wanted to stop her, but she was jumping this way and that, worse than a flea, and she refused to be caught. Because of the tickles the king laughed—*ha! ha! ha!*—and his big belly bounced up and down in a very funny way. *Ha, ha, ha!*

Then Cecina weighed in:

The king's belly is big and fat,
It'll be my palace in no time flat!

The king's mouth was open because he was laughing so hard, and Cecina jumped right in and slid down his throat.

The king's belly is big and fat,
It'll be my palace in no time flat!

You can just imagine how frightened His Majesty and all of his court were!

In the midst of the confusion, the old woman had disappeared.

And Cecina, from her palace, ordered, "Give me something to eat!" And the king had to eat for her, too.

"Give me something to drink!" And the king had to drink for her, too.

"Let me sleep!" And the king had to be still and silent, so that Cecina could sleep.

"Your Majesty," said one of the ministers, "could this be a curse cast on you by that thin, spindly woman whom we threw in prison? Let's have her brought in."

The guards opened the prison cell and found it empty. The woman must have escaped through the keyhole!

"And now what should we do?"

And Cecina, from her palace in the belly, cried, "Give me something to eat! Give me something to drink!"

Meanwhile, the king's subjects were grumbling about taxes, since it took a lot of things to fill that big belly of the king's! And it all had to be paid for.

The king issued a proclamation: whoever was able to extract Cecina from his stomach would become the royal prince and would be given as much money as he wanted!

But the town criers circulated in vain. And as Cecina grew, even if it wasn't very much, the king's big belly swelled up and looked like it was going to explode any minute.

The king begged her, "Cecina, sweetie, come out and I'll make you queen!"

"I'm happy in here, Your Majesty. Give me something to drink."

If he hadn't been afraid of dying, he would have split his belly open with his own hands.

And the people complained, "King Big-Belly is eating everything up! We're working for King Big-Belly now!"

As if King Big-Belly could do what he pleased! Only he knew what he was suffering, with Cecina in there ordering him around and demanding to be obeyed!

One day the old woman finally reappeared.

"Ah, you wicked old thing! Get your Cecina out of me, or you'll be in big trouble!"

"Your Majesty, I came with my doctors for that very purpose."

Her doctors were two dreadful-looking birds, bigger than turkeys and with arm's-length beaks that were as strong as steel.

"Your Majesty," said the old woman, "you'll have to lie down belly up in the middle of a plain."

The king, who had gotten so fat that he could no longer take even one step, ordered, "Roll me down there." And the people began to roll him like a barrel, down the stairs and through the streets, and they were sweating from the effort.

When they reached the plain and had placed the king belly up on the ground, one of the birds pecked him on the belly, and what do you think squirted out? A spray of unadulterated wine: all the wine that His Majesty had drunk in so many years.

The people filled up barrels, casks, kegs, vats, drums, bottles, and jugs; there weren't enough containers to hold it all. It was like being at a grape harvest. Everyone was guzzling it down and getting drunk.

And the king's belly deflated a little.

Then the other bird gave the king his peck, and out regurgitated all of the delicacies that the king had eaten in so many years: macaroni, juicy sausages, roast chickens, steaks, pastries, fruit—in short, everything imaginable. The people didn't know where to put it all. Everyone ate until they were bursting, as if it were Carnival.

And the king's belly deflated a little more.

Then the king said, "Cecina, sweetie, come out; I'll make you queen!"

Cecina stuck her head out of one of the holes, and replied, laughing, "Here I am."

And the king returned to his normal state.

They got married; but with that little pint-sized thing who had become his wife only because of all the fuss, the king considered himself free to go back to his pastime of hunting, and he would stay away for weeks on end. Cecina would weep,

Alas, this poor little thing,
She's a queen without a king!

The king couldn't tolerate her, because of all of that complaining. He went to a witch and said, "What do I need to do to get Cecina out of my sight?"

Majesty,
You can skin her or you can boil her in a pot,
Or eat her roasted, nice and hot.

Although the idea of eating her repulsed him, when he returned home he said to Cecina, "Tomorrow I'll take you hunting with me, and you'll have a good time." He wanted to take her out to the woods, where no one could see him.

But Cecina replied,

You can skin her or you can boil her in a pot,
Or eat her roasted, nice and hot.

"Thank you, Your Majesty!"

Alas, this poor little thing,
She's a queen without a king!

The king was dumbfounded. "How did she know that?"

He went back to the witch and told her what had happened.

"Your Majesty, when Cecina falls asleep, cut off a lock of her hair and bring it to me." But that evening Cecina didn't feel like going to bed.

"Cecina, come to sleep."

"Later, Your Majesty; I'm not sleepy right now."

The king waited and waited, and fell asleep before her. When he awoke the next morning, he saw that Cecina was already up.

"Cecina, didn't you sleep?"

"Those who watch over themselves will be saved. Thank you, Your Majesty."

Alas, this poor little thing,
She's a queen without a king!

The king was dumbfounded. "How did she know that?"

He went back to the witch and told her what had happened. "Your Majesty, invite King Crow; as soon as he sees her, he'll eat her up in one bite."

King Crow came. "*Caw! Caw! Caw! Caw!*" The minute he saw pint-sized Cecina, *caw! caw!* He ate her up in one bite.

"Thanks a million, King Crow. You can leave now."

"*Caw! Caw! Caw!* But before I leave, I need to eat your eyes." And with two pecks he scratched the king's eyes out.

The poor king was weeping blood.

"Cecina dead, and me without eyes! Ah, my Cecina!"

After some time, the same old woman reappeared. She was the fairy godmother of the princess of Spain.

"No need to worry, Your Majesty. Cecina is alive, and your eyes are stored in a safe place—they're in the princess of Spain's hump."

The king dragged himself back to the royal palace where that princess lived, and when he was at the door, he began to shout pitifully, "Ah, princess! Give me back my eyes!"

From the window the princess replied, "Marry a little hunchback? No, never!"

"Forgive me, princess, and give me back my eyes!"

From the window the princess replied,

You can skin her or you can boil her in a pot,
Or eat her roasted, nice and hot.

And then the king understood that the princess of Spain and Cecina were the same person; and he began to shout even more loudly, "Ah, princess! Ah, my Cecina! Give me back my eyes!"

The princess came down and said to him, "Here are your eyes."

The king looked at her with amazement. The princess was no longer a hunchback, and she looked exactly like Cecina, except that she was of normal stature.

And so he was forgiven, and soon thereafter she married him.

As a reminder of the past she always wanted to be called Cecina.

And so they lived happily ever after
But as for us, not so much laughter.

The Black Egg (L'uovo nero)

This tale contains many elements of ATU 441, Hans My Hedgehog. Here we find another of Capuana's kings, who is debased by having to deal with an out-of-control young rooster, who filthies and wreaks havoc on his living spaces but whom the king eventually resigns himself to adopting as his son, as if, perhaps, to say that the boundary between noble kings and dirt-pecking animals is at the best tenuous.

Once upon a time there was an old woman who earned her living by begging for alms, and everything that she got she split exactly down the middle: half for her, and half for her hen.

Every day at dawn the hen would start clucking; she had laid an egg. The old woman sold it for a penny and bought a penny's worth of bread. She would crumble up the crust for the hen, and she would eat the inside. Then she would go around again begging for alms.

But then there was a bad year. One day the little old woman returned home with nothing.

"Ah, my dear little hen! Nothing to put in our mouths today."

"We have to be patient. Tomorrow we'll eat."

The next day, at daybreak, the hen started to cluck. Instead of one egg, she had laid two, one white and the other black.

The old woman went out to sell them. She sold the white one right away; but no one wanted to believe that the black one was a hen's egg. The little old woman bought the usual penny's worth of bread, and returned home.

"Ah, my dear little hen! No one wants the black egg."

"Take it to the king."

The old woman took it to the king.

"What kind of egg is this?"

"A hen's egg, Your Majesty."

"What's your price?"

"Whatever your heart dictates, Your Majesty."

"Give her a hundred lire."

With those hundred lire, the little old woman thought that she was richer than His Majesty himself.

Around that same time the queen had acquired a hen, and she added the black egg to the eggs her hen was brooding. But the mother hen wouldn't have it.

"That egg has gone bad."

"That can't be, Your Majesty; the hen had laid it that same day."

"And yet nothing has come out of it."

"The queen needs to brood it."

This seemed strange. But the queen was curious, and said, "I'll brood it."

And she kept it close to her breast. After twenty-two days, she heard the shell breaking. A white chick came out, a real beauty.

"Your Majesty, Your Majesty! Make me some wine soup!" And it cheeped.

"Are you a cockerel or a pullet?"

"I'm a cockerel, Your Majesty."

"Sing."

"*Cock-a-doodle-doo!*"

It really was a cockerel. And it became the pastime of the whole court. But the bigger it grew, the more impertinent it became. At the table it would peck in the king's and queen's dishes; it scratched about in the ministers' plates, as if this were normal, and they didn't dare to say *shoo!* out of respect for the king; it walked through the rooms of the royal palace, roosting wherever it felt like it; and it left dirt all over the place and filled everything with droppings. And then, all day long, *cock-a-doodle-doo! cock-a-doodle-doo!* It was deafening. The people who lived in the palace couldn't take it anymore.

One day the queen had just had a new dress made: a marvelous dress that had cost an arm and a leg. Before she had a chance to wear it the cockerel went and soiled it.

The queen flew into a rage. "Dirty cockerel! This time I'll let it go, but do it once more and I'll show you!"

And she ordered another dress from the seamstress, even more lavish than the first. The seamstress applied herself to the task with diligence; just imagine what a dress she made! But before the queen had a chance to wear it, the cockerel went and soiled it.

The queen went off the deep end. "Dirty cockerel! I'll ruin you! Call the cook."

The cook presented himself. "Have a nice bowl of broth made from that cockerel."

In the kitchen they wrung its neck and put it on to cook. As soon as the pot began to boil, *cock-a-doodle-doo!* The cockerel had escaped, as if its neck had never been wrung and its feathers plucked and seared.

The cook ran off to the queen. "Your Majesty, the cockerel has come back to life!"

This was too strange of an occurrence, and after that the cockerel became precious. Everyone regarded it with respect; some were even a little frightened. And it took advantage of this. At the table it pecked in the plates of the king and queen more than ever; it scratched about in the ministers' plates, as if it were normal, and they didn't dare to say *shoo!* out of respect for the king; it roosted wherever it felt like; it left dirt all over, even on the royal throne, and filled it with droppings. And besides, night and day—*cock-a-doodle-doo! cock-a-doodle-doo!* It was deafening. And the people clenched their teeth and swore, "Dang that cockerel and the ones who are raising it!"

One day His Majesty had to write a letter to another king. He got paper, pen, and inkwell, wrote the letter, and left it on the table to dry. The cockerel went over and soiled it, right where the king's signature was.

"Dirty cockerel! This time I'll let it go, but do it once more and I'll show you!"

The king wrote the letter all over again, and left it on the table to dry. The cockerel went over and soiled it right where the king's signature was. The king went off the deep end. "Dirty cockerel! I'll ruin you! Call the cook."

The cook appeared. "Roast it for me for dinner."

In the kitchen they wrung its neck, skewered it, and put it on the spit.

When it was time for dinner, the cook served it at the table. His Majesty began to divide it up: a wing here, a thigh there, some breast here, the rump there. He saved the neck and the head with the comb and wattles for himself.

He had barely finished eating when from the depths of his stomach there burst a sound: *cock-a-doodle-doo!* There was general consternation. The court doctors were quickly summoned.

"We'll need to cut open the king's belly, but who's going to do that?"

And every now and then the cockerel would speak from the bottom of His Majesty's stomach: *cock-a-doodle-doo!*

"Summon the old woman for me," said the king.

At that very moment she was on her way to the royal place to beg for alms, and they escorted her up.

"Devil's witch! What sort of curse did you put on that egg? I ate the cockerel's head, and now it's singing in my stomach. If you don't get rid of it, consider yourself dead!"

"Your Majesty, give me one day's time." Then she returned straight home. "Ah, my dear little hen! I was summoned by the king. He ate the head of the cockerel, and now it's singing in his stomach. If I don't get rid of it, I'm going to die!"

"My dear little old woman, that's nothing. Tomorrow you'll take some chicken feed, return to the king, and you'll go, '*Billi! Billi!*' When the cockerel hears your voice, it will come out."

And that's what happened.

This was too strange of an occurrence. The cockerel became famous, and went back to behaving even worse than before.

One morning before dawn: "*Cock-a-doodle-doo!* Your Majesty, I want a hen."

"Alright, let's give him a hen!"

The following day, before dawn: "*Cock-a-doodle-doo!* Your Majesty, I want another hen."

"Alright let's give him another hen!"

In short, he wanted two dozen of them.

Another morning, before dawn: "*Cock-a-doodle-doo!* Your Majesty, I want some golden spurs."

"Bring on the golden spurs!"

The cockerel, who had become a handsome rooster, would strut around with those golden spurs, pecking here and there.

Another time, before dawn: "*Cock-a-doodle-doo!* Your Majesty, I want a double comb made of gold."

"Bring on the double comb made of gold!"

The king was beginning to get fed up; but the rooster, with those golden spurs and that double comb of gold, would strut around, pecking at this and at that.

Finally another morning, before dawn: "*Cock-a-doodle-doo!* Your Majesty, I want half of your kingdom; I have a crown, just like you!"

The king lost his patience. "Get this nasty, impertinent rooster out of my sight!"

But what could he do? It was useless to kill it; it kept on coming back to life. Taking it far away didn't resolve anything; it would return. Treating it nicely made things worse; it responded by mocking him: *cock-a-doodle-doo!* Desperate, the king sent for the old woman.

"If you don't get rid of this rooster, I'll have your head chopped off!"

"Your Majesty, give me one day's time."

She returned straight home. "Ah, my dear little hen! I was summoned by the king. 'If you don't get rid of this rooster, I'll have your head chopped off.' What am I supposed to answer him?"

Answer him: "Your Majesty, you have no children; adopt it as your child and it will calm down."

The king's back was up against the wall, and so he agreed to adopt it. But that didn't help much.

With all those hens, the royal palace had become a chicken coop. The king, the queen, the ministers, the ladies of the court, the servants, everyone was full of droppings from head to toe, and couldn't put up with it anymore. And besides, their heads were bursting with all that clucking and crowing.

The people clenched their teeth and swore, "Dang that rooster, those hens, and the ones who are raising them."

"Listen here, witch," said the king, "If in one day's time you don't sweep me clean of the rooster and all the hens, you'll pay with your head."

"Your Majesty, this is a job for the Fata Morgana; send for her."

The king sent for the Fata Morgana. She replied, "He who wants must go himself; he who wants not sends someone else."

So the king had to go in person.

"Your Majesty, you'll never have peace until that rooster becomes a man just like you."

"And what will it take for it to become a man just like me?"

"It will take three types of chicken feed. Dig three holes with your hands, and sow these three seeds. Harvest and thresh the grains, without mixing them, and then say,"

Cluck, cluck, cluck!
Whoever wants some, come try their luck!

"Then scatter this grain on the ground. When there's just one grain left, say":

Cluck, cluck, cluck!
Whoever wants some, come try their luck!

"Then scatter this other grain on the ground. When there's just one grain left, say":

Cluck, cluck, cluck!
Whoever wants some, come try their luck!

"Then scatter the last grain on the ground."

The king was careful to do everything exactly as told. When it was the right moment, he said,

Cluck, cluck, cluck!
Whoever wants some, come try their luck!

And half of the hens died.

Cluck, cluck, cluck!
Whoever wants some, come try their luck!

And the rest of the hens died.

Cluck, cluck, cluck!
Whoever wants some, come try their luck!

The rooster began to peck by itself, and as soon as it had pecked the last grain, it stepped back, stretched—*cock-a-doodle-doo!*—shook its feathers, and became a tall, handsome young man. The only things left of the rooster were the comb and the spurs. But that didn't matter.

The king said to his people, "I have no children, so this young man here will be the prince. Respect him as such."

"Long live the prince! Long live the prince!"

But under their breath the people were saying, "We'll see. When you're born a rooster you've got to crow."

After some months the prince grew melancholic. He wanted to be alone; he wouldn't talk to anyone.

"What's the matter, my son?"

"Nothing, Your Majesty."

He didn't want to mention it, he was embarrassed, but he had the greatest desire to go *cock-a-doodle-doo!*

They summoned the court physicians; they summoned physicians from outside the kingdom, too, the most talented. They couldn't understand what was going on.

"Perhaps the prince desired a wife?"

He did not desire a wife.

But then what did he desire? Whatever he wanted would be granted to him.

"I would like . . . to go *cock-a-doodle-do!*"

They had to let him, and he crowed the whole day long.

Then they cut off his comb, and he no longer had that desire. The people said, "We'll see. When you're born to a hen you're bound to go scratching."

After some months the prince became melancholic again. He wanted to be alone; he wouldn't talk to anyone.

"What's the matter, my son?"

"Nothing, Your Majesty."

He didn't want to mention it, he was embarrassed, but he had the greatest desire to go out and scratch around.

They called back the doctors, but they couldn't figure it out.

"Perhaps the prince desired a wife?"

He did not desire a wife.

But then what did he desire? Whatever he wanted would be granted to him.

"I would like . . . to go out and scratch around!"

And they had to let him do it.

Then they tore off his spurs, and he no longer had that desire.

The time came to give him a wife.

"Would you like the princess of Spain, my son?"

"Your Majesty, if I have to get married . . . I would like to marry a pullet!"

So they were back where they had started again?

The king was down in the dumps that day. He pulled out his saber and cut the prince's head off.

But instead of human blood, he shed chicken blood.

Then the little old woman appeared. "Your Majesty, it's over now." She stuck his head back on with some of her spit, and the prince came back to life.

Now that he was a real man, he calmed down, and shortly thereafter he married the princess of Spain. Then they became king and queen, and did some good.

And now the tale is over.

5

Emma Perodi (1850–1918)

The writer and journalist Emma Perodi, born in Florence, dedicated much of her professional life to children's literature. She produced numerous original tale collections, edited scholastic texts for use in elementary schools, and assumed editorial direction of one of the most important children's journals of the time, *Giornale per i bambini*. Her interest in the fairy tale expressed itself more in a creative re-elaboration of folk narrative than in the "archeological" bent and collecting activities of her contemporaries Giuseppe Pitrè and Vittorio Imbriani. Her collections include *Al tempo dei tempi . . . Fiabe e leggende del Mare, delle Città e dei Monti di Sicilia* (In Days of Old . . . Fairy Tales and Legends of the Sea, Cities, and Mountains of Sicily), *Fate e fiori* (Fairies and Flowers), *Il paradiso dei folletti* (The Paradise of Elves), *Le fate d'oro* (The Golden Fairies), *La Bacchetta Fatata* (The Enchanted Wand), *Le Fate Belle* (The Beautiful Fairies), *Nell'antro dell'orco* (In the Ogre's Cave), and her best-known work, *Le novelle della nonna: fiabe fantastiche* (Grandmother's Stories: Fantastic Fairy Tales, 1892).

The *Novelle* includes forty-five tales, most incorporating fairy-tale or fantastic motifs, and is framed by a realistic narrative of a year in the life of a Tuscan peasant family, the Marcuccis. The tales are told around the family hearth by the family matriarch, grandmother Regina ("Queen"), an idealized model of the tale-tellers so prized as sources by folklorists of the period. Regina's stories are regularly punctuated by the Marcuccis' everyday vicissitudes, which include marriages, changes in employment, and food shortages; the fantastic tales, which often incorporate similar events, thus obliquely offer the family counsel. Stylistically, too, the tales are marked by an expressive interplay between the real and the fantastic; by the overlay of religious and folkloric motifs; and by a predilection for the macabre, the paradoxical, and the uncanny, as in, for example, the tales "Il morto risuscitato" (Risen from the Dead), "Il teschio di Amalziabene" (Amalziabene's Skull), "La fidanzata dello scheletro" (The Skeleton's Fiancée), "Mona Bice e i tre figli storpi" (Lady Bice and Her Three Crippled Sons), "Il ragazzo con due teste" (The Boy with Two Heads), "L'impiccato vivo" (Hung Alive), "La sorte di Biancospina" (The Fate of Biancospina), and "Il lupo mannaro" (The Werewolf). Ultimately, the tales of the *Novelle* celebrate the pleasures of narration and the indeterminacy of the fantastic worlds that they represent, which to some degree undermines any straightforward didactic function that the tales purport to have.

Further Reading

Primary

Perodi, Emma. *Fiabe fantastiche: Le novelle della nonna*. Ed. and introd. Antonio Faeti. Turin: Einaudi, 1974. 394–406. [source text]

Secondary

Carli, Alberto. "La nuova veglia di lettura, la fiaba 'moderna' e l'Italia unita: Ferdinando Martini, Emma Perodi e Luigi Capuana tra oralità e scrittura." *History of Education & Children's Literature* 1, no. 2 (2006): 131–50.

Casentino in fabula. Cent'anni di fiabe fantastiche (1893–1993). "Le novelle della nonna" di E. P., Atti del Convegno, Popp, 18–19 settembre 1993. Ed. V. Agostini-Ouafi. Florence: Quaderni della Rilliana, 2000.

Faeti, Antonio. "Il crepuscolo dell'orco pedagogico." In *Fiabe fantastiche: Le novelle della nonna*, by Emma Perodi. Turin: Einaudi, 1974.

Scancarello, Walter, ed. *Su Emma Perodi: Nuovi saggi critici*. Pisa: Bibliografia e informazione, 2015.

The Enchantress (L'incantatrice)

This tale contains many common fairy-tale motifs, such as a Circe-like enchantress figure who transforms men into animal form (fish) and keeps them prisoners; three magic objects with miraculous properties—here, religious relics, which many people did believe had such powers; and a cross-dressed heroine with whom the enchantress falls in love.

In times gone by, when the Madonna, Jesus, and the saints performed miracles, there was in Arezzo—not quite in the city, but just outside the walls, near the church of the Graces—a girl by the name of Santina. This girl had a cousin called Gosto, and being relatives, the two of them had grown up with the idea of getting married one day. But when their parents came to their death, they were forced to hire themselves out as help, and in their adversity they had had the luck to end up at the same farm, working for the same employer.

The two of them could have gotten by happily, mutually helping each other, but instead they were always complaining.

"If we had at least enough to buy a couple of cows and a pig," Gosto would say, "we'd look for a little farm and we could get married!"

"Yes," Santina would answer, sighing, "but these are some times! It's crazy how expensive animals are, and there's no relief for poor people."

"I'm afraid we're going to have to wait a long time!" replied the young man. "In any case, I can't be accused of wasting money at the tavern."

"I'm afraid, too," said Santina.

They would repeat these complaints every day, and Gosto finally lost his patience. One morning he went to the girl, who was sifting wheat in the barnyard, and told her that he wanted to travel afar to find his fortune.

Santina was very disturbed by this news, and she did everything she could to hold him back; but Gosto, who was a resolute young man, wouldn't listen to her.

"Birds," he said, "always fly until they find a wheat field, and bees buzz around searching for flowers from which to make honey. Do you think that a man should have lower standards than those animals? I want to search, too, until I find what I'm missing, and by that I mean something to buy a couple of cows and a pig with. If you care for me, Santa, you mustn't oppose this decision of mine, which will expedite our marriage."

The girl understood that she needed to give in, and even though she felt her heart bleeding, she said to Gosto:

"Go, and may God help you! But before you leave, let me share with you what my parents left me."

Then she brought the young man over to a chest, opened it, and took out a little bell, a knife, and a club.

"These three relics," she said, "have never left my family. Here is Saint Romano's little bell: its ring can be heard at any distance, and it warns the friends of whoever possesses it of any danger he may be in. The knife belonged to Saint Donato: everything it touches is protected from the enchantments of sorcerers and the Demon. Finally, the walking stick is the one that the glorious Saint Francis had, and it leads you wherever you want to go. I'm giving you the knife so that you can defend yourself from evil spells, and the bell so that you can warn me of the dangers that you are in; the club I'll keep for myself, so that I may reach you if I need to."

Gosto thanked Santina, shed two big tears as he left her, and then headed toward the mountains. But as soon as he appeared at the entrance to a village, the poor people accosted him, thinking that he was a gentleman because he was dressed in clean clothes.

"This looks like a place made more for using up the few coins that I have than for adding to them," said Gosto. "Let's try something farther along."

And he walked, and then walked some more, and came to Romagna, a short distance from the sea.

While he was at the door of a tavern, about to go in, he heard two mule drivers who, as they were loading up their mules, were talking about the Enchantress of the Devil's Cliff. Gosto drew closer to the two men and asked them for an explanation. They answered that no one knew who the Enchantress was or where she came from, but only that she lived on a dangerous cliff and that she was richer than all of the kings on earth.

"Don't you follow the example of so many others," added one of the mule drivers, "who have gone to the Devil's Cliff to take possession of the Enchantress's treasures. Those who go to her never return."

When he heard this warning, Gosto was immediately stung by the desire for that adventure. The mule drivers did everything they could to hold him back, and when they saw that he was determined to go, they incited the townspeople, who crowded around him and began to shout, saying that no Christian soul could allow a young fellow to go off like that to his perdition.

Seeing the predicament he was in, Gosto said that he would abandon the enterprise. But since he was so poor, he begged those good souls, who showed such a lively interest in him, to take up a collection with whose proceeds he might buy a couple of steer and a pig.

When they heard this, the crowd dispersed, saying that the boy was stubborn and that there was no way to hold him back.

And so, once Gosto had been left to himself, he went to the seashore and got a boatman to take him to the Devil's Cliff.

This cliff was partially submerged in water, and in the middle there was a pool formed by seawater, and in the center of the pool there was a little island surrounded by seaweed and rose-colored lilies. While Gosto was walking around the edge of the pool, he saw, hidden in a tuft of grass, a little sky-blue boat that was rocking on the calm water. The little boat had the shape of a swan with its head folded under one wing.

Gosto, who had never seen anything of the sort, went closer so that he could look at the boat, and after he examined it from every side, he got in. But as soon as he stepped into it, the swan seemed to wake up: it pulled its head from under its feathers, extended its feet in the water, and moved swiftly away from the shore.

The boy cried out in fright, but the swan pushed forth rapidly toward the center of the pool. Then Gosto tried to jump into the water, hoping to swim to shore, but the swan dove down into the water and dragged with it the boy, who didn't dare to shout so that he wouldn't fill his mouth with that nauseating water. And so he had to keep silent, and in that way he arrived at the Enchantress's house.

The house was made out of the rarest seashells. It was accessed by a crystal staircase that had been created in such a way that when you climbed it, each step sang like a bird in the spring. Surrounding the house were vast gardens where forests of marine plants grew, and there were beds of green seaweed dotted with diamonds in the place of flowers.

The Enchantress was lying on a golden bed in the first room. She was dressed in a sea-green dress that was as fine and transparent as waves; her black hair was charmingly adorned with corals, and fell all the way down to her heels; her face was as white and rosy as the inside of a seashell.

Gosto's mouth fell open when he saw how beautiful she was; then the Enchantress arose with a smile and began to come toward him. Her gait was as light as a white wave coursing across the sea, or a cloud wafting through the air.

When she got close to Gosto she greeted him, saying, "May you be welcome. There is always room here for strangers and for handsome young men."

Gosto mustered up some courage and took a step forward; then the Enchantress asked him, "Who are you? Where do you come from? What are you looking for?"

"My name is Agostino," answered the boy. "I come from Arezzo and I'm looking for a way to buy a pair of steer and a pig."

"Well, then, come with me," said the fairy. "You mustn't worry about a thing, because you will have all you need to make you happy." She invited him into a second room whose walls were covered with pearls, where she prepared for him eight different varieties of wine, in eight silver pitchers. Gosto emptied all of the pitchers, and when they were refilled, he emptied them again; and the more he drank, the more beautiful the Enchantress appeared to him.

She reassured him, telling him that he shouldn't worry about ruining her, because the pool on the Devil's Cliff communicated with the sea, and all of the treasures swallowed by the sea during storms were carried there by a magic current.

"By my soul," said Gosto, who had become rather bold on account of the wine, "it's no wonder that the people on the coast speak badly of you! Rich people are always the target of envy; as for myself, I would ask for nothing more than half of what you possess."

"You will have it, Agostino, if you like," said the fairy.

"What do I need to do?" he asked.

"I'm the widow of a dwarf," she replied, "and if you like me, we can get married."

Gosto was astonished by this proposal. He, of all people, dirt poor, was supposed to marry the Enchantress, who was so beautiful and rich enough to offer him eight varieties of wine? It's true that he had promised Santina that he would marry her, but in this world, when you have the chance to get rich, you forget about that as well as other things.

And so he answered the fairy very politely, telling her that she wasn't the sort of person one could refuse, and that it would be a pleasure for him to be her husband.

The Enchantress then replied that she wanted to prepare the wedding banquet right away, and she set a table covered with every sort of food imaginable. There were many things that Gosto was familiar with, but also many others that he had never seen. Then she went over to a little fish pond at the back of the garden, and began to shout, "Oh, counselor! Oh, miller! Oh, sailor! Oh, soldier of fortune!"

Each time she shouted, on the surface of the water you could see a fish flash by, which she would catch in a steel net. When the net was full, the Enchantress went into a nearby room and threw the fish into a golden pan.

But instead of the sizzle of frying Gosto seemed to hear many little voices whispering.

"Tell me, Enchantress, who is that whispering in the golden pan?"

"It's the wood crackling," she answered, stoking the fire.

A moment later the little voices started up again.

"Tell me, Enchantress, who is that murmuring in the golden pan?"

"It's the oil frying," answered the fairy, stirring the pan.

But before long the little voices could be heard again.

"Tell me, Enchantress, who is that screaming?"

"It's the cricket outside here," said the fairy.

And she began to sing at the top of her lungs, so that Gosto heard nothing more.

However, what he had heard made him wonder, and since he was starting to be afraid, regret set in. "Dear Jesus," he said to himself, "how is it possible that I was so quick to forsake Santina for an Enchantress, who's probably the daughter of Satan! I wouldn't even dare to say my prayers with this woman here, neither in the evening nor in the morning; I'd be sure to go to hell and burn for all eternity."

While he was saying this, the fairy had put the fried fish on the table, and she urged him to eat, telling him that she was going to get another twelve varieties of wine for him.

Gosto took out the knife that Santina had given him and with a sigh prepared to start eating; but as soon as the blade that destroyed spells touched the golden plate, all of the fish stood up and turned back into men, who were dressed according to their professions. The counselor was wearing a toga, the miller was covered with flour, the sailor had a red beret, and the soldier of fortune had a multicolored uniform and a lance, and they all began shouting, "Save us, if you want to be saved!"

"Holy Mary! Who are these men who were screaming in the boiling oil?" exclaimed Gosto, astonished.

"We're poor souls, just like you," they answered. "We came to the Devil's Cliff in search of good fortune, we agreed to marry the Enchantress, and the day after our wedding she reduced us to the state that you saw, the same as she had done to our predecessors, who are in the fish pond."

"What do you mean?" exclaimed Gosto. "A woman who looks so young has already been widowed so many times?"

"And very soon you'll be turned into a fish, and risk being fried and eaten by your successors."

Gosto jumped up. He imagined that he was already in the golden pan, and he ran to the door, trying to escape before the return of the Enchantress. But as soon as she entered the room she understood everything. In the blink of an eye she threw the steel net over him, and he was transformed into a frog fish and brought to the fish pond, where all the other husbands were.

At that same moment the little bell around Gosto's neck began to ring by itself, and Santina heard it from Arezzo while she was spinning wool in the farmyard. At that sound she felt a stab in her heart, and she cried, "Gosto is in danger!"

And without waiting a moment longer or consulting anyone, she hurried off to put on her Sunday dress. Then she slipped on her shoes and left the farm, leaning on Saint Frances's walking stick.

When she reached a crossroad she drove the stick into the ground and said,

O stick, little stick of mine,
From our saint, poor and divine,
Bring me to my Gosto dear
With the help of God ever near.

The stick immediately changed into a horse that was curried, harnessed, and saddled, with bows on its ears and plumes on its head.

Santina got onto the horse; at first it started walking, then galloping, and finally it was running so fast that the gullies, trees, houses, and bell towers flew past the girl's eyes as if they were the spokes of a spinning wheel. But she didn't complain, since she knew that every step brought her closer and closer to her dear Gosto. In fact, she spurred the animal on, repeating, "Horses go slower than swallows, swallows go slower than the wind, and the wind slower than an arrow. But you, my dear little horse, you must go more swiftly than them all, if you love me, for a part of my heart is suffering, and it's the best part of my heart that is in danger."

The horse understood her perfectly and ran like a piece of straw carried away by the wind. But when it was halfway across the Apennine mountains, it stopped, because no horse had ever traveled such a steep and precipitous path as the one taken by Santina.

Santina understood why the horse had stopped, and said:

O horse, little horse of mine,
From our saint, poor and divine,
Bring me to my Gosto dear
With the help of God ever near.

As soon as the girl had completed this invocation, wings sprouted from the flanks of the horse, which transformed into a huge bird and began to fly higher and higher, until it reached the peak of a mountain. On that peak there was a clay nest covered in moss, in which a little bald, wrinkled man was crouched. When he saw Santina he began to shout, "Here's the beautiful girl who's come to save me!"

"To save you? But who are you, little man?"

"I'm Cencio, the husband of the Enchantress of the Devil's Cliff; it was she who banished me to this place."

"And what are you doing in that nest?"

"I'm brooding six stone eggs, and I will not be free until from these eggs are born six chicks."

Santa couldn't hold back her laughter. "Poor little rooster, how am I ever going to save you?"

"By saving Gosto, who is under the power of the Enchantress, you will also save me."

"Tell me what I can do, for goodness sake, and even if I had to do a tour of every shrine in the world on my knees, I would set off immediately."

"Alright, then, we'll need to do two things," the Dwarf replied. First, you must present yourself to the Enchantress disguised as a young man; then, you must remove her steel net, which she carries on her belt, and imprison her in it until the Day of Judgment.

"And wherever am I going to find man's clothes?" the girl asked.

"You'll soon find out, my pretty one!"

The Dwarf began to dig in the earth, and after digging and digging, he made a deep hole. Then he stopped abruptly, and said to Santina, "I can't do this anymore; but you're not tired and you can dig some more. There should be some bags down there that were taken from a knight by thieves. After robbing him they were captured and hung, but the stolen goods are still in the earth's safekeeping."

Santina continued to dig, and dug for so long that at the end she found the leather bags intact. Inside there was an elegant velvet tunic, a plumed cap, a belt, pants, and a sword.

When Santina had put on the elegant clothing, she looked just like a knight.

She thanked the Dwarf, who gave her some more instructions about what to do, and then the bird with the enormous wings brought her in a single flight all the way to the Devil's Cliff.

When she arrived, she said,

O Bird, you bird so fine,
Go back to being the stick of mine,
Now I'm here with my Gosto dear
With the help of God ever near!

Then she saw the boat in the shape of a swan and got in, and the swan brought her to the Enchantress's place.

At the sight of the handsome, elegantly dressed knight, the Enchantress was quite delighted, and exclaimed, "What the devil? I've never seen such a handsome young man on this island, and I want to give him a joyous and gracious welcome."

She went up to Santina, saying, "My heart! My love!" Then she served her some refreshment, and when the girl found Saint Donato's knife on the table, where it had been left by Gosto, she took it so that she could make use of it in case of need. Then she followed the Enchantress into the garden.

The fairy showed her the gardens with the diamond flowers, the fountains of fragrant water, and above all the fish pond, where fish of every color were swimming. Santina contemplated them with great admiration, and sat down at the edge of the pond so that she could take a closer look.

The Enchantress took advantage of the moment to ask her if she would be happy to stay forever in her company, and Santina answered that she yearned for nothing else, that this was her sole desire.

"And so you would marry me right away?" asked the fairy.

"Yes, on the condition, though, that you allow me to fish for one of these beautiful fish with the steel net that you wear on your belt."

The Enchantress had no suspicions, believing that this wish was a mere whim on the part of the young man, and so she gave him the net and said, smiling, "Let's see what you'll fish, handsome fisherman!"

"I'll fish the Devil!" exclaimed Santina, throwing the net over the Enchantress's head. "In the name of the Redeemer of all men, accursed witch, may you now become in appearance what you are in reality."

The Enchantress could do no more than let out a scream, which ended in a strangled groan, because Santina's wish had been fulfilled, and the lovely fairy of the waters had been transformed into a horrid old woman, wrinkled and drooling.

Santina pulled the net closed and quickly threw it into a well; she put a stone with the sign of the cross on top, so that, like a tombstone, it could not be lifted until the Day of Judgment.

Then she rushed back to the fish pond, but the fish had already gotten out and were coming toward her in a long procession, shouting with their raspy little voices, "Here is our master, he who has freed us from the steel net and the golden frying pan."

"And he will also give you back your human appearance," said Santina, taking the knife of Saint Donato out of her pocket.

But just as she was about to touch the first fish with it, she saw a green frog with a little bell around its neck next to her on the grass. The frog was crying and pressing its heart with its little front legs; at the sight of this, Santina felt a rush of blood to her heart and exclaimed, "Is that you, my dear Gosto, my promised one, my darling?"

"Yes, it's me," answered the frog.

Santina immediately touched him with the blade she had at her belt, and Gosto took on a human appearance. They embraced, laughing and crying at the same time. The tears were the expression of past sorrows; the laughter, of future hopes.

Then the girl touched all the other fish, which turned back into men, just as they had been before the enchantment.

As she was about to leave, she saw the little man of the mountain arrive. He was seated on the nest, which was pulled by six cockroaches that had been born from the six stone eggs.

"Here I am, pretty girl!" he exclaimed, when he caught sight of Santina. "The spell that kept me confined to the peak of the mountain is now broken, thanks to you." And to demonstrate his gratitude, he guided her down into the palace cellars, where the Enchantress kept her treasures hidden, and he told her to take what she wanted. Santina and Gosto filled their pockets with precious gems, and the girl ordered the stick to become a ship big enough to take all the people that she had saved to the coast of Romagna. The stick of Saint Francis obeyed at once, and before the vessel set sail, Santina touched the Devil's Cliff with the knife of Saint Donato, and the cliff collapsed into the eddies of the sea.

After a few days, Santina and Gosto returned to the farm of the Graces, near Arezzo, and instead of buying just a pair of steer and a pig, they purchased a great quantity of land and celebrated their wedding in grand splendor. In attendance at the ceremony were all of the people freed by Santina, who, after they received lavish gifts from the bride and groom, went back to their homes, blessing the young lady's presence of mind.

Santina was a good wife, just as she had been a good betrothed, and she raised her children with love. They, in turn, rose to high positions, and when they were appointed nobility by the emperor, they put a knife, a little bell, and a walking stick on their coat of arms. Thanks to them three churches were created in Romagna in honor of Saint Romano, Saint Donato, and Saint Francis, the guardian saints of their mother.

The knife, the little bell, and the walking stick lost all of their powers as soon as Gosto and Santina's family was rich and happy, but their descendants retained the couple's loyalty and prudence, which had been the true talismans of Santina, who died at a very old age with the aura of a saint about her, and was honored by her grateful family with a marble tomb.

6

Grazia Deledda (1871–1936)

The self-taught Italian writer and folklorist Grazia Deledda was born in Nuoro, Sardinia, and published over forty volumes, primarily novels and short stories. She won the Nobel Prize for Literature in 1926; noteworthy novels include *Elias Portolu* (*Elias Portolu*, 1903), *Canne al vento* (*Reeds in the Wind*, 1913), *La madre* (*The Mother*, 1920), and the autobiographical *Cosima* (1937). Much of her early writing was in the style of Italian regional realism and as such integrated Sardinian customs, traditions, and folklore into its texture. Deledda's Sardinia often appears as a mythical place cut off from the world of history, a dimension in which time seems to have come to a halt and the mysterious forces of fate make it difficult for characters to resist or shape their own destinies.

Deledda's interest in the traditional cultures of Sardinia, as well as her belief that, in this context, "Sardinia is the Cinderella of Italy and still awaits its fairy godmother," led her to gather and edit material that she started publishing in the early 1890s (cit. in Gunzberg 114). In 1892 she began to collaborate with the folklorist Angelo De Gubernatis, who then recruited her for the new Italian Society for Folklore. A collection of Sardinian legends appeared in the journal *Vita sarda* (Sardinian Life, 1893); during the same period the lengthy ethnographic study "Tradizioni popolari di Nuoro" (Popular Traditions of Nuoro) was published in the journal *Rivista delle tradizioni popolari italiane* (1893–95). In the latter she covered topics such as proverbs and popular sayings, names, curses and oaths, popular poetry, nursery rhymes and lullabies, riddles, games, superstitions and popular beliefs, and rituals and festivities.

Deledda's editing and, as in the case of the tales published here, original reworking of popular material demonstrated her interest in the intersections between legends and other narratives (e.g., fairy tales), fantastic and realistic modes, and historical and supernatural or mythical characters, as well as her attraction to themes common to folk narrative, such as transgression, negotiation of violent passion, and socialization. At the same time, her tales evidence a strong sense of place, as is underlined by many references to the stark landscapes of the author's native island. The style and rhythm of these tales are at once poetic and evocative of the ballads and oral storytelling in which Deledda might have heard similar stories.

Further Reading

Primary

Deledda, Grazia. *Fiabe e leggende*. Ed. Bruno Rombi. Milan: Rusconi, 1994. 169–78, 209–12. [source text]

Secondary

Gunzberg, Lynn. "Ruralism, Folklore, and Grazia Deledda's Novels." *Modern Language Studies* 13, no. 3 (1983): 112–22.

Mazzoni, Cristina. "A Fairy Tale Madonna: Grazia Deledda's 'Our Lady of Good Counsel.'" *Spiritus: A Journal of Christian Spirituality* 19, no. 1 (2019): 131–45.

Mazzoni, Cristina. "'The Loving Re-education of a Soul': Learning from Fairy Tales through Grazia Deledda and Cristina Campo." *Quaderni d'Italianistica: Official Journal of the Canadian Society for Italian Studies* 29, no. 2 (2008): 93–109.

Our Lady of Good Counsel (Nostra signora del Buon Consiglio)

This fairy tale, like many of Deledda's, includes original arrangements of common fairy-tale motifs, such as a male relative—often a father or brother, here an uncle—who desires an incestuous relationship (ATU 510B, Peau d'Asne, of which Basile's "The She-Bear" is an early example) or an envious relative who substitutes a newborn baby with an animal to delegitimize the mother. Here, as in other tales, religious figures stand in for magic helpers (e.g., fairy godmothers), attesting to Sardinian and Italian popular traditions that syncretically draw on both secular and Christian folklore. Also of note are realistic details such as the backdrop of the war with Spain; because of its location, Sardinia was for centuries a contested area between Spain and Italy.

Once upon a time in a village in Sardinia that you have never passed through and probably will never pass through, there lived a bad man who did not believe in God and who never gave alms to the poor.

This man's name was Don Juanne Perrez. He was of Spanish origin, and he was as ugly as the demon.

He lived in a huge house that was dark and mysterious and that contained a hundred and one rooms, and with him lived his little fifteen-year-old niece named Mariedda, who was there to serve him.

Mariedda was as good, beautiful, and devout as her uncle was bad, ugly, and wicked. Mariedda had the most beautiful black hair in all of Sardinia, and one of her eyes looked like the morning star, the other the evening star.

Don Juanne had no affection for Mariedda, just as he felt no affection for any Christian on earth. If he could have, he would have gouged out those lovely big eyes; it was only because of one small twinge of conscience that he didn't have the courage to harm her. But when she turned fifteen he thought he'd get rid of her by marrying her off to an ugly man from the village.

She refused to agree to this unhappy marriage, though, and to avenge himself for this humiliating rejection, one night the ugly man of the village tore up all the plants in Don Juanne's garden and left a pair of horns and two huge squash on the doorstep of the house where Mariedda and her uncle lived.[1] And every night he would pass by under their windows, singing dirty songs.

It's impossible to describe Don Juanne's rage, and the loathing that he began to harbor for poor Mariedda. Suffice it to say that one day he took her into the most remote room of the house, and said to her: "You didn't want Pietro Stonehead for your husband. Alright then! Since you absolutely must get married, prepare yourself to marry me."

The poor thing was left, as they say, speechless. Then she exclaimed, "What sort of business is this? Aren't you my uncle? Since when can uncles marry their nieces?"

"Shut up, you little tease! The pope gave me the permission to marry whomever I want, and to get married without a priest, too. Think carefully about your options. Either the man from the village or me. I'll let you have the whole night to decide."

And he left, locking her inside.

As soon as she was alone, Mariedda began to cry and to pray fervently to Our Lady of Good Counsel, asking her to help and guide her.

And lo and behold, as soon as night had fallen, a magnificent lady appeared. She was surrounded by light and clothed in a white satin dress and a blue cloak, with a gold tiara similar to that of the queen of Spain.

How had she gotten in?

Mariedda couldn't figure it out, and as she stood there with her mouth hanging open and looked at the beautiful lady, the latter said to her in a voice that was like the music of a viola, "I am Our Lady of Good Counsel, and I heard your prayer. Listen to me, Mariedda: ask your uncle for eight days' time, and if he hasn't changed his mind by then, call on me again. Always stay good, and my help and counsel will never be lacking."

---

1. Horns would connote that someone in the house has been sexually betrayed; the squash is perhaps a reference to the male genitals.

That said, she disappeared, leaving a trace of moonlight and a scent of jasmine in the room.

Mariedda felt an intense joy, and prayed all night; the next day she asked her uncle for eight days' time. Even if reluctantly, Don Juanne granted her this; in the meantime, he kept her locked in that remote room, in which the moonlight and the scent of jasmine lingered, so that she couldn't escape. But when the eight days had passed, he asked her if she had decided, since he absolutely wanted to marry her the next day.

When she was alone again, Mariedda started to cry and to pray, and the Blue Lady immediately reappeared, this time with a gold brocade dress and a pearl tiara like that of the queen of France.

"Go to sleep, Mariedda, and have no fear," she said, in a voice that was like the song of a nightingale. "Take this rosary, which has the power to heal the sick, and even in times of good fortune do not forget me, if you do not want bad luck to befall you." At that she vanished, leaving in the room a trace of the light of spring dawns and a fragrance of carnations.

Mariedda hadn't been able to say a single word. Hopeful and ecstatic, she kissed the mother-of-pearl rosary that the Divine Lady had left for her, put it around her neck, and went calmly to sleep, without asking herself what might happen the next day.

The next day she woke in the middle of a thicket, near a swamp, and right away she thought that her Saint Protectress must have transported her there during her sleep. She got up and recited her usual prayer, and then set off toward a city that she could see in the distance, through the rosy vapors of the splendid morning.

She walked, and then walked some more, and she saw a little fisherman with bare feet and a fishing line on his shoulder who was on his way to go fishing in some little ponds nearby. She asked him: "Kind fisherman, if you please, what's the name of this city?"

The fisherman didn't answer, and began to sing:

I fish eels, and hunting geese is my plan;
That city down there is named Oristan.[2]

2. In the original, Othoca, an ancient name for the Sardinian city of Oristano.

"Alright, then!" thought Mariedda. "We're in Oristano."

She walked, and then walked some more, and entered the city, where she immediately began to look for a family where she might find a job as a servant. But it was useless: after three days and three nights of going from one door to another, famished and dead tired, Mariedda still hadn't found a mistress. But she did not despair, and continued to pray to the lovely Lady of Good Counsel for help.

Now on the fourth day, when she was passing by the royal palace, she saw a large group of people who were speaking in a subdued manner among themselves, pale faced and full of sorrow.

"Kind soldier," she asked a young squire, who was also sad, "what is happening?"

"The son of the Judge of Arborea is dying, and no doctor is able to cure him."

The Judge was the king of Arborea, and therefore his son was the crown prince, and the most handsome knight in all of Sardinia.

Mariedda was shaken by the distressing news and was about to say an Ave Maria for the moribund prince when, touching the beads on her rosary, she remembered with joy that it had the power to heal the sick. Without saying anything, she passed through the crowd and managed to gain entrance to the royal palace, but then a captain of the guards stopped her and arrogantly asked her what she wanted.

"I've come to heal Don Mariano, the sick prince," she humbly answered. "I have a marvelous medicine that cures even the dying."

So the arrogant captain brought her in to the Judge, an old king with a beard down to his knees, to whom Mariedda had to repeat the reason for her presence. The Judge was moved by the beauty of the little stranger, and even more by the promise that she made. He said to her, "I'm warning you, star-eyed maiden, if you deceive us we will cut your head off."

"And if I save the prince?"

"We'll give you whatever you want."

That said, it was he himself who brought her in to see the dying prince. And just in time; a few more moments and everything would have been lost.

But the niece of Don Juanne Perrez put her rosary around the prince's neck and, kneeling on the deerskin that lay in front of the bed, she prayed fervently. And then all of the onlookers, white faced and full of marvel, witnessed an extraordinary miracle.

Don Mariano was opening his eyes, his beautiful brown long-lashed eyes. Little by little his cheeks became as rosy as the oleanders in the royal gardens; his brow glowed with life; he smiled; he rose, saying:

"My dear father, I am reborn. Who saved me?"

The Judge was crying with joy; he was crying so hard that his beard dripped tears like a tree bathed by rain.

"She's right there!" he replied, helping Mariedda to her feet and pointing at her.

"You must be a fairy," said the prince, as he embraced her. "Your eyes are like moonlight. You will be my wife."

In fact, shortly thereafter she became Her Lady the Judge of Arborea—that is to say, as soon as the brocaded dresses that stood up by themselves because all of the gold and silver on them had arrived from France and Flanders, together with the veils and the cloaks, all for Mariedda.

And she was so happy that she began to forget the advice of Our Lady of Good Counsel, namely, that she was supposed to pray to her and remember her even in good fortune.

After a year, Mariedda had entirely forgotten her Heavenly Protectress. The miraculous rosary was hanging in the royal chapel, among the other relics, and Her Lady the Judge went down there rarely, instead spending her time in parties, hunting expeditions, tournaments, and listening to the songs, lutes, and mandolins of the troubadours who were not lacking in the court of Arborea.

Now it came to pass that the Spaniards invaded the kingdom of Arborea, and Don Mariano, Mariedda's husband, had to leave with his army to defend his lands and oust the invaders. He departed and left Mariedda, who was about to become the mother of a fair little prince.

"Farewell, my beautiful friend," he said to her, kissing her forehead, before he mounted his great white horse with its red saddlecloth. "Keep your spirits up, and make sure that upon my return I find a new little prince, as handsome and strong as . . ."

"As you, my beautiful friend!" answered Lady Mariedda with pride.

During the war, Don Mariano stayed far from the capital, his old father, and his wife for a long time. A few months after his departure the latter became the mother of a beautiful baby who was the color of a rose and had little hands and feet that looked like flowers.

You need to know, however, that there was someone who was anxiously awaiting the day the beautiful baby would be born, so that he could demolish all of the happiness of Her Lady the Judge, Mariedda.

That person was Don Juanne Perrez. Now listen.

After his niece's disappearance, he had begun to hate her fiercely, and had vowed to get revenge. But however hard he searched for her around Logudoro and in the nearby lands, no one had ever heard of the star-eyed girl or seen her. And Don Juanne was already starting to believe, with a sort of wicked joy, that the demon had taken her, when, while visiting Oristano for the prince's marriage, he saw with wonder and annoyance that the bride was Mariedda!

What did he do then? He returned to his village and sold everything he owned. He even sold his soul to the devil, so that he would assist him in his vendetta. Then he dressed up as a doctor, with a long white beard and a black robe, dressing like that because he had read in an old book that Claudius Galenus, an ancient doctor, had clothed himself in that manner. Thus disguised, Don Juanne Perrez set off for Oristano again, passing himself off as a doctor who had just arrived from Germany, and who had studied in Regensburg.

And he was so insistent that they finally took him on as court doctor.

Mariedda didn't recognize him. For this reason, when the beautiful baby mentioned above was born, the false doctor was summoned; and the false doctor, who was waiting for this opportunity to get his revenge, hid the beautiful baby and deftly substituted him with an ugly, mangy black puppy that he had prepared. And he performed this cowardly action so deftly that not even Mariedda noticed.

Don Juanne did not kill the beautiful baby but let him die of hunger; for this reason, still today in many parts of Sardinia hunger is called Sir Juanne, in memory of this fact.

Meanwhile, everyone in the royal court was in a state of deepest sorrow and fear, because no one had ever seen anything like this, and Mariedda's grief and humiliation had brought on a fever. It would have been one thing if a commoner had become the mother of an ugly, mangy black puppy—Good God! That would have been acceptable, because in those days there were witches who married the devil, and from those horrible marriages even puppies or scorpions could be born. But Her Lady the Judge, who had brocaded dresses that stood up by themselves, there was so much gold and silver!

Enough said. Don Mariano received written notice and, for the first time in his life, he cried with sorrow. And perhaps he would have forgiven Mariedda, except that when the news spread through the Spanish battlefield, it aroused so much hilarity and joking at the expense of the enemy prince that he flew into a rage and wrote to his majordomo, telling him to seize Her Lady the Judge and the little monster and to take them to a place far, far away, somewhere from which they could never return, because he was repudiating her.

The majordomo obeyed, and one night Mariedda found herself being taken far, far away, to a deserted and silent countryside. In her arms she squeezed the puppy, for whom she had developed a deep love.

All alone in that deserted and silent countryside, at that terrible hour of desperation, she finally remembered her past; she remembered Our Lady of Good Counsel and fell to the ground crying, asking for mercy and forgiveness.

And then, just like in the dark and remote room of Don Juanne's house, a golden light began to shine brightly, and the Madonna appeared, with her white dress and blue cloak and the tiara similar to that of the queen of Spain.

"Mariedda, Mariedda," she said in a voice so sweet that it consoled the poor, distressed girl, "you forgot about me, and for that reason you encountered misfortune. But I do not abandon those who are in distress, and I am the mother of all who suffer."

With her forehead on the ground, Mariedda wept and prayed.

"Mariedda," continued the Madonna, "walk, and keep on walking. You will find a house that will be yours, and nothing will be lacking. Live there until your day arrives, and never forget me again."

After saying this, she vanished. A light like the rising sun spread across the desolate countryside; hedges bloomed, streams sparkled, a sweet scent of mint floated through the air, and a row of yellow-beaked blackbirds sang on a nearby wall.

When she raised her forehead from the ground, Mariedda found in her arms not the black puppy, but a beautiful baby the color of a rose, whose little hands and feet looked like flowers. For a moment, she thought about going back to the court with the baby. But the words of Our Lady of Good Counsel were stuck in her mind, and she immediately continued walking across the great plain, which was now suddenly in bloom.

She walked and walked, and walked even farther, and after many long hours she found herself in front of a pretty little green house, hidden in a little wood of orange trees and rose bushes. Big balls of gold hung from the orange trees, and large flowers of coral climbed from the rose bushes. Mariedda knocked.

A maid clothed in traditional dress, with a flaming scarlet skirt, a green and gold brocaded bodice, and a long white veil on her head, opened the door and said, curtsying:

"Are you the mistress that we're expecting?"

"Yes," answered Mariedda, smiling.

And from that day on, in fact, she was the mistress of the little green house hidden among the orange trees and rose bushes.

No one ever passed by there; the world was far, far away, and yet nothing was ever lacking in the little house: there was always bread that looked like gold, water like silver, wine like coral, oil like amber, honey like topaz, milk like snow. Mariedda was always praying, as she waited for the promised day in which she hoped to see her beloved husband again. Meanwhile the beautiful baby, whose name was Consiglio,[3] was growing like the orange trees in the little wood, and he would laugh and gallop around on horses made of reeds, which he would make twirl at breakneck speed, even if their bodies were all tails.

Five years went by. Finally, one day a party of hunters who had lost their way in that uninhabited countryside passed by the little house, and asked Mariedda for hospitality.

Imagine Mariedda's trepidation, surprise, and joy when she saw that her husband was the head of those hunters!

"The day has come!" she thought, anxiously. She wasn't recognized, though, because she had changed, and she was in traditional dress. But she graciously welcomed the hunters, among whom there was also Don Juanne, the devil's doctor.

They were all enchanted by the warm welcome and by the beauty of Mariedda and of Consiglio. At the table Don Mariano, who was seated next to the mistress of the house, told her the story of his misfortune. He said that he had regretted his atrocious order and had had his poor bride searched for across all of the mountains and valleys of Sardinia, and that because he had not been able to find her he was now the most unhappy man on earth, and was tormented by remorse and by memories.

3. "Counsel," named after Mariedda's benefactress.

Mariedda was moved by this story, and she decided to reveal herself before the hunters left.

Meanwhile, something extraordinary happened, which demonstrated how God's justice is revealed in the smallest things. Listen. One of the gold teaspoons from the dinner set had fallen on the ground. Consiglio, who was playing under the chairs, picked it up and hid under the table, where as a joke he put it in Don Juanne's embroidered slipper of Moroccan leather. Then he left the room and was put to bed by the maid.

When the table was being cleared, it was noticed that a gold teaspoon was missing, but it was nowhere to be found.

"My dear prince," said Mariedda, then, to the prince, "I offered you and your knights hospitality. Why, then, do you repay me in this fashion?"

And she told him about the gold teaspoon, which had without doubt been stolen by one of the hunters.

Don Mariano flew into a rage, and taking out his sword, shouted: "Knights, someone here has stolen something. Confess your shameful action, or else you will have cause for bitter regret."

They all denied it; Don Mariano continued, "Alright then, my dear lords! I will search each one of you myself, and woe to the ignoble traitor who has repaid the hospitality of this noble lady in such a manner, for I will run him through with my sword."

No sooner said than done. He searched all of the hunters, and he found the gold teaspoon in Juanne's embroidered slipper of Moroccan leather. The latter professed his innocence, but in vain.

"Sir," said the prince to him, "you will die by my hand."

And he was about to kill him when Mariedda, moved to pity, asked for clemency for him and then revealed who she was, to the prince's great happiness.

Greatly affected by this scene, Don Juanne threw himself at the feet of his niece, who had saved him, and confessed his misdeeds.

Mariedda and the prince pardoned him, but as penance they did oblige him to live the rest of his life in the little green house hidden among the orange trees and rose bushes, so that he could repent and atone for his sins in solitude. We don't know if he actually repented, but we do know that he never moved from there, whereas Mariedda, Consiglio with his reed horse, the maid with her costume and her veil, Don Mariano, and all the other hunters returned to the court, where they were welcomed with great festivities, and where they lived happily for a long time afterward.

When they were passing by the ponds, that fisherman who had sung when Mariedda arrived in Oristano the first time now sang these words:

Birds that fly, birds that fly,
In my company, unafraid,
Go, and return by and by,
For the king and the queen peace have made.

Fairy Tale (Fiaba)

This tale, like others by Deledda, is dominated by the melancholic sense that in the world here described there is no place for the traditional happy endings of fairy tales.

The little princess, seated near the recessed window in her drawing room, was watching the clouds rise from the distant sea, and she was asking herself why she was alive.

The little princess was twenty years old, but looked both older and younger than that, with her jet-black hair already streaked with silver here and there and her fresh but ivory-pale face. Her father and brothers had died in war and her fiancé, a Spanish prince, had abandoned her because the fortune that she had inherited was not as great as he had hoped. And so, cloistered in a castle near the sea, she asked herself why she was alive. She no longer suffered, but occasionally she longed for the time when at least she did suffer, when her pain would burst inside her with the rumble and crash of a hurricane, but also with the blaze of lightning. Back then, her pride made its way through the whirlwind like a chained lion; she roared, she tried to sink her teeth into her pain; and sometimes she won. But time, that unsolicited good doctor, had extracted the little princess's ailing heart from her breast, piece by piece; and now everything was quiet and everything was empty inside her, and she longed for the days when at least she could suffer. Now the days went by like this: they were neither good nor bad, and they were long, even if it was winter. But it was a mild winter, warmed by the breath of the sea; the oak trees in the wood beneath the castle still had their dry golden leaves, and when the wind blew you could see the grass sparkle like green water through the trees. And in the evening the sky was so limpid that even through the closed glass of the window it seemed to the little princess that she could discern the stars wheeling through space. On that evening, though, clouds were rising from behind the wood, up from the sea; they were already spring clouds, light yellow and rose tinged with blue, and for the first time after so many months, the little princess, when she asked herself why she was alive, felt like crying. Why, and for whom was she crying? This question kept the tears suspended on her eyelids like dewdrops on spiderwebs. But at one point a tear fell onto her breast, and from her breast bounced down to her lap; at that moment she understood that she was crying for herself, and a thousand more tears fell from her eyes, onto her breast, her lap, all the way down to her feet.

Then she seemed to remember someone who was waiting for her help; she stopped crying and remembered that it was she herself who was waiting for her help. She stood up, and decided to get married, and to have children to whom she would give the names of her brothers who had died in war: children who when they grew up would also go off to die in war. But this time she wanted a poor husband, so that her riches would seem greater than those of the king of Spain; and she wanted to know this husband well beforehand, not like the other time with the prince, when they had never met.

She summoned the Chief Guard.

"I want to get married; I'm tired of spending my evenings alone, now that I can open the balcony windows and the nightingale is starting to sing. But I want someone who is poor; he must, though, be clean and he must not curse."

"That will be difficult," said the Chief Guard, who had traveled the world. Nonetheless, that very night he began the search for the poor, clean, and proper-tongued husband.

After searching high and low for seven weeks, the men returned. The Chief Guard went in to see the little princess. The window was open and the air was fragrant with elderberry flowers.

"After searching high and low, we found the poor, clean, and sweet-speaking young man here below the castle, down by the sea's edge: he's a fisherman, and no one knows where he came from. He lives in a reed hut that's enclosed by a rose garden, and he has a boat with a yellow sail with Christ painted on it; he is handsome."

"Good, then," said the little princess.

"But he doesn't want to get married."

The little princess didn't say anything. She thought that perhaps the poor fisherman was ashamed to come up to see her, and she decided to go down to him.

She dressed in country clothes, with a veil on her head, and she thought about the joy the poor man would feel when he found out he was going to marry a rich woman. She walked, and walked; her little feet were so used to smooth floors that it took her a long time to arrive. And yet the spot was so close that you could hear the servants singing as they sifted the floor in the castle to make the guards' bread.

There was the hut, the reeds still green; there it was, like a big basket forgotten in the middle of the wild rose garden. And the wild roses were full of buds that were starting to bloom, but very slowly, so as not to reveal their beauty all at once.

The sea was blue, and on the golden sail fluttering on the boat the painted Christ seemed to be turning to dispense blessings, first to one side and then the other.

The fisherman had just returned, and he was unloading a basket full of silvery fish. He turned, standing on the shore, and his eyes were so blue that they made the sky and the sea behind his head turn pale. Seeing the country-woman, he greeted her and invited her into his hut.

"I was waiting for you," he said to her.

She began to tremble.

"You want me, then?"

"Of course I want you. Now that the sea is calm and the nightingale's song in the tamarisk trees sounds like a mermaid's song, it will be sad to be alone. But you came."

She didn't dare to look at him, she liked him so much. Before him she felt humble, like a real countrywoman. The she said, humbly, "They said you didn't want to get married."

"Yes," he said, bending over to gather up the fish that, still alive, were leaping out of the basket and flopping around on the ground, "they had suggested a little princess who lives nearby, but I don't want her. I am a prince," he said, lifting his handsome face up through the hair that hung over his cheeks like clusters of ripe grapes. "I was supposed to marry a princess whom I loved, but my head minister wouldn't allow me to marry her, because on her father's death his fortune ended up not being as great as had been thought. And then out of spite I went away, and made a vow to live as a poor man and to marry a woman who was born poor."

"I am that little princess whom you were supposed to marry; and I want you as you are, a poor man."

"But I cannot marry you, because of that vow. I'm sorry."

She stood up and left; her pride made her walk quickly, even if her little feet were used to smooth floors. And as revenge, she gave the Chief Guard the order that no girl who had been born poor should ever be allowed to cross the wood and arrive at the tamarisk grove by the beach.

And so once again she sat in front of the recessed window in her sitting room, and asked herself why she was alive.

The entire wood was in flower, and in the rose garden the blooming roses revealed themselves to the sun like a lover reveals herself to her beloved, in all of their beauty. You could hear the murmur of the sea, and the servants sang languidly. And then, right at that moment, the murmur and the singing ceased.

Everything seemed dead, dead with love. The poor prince sat by the sea, motionless, in front of his boat on whose sail the painted Christ bowed his head; he too was dead. There he sat, the poor prince, with his elbows on his knees and his hands squeezing bunches of his hair. The girl who was born poor did not appear, and he thought, inevitably, about the little princess, though he was determined to keep his vow not to have her.

And she, too, thought about him up there, because he was the only poor, clean, and sweet-tongued young man who had been found after all those travels. But since he wouldn't have her, she asked herself why she was alive, and longed for the winter days when, at least, the window would be closed. Now the window was open, and you could hear the nightingale singing. And its song filled the night with everything that those two—seated, silent, distant—were unable to say.

7

Guido Gozzano (1883–1916)

Guido Gozzano, born in Turin, is best known as a poet and the foremost exponent of the *crepuscolarismo* ("twilight-ism") literary movement, which embraced a poetics of humble simplicity and a refusal of the grand ideals and rhetoric in vogue as Italy waged its colonialist campaign in Libya and prepared to enter World War I. Common themes in his poetry include ennui, loneliness and melancholy, and disillusion with the present. Gozzano's two most important volumes of poetry, *Via del rifugio* (*The Road to Shelter*) and *I colloqui* (*The Colloquies*), were published in 1907 and 1911, respectively; during this same period he also began to publish original fairy tales, first in 1909–14 in the children's journals *Corriere dei piccoli* and *Adolescenza* and then in the volumes *I tre talismani* (The Three Talismans, 1914) and *La principessa si sposa* (The Princess Gets Married, 1916).

In a sense, fairy tales were a natural expression of Gozzano's preoccupation with the ephemerality of human experience and fascination with the mythical, timeless dimension of prehistory or—in the context of a human life—childhood, which permeated his poetry. His fairy tales, though sometimes proposing new arrangements of familiar motifs, generally incorporate the formulaic elements of magic, supernatural creatures, repeated trials, and indeterminate temporal and spatial settings. But they also can surprise the reader for their delicate representation of human sentiment, playful and grotesque elements (such as the fluttering hands and the "sheet game" in "The Silver Hare"), and overall lightness of tone, which is even personified in one of his tales, "Piumadoro and Piombofino," in the form of a princess so light that she risks floating away. It is tempting to suggest that the various odd ailments and sense of transience that prevail in his tales may have to do with his decade-long battle with tuberculosis, which caused his death when he was thirty-two years old.

Further Reading

Primary

Gozzano, Guido. *Fiabe e novelline*. Ed. Gioia Sebastiani. Palermo: Sellerio, 2003. 48–60, 63–75. [source text]

Secondary

Mazzoni, Cristina. "Of Golden Feathers and Light Reading: Guido Gozzano's 'Piumadoro e Piombofino.'" *Quaderni d'Italianistica: Official Journal of the Canadian Society for Italian Studies* 29, no. 1 (2008): 105–24.

Sebastiani, Gioia. "Gozzano e le fiabe." In *Fiabe e novelline*, by Guido Gozzano. Palermo: Sellerio, 2003. 207–22.

The Silver Hare (La lepre d'argento)

This tale contains elements of ATU 403C, The Substituted Bride. As in many of Gozzano's tales, delightfully strange details abound, such as the bedroom bouncing game that Prince Aquilino must endure in order for his promised bride to change back into her human form.

When witches used magic brews
To prepare their spells just so
(listen up, all of you!)
there was, back then, long ago . . .

. . . a prince named Aquilino, who was twenty years old and wanted to take the most beautiful princess in the world for his wife. He issued the marriage proclamation, and hundreds of portraits arrived, which he had exhibited in the galleries of the castle, and there he meditated on the beautiful ladies who smiled at him from the large gilt frames.

He settled on Nazzarena, princess of Bikarìa, and the wedding was arranged through ambassadors.

Grand preparations were made for the ceremony in Aquilino's castle, and at dawn on the longed-for day the prince was already at the lookout post on top of the highest tower. The procession was scheduled to arrive shortly; soon he would see the renowned beauty for the first time.

But the procession did not arrive.

The only thing that appeared was a single carriage, from which a hunchbacked, bearded little old man got out.

"I am the king of Bikarìa. And this is my daughter Nazzarena, whose hand you have asked for in marriage."

Aquilino wasn't able to hide his disappointment. The princess was a dwarf, she was pale and wrinkled, and she didn't in the least resemble the portrait he had chosen.

The little old man noticed his reaction.

"The fatigue of the journey and the excitement have worn her out. But she'll recover, and you'll find her as beautiful as you had hoped."

Aquilino wanted to call off the wedding, but he had given his word and he had to keep it.

He did ask that the ceremony be delayed two days, and he hosted the old man and his daughter in the castle.

The next morning, as a distraction from his unhappiness and disappointment, the prince went out alone to hunt, a lovely jewel-studded golden rifle at his side. He walked through fields and meadows until he reached a thousand-year-old forest.

A silver hare appeared across his path; it was grazing on grass and stared at him, not at all frightened. The prince aimed his weapon and fired. But after the smoke dispersed, the hare reappeared in the same spot, unharmed and calm.

The prince advanced. The hare fled, and then came to a halt after a short distance, staring at him with its calm human eyes. Aquilino shot again. The smoke cleared and the hare reappeared, calm and intact, seated on its haunches; with one ear up and the other lowered, its eyes imploring and its nose trembling, it leaned toward him. But as soon as the prince threw his weapon down and moved toward the hare, it leaped away and disappeared among the tree trunks. Aquilino was puzzled.

It had to do with a curse.

He leaned against the trunk of a giant tree, thinking again of the gentle gaze of the invulnerable victim. And he seemed to hear a far-off echo of music and voices that was coming from behind him, from inside the trunk. He turned, and walked around the tree: there was no one there. He leaned back against the trunk. And he heard the sound and the voices again.

He knocked on the bark with his fist, impatiently.

The bark creaked, and then split down the middle and swung open on both sides, and there before the astonished prince appeared a dazzling staircase. He climbed the first steps, as if in a dream, and heard the bang of the door closing. The palace was immense. There was an endless succession of staircases, vestibules, corridors, loggias, and rooms, all richly decorated with marble, porphyry, jasper, and jewels. Aquilino advanced as if in a dream.

Night fell, and no one appeared in the enchanted palace. The only things there were two hands that guided him on, one carrying a lamp and the other gesturing to him to follow. In this manner they arrived at an immense dining room. Aquilino sat down at the table, and the two hands began to bring him delectable foods and wines.

He watched those two flying, detached hands, and he tried to grab them when they came close to him, but they would set down the plates and then flutter away like butterflies. He ate, and then began to feel sleepy and got up to go off to sleep. The two hands preceded him to a chamber lined in crimson damask, made a gesture of farewell and of good wishes, and disappeared.

He tucked himself in between the fine sheets and fell asleep. He dreamed of seeing Princess Nazzarena again, not the one brought by the bearded hunchback, but as she had appeared in the painting, blond and very beautiful.

Then all of a sudden he was awakened by loud chattering. He half-opened his eyes. The room was illuminated, and a great many hands, just like the ones the evening before, were fluttering around, crossing each other's paths, and pointing toward him.

"What game are we playing?"

"Ball."

"Shall we play ball with that fellow who's sleeping?"

"Who is it that's sleeping?"

"Over there in the bed, can't you see?"

And through his half-closed eyes, the prince saw the hands move closer. They took hold of the sheets and, holding the edges tautly, began to bounce him up and down, with hoarse laughter and piercing hisses.

He kept his eyelids closed, pretending to sleep.

"He won't wake up!"

"We'll wake him up! We'll wake him up!"

And they doubled the frenzy of their cruel game.

At the rooster's first crow, the hands bounced him back onto the bed, and disappeared.

Aquilino was rubbing his aching bones when he heard a rustling sound, and saw that the silver hare was there next to him. Instead of its four paws it had two feet and two lily-white hands, those of a woman.

"Prince Aquilino, I am Princess Nazzarena, whom your heart chose as your companion. When I reached the forest with my entourage, a sorcerer transformed me, imprisoning me and all of my people in this castle. I will be rescued from this state if you spend two more nights like last night in here. The sorcerer is the same one who came before you and tried to get you to marry his little dwarf."

The hare disappeared.

Aquilino waited anxiously for the second evening. He ate, served by the flying hands, went to bed, and fell asleep. He woke up to the loud chattering: a large number of hands took him from his bed, lifted up the sheets, and began the game, and it was even more furious than the previous evening.

"He won't wake up!"

"If he doesn't wake up, we're done for!"

Then the hands bounced him up one last time, and he was left hanging on a nail on one of the ceiling beams. The hands disappeared, hissing.

Aquilino opened his eyes and saw the silver hare. By now its whole body was that of a woman; only its head was still that of a hare, and it looked at him with sweet human eyes.

"Poor prince! Suffer one more night for my sake, and we'll be safe."

The third night arrived. The hands appeared again, more frenzied than ever.

"Shall we play?"

"Let's play!"

"But tonight we have to end things!"

"We have to end it!"

And the cruel bouncing began.

Aquilino flew up, hit the ceiling, was left sticking there like a pie, and then fell back down onto the stretched sheet, where he was bounced again, amid the infernal laughter. And he didn't open his eyes out of love for Nazzarena.

"He's not waking up! We're done for!"

"We're done for!"

"It's dawn! We're done for!"

The frenzied hands moved over to the window, stretched out the sheet, and bounced Aquilino up to a dizzying height. He rose, and rose some more; he fell, and continued falling for ten minutes. Then he hit the grass, felt his bruised bones, and opened his eyes, still alive. He was at the foot of the enchanted tree.

Next to him was his true promised one, Nazzarena, more beautiful than any beauty ever before seen. And with her she had a train of carriages, ladies, and knights, all of whom had at the same moment been freed from the sorcerer's curse.

The prince brought her to his castle and gathered all of his court in the hall of the Grand Council. Then he had the bearded hunchback and his disgusting daughter brought forth, and, addressing the ministers, said, "I ordered a trunk of gold and jewels; a crook stole it from me on its way here and substituted it with another worm-eaten one. Fortune dictates that I find the first one. Which should be my preference?"

"The first!" ruled the court.

"And what should I do with the thief and the worm-eaten trunk?"

"Burn them on the same stake!"

And that's what was done. The sentence and the wedding took place amid the applause of all the people.

Piumadoro and Piombofino (Piumadoro e Piombofino)

This tale is quite similar to George MacDonald's 1864 "The Light Princess," as well as Luigi Capuana's 1894 "Piuma d'oro." It is a charmingly explicit allegory of the trials of adolescence from both male and female perspectives; it is notable that Piumadoro, the heroine, saves Piombofino from sinking irrevocably into a fate of "heaviness."

I.

Piumadoro—Golden Feather—was an orphan and lived with her grandfather in a hut in the woods. Her grandfather was a coal man, and she would help him gather sticks and make coal. The little girl grew up to be kind, well loved by her friends and by the little old ladies who lived in the cottages nearby, and beautiful, as beautiful as a queen.

One spring day she saw a pure white butterfly on the pot of carnations on her windowsill, and she cupped it in her hand.

"Have mercy on me and let me go!"

Piumadoro let it go.

"Thank you, my pretty little girl. What is your name?"

"Piumadoro."

"My name is Pieris of the Hawthorn. I'm going off to deposit my larvae in a far-off land. Perhaps one day I'll pay you back."

And the butterfly flew off.

Another day, when she was walking on a path, Piumadoro had snatched up some lovely, snowy fluff carried by the wind, and was already plucking apart the airy silk.

"Have mercy on me and let me go!"

Piumadoro let it go.

"Thank you, my pretty little girl. What is your name?"

"Piumadoro."

"Thank you, Piumadoro. My name is Achene of the Thistle. I'm going off to deposit my seeds in a far-off land. Perhaps one day I'll pay you back."

And the fluff flew off.

Another day Piumadoro snatched an emerald beetle from the heart of a rose.

"Have mercy on me and let me go!"

Piumadoro let it go.

"Thank you, my pretty little girl. What is your name?"

"Piumadoro."

"Thank you, Piumadoro. My name is Rose Chafer. I'm looking for the roses of a far-off land. Perhaps one day I'll pay you back."

And the beetle flew off.

II.

When she was about fourteen something strange happened to Piumadoro. She started to lose weight.

She was still the same lovely blond girl, and she was still flourishing, but every day she got lighter.

At first she thought nothing of it. It amused her, actually, to let herself drop from the branches of the tallest trees and then float down, slowly, slowly, ever so slowly, like a sheet of paper. And she would sing:

I adore none but Piumadoro . . .
Oh! Piumadoro,
pretty little girl, one day you shall be queen!

But as time passed she became so light that her grandfather had to tie four large rocks onto her skirt so that the wind wouldn't carry her off. And then even the rocks were no longer enough, and her grandfather had to keep her shut up in the house.

"Piumadoro, my poor child, this must be some kind of curse!"

And the old man sighed. Piumadoro grew bored, shut up like that in the house.

"Blow on me, grandfather!"

And to amuse her, her grandfather would blow her high up into the room. Piumadoro would go up and then come down, as slowly as a feather.

I adore none but Piumadoro . . .
Oh! Piumadoro,
pretty little girl, one day you shall be queen!

"Blow on me, grandfather!"

And her grandfather would blow hard and Piumadoro would drift lightly up, all the way to the roof beams.

Oh! Piumadoro,
pretty little girl, one day you shall be queen!

"Piumadoro, what are you singing?"

"It's not me. It's a voice that sings inside me."

In fact, Piumadoro heard the words being repeated by a sweet and very distant voice.

And the old man would blow, and sigh, "Piumadoro, my poor child, this must be some kind of curse!"

III.

One morning Piumadoro awoke lighter and more bored than usual.

"Blow on me, grandfather!"

But the old man didn't answer.

Piumadoro went over to her grandfather's bed. Her grandfather was dead.

Piumadoro cried.

She cried for three days and three nights. On the fourth day at dawn she wanted to call for someone. But she had barely opened the door to the house when the wind snatched her away and carried her up high, higher, and then even higher, like a soap bubble . . .

Piumadoro let out a cry and closed her eyes.

She dared to open them, little by little, and she looked upward, through her head of thick, loose hair. She was flying at a dizzying altitude.

Gliding by below her she could see green countrysides, silver rivers, dark forests, cities, towers, abbeys so miniscule that they looked like toys . . .

Once again Piumadoro closed her eyes with fear. She wrapped herself in her immense hair and settled into it, as if it were the quilt on her bed, allowing herself to be transported.

"Be brave, Piumadoro!"

She opened her eyes. There were the butterfly, the beetle, and the fluff.

"The wind will carry us with you, Piumadoro. We will follow you and help you, whatever your destiny may be."

Piumadoro felt reborn.

"Thank you, my friends."

I adore none but Piumadoro . . .
Oh! Piumadoro,
pretty little girl, one day you shall be queen!

"Who is it that has been singing in my ear all this time?"

"You'll find out this evening, Piumadoro, when we reach the Fairy of Adolescence."

Piumadoro, the butterfly, the beetle, and the fluff continued on their journey, transported by the wind.

IV.

Toward evening they reached the Fairy of Adolescence's house and entered through the open window.

The good fairy received them graciously. She took Piumadoro by the hand, and they passed through immense rooms and corridors that never ended. Then the fairy took a round mirror out of a golden case.

"Look in here."

Piumadoro looked. She saw a marvelous garden, palm trees, and other tropical trees and flowers that she had never seen before.

And there in the garden was a young man dressed like a king, as beautiful as the sun. The young man sat in a golden cart that five hundred pair of oxen were barely able to pull, and he was singing:

Oh! Piumadoro,
pretty little girl, one day you shall be queen!

"The person you see there is Piombofino—Fine Lead—prince of the Isles of Fortune, and it is he who has been calling you for so long with his song. He is the victim of a curse that is the opposite of yours. Five hundred pair of oxen strain to pull him. He is growing heavier and heavier. The curse will be broken the moment you exchange your first kiss."

The vision disappeared and the good fairy gave Piumadoro three grains of wheat.

"Before you reach the Isles of Fortune the wind will blow you over three castles. In each castle an evil fairy will appear before you and will attempt to attract you with threats or with flattery. Each time you must drop one of these grains."

Piumadoro thanked the fairy, went out the window with her companions, and resumed her journey, transported by the wind.

V.

Toward evening they were within sight of the first castle. The Multicolored Fairy appeared on the turrets and gestured with her hands. Piumadoro felt herself attracted by a mysterious force, and she slowly began to descend. She seemed to be able to discern the smiling faces of people she knew in the garden: her companions and the little old ladies from her native woods, and her grandfather, who was waving to her.

But the beetle reminded her of the warning given by the Fairy of Adolescence, and Piumadoro dropped a grain of wheat. The smiling people immediately changed into demons and sorceresses crowned with hissing serpents.

Piumadoro rose back up into the air with her companions, and she understood that that was the Castle of Lies, and that the grain she had thrown down was the grain of Prudence.

They traveled for two more days. Toward evening they were in sight of the second castle.

It was a castle the color of bile, streaked with blood. Up on the turrets the Green Fairy was throwing herself about furiously. A throng of livid people gestured menacingly from the battlements and the courtyards.

Piumadoro began to descend, attracted by the mysterious force. In a state of terror, she dropped the second grain. As soon as the grain touched the earth the castle turned into gold, and the fairy and her guests took on a benevolent and smiling appearance, stretching out their hands to Piumadoro in greeting. She rose up again and set off on her way, transported by the wind. And she understood that that had been the grain of Goodness.

She traveled and then traveled some more, and two days later reached the third castle. It was a marvelous castle, made of gold and precious stones. The Blue Fairy appeared on the towers, making benign gestures toward Piumadoro.

Piumadoro felt attracted by the invisible force. As she neared the earth she heard a confused clamor of laughter, songs, and music; in the immense gardens she discerned groups of scintillating ladies and gentlemen occupied in banquets, dancing, jousts, and theatrical performances.

Piumadoro was bedazzled. She was about to go down when the beetle reminded her of the warning she had been given by the Fairy of Adolescence and, reluctantly, she dropped the third grain of wheat. As soon as it touched the ground, the castle turned into a cave, the Blue Fairy into a dreadful hag, and the ladies and gentlemen into ragged and desperate paupers who were running through rocks and brambles, crying. As she rose back up into the air with a leap, Piumadoro understood that this was the Castle of Desires and that the grain she had thrown down was the grain of Wisdom.

She continued on her way, transported by the wind.

The butterfly, the beetle, and the fluff followed her faithfully, inviting all of their comrades that they met along the way to accompany them. And so Piumadoro soon had a train of multicolored butterflies, a cloud of snow-white fluff, and a dazzling troop of emerald-green beetles.

They traveled, and traveled, and traveled, and then the earth ended, and Piumadoro, looking down, saw an infinite expanse of blue. It was the sea.

The wind calmed and at times Piumadoro would fly down so low that she grazed the lily-white foam with her hair. Then she would let out a cry, and the ten thousand butterflies and ten thousand beetles would lift her up with the tremor of their tiny wings.

They traveled in this manner for seven days.

At dawn on the eighth day the golden minarets and the tall palm trees of the Isles of Fortune appeared on the horizon.

VI.

At the Royal Palace everyone was desperate.

With his weight, Prince Piombofino had broken through the floor of the Hall of the Great Council and was now buried up to his waist in its mosaics. Blond, blue-eyed, and dressed completely in red velvet, Piombofino was as beautiful as a god, but the spell became more and more perverse every day.

By this time the weight of the young man was so great that all the oxen of the kingdom weren't enough to move him an inch.

Doctors, fortune-tellers, palm readers, necromancers, and alchemists had been summoned, in vain, to visit the enchanted crown prince.

I adore none but Piumadoro . . .
Oh! Piumadoro,
pretty little girl, one day you shall be queen!

And Piombofino sank even deeper, like a bronze mortar into the sand of the sea.

A sorcerer had predicted that all efforts would be useless unless help came in the form of the crossing of certain well-disposed stars.

The queen ran to the window at every moment and consulted with the astrologers of the towers in a loud voice.

"Master Simone! What do you see there on the horizon?"

"Nothing, Your Majesty . . . The Holy Christian fleet returning from the Holy Land."

And Piombofino sank deeper and deeper.

"Master Simone, what do you see now?"

"Nothing, Your Majesty . . . A Venetian galley loaded with ivory."

The king, the queen, the ministers, and the ladies were desperate.

By this time only Piombofino's head was visible; and as he sank he sang:

Oh! Piumadoro,
pretty little girl, one day you shall be queen!

All of a sudden the voice of Master Simone was heard:

"Your Majesty! There's a shooting star on the horizon! A star shining in the middle of the afternoon!"

Everyone rushed to the window, but before they got there the huge glass pane at the end of the room opened as if by magic, and Piumadoro, with all her entourage, appeared before the shocked royal court.

The fluff had woven her a dress of the lightest gauze, and the butterflies had colored it with gems. The ten thousand beetles, transformed into ten thousand tiny pages dressed in emerald, flanked the young lady, who entered smiling, as beautiful and majestic as a goddess.

Once Piombofino had received the first kiss from her, he returned to his normal state and leaped to his feet, free and disenchanted, amid the shouts of joy of the exultant royal court.

They prepared festivities unlike any seen since. And eight days later, Piumadoro the coal girl married the prince of the Isles of Fortune.

PART V

Italo Calvino's Fiabe Italiane (Italian Folktales)

Italo Calvino (1923–85)

The Italian writer, critic, and editor Italo Calvino, author of the monumental *Fiabe italiane* (*Italian Folktales*, 1956), was born in 1923 in Cuba to Italian parents and spent his youth in San Remo, on the Ligurian Riviera. During World War II he fought in the Resistance, and in 1947 he began working for the Turin press Einaudi, where he published his first works.

Calvino is one of the most influential and widely read literary figures of the twentieth century. His fame derives principally from his short stories and novels, which demonstrate his consummate ability to unite brilliant storytelling with reflection on the nature of the combinatorial mechanics of narration itself. From his earliest works, Calvino sensed an affinity between the interplay of variety and repetition present in folktales and fairy tales and the narrative dynamic that he aspired to in his own writing, in which the marvelous and the everyday merge in stories structurally informed by familiar folkloric paradigms. Calvino's use of the "once upon a time" marvelous is, however, in many of his fictional works directed toward finding meaning in the here and now through an engaged investigation of the human condition. His first novel, *Il sentiero dei nidi di ragno* (*Path to the Nest of Spiders*, 1947), is a tale of the Resistance as seen through the eyes of a young boy; the trilogy *I nostri antennati* (*Our Ancestors*), which includes *Il visconte dimezzato* (*The Cloven Viscount*, 1952), *Il barone rampante* (*The Baron in the Trees*, 1957), and *Il cavaliere inesistente* (*The Nonexistent Knight*, 1959), consists of allegories on modern life populated by fabulous heroes; and the stories of *Marcovaldo* (1963), which feature the encounters of the bewildered Marcovaldo and family with contemporary urban life, have the flavor of dystopic fairy tales. Even if later works such as *Le città invisibili* (*Invisible Cities*, 1972), *Se una notte d'inverno un viaggiatore* (*If on a Winter's Night a Traveler*, 1979), and *Palomar*

(*Mr. Palomar*, 1983) move away from the fairy tale in content, formally they continue to draw on its narrative potentialities.

The 1950s witnessed in Europe a revival of interest in folk traditions. In Italy, which had been a nation for less than a century and a republic only since the end of World War II, the need for a creative re-elaboration of these traditions was especially felt. In 1954 Calvino was asked by Einaudi to compile a collection of Italian folktales, and the *Fiabe italiane* were published two years later. The collection contains two hundred tales, the same number as in the Grimms' *Children's and Household Tales*, and Calvino's guiding criteria in choosing the tales were both variety of major tale types—his work includes about fifty—and geographical representation—there are tales from all twenty Italian regions, plus Corsica. Fairy tales that incorporate magic predominate, though religious and local legends, novellas, animal fables, and anecdotes also appear. Calvino did not use informants but selected his materials primarily from nineteenth-century anthologies such as Giuseppe Pitrè's *Fiabe, novelle e racconti popolari siciliani* (Fairy Tales, Novellas, and Popular Tales of Sicily, 1875) and Gherardo Nerucci's *Sessanta novelle popolari montalesi* (Sixty Popular Tales from Montale, 1880). The recasting of this material by imposing "stylistic unity," integrating variants so as to produce the "most unusual, beautiful, and original texts," and in some cases translating tales originally told or transcribed in dialect into Italian has been compared to the Grimms' project, although Calvino openly discussed his "halfway scientific" method and indicated the specific changes he made in the abundant notes to the collection. In the words of a Tuscan proverb that Calvino quotes, "The tale is not beautiful if nothing is added to it"; in his own words, "I have the right to produce variants, too."

In the introduction to his *Folktales*, Calvino maintains that Italian tales are as varied and rich as those of Northern Europe; they are endowed with an "unparalleled grace, wit, and unity of design" and possess certain unique features, such as enterprising and active female protagonists, an acute sense of beauty, "a continuous quiver of love" and sensuality, the preference for harmony and the "healing solution" over cruelty, a "tendency to dwell on the wondrous," and an ever-present dialectic between the fantastic and the real (xxxix). Fairy tales are, for Calvino, not only the thematic and structural model for all stories but a key to interpreting the world. The magic they showcase is a complement to human strengths we all possess; even further, they reflect, symbolically, authentic social and political desires and tensions. This is what Calvino means when he says that "folktales are real": they treat, quite simply, of the human condition.

> [Fairy tales] are the catalog of the potential destinies of men and women, especially regarding the stage of life when destiny is formed, i.e., youth: from birth, which itself often foreshadows the future; to the departure from home; and finally, to the trials of growing up, attaining maturity, and confirming one's humanity. In this rapidly sketched design there is everything: the drastic division of humans into kings and poor people, even if they are in essence equal; the persecution of the innocent and their subsequent vindication, a dialectic inherent in every life; love unrecognized when first encountered and then no sooner experienced than lost; the common fate of being subject to spells or, in other words, having one's existence predetermined by complex and unknown forces; but also the elementary duty of struggling to liberate oneself and to determine one's own fate, together with the duty of liberating others, since we can only free ourselves by freeing others. Fairy tales teach us that we must be loyal in our commitments and pure of heart, for these are the basic virtues that lead to salvation and triumph. And that beauty is a sign of grace, and that it can be masked by the humble, ugly guise of a frog. Above all, fairy tales show us how everything—men, beasts, plants, things—is connected, the infinite possibility of transformation of all that exists. (xviii)

Calvino's last work, published posthumously, was *Six Memos for the Next Millennium* (1988), a series of lectures that was to be delivered at Harvard University. It should come as no surprise that the six qualities that are for Calvino the essence of literature—lightness, quickness, exactitude, visibility, multiplicity, and consistency—find themselves at home in the fairy tale as well.

Further Reading

Primary

Calvino, Italo. *Fiabe italiane.* 2 vols. Turin: Einaudi, 1956. 1:3–4, 100–103, 229–35, 277–82, 359–60; 2:456–59, 476–77. [source text]

Calvino, Italo. *Italian Folktales*. Trans. George Martin. New York: Harcourt Brace Jovanovich, 1980.

Secondary

Bacchilega, Cristina. "Calvino's Journey: Modern Transformations of Folktale, Story, and Myth." *Journal of Folklore Research* 26, no. 2 (1989): 81–98.

Beckwith, Marc. "Italo Calvino and the Nature of Italian Folktales." *Italica* 64, no. 2 (1987): 244–62.

Benson, Stephen. *Cycles of Influence: Fiction, Folktale, Theory*. Detroit: Wayne State University Press, 2003.

Bronzini, Giovanni Battista. "From the Grimms to Calvino: Folk Tales in the Year Two Thousand." In *Storytelling in Contemporary Societies*, ed. Lutz Röhrich and Sabine Wienker-Piepho. Tübingen, Narr, 1990. 189–98.

Dauntless Little John (Giovannin senza paura)

Translated by George Martin

This is the familiar ATU type 326, The Youth Who Wanted to Learn What Fear Is, and the tale that opens Calvino's Italian Folktales. *In its role as overture to the collection, it contains the important warning to be skeptical about overly triumphant vanquishing of obvious enemies; the most perilous situations involve confronting the subtle monsters that are not only among us but intimately part of ourselves. This seems especially relevant in the Italian postwar context in which the* Folktales *were published, when it was becoming increasingly clear that a part of the political and cultural legacy of fascism had not been entirely dispersed but merely reabsorbed.*

There was once a lad whom everyone called Dauntless Little John, since he was afraid of nothing. Traveling about the world, he came to an inn, where he asked for lodgings. "We have no room here," said the innkeeper, "but if you're not afraid, I will direct you to a certain palace where you can stay."

"Why should I be afraid?"

"People shudder at the thought of that palace, since nobody who's gone in has come out alive. In the morning the friars go up with the bier for anyone brave enough to spend the night inside."

So what did Little John do but pick up a lamp, a bottle, and a sausage, and march straight to the palace.

At midnight he was sitting at the table eating, when he heard a voice in the chimney. "Shall I throw it down?"

"Go ahead!" replied Little John.

Down the chimney into the fireplace fell a man's leg. Little John drank a glass of wine.

Then the voice spoke again. "Shall I throw it down?"

"Go ahead!" So another leg dropped into the fireplace. Little John bit into the sausage.

"Shall I throw it down?"

"Go ahead!" So down came an arm. Little John began whistling a tune.

"Shall I throw it down?"

"By all means!" And there was another arm.

"Shall I throw it down?"

"Yes!"

Then came the trunk of a body, and the arms and legs stuck onto it, and there stood a man without a head.

"Shall I throw it down?"

"Throw it down!"

Down came the head and sprang into place atop the trunk. He was truly a giant, and Little John raised his glass and said, "To your health!"

The giant said, "Take the lamp and come with me." Little John picked up the lamp, but didn't budge. "You go first!" said the giant.

"No, after you," insisted Little John.

"After you!" thundered the giant.

"You lead the way!" yelled Little John.

So the giant went first, with Little John behind him lighting the way, and they went through room after room until they had walked the whole length of the palace. Beneath one of the staircases was a small door.

"Open it!" ordered the giant.

"You open it!" replied Little John.

So the giant shoved it open with his shoulder. There was a spiral staircase.

"Go on down," directed the giant.

"After you," answered Little John.

They went down the steps into a cellar, and the giant pointed to a stone slab on the ground. "Raise that!"

"You raise it!" replied Little John, and the giant lifted it as though it were a mere pebble.

Beneath the slab were three pots of gold. "Carry those upstairs!" ordered the giant.

"You carry them up!" answered Little John. And the giant carried them up one by one.

When they were back in the hall where the great fireplace was, the giant said, "Little John, the spell has been broken!" At that, one of his legs came off and kicked its way up the chimney. "One of these pots of gold is for you." An arm came loose and climbed up the chimney. "The second pot of gold is for the friars who come to carry away your body, believing you perished." The other arm came off and followed the first. "The third pot of gold is for the first poor man who comes by." Then the other leg dropped off, leaving the giant seated on the floor. "Keep the palace for yourself." The trunk separated from the head and vanished. "The owners of the palace and their children are now gone forever." At that, the head disappeared up the chimney.

As soon as it was light, a dirge arose: "Miserere mei, miserere mei." The friars had come with the bier to carry off Little John's body. But there he stood, at the window, smoking his pipe!

Dauntless Little John was a wealthy youth indeed with all those gold pieces, and he lived happily in his palace. Then one day what should he do but look behind him and see his shadow: he was so frightened he died.

(This is the only tale in the collection whose geographical origin is not indicated. For all of the other tales, Calvino indicates the region of origin.)

The Crab Prince (Il principe granchio)

Translated by George Martin

This is a curious aquatic version of ATU 425A, The Animal as Bridegroom. Aptly, it hails from Venice, the city of water.

There was once a fisherman who never could catch enough fish to buy food for his family. One day though, when he went to pull up his nets, he felt a weight almost too heavy to move, but he tugged and tugged and found a crab so enormous that one pair of eyes was not enough to take it all in. "Oh, what a haul at last! Now I can buy food for my children!"

He took the crab home on his back and told his wife to put the pot on the fire, for he would return shortly with food. Then he carried the crab to the king's palace.

"Your Highness," he said to the king, "I've come to see if you will kindly buy this crab from me. My wife has put the pot on the fire, but I have no money to buy anything to go in it."

The king replied, "But what would I do with a crab? Can't you sell it to someone else?"

Just then the king's daughter came in. "Oh, what a fine crab, what a fine crab! Please buy it for me, Papa, please! We'll put it in the fishpond with the mullets and the goldfish."

The king's daughter was fascinated by fish and would sit for hours on the rim of the fishpond in the garden watching the mullets and the goldfish swim about. Her father could refuse her nothing, so he bought the crab. The fisherman put it into the fishpond and received a purse of gold coins that would feed his children for a whole month.

The princess never tired of watching the crab and spent all her time by the fishpond. She had become thoroughly familiar with him and his ways, noticing that from noon until three o'clock he always disappeared and went off goodness knows where. One day the king's daughter was there studying her crab, when she heard the doorbell ring. She looked down from her balcony, and there was a poor tramp asking for alms. She threw down a purse of money, but it flew past him into a ditch. The tramp went into the ditch after it, plunged under water, and began to swim. The ditch connected with the king's fishpond by an underground canal which continued on to no telling where. The tramp followed it and came out in a beautiful basin in the middle of a large underground hall hung with tapestries and containing a table sumptuously laid. The tramp stepped from the basin and hid behind the tapestries. At the stroke of noon, up popped a fairy in the middle of the basin, seated on the back of a crab. She and the crab jumped out of the water into the hall, the fairy tapped the crab with her wand, and there emerged from the crab shell a handsome youth. The young man took a seat at the table and the fairy tapped her wand, producing food in the dishes and wine in the bottles. When the youth had finished eating and drinking, he reentered the crab shell, which the fairy touched with her wand, and the crab took her onto his back once more, jumped into the basin, and disappeared underwater with her.

Then the tramp came out from behind the tapestries, dove into the water, and swam back to the king's fishpond. The king's daughter was there looking at her fish and, seeing the vagabond's head bob up, she asked, "What are you doing here?"

"Princess," said the tramp, "I have a wonderful thing to relate to you." He came out of the pond and told her the whole story.

"Now I understand where the crab goes from noon to three o'clock!" exclaimed the king's daughter. "Fine, tomorrow at noon we shall go together and see."

So the next day they both swam the underground canal from the fishpond to the underground hall and hid behind the tapestries. Exactly at noon, up popped the fairy on the crab's back. She tapped her wand and out stepped the handsome young man from the crab shell and took his place at the table. The princess, who already liked the crab, was charmed with the young man and immediately fell in love with him.

Seeing the empty crab shell right there next to her, she hid inside it.

When the youth got back into the shell he found the beautiful maiden there. "What have you done?" he whispered. "If the fairy learns of this, she will put us both to death."

"But I want to free you from the spell!" whispered the king's daughter. "Tell me what I must do."

"Impossible," said the young man. "Only a maiden who loved me enough to die for me could break the spell."

"I am that maiden," said the princess.

While this conversation was taking place inside the crab shell, the fairy seated herself on the crab's back, and the youth, working the crab claws as usual, carried her through the underground waterways to the open sea, without her suspecting that hidden inside with him was the king's daughter. On the way back to the fishpond after leaving the fairy at her destination, the young man, who happened to be a prince, explained to his beloved close beside him in the crab shell what to do to free him. "You must climb up on a rock on shore and play and sing. The fairy is enthralled by music and will emerge from the sea to listen to you and say, 'Play on, lovely maiden, your music is so delightful.' And you will reply, 'I certainly shall, if you give me the flower in your hair.' When you have that flower in your hand, I will be free, since the flower is my life."

Meanwhile the crab had reached the fishpond, and he let the king's daughter out of the shell.

The tramp had swum back by himself and, finding no princess, saw himself in serious trouble. But the maiden emerged from the fishpond, thanked him, and gave him a handsome reward. Then she went to her father and told him she wanted to study music and singing. The king, who never refused her anything, sent for the finest musicians and singers to give her lessons.

As soon as she had learned music, the daughter said to the king, "Papa, I want to go and play my violin on a rock by the sea."

"On a rock by the sea? Have you lost your mind?" But, as usual, he gave in to her and let her go with eight maids of honor dressed in white. As a precaution, he had her followed at a distance by a few armed soldiers.

Seated on a rock, with her eight maids of honor in white dresses on eight rocks around her, the king's daughter played her violin. From the waves rose the fairy. "How beautifully you play!" she said. "Play on, play on, it delights me so to hear you!"

The king's daughter said, "Indeed I shall, if you make me a present of that flower you are wearing in your hair, for I love flowers to distraction."

"I will give it to you if you can fetch it from where I throw it."

"I will fetch it," she assured the fairy, and started to play and sing. When the song was over, she said, "Now give me the flower."

"Here you are," said the fairy, and threw it as far as she could out to sea.

The princess dove into the sea and swam toward the flower floating on the waves. "Princess, princess! Help! Help!" screamed the eight maids of honor standing up on the rocks, with their white veils billowing in the wind. But the princess swam on and on, disappearing in the waves and coming back up; she was beginning to doubt whether she would reach the flower, when a big wave swept it right into her hand.

In that instant she heard a voice beneath her, saying, "You have given me back my life, and will be my bride. Now don't be afraid. I am under you and will carry you to shore. But say nothing of this, not even to your father. I must go and tell my parents, and within twenty-four hours I'll come and ask for your hand."

"Yes, yes, I understand" was all she could answer, since she was out of breath, while the crab underwater carried her to shore.

So when she got back home, all the princess told the king was that she had enjoyed herself immensely.

The next day at three, there was a roll of drums, a flourish of trumpets, a prancing of horses, and in walked a majordomo saying the son of his king requested an audience.

The prince put the customary request to the king for the princess's hand and then told the whole story. The king was somewhat taken aback, for he had been in the dark about everything. He sent for his daughter, who came running in and threw herself into the prince's arms, exclaiming, "This is my bridegroom, this is my bridegroom!" The king realized there was nothing to do but conclude the marriage as soon as possible.

(*Venice*)

Bellinda and the Monster (Bellinda e il mostro)

Translated by George Martin

This is one of the many ATU 425 (The Search for the Lost Husband) tales in Calvino's collection, here present as the Beauty and the Beast version (ATU 425C). As has been noted by Renato Aprile, in his Indice delle fiabe popolari italiane di magia, *this type, which harkens back to the ancient Cupid and Psyche tale, is one of the most widespread among Italian fairy tales. Calvino's version includes many of the same motifs as the early, best-known version, Madame de Beaumont's "La Belle et la bête" (1756). These include both major plot elements such as the family's middle-class status and the merchant father's economic downfall and smaller details such as Bellinda's dismay at seeing her familiar monster transformed into a "handsome gentleman" and the punishment of the sisters by having them turned into statues.*

Once upon a time in Leghorn there was a merchant who had three daughters: Assunta, Carolina, and Bellinda. He was rich, and had brought his girls up in the lap of luxury. They were all three beautiful, but the youngest was so bewitchingly lovely that they had given her the name of Bellinda. Not only was she beautiful, but also kind, modest, and wise—every bit as much as her sisters were haughty, stubborn, spiteful, and always full of envy to boot.

When the girls were older, the richest merchants in town went and proposed to them, but Assunta and Carolina scornfully dismissed them. "Never will we marry a merchant!"

Bellinda, however, always had a courteous reply for her suitors. "I can't marry just now, for I'm still too young. We'll speak further of the matter when I get older."

As the saying goes, life is full of surprises. The father lost a ship with its entire cargo, and in no time he was ruined. Of all his former possessions, the only thing left was a cottage in the country. The only choice he now had was to move there with his daughters and till the soil as a farmer. Just imagine the faces the two older girls made upon hearing that. "No, indeed, Father," they said, "we're not about to move to the country. We're staying right here in town. Certain gentlemen of consequence have proposed to us."

But just let them seek out the gentlemen now! On hearing that the young ladies were left without a cent to their name, the sometime suitors all stole away, saying, "It serves them right! That will teach them a lesson. Now they'll get off their high horse." But equal to the men's delight over Assunta and Carolina's misfortune was everyone's sympathy for poor Bellinda, who had never turned up her nose at anyone. Two or three youths even asked her to marry them just as she was, beautiful and penniless. She wouldn't hear of it, however, for her heart was set on helping her father, whom she couldn't think of abandoning now. As things stood, she was the one who rose early in the country, did the housework, got dinner for her sisters and her father. Her sisters, however, always rose at ten o'clock and didn't lift a hand all day long. They were forever out of sorts with Bellinda, and called her "country wench," for taking such a wretched life in her stride from the start.

One day the father got a letter saying that his ship, which he had given up for lost, had reached Leghorn with part of its cargo intact. The older sisters, imagining they'd be back in town in no time and rich again, went wild with joy. Their father said, "I'm going to Leghorn now to see about recovering what is due me. What shall I bring you as a present?"

Assunta said, "I want a beautiful silk gown the color of air."

Then Carolina said, "Bring me, instead, a peach-colored gown."

Bellinda, however, remained silent and asked for nothing. Her father repeated his question, and she said, "Now is no time to be spending so much money. Just bring me a rose, and I'll be happy." Her sisters poked fun at her, but she paid no attention.

The father went to Leghorn, but just as he was about to claim his cargo, up rushed other merchants to prove he owed them money and that these goods were therefore not his. After much wrangling, the poor old man was left empty-handed. But not wanting to disappoint his daughters, he drew out the little money remaining to him and bought the air-colored gown for Assunta and the peach-colored one for Carolina. Then he hadn't a cent left. The rose for Bellinda was such a little thing, he decided, that it really made no difference whether he bought it or not.

Thus he headed back to the country. He walked and walked until nightfall; entering a forest, he soon lost his way. To make matters worse, snow began falling and a strong wind arose. The merchant took refuge under a tree, expecting to be torn to bits any moment by the wolves whose howling came from all directions. While he stood there glancing around, he caught sight of a light in the distance. He made his way toward it and at length saw a handsome palace all lit up inside. The merchant went in, but not a soul was anywhere to be seen; no matter where he looked, there was absolutely no one. A fire burned brightly in the fireplace, and the merchant, who was soaking wet, paused to warm himself. Somebody will surely come in now, he thought. He waited and waited, but not a living soul appeared. The merchant saw a table laden with delicacies of every variety, so he sat down and dined. Then he took up the lamp and passed into another room, where a fine bed had been carefully made; after undressing, he climbed into it and went to sleep.

When he woke up next morning, he couldn't believe his eyes: there on the chair beside the bed lay a brand-new suit of clothes. He dressed, went downstairs and out into the garden. A magnificent rosebush was blooming in the middle of a flowerbed. The merchant remembered his daughter Bellinda's wish and decided he could now fulfill this one too. He selected the most beautiful rose and plucked it. At that moment a roar came from behind the rosebush, and in the midst of the roses appeared a monster, so ugly that the mere sight of it was enough to reduce a person to ashes. It exclaimed, "How dare you steal my roses after I've lodged you, fed you, and clothed you! You shall pay for that rose with your life!"

The poor merchant fell to his knees and explained that the flower had been intended for his daughter Bellinda, who wanted no present but a rose. Hearing the story, the monster calmed down and said, "If you have such a daughter, bring her to me. I will keep her here with me, and she will live like a queen. But if you don't send her, I will pursue you and your family wherever you happen to be."

Quaking in his boots, the little old man could hardly believe it when he was told he was free to go. But first the monster had him go back inside the palace and pick out all the jewels, gold objects, and brocades that captured his fancy. These things filled a chest, which the monster would send to the merchant's house.

As soon as the merchant got back to the country, his daughters ran out to meet him. Simpering, the two older girls asked him for their presents. Bellinda, though, was truly happy over his return and as gracious as ever. He gave one of the dresses to Assunta, the other to Carolina. Then he looked at Bellinda and burst into tears as he handed her the rose and told her exactly what had happened.

The older sisters were quick to speak out. "We said so! Bellinda and her crazy ideas! A rose, mind you! Now we'll all have to suffer the consequences!"

Calm as usual, Bellinda said to her father, "The monster promised to harm none of you if I go to him? In that case I'll go, since it's better for me to sacrifice myself than for all of us to suffer."

Her father said that never, never would he take her there, and her sisters insisted she was crazy. Bellinda, though, would hear no more. She put her foot down and declared she was going.

The following morning, then, father and daughter set out at dawn. Earlier, however, upon arising, the father had found at the foot of his bed the chest with all the treasures he had selected at the monster's palace. Making no mention of it to the two older girls, he hid it under the bed.

They arrived at the monster's palace in the evening and found it all lit up. They went inside. On the first floor was a table laid for two, full of heavenly delights. Although Bellinda and her father had little appetite for these things, they nevertheless sat down to taste a few dishes. When they had finished eating, a great roar was heard, and in came the monster. Bellinda was speechless: he was far uglier than she had dared imagine. But little by little she took heart, and when the monster asked if she'd come of her own will, she answered quite frankly that she had.

The monster seemed pleased. He turned to the father, handed him a traveling bag full of gold, and ordered him to leave the palace at once and never set foot there again; the monster would see to it that the family had everything they needed. Heartbroken, the poor father kissed his daughter goodbye and returned home, pitifully weeping.

Left by herself (since the monster had bid her good night right after her father's departure), Bellinda undressed and got into bed and slept peacefully the whole night long knowing she had saved her father from no telling what catastrophes.

Next morning she arose refreshed and confident, and decided to look around the palace. On the door of her room was written *Bellinda's Room*. On the door of her wardrobe was written *Bellinda's Wardrobe*. In each of the beautiful frocks was embroidered *Bellinda's Frock*. And all around were placards that read:

Queen art thou here,
Thy every wish to us is dear.

In the evening when Bellinda sat down to dine, the customary roar was heard, and in walked the monster. "May I join you?" he asked.

Naturally polite, Bellinda replied, "You are the master."

"No," he said, "you are in charge here. The whole palace and everything in it are yours." He was silent for a while, as though lost in thought. Then he asked, "Am I really so ugly?"

Bellinda answered, "Ugly you are, but you have a kind heart which makes you almost handsome."

Then he asked, all of a sudden, "Bellinda, would you marry me?"

She trembled all over, not knowing what to reply. She thought, If I turn him down, goodness knows how he will feel. Then she took heart and said, "To tell the truth, I'm not really interested in marrying you."

The monster made no comment, but bid her good night and went away sighing.

Three months passed. And every evening during that time, the monster came and asked Bellinda the same thing, if she would marry him, and then went away sighing. The girl was now so used to it that she would have been hurt if he had missed one evening.

Every day Bellinda strolled in the garden, and the monster told her about the magic of the plants. Among the trees was a leafy one known as the tree of weeping and laughter. "Whenever its leaves turn upward," explained the monster, "that means there's joy in your family; when they droop, there is weeping at home."

One day Bellinda noticed the tree of weeping and laughter with all its leaves pointed upward. She asked the monster, "Why is it so jubilant?"

"Your sister Assunta is going to get married."

"Could I go to the wedding?"

"Of course," answered the monster. "But come back in a week, or else you'll surely find me dead. Take this ring. Whenever the stone clouds up, that means I'm sick, and you must rush back to me at once. Now gather together whatever things in the palace you'd like to take along as wedding presents, and put them in a trunk this evening at the foot of your bed."

Bellinda thanked him and took a trunk and filled it with silk gowns, fine lingerie, jewels, and gold coins. She put the trunk at the foot of her bed and went to sleep. In the morning she woke up in her father's house, and there with her was the trunk she had packed the night before. Everybody gave her a hearty welcome, even her sisters. But when they learned she was so happy and rich and the monster so kind, they were again green with envy, since they were far from wealthy themselves, in spite of the monster's presents; and to make matters worse, Assunta was marrying a mere carpenter. As spiteful as ever, they got Bellinda's ring away from her under the pretext of wearing it themselves a little while; then they hid it. Bellinda was quite upset over not being able to see the stone, and at the end of a week she wept and pleaded so with her sisters that her father ordered them to return the ring at once. As soon as she got it back she noticed the stone had become somewhat cloudy, so she left immediately for the palace.

The monster failed to appear at mealtime, and Bellinda grew worried; she looked all over for him and called and called. Only at dinner did he turn up, with a somewhat pained expression. "I was ill," he said, "and if you'd come any later, you wouldn't have found me alive. Don't you love me any more?"

"Of course I love you," she replied.

"And you would marry me?"

"That, no!" exclaimed Bellinda.

Two more months went by and the leaves again pointed upward on the tree of weeping and laughter, since this time Carolina was getting married. Bellinda went home once more with the ring and another trunk of treasures. Her sisters pretended they were glad to see her. Assunta was now meaner than ever, since her carpenter husband beat her every day. Bellinda told her sisters what a risk she had run by staying too long on her last visit, and said she couldn't tarry this time. But once more the sisters stole the ring. When they finally returned it, the stone had completely clouded over. Bellinda rushed home in alarm, but the monster showed up for neither lunch nor dinner. He came in next morning looking quite weak, and said, "I was ready to die. If you are late another time, it will be the end of me."

A few more months went by. One day, the leaves of the tree of weeping and laughter were drooping, and the tree appeared completely withered. "What's the matter at home?" Bellinda cried.

"Your father is dying," answered the monster.

"Let me go to him! I promise I'll come back on time!"

The joy of having his youngest daughter at his bedside put the poor merchant on the road to recovery. Bellinda stayed by him day and night but one day while washing her hands she left the ring lying on the washstand and then couldn't find it when she went to put it back on.

Frantic, she looked everywhere for it, and pleaded with her sisters to return it. When she finally recovered it, the stone was all black except for a tiny dot on the edge.

She hastened to the palace, but it was pitch-dark and looked as though it had been vacant for the last hundred years. Screaming and crying, she called and called the monster, but there was no answer. She looked everywhere for him; as she was running through the garden she suddenly saw him lying under the rosebush and breathing what seemed to be his last. She got down on her knees and listened to his heart: it was still beating but very feebly. Then she kissed him and sobbed, "Monster, if you die, I'll be lost without you! If only . . . if only you could go on living, I'd marry you at once to make you happy!"

She had not finished speaking, when all at once the whole palace lit up and music and song poured from every window. Bellinda turned around, amazed. When she faced the rosebush again, the monster had vanished, and in his place, among the roses, stood a handsome knight. He bowed and said, "Thank you, dear Bellinda, for freeing me."

Bellinda was dumbfounded. "But I want the monster," she said. The knight knelt at her feet and said, "Here is the monster. I was under a spell and obliged to remain a monster until a beautiful maiden promised to marry me the way I was."

Bellinda gave her hand to the youth, who was a king, and together they walked to the palace. At the door stood her father, who embraced her, and her two sisters. The sisters, out of spite, remained outside and became statues on each side of the door.

The young king made Bellinda his wife and queen, and they lived happily ever afterward.

(*Montale Pistoiese*)

Buffalo Head (Testa di bufala)

Translated by George Martin

This tale, which Calvino calls "one of the most suggestive and mysterious tales to be found in Italy," has elements of ATU 710, Our Lady's Child, and bears similarities to Basile's "Goat-Face."

A farmer was angrily hoeing the wretched soil of his field, when his hoe struck something hard. He dug gently around it, unearthing a buffalo head twice as big as any other buffalo head. Its horns stood up, its fur gleamed, and its eyes were open and bright, so that it really looked as if it were alive. It was alive, in fact, for when the farmer made ready to bring his hoe down on the ugly thing with all his might, the head opened its mouth and spoke. "Stop! Don't kill me. I will be the making of one of your daughters if you spare me."

Suspecting that magic was in play here, the farmer carefully picked up the head and carried it to the edge of the field, where he put it down and covered it with his coat. When his elder daughter brought him his midday meal, he said to her, "Go look at what's under my coat."

The girl lifted the coat and let out a scream. "Oh, what a hideous monster!" She went flying back home, screaming all the way.

Seeing her return so frightened her mother thought something might have happened to her husband, so she said to her middle daughter, "Go to your father and find out if he needs anything."

She too was directed by her father to look under the coat, and she too fled like lightning, screaming at the top of her voice. "What a dreadful snout!"

The mother then called her youngest daughter, who was also the smartest and most courageous of the three, and sent her to the field. When her father told her to look under the coat, the little girl obeyed. A smile spread over her face, and she reached out and petted the buffalo head. "My, what a pretty little head! What fine horns! What fine whiskers! Papa, where did you find this wonderful buffalo head?"

At those compliments, the buffalo head looked up and whined happily. "Would you come and live with me, you lovely child?"

"If Papa lets me, I'll come right now."

The farmer didn't have the heart to refuse. The buffalo head led the way, capering on its horns, while the child followed dancing and clapping for joy.

In a clearing in the heart of the woods was a trapdoor. Buffalo Head opened it with one of her horns and sprang through it. Reaching the bottom, she called to the little girl, "Remove your wooden shoes and come on down. Be careful, though, for the steps are glass." The child went down the glass steps and found herself in a princely drawing room, and there in an armchair sat Buffalo Head.

The little girl was quite happy in this underground home. Buffalo Head was even better to her than any real mother would have been, teaching her how to keep house, cook and iron, along with many other things. The child was good at everything, even reading and writing. She grew by leaps and bounds, and before you knew it she had become a beautiful maiden and so fond of Buffalo Head that she called her "Mamma."

The girl had not been in this hole too many years before she began saying, "Mamma, let me go up to the clearing for a little fresh air."

Buffalo Head didn't think much of the idea, but the girl kept on begging until Buffalo Head finally gave her a silver dress and a stool and told her she could sit in the clearing and knit.

While she was knitting in the clearing, a hunter who had lost his way came by and saw her. He was the son of the king of that territory. He got to talking to her, and in no time he was in love with the maiden.

"Beautiful maiden," he said, "you delight me in every way imaginable. If you have no objections, I would like to marry you."

"I have no objections myself," she replied, "but I must first see what my mother has to say." She walked back to the trapdoor and disappeared down the glass staircase.

Buffalo Head did not say no, but, "Do as you like. If you wish to leave me, then leave. But remember to be grateful. I'm responsible for all the good that has come your way, even the king's son who just asked you to marry him."

The king's son promised to return in a week with maids of honor and knights and royal carriages to take his bride away. Meanwhile, with Buffalo Head's help, the bride-to-be got her trousseau ready, and it was a trousseau fit for a queen. "Remember, now," Buffalo Head told her repeatedly, "when you leave this home, see that you leave nothing behind you. If you forget something, great misfortune could overtake you."

But when the king's son arrived with his train, the bride was so excited and distracted that not only did she leave her comb behind, she also forgot to bid Buffalo Head farewell and ran off without even closing the trapdoor behind her.

The bridal party had already traveled a great distance, when the bride suddenly clapped her hand to her forehead. "We must go back, we must go back, Majesty! I have forgotten my comb."

The king's son replied, "Are you afraid there'll be no combs in my palace? Or that the shops in town will have none?"

"I'm afraid something awful will happen to me," she said in a tearful voice, "since Mamma told me to leave none of my things behind if I didn't want to have bad luck. Please, Majesty, let's go back." So the prince ordered the horses turned about, and they rode back into the woods.

The trapdoor was still wide open. The bride ran downstairs and started looking for her comb.

"Oh, you'd already gone off?" asked Buffalo Head.

"Yes, Mamma, and in the excitement of getting away I forgot my comb, and now I can't find it."

"You forgot your comb, did you?" said Buffalo Head. "Just your comb? Go look in your dresser drawer."

Quite upset by now, the bride pulled out a drawer and bent over to rummage through it. When she stood back up and saw herself in the mirror, she let out a scream: her head had changed into a large buffalo head. "Mamma, Mamma! Something terrible has happened to me! Come here quick! Help me!"

Buffalo Head said, "There is nothing I can do. This is what you get for being ungrateful. You went off without even telling me goodbye."

"What will my bridegroom now say?"

"He will have to take you as you are, for he promised to marry you."

In short, all the maiden could do was wind a thick veil around her head and return to the prince. "Why on earth are you all muffled up?" he asked her. The girl explained that her eyes had suddenly become sore and swollen.

At court, the prince's mother and all the noble ladies could hardly wait to see this great beauty. But, under the pretext of sore eyes, she arrived heavily veiled and showed her face to no one. At last came the hour when she was alone with the prince and had to lift the veil. Imagine his surprise on discovering that his bride had become a monster! He pressed his hands tightly over his eyes and refused to take a second look. His first thought was to have her burned at the stake, but then he consulted his mother, who persuaded him to close up the poor thing in the palace attic instead. The rumor spread through the court that he kept her locked up out of jealousy. Only his mother knew his secret and sympathized with him the sadder he became. One day she said to him, "Dear son, you will have to get rid of that buffalo head and start looking around for a bride who is worthy of you."

"How can I get rid of her when I've already promised to marry her?"

"There's a way, I assure you," said his mother. "At the court, there are two graceful young ladies whose sole dream is to marry you. Let us have a contest between them and the buffalo head to see who spins a pound of flax the best, in only one week. The winner will be your bride."

The prince followed the suggestion. The noble ladies shut themselves up in separate rooms and went to work at once painstakingly spinning their pound of flax. The poor bride, however, did nothing but sit and weep over her misfortune. Saturday evening she slid down a rope and ran to Buffalo Head's trapdoor in the woods. "Mamma," she whined, "please help me. Get me out of this mess, please. I know you can! After showing me so much kindness, you have made me the most miserable girl alive."

Buffalo Head replied, "You think ingratitude is nothing? I'm sorry but I can't help you. I can only give you this walnut. Offer it to the king's son tomorrow and tell him to eat the kernel in exchange for the pound of flax he gave you to spin."

On Sunday the noble ladies took their finely spun yarn to the queen to judge. "Not bad!" she commented. "But it's not perfect, either; it's not completely uniform. Let's now have a look at this other one's work."

The bride came forward with the walnut. "Do you want to make a fool of me too?" said the king's son. He nevertheless cracked open the nut and found a skein of thread perfectly spun from a pound of flax and finer than any you ever saw.

But the queen remarked, "The thread is fine indeed; that, we cannot deny. But would you marry a monster solely because of the wonder she's worked with a pound of flax? There must be a second test. This time we'll give these ladies a week to make a linen shirt, and the best seamstress will be your bride."

Once more the ladies were in their rooms and bent over their work: stitch by stitch, minute by minute, they worked. But the bride wept without cease and didn't even go near her material. Saturday evening she slipped down the rope and back to Buffalo Head. "Mamma, please help me! Forgive me for going off without saying goodbye. Have you really ceased to love your daughter?"

"Can't you do anything but weep and complain?" said Buffalo Head. "It's certainly not my fault you're in this predicament. You can't say I didn't warn you in time. All I can give you is this hazelnut. Take it to the king's son to crack open and eat. If he doesn't like it, let him spit it out!"

When the king's son cracked the hazelnut, out came a shirt embroidered entirely in gold, with certain stitches so close and fine that no human eye could see them.

The queen spoke. "We shall now have the final test. One week from today a grand ball will take place. Order these three ladies to get ready for it, and the most beautiful will be your bride."

As soon as they got back to their rooms, the two noble ladies each began exerting all their skill to become the most beautiful. They were so busy rubbing down their bodies with aromatic oils, making up their faces, setting their hair in every way imaginable, and trying on dress after dress, that they had no time to sleep. And could looking glasses be worn out from use, nothing of theirs would have remained at the end of that week. As for the bride, what more would you expect her to do, with that bunglesome buffalo head on her shoulders, than cry all week long and then slip back on Saturday night to the trapdoor in the woods.

"You've come back to bawl?" asked Buffalo Head.

"Mamma, what on earth will I do now? If you don't forgive me right away, I will lose my bridegroom for good."

"You brought this all on yourself. You ran off like a dog, and after all the nice things I'd done for you."

"I didn't do it on purpose, Mamma, don't you see? I was too happy and excited to realize what I was doing that day."

"And now, if you had that day to live over, what would you do?"

"Oh, Mamma, I would hug and kiss you goodbye, and I wouldn't leave any of my belongings behind, and I would close the trapdoor securely when I went out."

"All right, then, I forgive you," said Buffalo Head. "Go look for your comb."

The bride went to the dresser, opened her drawer, rummaged through it, and found the comb. How great was her amazement, as she stood up again, to see her original head in the mirror, but twice as lovely now as before! Jumping and screaming for joy, she ran to Buffalo Head and hugged and kissed her, thanking her over and over for her kindness.

On Sunday the whole court gathered in the royal ballroom before the king and queen seated on the high throne and their son standing at the foot of the steps. The three ladies came forward, heavily veiled from head to foot. The prince lifted the first one's veil and muttered, "What's this? She's nothing but padding from top to bottom!"

The second lady moved up, and the prince lifted her veil. "My word! This one is all ribbons and paint!" He dared not lift his bride's veil, but when he did lift it at last, he was dumbfounded. "That's my wife! That's how she looked the first time I ever saw her, knitting out in the heart of the woods. Only, she's far lovelier now than then! Mother dear, I've made my choice, I will marry this kind and beautiful maiden."

He took her by the hand and drew her onto the throne beside him, while the whole court hailed her as their future queen. From that day on they were together and as happy as happy could be.

(*Montale Pistoiese*)

Apple Girl (La ragazza mela)

Translated by George Martin

Here we have a botanical girl (ATU 407, The Girl as Flower) in the form of an apple. The best-known tales of this type in Italy are Basile's "The Myrtle" and Pitrè's "Rosemary."

There was once a king and a queen who were very sad because they had no children. The queen kept asking, "Why can't I bear children the same as the apple tree bears apples?"

Now it happened that instead of bearing a son, the queen gave birth to an apple, but an apple redder and more beautiful than any you ever saw. The king placed it on a gold tray on his balcony.

Across the street from the king lived a second king, who happened to be standing at his window one day and saw, on his neighbor's balcony, a beautiful maiden as fair and rosy as an apple bathing and combing her hair in the sun. Open-mouthed, he stood staring at her, never having seen so lovely a maiden. But the minute the girl realized she was being observed, she ran back to the tray and disappeared inside the apple. The king had fallen madly in love with her.

He racked his brains and ended up crossing the street and knocking on the door, which the queen answered. "Majesty," he said to her, "I have a favor to ask of you."

"By all means, Majesty," replied the queen. "Any way neighbors can help one another out . . ."

"I would like to have that magnificent apple on your balcony."

"Do you know what you're asking, Majesty? I'm that apple's mother, mind you, and I had to wait a long time before I had her."

But the king wouldn't take no for an answer, so the other king and queen had to grant his wish, in order for them all to remain good neighbors. Thus he went home with the apple, which he took straight to his own room. He put out everything necessary for her toilette, and the maiden would emerge every morning to bathe and arrange her hair while he looked on. That was all she did. She neither ate nor talked; she only bathed and arranged her hair, then went back inside the apple.

The king lived with his stepmother, whose suspicions were aroused by her stepson's constant seclusion in his room. "I'd give anything to know what my son is up to!"

War broke out, and the king had to go off and fight. It broke his heart to leave his apple. He called his most trusted servant to him and said, "I'm leaving the key to my room with you. See that nobody goes in. Put out water and a comb every day for the apple girl, and make sure she has everything she needs. And don't forget, she tells me everything." (That wasn't so, the girl never said a word, but the king thought it wise to tell his servant the contrary.) "If a hair of her head is harmed during my absence, you'll pay with your life."

"Have no fear, Majesty, I will look after her to the very best of my ability."

As soon as the king was gone, the stepmother queen went to all lengths to get into his room. She put opium into the wine of his servant and stole the key from him when he fell asleep. She unlocked the door and turned the room upside down in search of clues to her stepson's strange behavior; but the more she searched, the less she found. The only thing out of the ordinary in the room was that splendid apple in a golden fruit bowl. "It must be this apple that is always on his mind!"

Queens, as you well know, always have a small dagger concealed in their sashes. She took out her dagger and began pricking the apple all over. Out of every wound flowed a rivulet of blood. The stepmother queen grew frightened, ran away, and replaced the key in the sleeping servant's pocket.

When the servant awakened, he had no idea what had happened to him. He ran into the king's room and found blood all over the place. "Oh, my goodness, what will I do now?" he exclaimed and fled.

He went to an aunt of his who was a fairy and possessed all the magic powders. The aunt took a powder suitable for apples under spells and another for bewitched maidens, and blended them.

The servant returned to the apple and sprinkled all the wounds with the mixture. The apple burst open, and out stepped the maiden in bandages and plaster casts.

The king came home, and for the first time, the maiden spoke. "Would you believe that your stepmother stabbed me all over with her dagger? But your servant has nursed me back to health. I am eighteen and was under a spell. If you like, I will be your bride."

"If I like! Indeed I do!"

The wedding was celebrated, to the great joy of both palaces. The only person missing was the stepmother, who fled and was never heard of again.

Merrily through life they went,
But were only content
To give me one cent
I never spent.

(*Florence*)

Bella Venezia

Translated by George Martin

This is an earthy, realistic version of ATU 709, Snow White. It features an industrious, middle-class mother (not a stepmother) who is a penny-pinching innkeeper, travelers from various Italian cities, and a Snow White character who sojourns with robbers. The bandits of the Abruzzo region were legendary.

A mother and a daughter kept an elegant inn, where kings and princes passing through town would stop. The innkeeper's name was Bella Venezia, and while travelers sat at the table, she would strike up a conversation. "What town do you come from?"

"From Milan."

"Did you ever see any woman in Milan lovelier than I am?"

"No, I've never seen a soul lovelier than you."

When it came time to settle the accounts, Bella Venezia would say, "Normally that would be ten crowns, but you need give me only five"—for she charged anyone only half-price when he told her he'd never seen a lovelier woman than herself.

"Where are you from?"

"Turin."

"And is there anyone in Turin lovelier than I am?"

"No, a woman lovelier than you I have never seen."

Then, at reckoning time, Bella Venezia said, "Normally I charge six crowns, but you need give me only three."

One day the innkeeper was asking a traveler the usual question, "And did you ever see a lovelier woman than myself?" when her daughter went through the room. And the traveler replied, "Indeed I have."

"Who?"

"Your daughter."

This time in making up the bill, Bella Venezia said, "It's normally eight crowns, but I'm asking you for sixteen."

That evening the mistress called in the kitchen boy. "Go to the sea shore, build a hut with just one tiny little window, and close up my daughter in it."

Thus Bella Venezia's daughter was imprisoned day and night in that hut by the sea. She heard the breaking of the waves, but was able to see no one other than the kitchen boy, who came to her daily with bread and water. But in spite of being shut up there, the maiden grew lovelier by the day.

A stranger riding along the beach on horseback saw that hut all boarded up and drew closer. He peeped through the tiny window and made out in the dimness the most beautiful maidenly face he had ever laid eyes on. A bit frightened, he spurred his horse and galloped off.

That night he stopped at Bella Venezia's inn.

"What town are you from?" asked the innkeeper.

"Rome."

"Did you ever see anyone lovelier than myself?"

"I certainly have," replied the stranger.

"Where?"

"Closed up in a hut by the sea."

"Here's your bill. It's only ten crowns, but I want thirty from you."

In the evening Bella Venezia asked the kitchen boy, "Listen, would you like to marry me?"

The kitchen boy couldn't believe his ears.

"If you want to marry me," continued Bella Venezia, "you must take my daughter into the woods and kill her. Bring me back her eyes and a bottle of her blood, and I'll marry you."

The kitchen boy was eager to marry the mistress, but he didn't have the heart to kill her daughter, who was all beauty and goodness. So he took the girl to the woods and left her. To get eyes and blood to carry back to Bella Venezia, he killed a lamb, which is innocent blood. And the mistress married him.

Alone in the woods, the girl screamed and cried, but no one heard her. Toward nightfall she spied a light in the distance. Drawing near, she heard many people talking and, frightened to death, hid behind a tree. It was a rocky, desolate place, and twelve robbers had come to a halt before a white boulder.

One of them said, “Open up, desert!” and the boulder swung outward like a door. The inside was all lit up like a large palace. The twelve robbers went in, and the last one said, “Close up, desert!” and the boulder swung to. The girl hidden behind the tree bided her time. In a little while, a voice inside said, “Open up, desert!” The door opened, and out filed the twelve robbers, the twelfth ordering, “Close up, desert!”

Once the robbers were out of sight, the girl went to the white boulder and said, “Open up, desert!” and the door swung open for her. She stepped into the lighted interior and commanded, “Close up, desert!”

Inside was a table laid for twelve, with twelve plates, twelve loaves of bread, and twelve bottles of wine. In the kitchen twelve chickens were on a spit ready to roast. The girl tidied up the place, made the twelve beds, and roasted the twelve chickens. Hungry by then, she ate a wing from every chicken, took a bite of every loaf of bread and a sip of wine from every bottle. When she heard the robbers coming back, she hid under a bed. The twelve bandits didn't know what to think when they saw the house so tidy, the beds made, and the chickens roasted. Then they noticed a wing missing from every chicken, a bite from every loaf, and a sip from every bottle, and said, “Somebody must have come in here.” Tomorrow it was agreed one of them would remain behind to stand guard.

The smallest of the robbers stayed, but he went outside to watch while the girl meanwhile came out from under the bed, put everything in order, ate the twelve chicken wings, the twelve chunks of bread, and drank the twelve swallows of wine.

“You're good for nothing!” said the ringleader, when he returned and saw that the house had been visited again. He assigned someone else to stand guard the next day. But this man also remained outside, while the girl was indoors. So for eleven days straight every robber tried keeping watch, but failed to discover the girl and was bawled out by all the others for being so stupid.

On the twelfth day, the chief decided to stand guard. Instead of watching outside, he remained inside and thus saw the girl come out from under the bed. Grabbing her by the arm, he said, “Don't be afraid. Now that you are here you can stay, and we will treat you as our little sister.”

So the girl remained with the robbers, keeping house for them, and every evening they brought her jewels, gold pieces, rings, and earrings.

The youngest robber delighted in dressing up as a grand nobleman to commit his robberies, and he would stop at the best inns. He thus went to Bella Venezia's one evening for dinner.

"Where do you come from?" asked the innkeeper.

"From the heart of the forest."

"Have you ever seen any woman lovelier than myself?"

"I certainly have," replied the robber.

"Who is she?"

"A girl we have with us."

So Bella Venezia knew her daughter was still alive.

Every day an old woman would come to the inn asking for alms, and this old woman was a witch. Bella Venezia promised one-half of her fortune to the witch if she could track down and kill that daughter.

One day while the robbers were out, the girl was standing at the window singing, when an old woman came by and said, "Brooches for sale! Brooches for sale! Lovely maiden, may I come in? I'll show you a pin that's a real gem, for your hair."

The maiden invited her in, and the old woman, going through the motion of showing her how nice a pin would look in her hair, thrust it into her scalp. The girl died.

When the robbers came home and found her dead, they all burst into tears, tough as they were. They chose a tall tree with a hollow trunk and buried her inside it.

Now the king's son was out hunting. He heard the dogs barking and, moving closer, saw them all scratching on the trunk of a tree. The king's son looked inside and found a very beautiful maiden who was dead.

"If you were alive, I would marry you," he said. "Even though you are dead, I can't tear myself away from you." He sounded his hunting horn, assembled his hunters, and had her taken to the royal palace. Without his mother the queen's knowledge, he had the beautiful maiden put in one of the rooms and would stay there the whole day admiring her.

Suspicious, the mother burst into the room. "So that's why you didn't want to come out! But she's dead! How could you possibly be interested in her?"

"Dead or not, I can't live apart from her!"

"You can at least have her hair fixed!" said the queen, and sent for the royal hairdresser. He came and, combing her hair, broke his comb. He picked up another comb and broke that one too. Thus, one right after the other, he broke seven combs. "What on earth does this girl have in her head?" asked the royal hairdresser. "I shall take a look." And he touched the head of a pin. He pulled ever so gently and, as the pin came out, the maiden regained her color, opened her eyes, drew her breath, said, "Oh," and stood up.

The wedding was celebrated. Tables were also set up in the streets. Whoever wanted to eat, ate; whoever didn't want to, didn't.

O Lord!
A hen for every sinner!
And for me, sinner of sinners,
A hen and several roosters!

(*Abruzzo*)

The False Grandmother (La finta nonna)

Translated by George Martin

This is a delightful version of Little Red Riding Hood (ATU 333) featuring grateful objects, cannibalism, and the indelible final image of the enterprising young heroine making faces at the ogress from the riverbank.

A mother had to sift flour, and told her little girl to go to her grandmother's and borrow the sifter. The child packed a snack—ring-shaped cakes and bread with oil—and set out.

She came to the Jordan River.

"Jordan River, will you let me pass?"

"Yes, if you give me your ring-shaped cakes."

The Jordan River had a weakness for ring-shaped cakes, which he enjoyed twirling in his whirlpools.

The child tossed the ring-shaped cakes into the river, and the river lowered its waters and let her through.

The little girl came to the Rake Gate.

"Rake Gate, will you let me pass?"

"Yes, if you give me your bread with oil."

The Rake Gate had a weakness for bread with oil, since her hinges were rusty, and bread with oil oiled them for her.

The little girl gave the gate her bread with oil, and the gate opened and let her through.

She reached her grandmother's house, but the door was shut tight.

"Grandmother, Grandmother, come let me in."

"I'm in bed sick. Come through the window."

"I can't make it."

"Come through the cat door."

"I can't squeeze through."

"Well, wait a minute," she said, and lowered a rope, by which she pulled the little girl up through the window. The room was dark. In bed was the ogress, not the grandmother, for the ogress had gobbled up Grandmother all in one piece from head to toe, all except her teeth, which she had put on to stew in a small stew pan, and her ears, which she had put on to fry in a frying pan.

"Grandmother, Mamma wants the sifter."

"It's late now. I'll give it to you tomorrow. Come to bed."

"Grandmother, I'm hungry, I want my supper first."

"Eat the beans boiling in the boiler."

In the pot were the teeth. The child stirred them around and said, "Grandmother, they're too hard."

"Well, eat the fritters in the frying pan."

In the frying pan were the ears. The child felt them with the fork and said, "Grandmother, they're not crisp."

"Well, come to bed. You can eat tomorrow."

The little girl got into bed beside Grandmother. She felt one of her hands and said, "Why are your hands so hairy, Grandmother?"

"From wearing too many rings on my fingers."

She felt her chest. "Why is your chest so hairy, Grandmother?"

"From wearing too many necklaces around my neck."

She felt her hips. "Why are your hips so hairy, Grandmother?"

"Because I wore my corset too tight."

She felt her tail and reasoned that, hairy or not, Grandmother had never had a tail. That had to be the ogress and nobody else. So she said, "Grandmother, I can't go to sleep unless I first go and take care of a little business."

Grandmother replied, "Go do it in the barn below. I'll let you down through the trapdoor and then draw you back up."

She tied a rope around her and lowered her into the barn. The minute the little girl was down she untied the rope and in her place attached a nanny goat. "Are you through?" asked Grandmother.

"Just a minute." She finished tying the rope around the nanny goat. "There, I've finished. Pull me back up."

The ogress pulled and pulled, and the little girl began yelling, "Hairy ogress! Hairy ogress!" She threw open the barn and fled. The ogress kept pulling, and up came the nanny goat. She jumped out of bed and ran after the little girl.

When the child reached the Rake Gate, the ogress yelled from a distance; "Rake Gate, don't let her pass!"

But the Rake Gate replied, "Of course I'll let her pass; she gave me her bread with oil."

When the child reached the Jordan River, the ogress shouted, "Jordan River, don't you let her pass!"

But the Jordan River answered, "Of course I'll let her pass; she gave me her ring-shaped cakes."

When the ogress tried to get through, the Jordan River did not lower his waters, and the ogress was swept away in the current. From the bank the little girl made faces at her.

(*Abruzzo*)

The Forest on the Superhighway (Il bosco sull'autostrada)

Translated by William Weaver

The title character of the short, dystopic tales of Calvino's Marcovaldo *(published as a volume in 1963 but written over the previous ten years) is an urban migrant for whom the city becomes a forest of inhumanity and monstrous forces and objects, a figure, in Calvino's words, for contemporary man himself, who "has lost all harmony with his surroundings."*

Cold has a thousand shapes and a thousand ways of moving in the world: on the sea it gallops like a troop of horses, on the countryside it falls like a swarm of locusts, in the cities like a knife-blade it slashes the streets and penetrates the chinks of unheated houses. In Marcovaldo's house that evening they had burned the last kindling, and the family, all bundled in overcoats, was watching the embers fade in the stove, and the little clouds rise from their own mouths at every breath. They had stopped talking; the little clouds spoke for them: the wife emitted great long ones like sighs, the children puffed them out like assorted soap-bubbles, and Marcovaldo blew them upward in jerks, like flashes of genius that promptly vanish.

In the end Marcovaldo made up his mind: "I'm going to look for wood. Who knows? I might find some." He stuffed four or five newspapers between his shirt and his jacket as breastplates against gusts of air, he hid a long, snaggle-tooth saw under his overcoat, and thus he went out into the night, followed by the long, hopeful looks of his family. He made a papery rustle at every step; the saw peeped out now and then above his collar.

Looking for wood in the city: easier said than done! Marcovaldo headed at once toward a little patch of public park that stood between two streets. All was deserted. Marcovaldo studied the naked trees, one by one, thinking of his family, waiting for him with their teeth chattering.

Little Michelino, his teeth chattering, was reading a book of fairy-tales, borrowed from the small library at school. The book told of a child, son of a woodsman, who went out with a hatchet to chop wood in the forest. "That's the place to go!" Michelino said. "The forest! There's wood there, all right!" Born and raised in the city, he had never seen a forest, not even at a distance.

Then and there, he worked it out with his brothers: one took a hatchet, one a hook, one a rope; they said good-bye to their Mamma and went out in search of a forest.

They walked around the city, illuminated by street-lamps, and they saw only houses: not a sign of a forest. They encountered an occasional passer-by, but they didn't dare ask him where a forest was. And so they reached the area where the houses of the city ended and the street turned into a highway.

At the sides of the highway, the children saw the forest: a thick growth of strange trees blocked the view of the plain. Their trunks were very very slender, erect or slanting; and their crowns were flat and outspread, revealing the strangest shapes and the strangest colors when a passing car illuminated them with its headlights. Boughs in the form of a toothpaste tube, a face, cheese, hand, razor, bottle, cow, tire, all dotted with a foliage of letters of the alphabet.

"Hurrah!" Michelino said. "This is the forest!"

And, spellbound, the brothers watched the moon rise among those strange shadows: "How beautiful it is . . ."

Michelino immediately reminded them of their purpose in coming there: wood. So they chopped down a little tree in the form of a yellow primrose blossom, cut it into bits, and took it home.

Marcovaldo came home with his scant armful of damp branches, and found the stove burning.

"Where did you find it?" he cried, pointing to what remained of a billboard, which, being of plywood, had burned very quickly.

"In the forest!" the children said.

"What forest?"

"The one by the highway. It's full of wood!"

Since it was so simple, and there was need of more wood, he thought he might as well follow the children's example, and Marcovaldo again went out with his saw. He went to the highway.

Officer Astolfo, of the highway police, was a bit shortsighted, and on night duty, racing on his motorcycle, he should have worn eyeglasses; but he didn't say so, for fear it would block his advancement.

That evening, there was a report that on the superhighway a bunch of kids was knocking down billboards. Officer Astolfo went out to inspect.

On either side of the road, the forest of strange figures, admonishing and gesticulating, accompanied Astolfo, who peered at them one by one, widening his near-sighted eyes. There, in the beam of his motorcycle's headlight, he caught a little urchin who had climbed up on a billboard. Astolfo put on the brakes. "Hey, what are you doing there? Jump down this minute!" The kid didn't move and stuck out its tongue. Astolfo approached and saw it was an ad for processed cheese, with a big child licking his lips. "Yes, of course," Astolfo said, and zoomed off.

A little later, in the shadow of a huge billboard, he illuminated a sad, frightened face. "Don't make a move! Don't try running away!" But nobody ran away. It was a suffering human face painted in the midst of a foot covered with corns: an ad for a corn-remover. "Oh, sorry," Astolfo said, and dashed away.

The billboard for a headache tablet was a gigantic head of a man, his hands over his eyes, in pain. Astolfo sped past, and the headlight illuminated Marcovaldo, who had scrambled to the top with his saw, trying to cut off a slice. Dazzled by the light, Marcovaldo huddled down and remained motionless, clinging to an ear of the big head, where the saw had already reached the middle of the brow.

Astolfo examined it carefully and said: "Oh, yes. Stappa tablets! Very effective ad! Smart idea! That little man up there with the saw represents the migraine that is cutting the head in two. I got it right away!" And he went off, content.

All was silence and cold. Marcovaldo heaved a sigh of relief, settled on his uncomfortable perch, and resumed work. The muffled scrape of the saw against the wood spread through the moonlit sky.

PART VI

Something Old, Something New

Fairy Tales for Our Times

1

Gianni Rodari (1920–80)

Gianni Rodari is one of Italy's most renowned and beloved children's authors. He was born in Omegna, in the northwestern region of Piedmont, and was trained as an elementary school teacher. After a brief period of teaching when he was a young man, he spent most of his life as a journalist and writer. His numerous books for children, which often encompass fairy-tale themes, adopt irony and humor to subvert conventional narrative formulas and incorporate pedagogical strategies aimed at liberating the imagination and encouraging creativity. In the preface to *Grammatica della fantasia. Introduzione all'arte di inventare storie* (*The Grammar of Fantasy: An Introduction to the Art of Inventing Stories*), Rodari stresses that the use of these techniques is much more than a mere exercise; it is a way to ensure that children grow to become free and engaged citizens: "'Every possible use of the word for everyone' seems like a good motto, with a nice democratic sound. Not because we're all artists, but so that none of us will become a slave" (6).

Like many people of his generation, Rodari was formed by his coming of age during Italian fascism. He fought in the Resistance during World War II and after the war became active in the Italian Communist Party; although he would break with the party later on in life, he remained faithful to a utopian socialist vision. Initially, he began to write for the party newspaper, *L'Unità*, where he was asked to edit a section dedicated to children, and it was here that he first published pieces for a young audience: his earliest work, *Libro delle filastrocche* (Book of Nursery Rhymes, 1950), dates from this period. He was involved with other newspapers and journals as well, in particular with the nonparty leftist daily *Paese Sera*, for which he wrote from 1958 until his death.

Rodari had discovered surrealism early on, and many of his works are infused with an interest, shared with that movement, in testing the limits of linguistic and logical verisimilitude and in juxtaposing realistic and marvelous scenarios. In his case, this became a way of underscoring the absurd and nonsensical contradictions of modern life, in particular in its social and political dimensions, and of imagining other possible models, of moving from "a passive acceptance of the world to the ability to criticize it, and then to the commitment to transform it" ("Pro e contro" 155).

The 1950s and the 1960s were the most intense period of literary production for Rodari. *Le avventure di Cipollino* (The Adventures of Little Onion, 1957) features fruit and vegetable protagonists engaged in a bitter class conflict with a tyrannical Prince Lemon. *Favole al telefono* (*Telephone Tales*, 1962) is framed by the story of a traveling salesman who calls home every night when he is on the road and tells his daughter a story short enough to keep his telephone bills manageable; the result is eighty narratives of one to two pages. Other works from this period include *Filastrocche in cielo e in terra* (Nursery Rhymes in the Sky and on the Ground, 1960) and *Il libro degli errori* (The Book of Errors, 1964). In the 1960s Rodari was active in educational reform movements and cooperatives; in particular, the child-centered, experiential "Reggio Emilia" approach to preschool and primary education is based on many of the same concepts that fuel Rodari's work. In 1970 Rodari was the first Italian recipient of the prestigious Hans Christian Andersen Award.

In 1973 Rodari published *Grammatica della fantasia* (*The Grammar of Fantasy*), a manual of active, creative pedagogical techniques that was the end product of a seminar held in Reggio Emilia in 1972 on the valorization of creativity in preschool and K–8 schools. Its forty-four short chapters describe activities designed to cultivate children's curiosity, imagination, and sense of play. Rodari's larger objective is, once again, to encourage children to have an active role in the construction of their own lives from the earliest age so that they can become, later in life, not only consumers but also active producers of culture. In the substantial section on fairy tales (chapters 15–24 and 38), Rodari underlines especially how this narrative form can so easily inspire a wide range of liberating play. Other notable works of the last years of Rodari's life include *Venti storie più una* (Twenty Stories Plus One, 1969), *Novelle fatte a macchina* (*Tales Told by a Machine*, 1970), *Tante storie per giocare* (Lots of Stories for Play, 1971), and *C'era due volte il barone Lamberto* (*Lamberto, Lamberto, Lamberto*, 1978).

Further Reading

Primary

Rodari, Gianni. *Grammatica della fantasia. Introduzione all'arte di inventare storie.* Turin: Einaudi, 1973. 54–58, 71–80. [source text]

Rodari, Gianni. *Tante storie per giocare* (Lots of Stories for Play). Rome: Editori Riunti, 1971. 19–23 ("Clever Pinocchio"). [source text]

Rodari, Gianni. *Venti storie più una* (Twenty Stories Plus One). Rome: Editori Riuniti, 1969. 74–80 ("Nino and Nina"); 81–85 ("The House of Three Buttons"). [source text]

Rodari, Gianni. *The Grammar of Fantasy: An Introduction to the Art of Inventing Stories.* Trans. Jack Zipes. New York: Enchanted Lion Books, 2021.

Rodari, Gianni. "Pro e contro la fiaba." *Il cane di Magonza.* Ed. Carmine De Luca. Rome: Editori Riuniti, 1982. 141–55.

Secondary

Boero, Pino. *Una storia, tante storie: Guida all'opera di Gianni Rodari.* Torino: G. Einaudi, 1992.

Califano, Francesca. "Political, Social, and Cultural Divisions in the Work of Gianni Rodari." In *Divided Worlds: Studies in Children's Literature*, ed. Mary S. Thompson and Valerie Coghlan. Dublin: Four Courts Press, 2007. 149–58.

Roghi, Vanessa. *Lezioni di Fantastica: Storia di Gianni Rodari.* Bari: Laterza, 2020.

Salvadori, Maria Luisa, and Alessandra Asteriti Mathys. "Apologizing to the Ancient Fable: Gianni Rodari and His Influence on Italian Children's Literature." *The Lion and the Unicorn* 26, no. 2 (2002): 169–202.

Zipes, Jack. "Celebrating the Unknown Famous Gianni Rodari." *Marvels & Tales* 34, no. 1 (2020): 83–89.

Zipes, Jack. "Introduction." In *The Grammar of Fantasy: An Introduction to the Art of Inventing Stories*, by Gianni Rodari. New York: Teachers and Writers Collaborative, 1996.

Nino and Nina (Nino e Nina)

This is a version of ATU 327A, Hansel and Gretel, set in the bustling and impersonal "forest" of metropolitan Milan. The starting point for the tale is the same as in more traditional versions—extreme poverty—but here the context is 1960s Italy, when waves of mass migration from the rural south of Italy to Rome and the industrial cities of the north led to the creation of housing projects and shanty towns for the newly arrived members of the working and sub-proletarian classes. Here, the role of the witch (as in the Grimms' and other versions) is taken by a benevolent baker who eventually, through an act of solidarity, helps the whole family change the course of their life (Rodari's own father was a baker). Many of Rodari's tales are concerned with social justice and reach their happy endings by means of just this sort of collaborative effort.

A poor man lived with his family in a run-down hovel at the edge of the city. He was unemployed, his wife was ill, and the cupboard was often bare. One evening, he put his two children to bed very early, since he had nothing to give them for dinner, and he sat next to them, waiting for them to fall asleep. Nina, the younger of the two, dozed off almost immediately, and in her sleep she thrashed about as if she were having a bad dream. The older child, Nino, wasn't sleepy, but closed his eyes anyway, so that his father wouldn't see that he was hungry. The poor man sighed, went back to his wife, and said, "We can't go on like this. Those two little ones will get sick without anything to eat, and we won't even be able to have them treated because we have no money for a doctor. Tomorrow morning I'll bring the children to the city to see the Duomo, and I'll find a way to abandon them there. Some good soul will take care of them."

The sick woman burst into loud tears. "Don't cry," said her husband, "or they'll wake up. Believe me, there's nothing else that we can do. It'll be for their own good."

But Nino wasn't sleeping, and he had heard everything. He waited for his parents to turn off the light, he waited for everything to grow still, and then he tiptoed out of the hovel, gathered some pebbles, and filled the pockets of his little jacket with them. "I'll plant a trail of pebbles on the road," he thought, "like children in fairy tales do when they're abandoned in the woods. That way me and Nina will be able to find our way back home, and mama will be happy."

The next morning their father woke Nina and Nino up with a cheerful and festive face: "Come on, come on, hurry it up, we're going to the city to see the Duomo." The children got dressed quickly; Nino touched his pockets and felt the pebbles and wasn't afraid.

But their father had decided, as a surprise before he abandoned them, that they would take the streetcar, and he spent his last money on the three tickets. It was a miserable day; there was a gelid drizzle and people were saying, "If the wind dies down, it's going to start snowing."

The windows of the streetcar were all closed, and Nino wasn't able to leave his trail of pebbles. "Never mind," he thought, "I'll just have to make sure papa never gets out of my sight. I'll let him walk off a little way, and then I'll follow him without letting him see me."

"Look," their father was saying in the meantime, "look at all of these wonderful things: so many big buildings, so many cars. The city is beautiful!"

The city wasn't only beautiful, it was immense. It appeared to stop at the end of the street where the streetcar ran, with its cheerful rumble; but instead, at the end of that street another one began, and then another one, and wide, tree-lined avenues branched out in every direction, and in each avenue, in each street, in each square there were streetcars, automobiles, delivery trucks, and people, people, people everywhere. Was it possible that there were so many people in the world?

Nino and Nina looked out the window with their mouths open, enchanted.

Finally, their papa told them that it was time to get off, and the Duomo was right there in front of them. It was made entirely of marble, it was gray and shiny with rain, and at the top there was a forest of spires, strange spindly marble trees whose leaves were the clouds in the sky.

They went into the Duomo, holding hands, and walked in silence among the tall, mysterious columns. The columns, too, seemed to form a large forest, though it was nearly impossible for the eye to distinguish how their branches intersected, way up high, to support the ceiling.

Nino was holding his sister's hand on one side and his papa's on the other, and he felt his papa's hand squeeze his own, more and more tightly. Then his papa said, "Alright, wait here just a second for me; you can take a look at that pretty statue. Be good and don't be afraid; I'll come back right away."

"Yes, father," said Nina. Nino didn't say anything. He looked at his father, who was stroking his hair, and forced himself to smile at him. Then he saw him move off almost at a run, turn around, start walking again, and hide behind a column.

"When he comes out from behind that column," Nino thought to himself, "we'll follow him." He waited, and waited, but his papa didn't reappear. Nino ran to the column, pulling his little sister behind him. Their papa was no longer there. "Maybe I had my eye on the wrong column," thought Nino. They wandered in vain from one column to another, up and down the immense naves. "I'm tired," said Nina at a certain point. "Why isn't papa coming back?"

Nino sat her down on a pew, and after a moment the little girl put her head down on his knees and closed her eyes. "I'll let her sleep a little," thought Nino, "then we'll go out and look for the way home." Instead, he was tired and anxious, and he fell asleep, too.

They were awakened by someone shaking them rather roughly and by a voice that was saying, "What are you doing here? Do you think the Duomo is a dormitory?" They opened their eyes at the same time and saw a little old woman wrapped in a long black shawl. Her glasses sparkled frighteningly on her wrinkled face. Nina burst into tears. Nino got up, helped his sister to her feet, and then pulled her away by the arm.

"Where are you going? Come over here," the little old woman ordered, pointing a threatening finger at them. Or maybe she wasn't threatening them; maybe she was actually begging for alms. But in any case, the two children were frightened and ran away, and the old woman couldn't run fast enough to catch up to them. She shook her head, puzzled, and looked around as if she were searching for help. But all she saw was a tourist reading his book. "Little tramps," the old lady thought. And she went off on her own business.

In the meantime, Nina was asking, "Was that the witch?" as they walked hand in hand through the crowds on the sidewalk. "No," said Nino, "witches don't live in cities." "Where are we going?" asked Nina again. "Home." "But we need to take the streetcar to go home," the little girl reasoned. "Why don't we take the streetcar?" "Because we don't have any money." "Can't we ask the owner of the streetcar to do us a favor and take us for free? We're such little children, we won't take up much room." "There are so many different streetcars, I'm not sure which to take." "But the owner of the streetcar must know!"

They wandered for hours and hours in the hostile forest of houses, amid the roar of the traffic, numbed by the cold and their confusion. Every now and then Nina would start to whine, complaining that she was hungry, cold, tired. Nino would let her rest for a few minutes against a wall, in a doorway, on the running board of a parked car. But the sight of a policeman in the distance or a suspicious look on the part of a passerby was enough to drive them out of their temporary refuge.

Toward evening it began to snow. Nino and Nina looked for shelter in a covered walkway, between two alleyways. There was a pile of wooden crates in there, under a portico of damp, dark stone. "We'll make ourselves a hut," said Nino. And in fact, they did. They moved some empty crates and found two that were bigger than the rest; they put them together, covered them with another crate, and ended up with a cozy little shelter. Nina got into one of the crates, Nino in the other. But they continued to hold hands, to keep their courage up. No one passed by there, the sounds of the traffic were muffled by the snow, and it was just like being in a hut in the woods. And night was falling around them in a sweet and maternal way, in spite of everything. The two children whispered between themselves for a little while, and then slowly fell asleep.

Those crates belonged to a baker, and the door to his shop was right next to them. A few hours after midnight, the baker got up to make his first batch of bread. He was in a bad mood because his shop boy had quit and he had to do everything by himself: light the oven, mix and knead the bread, put the bread in the oven.

At a certain point he needed to go out under the portico to look for something. He thought he heard a strange noise, as if someone were snoring lightly. The noise was the sound of Nina breathing, for after roaming the streets all day, she had caught a nasty cold.

"What's this under here?" muttered the baker. In his sleep Nino must have heard the voice, because he began to toss and turn in his crate, knocking it with his shoes. "Who goes there?" said the baker, more loudly this time, picking up an iron bar.

He peered into the darkness without moving. Then he decided to look behind the crates, and he discovered the two children sleeping. He bent over them, curious. Nino was the first to wake up. In the semidarkness of the portico he saw, at a hand's length from his own eyes, the baker's dark and severe eyes, his big moustache, his white apron. He let out a cry. Nina was awoken by his cry; terrified, she burst into tears and started shouting, "Mama! Mama!"

"Come on, come on," said the baker gruffly, "come out of there, now!" Nino was the first to obey, gently urging his sister, "Let's do what he says, and maybe he won't hurt us." Nina was convinced that that big fat scary hulk of a man was the ogre in person, and she didn't even dare to whisper.

The baker took them inside, sat them down on a half-empty flour sack, and turned around to check how hot the oven was. At the sight of the flames, Nina hugged her brother as tightly as she could and whispered in his ear, "I don't want him to stuff me in the oven!"

Nino didn't know how to reply to that; he patted her on the back and kissed her hair, as he had seen his mama and papa do so many times. Every so often the baker said something to them, but they were too terrified to reply. He opened and closed the oven door many times, and each time Nina thought her final hour had arrived. But then the baker continued to work, paying no attention to them. The room was warm and quiet, and little by little an extraordinary scent began to waft through the air, a warm and mysterious smell. Nino seemed to recognize that smell, that good, familiar fragrance, but he dared not give it a name. The two children had now calmed down a little, and, with their arms still around each other, they watched the baker working.

Suddenly the big hulk of a man came toward them. He was carrying two golden, steaming forms of bread. "Are you hungry?" he asked. "Go on, take them. They're just two rolls; are you afraid they'll bite?" Nino took the two pieces of bread and gave one to his sister. They almost burned his hands, but the fragrance was so intense that it gave him a headache.

They hadn't eaten for such a long time, and never in their lives had they tasted such delicious bread. They ate the two rolls, then another two, then another two. The big baker said nothing, but when he saw that they had finished, he went and got more rolls from a basket.

"When was the last time the two of you had something to eat?" he boomed, after bringing them their sixth roll each. And then Nina started to laugh; in fact, she sprung to her feet and started jumping around the shop as if she were crazy. Nino, too, smiled at the kind man and thought to himself, "Imagine, we mistook him for an ogre!"

At around six in the morning the baker's wife came down to open up the shop. Her husband showed her the two children, and she scolded him for not having called her right away. "Can't you see that they're feverish?" "Yes," said the baker, "they have the eating fever."

But the baker's wife would have none of that; she took the two children and brought them upstairs, where she tucked them into bed. And they were still in bed when their papa arrived. After abandoning them he had returned to look for them, but he was too late, and after that he had gone from one police station to another, trying to get some word of where they were. He had finally been given the baker's address by an officer.

"Keep quiet, now," the baker's wife said to him, "don't wake them up. I called the police because it was my duty, but I didn't allow even the officers to wake them up. And now I think I have the right to hear the whole story. Out with it, then; come here and tell me what happened."

"What do you want me to tell you?" the poor man asked fearfully. "Everything," pronounced the baker's wife. The baker listened to the story, too, twisting his moustache. Then he said, "Well, I don't have an assistant at the moment, and I need someone to make deliveries to my customers. If you're happy with it, it's a job like any other."

Then the poor man started to cry, and he cried for all those days when he had had to swallow his tears so that his family wouldn't see. He accepted the position, and he always remembered that Nino and Nina had been the ones to find it for him, just like what happens in fairy tales, when abandoned children return home with a treasure.

The House of Three Buttons (La casa dei tre bottoni)

This tale features a "tiny house," before they became trendy! As in many of Rodari's original tales, the theme of social justice is again foremost; here, a king humbled by witnessing all the suffering that goes on his kingdom undergoes a radical change in lifestyle and becomes a roving benefactor.

Once upon a time there was a carpenter whose name was Three Buttons. Maybe his name was also Giacomo or Napoleon, but he had had the nickname of Three Buttons for so long that no one, not even him, remembered his real name any more.

He lived in a very poor town, where the people certainly did not have money to order new furniture. If he was lucky, in a year he would get an order for a table and four chairs, and the year after barely an order for a footstool.

"Don't you want a wardrobe?"

"Hmm, no telling how much that would cost."

"A chest of drawers?"

"Hmm, no telling how much that would come to."

"A coatrack?"

"Brilliant; what are we supposed to hang on it?"

The few clothes they had they wore on their backs.

Three Buttons thought, "I'd better move to another town. But if I go to a new town I'll have to buy a house, or at least rent one. I'd better make myself a little wooden house and put some wheels on it: that way I can take it with me everywhere, and when I've made my fortune I'll get married, and when I'm married I'll give it to my children to play in."

No sooner said than done; he set to work. He was a good carpenter, hard work didn't bother him, and he wasn't afraid to hit his fingers with the hammer.

Three Buttons was also small. And thin, too. He didn't need a house that was too big. And, in fact, the house he made was very small: he, his hammer, and his plane could fit inside it, but not the saw; he had to hang the saw on a nail outside the door. Above the door he painted his name: "Three Buttons." He put four wheels under the house, and attached a shaft to pull it.

"Look, look," the people said. "Three Buttons has made a house with a handle on it."

And they laughed. But Three Buttons pretended not to hear.

When he left, pulling his house on wheels behind him, the people would say, "Look, look. Three Buttons has made himself a trailer. Where are you going to put the gas, if there's no gas tank? Are you going to drink it?"

Three Buttons tipped his hat to say goodbye, and left. The house was light. When the road went downhill, Three Buttons got aboard, as if it were a little wagon, and off he went!

After rambling and racing along, evening fell, and Three Buttons stopped in a meadow.

"I'll sleep here. I've gone far enough for today."

A few hours later he was awakened by rain beating on the roof. A storm had broken, and lightning was flashing everywhere.

"Listen to how it's thundering," said Three Buttons to himself.

But it wasn't only thunder. Someone was knocking on the walls of the little house, knocking, knocking, and a voice was pleading:

"Open up, please. Open up, Three Buttons!"

"Who's there?"

"I'm getting all wet. Let me in."

"Let's give it a try," said Three Buttons, opening the little door. "I custom-made the house for myself, but if you can fit, all the merrier."

"Where there's room for one, there's room for two."

A little old man came in, wrung out his beard to get rid of all the water, and lay down.

"You see: I fit."

"I see, I see. But who are you?"

"I'm your uncle Caramella. I'm all alone now, there's no one left to give me a bowl of soup, and I thought of you. You can imagine how upset I was when they told me in the village that you had left. Luckily, the children saw which road you took, and pointed me in that direction. You've built yourself a new house, huh? So things are going well for you?"

"Quite well, quite well," said Three Buttons.

"Good for you; happy to hear that," said Uncle Caramella. "Now you'll have to excuse me, but I need to sleep. We'll talk tomorrow morning."

"Have a good rest," said Three Buttons. He stayed awake, though, scratching his head and thinking, "Poor old man, I bet he didn't even have dinner. Just like me."

And it kept on thundering, thundering. But it wasn't only thunder. There was someone knocking on the door, and a voice was begging:

"Open up, please. Open up!"

"Who's there?"

"A poor woman with her three children. The storm took us by surprise as we were on the road, and we have no shelter."

"Come in," said Three Buttons, opening the door, "if you can. I custom-made the house for myself, but if you can fit, all the merrier."

"Where there's room for two, there's room for three. I'll hold the children in my arms."

The woman came in, her children came in, they lay down and went to sleep, and there was room for everyone.

"Thank you so much," said the woman. "It's really nice in here."

"Pardon my asking, but where were you going in this terrible weather?"

"I was heading for a disaster, that's where I was going," said the woman, starting to cry. "I'm a recent widow, I've got these children, I could no longer pay the rent, and the landlord evicted me. There's no telling what will become of us tomorrow."

"Don't worry about that now. Try to get some sleep."

Three Buttons couldn't sleep, though, because he was thinking, "Poor woman and poor little children. I bet they didn't even have dinner. Just like me and Uncle Caramella."

The storm kept up. The rain poured down without reprieve. The thunder boomed from one end of the earth to the other. And every now and then someone would knock on the little door looking for shelter, and Three Buttons would let them in, saying:

"Where there's room for five, there's room for six . . . Where there's room for six, there's room for seven . . . Where there's room for eleven, there's room for twelve . . ."

Once it was a woodsman whose shack had been swept away by the flooding stream. Another time it was two young men who were on their way abroad to look for work. Then, an old man who had been kicked out of his house because he was no longer able to work. Then, one of the king's servants who had been kicked out of the royal palace because he had gotten sick and the head butler had refused to take care of him.

Before dawn, when the sky was darkest and the thunder the most violent, an imperious fist knocked on the door so hard that the little house shook.

"Open up!"

"You might add 'please,'" thought Three Buttons, surprised. But he opened anyway and there in front of him was . . .

"Let me in!"

But could it really be . . .

"Let my horse in, too!"

There was no doubt about it: his cloak was soaking wet, but his crown was shining, as if the storm had polished it. It was the king!

"Where there's room for twelve, there's room for thirteen," murmured Three Buttons, bowing. And he added, to himself, "And where there's room for a king, there's room for his horse, too."

"From the outside," the king said, "your house looked much smaller."

The king went in and looked around, during the flashes of lightning.

"Actually," explained Three Buttons, "I custom-made it for myself."

"What kind of wood did you use?"

"Chestnut, Your Majesty."

"Chestnut isn't flexible like rubber. There's something I don't understand."

"And thank goodness for that," said Three Buttons. "Otherwise how could all these people fit in here?"

His Majesty King Bernardino IV reflected on that for a long time.

"Maybe it's not a question of wood, but of heart," he said.

"What do you mean?"

"A heart is as small as a fist, but if you want to you can put all the people in the world inside of it and there's still room to spare. It's clear that you built this house with your heart."

Three Buttons was silent.

"Who are these people?" asked the king, pointing to the small crowd that was sleeping.

"Well, that's Uncle Caramella, that's a widow with her children, that's . . ."

Three Buttons explained it all to King Bernardino, and as he listened the king became sadder and sadder.

When he noticed his sick servant, who was groaning in his sleep, he took off his crown as if all of a sudden it had become too heavy to wear.

"I thought I was a good king," he said, "and look at all these miserable people. What have I done for these people? Much less than you have; at least you offered them a roof over their heads for a night. It's time for me to go."

"Out into this storm, Your Majesty?"

"No, that's not what I meant. It's time for me to retire. If you don't know how to rule so that everyone is happy, it's better to take the crown off your head."

He thought a little more, and then said, "But there is still something I can do. As soon as the storm is over, come with me, all of you. From what I see, you're a fine carpenter, and there will be no lack of work for you at the royal palace. We'll see to the others, too. Those who need to be taken care of will be; those who need to find a job will find one. In exchange, you'll give me your house on wheels, and I'll use it to travel around my kingdom in search of people who need my help. Agreed?"

No one knows what Three Buttons answered, because at that very moment there was an urgent honk of a horn.

During the night the wind had pushed the little house right into the road, and a bus couldn't get by.

"Hey, you," the driver shouted, "hey, you gypsies, wake up! Pull over to the side a little."

The people looked out the windows and laughed. "That's Three Buttons's house . . ."

"House? You mean trailer!"

"Wake up, Three Buttons!"

Three Buttons came out of the little house, and the first thing he noticed, with relief, was that it was no longer raining. After him Uncle Caramella came out, combing his beard. After Uncle Caramella, the widow came out, then her three children, the youngest crawling on all fours.

"That's not a house," the people laughed, "it's a magician's hat! No doubt a white rabbit will pop out at the end!"

Out came more people, and then some more.

"But how did you all manage to fit in there without getting squashed like sardines?"

"Look! There's a horse, too! A white horse! Forget the rabbits . . ."

But after the horse, the king in person came out. At that point everyone became silent. The bus driver bowed down so low that he was close to breaking his back in two.

"Come on, now, none of this fuss," said the king. "Let these good people get on the bus. I'll pay for their tickets. You can attach Three Buttons's little house to the back of the bus, using the tow line. I'll follow behind on my horse, and I'll tell you where you need to stop."

If history books tell the truth, that was the first time the bus arrived in the capital city escorted by the king on his horse. And it was also the last.

Three Buttons married the widow, and made another little wooden house on wheels, exactly the same as the first, for his children to play in. It was very small, but all the children of the city could fit into it, and if a cat showed up at the last minute, there was room for him, too.

Clever Pinocchio (Pinocchio il furbo)

Tante storie per giocare *is a collection of 1960s "hypertexts" that are all structured like this one. The reader is asked to choose the ending he or she likes best and, implicitly, to consider how the overall message of the story changes depending on the ending. At the end of the volume, in an author's note, Rodari expresses his own preference.*

Once upon a time there was Pinocchio. But not the one from the book about Pinocchio; a different one. He was made of wood, too, but he wasn't the same. Geppetto hadn't made him; he had made himself.

He told lies, too, like the famous puppet, and every time he told them his nose grew longer, right before your eyes. But he was a completely different Pinocchio, which is the reason why, in fact, when his nose grew longer, instead of being scared, crying, asking his little fairy for help, etc., he took a knife or a saw and cut off a good piece of nose. It was made of wood, right? So he didn't feel any pain.

And since he told a lot of lies, a whole lot of them, in a very short time he found his house full of pieces of wood.

"Fantastic!" he said. "With all this nice seasoned wood I'll make myself some furniture and save myself the expense of a carpenter. Yes, I will!"

He was good at it, there's no doubt about that. He set to work and made himself a bed, a wardrobe, chairs, bookshelves, a bench. Finally, he was making a stand to put his television on when he ran out of wood.

"I see," he said, "we need another lie."

He ran outside to find the right sort of guy. A little country fellow was trotting along on the sidewalk—the type who's always late for the bus.

"Good morning. Do you have any idea how lucky you are?"

"Me? How come?"

"You don't know yet?! You've just won a hundred million in the lottery; the radio announced it five minutes ago."

"That's not possible!"

"What do you mean, it's not possible? Excuse me, but what's your name?"

"Roberto Bislunghi."

"You see? They said your exact name on the radio: Roberto Bislunghi. And what do you do for work?"

"I sell salami, notebooks, and lightbulbs at San Giorgio di Sopra."

"Well, then, there's no doubt about it; the winner is none other than you. A hundred million. My most heartfelt congratulations!"

"Thank you, thank you . . ."

Mr. Bislunghi believed it, but couldn't believe it; in any case, he was quite excited and had to go into a café to drink a glass of water. Only after he was done drinking did it occur to him that he had never bought lottery tickets and that there had to be a mistake. But by then Pinocchio had returned home, satisfied. The lie had made his nose grow enough to make the last leg of the TV stand. He sawed, he nailed, he planed: there, it was done. A stand like that? It would take a good twenty thousand lire to buy it and pay for it. A nice savings.

When he had finished furnishing the house, he decided to go into business. "I'll sell wood and become rich."

And, indeed, he was so quick to tell lies that in no time at all he became the owner of a big factory that employed a hundred workers and twelve accountants who kept the books. He bought himself four automobiles and two cargo trucks. The trucks weren't for driving around and having fun, but for transporting the wood. He sent wood abroad, too, to France and to Prankland.

And out came lies and more lies, and his nose never tired of growing back. Pinocchio became richer and richer. Now there were 3,500 workers and 420 accountants who kept the books.

Unfortunately, with all those lies his imagination was getting depleted. For new inspiration he had to go around listening to the lies of others and then copy them down: lies told by adults, lies told by children . . . But they were minor lies, and they made his nose grow only a few centimeters at a time.

So Pinocchio decided to hire a prompter, for a certain amount per month. The prompter spent eight hours a day in his office thinking of lies and writing them down on countless little slips of paper, which he then passed on to his boss.

"Say that the cupola of Saint Peter's was built by you."

"Say that the city of Forlimpopoli has wheels and can roll around the countryside."

"Say that you went to the North Pole, you made a hole, and you came out at the South Pole."

The prompter earned a fairly good salary, but on account of inventing lies, by the evening he would have a headache.

"Say that Mount Blanc is your uncle."

"That elephants neither lie down nor stand up when they sleep, but sleep balanced on their proboscis."

"That the Po River is tired of flowing into the Adriatic, and wants to flow into the Indian Ocean."

Now that he was rich and super-rich, Pinocchio no longer sawed his nose himself: two specialized workmen with white gloves served him, with a golden saw. These workmen were paid twice by their boss: once for the work they did, and another time to remain silent. Every now and then, when the day had been particularly fruitful, he also paid for a glass of mineral water for them.

First Ending

Pinocchio grew richer by the day. But you mustn't think he was stingy. Sometimes, for example, he would give the prompter a small gift: a mint, a little licorice stick, a stamp from Senegal . . .

The town was very proud of him. They wanted very badly for him to become mayor, but Pinocchio didn't accept because he didn't feel like taking on that serious responsibility.

"But you can do a lot for the town," they said to him.

"I will, I will anyway. I'll donate a preschool, providing that it's named for me. I'll donate a bench for the public gardens, so that the old workmen can sit somewhere when they're tired."

"Hurray for Pinocchio! Hurray for Pinocchio!"

They were so happy that they decided to dedicate a monument to him. And they built it out of marble, in the main square. It represented a three-meter-tall Pinocchio who was giving a coin to a little orphan who was ninety-five centimeters tall. The band played nearby. There were fireworks. It was a memorable celebration.

Second Ending

Pinocchio grew richer by the day, and the richer he grew, the stingier he became. The prompter, who struggled to invent new lies, had been asking him for a raise for a while. But Pinocchio always found an excuse to refuse.

"Huh, it's easy for you to talk about raises. Yesterday, though, you slipped me a two-bit lie: my nose grew twelve millimeters in all. Twelve millimeters of wood isn't even enough to make a toothpick."

"I have family," said the prompter. "The price of potatoes has increased."

"But the price of *panettone* has decreased: why don't you buy *panettone* instead of potatoes?"

The prompter started to hate his boss. And along with the hate was born a desire for revenge.

"I'll show him," he grumbled to himself, while he scribbled his daily slips of paper without the least enthusiasm.

And so it happened that on one of those slips of paper he wrote, almost without realizing it, "The author of *The Adventures of Pinocchio* is Carlo Collodi."

That slip of paper ended up with all the other ones that were covered with lies. Pinocchio, who had never read a book in his life, thought it was a lie like all the others, and he made a point of remembering it so that he could rattle it off to the first person who came along.

That was how, for the first time in his life and out of pure ignorance, he told the truth. And as soon as he told it, all of the wood produced by his lies became sawdust and shavings, and all of his riches vanished, as if the wind had blown them away. And Pinocchio found himself poor, in his old house with no furniture, and without even a handkerchief to dry his tears.

Third Ending

Pinocchio grew richer by the day, and he would have definitely become the richest man in the world if one day a little man who knew his business hadn't shown up in those parts. Actually, he knew everything, and he also knew that Pinocchio's riches would go up in smoke the day he was forced to tell the truth.

"Mister Pinocchio, this and that: be very careful never to tell even the smallest truth, not even by mistake, or the party will be over. Got it? Good, good. By the way: is that villa yours?"

"N-no," said Pinocchio.

"Then I think I'll take it: it looks like it was custom-made for me. Are those factories yours?"

"N-no," Pinocchio said reluctantly, to avoid telling the truth.

"Wonderful; then I'll take them . . ."

With that system, the little man took the automobiles, the cargo trucks, the television, the golden saw. Pinocchio's mood grew darker and darker, but he would have cut his tongue off before he told the truth.

"By the way," the little man finally said, "is that your nose?"

Pinocchio snapped back, "Of course it is! And you'll never be able to take it away from me! This nose is mine, and anyone who touches it is in big trouble!"

"That's the exact truth," the man smiled.

And at that moment all of Pinocchio's wood turned to sawdust, all of his riches were reduced to dust, and a great wind arrived and carried every last thing away, even the mysterious little man, and Pinocchio ended up alone and poor, without even a cough drop to put in his mouth.

Author's note on the endings: *The first ending is wrong, because it's not right that clever Pinocchio, after all those scams, is celebrated as a benefactor. I'm undecided between the second and the third. The second is wittier, the third meaner.*

From *The Grammar of Fantasy: An Introduction to the Art of Inventing Stories* (*Grammatica della fantasia. Introduzione all'arte di inventare storie*)

These are the only selections in this volume that are not fairy tales. I include them not only because they provide insight into Rodari's unique take on fairy tales but also because the pedagogical techniques described here are wonderfully effective in the classroom, even today and even with young adults.

At the heart of Rodari's creative storytelling techniques is the "fantastic binomial," a concept and practice inspired by the surrealist technique of "systematic disorientation," in which, by juxtaposing two words between which there is generally not an association, "words are not taken in their daily meaning, but freed from the verbal chains in which they usually live . . . finding themselves in conditions better adapted to generate a story." Rodari gives the example of the binomial "dog" and "armoire" and outlines stories that can emerge from situations involving "a dog with an armoire," "a dog's armoire," "a dog on the armoire," "a dog in an armoire," and so forth (19–20). Besides the chapters translated here, other chapters that focus on a similarly disruptive use of fairy tales include "Popular Fairy Tales as Raw Material," "Fairy Tales Upside Down" (in which introducing an "error" in the story leads to it developing in unforeseen directions, such as "Cinderella is a good-for-nothing who makes her patient stepmother despair and steals her virtuous stepsisters' boyfriends"), "What Happened After" (in which an invented epilogue may undermine the basic premise and/or "message" of the better-known classic version of a tale), "Fairy-Tale Salad" (in which characters and elements from different fairy tales mix and mingle, such as "Pinocchio ends up in the seven dwarfs' cottage, becoming the eighth of Snow White's companions and injecting his own vital energy into the old story"), "Fairy Tales Revisited" (in which new people and places are grafted onto the same formula or "functions" of a classic tale, as in Rodari's own version of Hansel and Gretel in this section), "Franco Passatore Puts Cards on the Fable" (in which participants create and use storytelling cards similar to the "Propp's cards" in the chapter included here), and "Fairy Tales in an Obligatory Key" (in which an entire fairytale is transposed to a different time and/or space, such as "Tell the story of the Pied Piper of Hamelin setting it in Rome, 1973"). Many of these playful creative techniques are familiar to us today, as they are frequently implemented in the creation of "fractured fairy tales," though they weren't nearly as common in the 1960s, when Rodari had the classroom experiences he mentions.

I have cut small portions of the text, mostly parenthetical references that are not pertinent to the main themes.

Getting Stories Wrong

"Once upon a time there was a girl named Yellow Hood."

"No, Red!"

"Oh, that's right; Red. So, her father calls her over and . . ."

"No, not her father, it was her mother."

"Right. She calls her over and says, 'Go to your aunt Rosina's, and bring her . . .'"

"Go to your grandmother's, she told her, not to your aunt's!"

This is the framework of the old game of "getting stories wrong" that can take place in anyone's house, at any time. I used it myself, many years ago, in my *Telephone Tales.*

It's a more serious game than it might seem at first glance. But it has to be played at the right time. As far as stories go, children remain conservative for a fairly long time. They want to listen to stories with the same words they heard the first time, so that they can have the pleasure of recognizing them, learning them from top to bottom in the right sequence, reliving the emotions they felt at the first meeting, in the same order: surprise, fear, gratification. They need order and reassurance: the world mustn't get too far away, and too abruptly so, from the tracks on which, with so much effort, they are setting it in motion.

And so it might be that at first the game of getting the stories wrong irritates them, because it makes them feel like they're in danger. They're prepared for the appearance of a wolf, but the appearance of something new makes them anxious, because they don't know if it will be friendly or not.

At a certain point—maybe when Little Red Riding Hood doesn't have much left to say to them, when they're ready to leave her behind just as they would an old, worn-out toy—they will accept the fact that the old story can give birth to parody. In part, this sanctions the separation, but the new point of view also renews interest in the original story itself; it brings it back to life, though on another track. The children are longer playing as much with Little Red Riding Hood as with themselves: they dare themselves to confront freedom, without fear; to assume risky responsibilities. Therefore, it's necessary to be prepared for a healthy excess of aggressiveness, and for unbounded leaps into the absurd.

In some cases the game will be of therapeutic efficacy, helping children to release themselves from certain fixations. The game downplays the wolf, makes fun of the ogre, ridicules the witch, establishes a more clear-cut boundary between the world of real things—where certain liberties are not possible—and the world of imaginary things. This has to occur sooner or later, in any case: definitely not before the wolf, the ogre, and the witch have fulfilled their deep functions, but not too late, either.

Another serious aspect of the game consists in the fact that those who participate are forced to carry out, at an intuitive level, a full-fledged analysis of the fairy tale. Alternative elements or parody can find their place only at certain points of the tale and not others: at those precise points that characterize or structure the fairy tale, but not during its more uneventful verbal transitions from one significant node to another. The operations of deconstruction and reconstruction are, in this game, simultaneous. And they are, to be exact, operative interventions, not abstractly logical ones.

The end result is a "pointillist" invention, one that rarely leads to a new synthesis with its own new logic but instead favors wandering among fairy-tale themes without a precise destination. It's more doodling than drawing. But we all know how very useful doodling can be.

Little Red Riding Hood in a Helicopter

I've seen this game played in a number of schools. The children are given a few words on the basis of which they have to invent a story. A series of five words, for example, that suggest the story of Little Red Riding Hood: "little girl," "woods," "flowers," "wolf," "grandmother." The sixth word breaks the sequence: for example, "helicopter."

With this game, or exercise, teachers, or other authors of this experiment, can measure the children's ability to react to an element that is new and, with respect to a certain series of events, unexpected; to absorb the new word into a well-known story; and to get familiar words to react to the new context in which they find themselves.

If we take a closer look at this game, it takes the form of a "fantastic binomial": on the one hand there's Little Red Riding Hood, and on the other the helicopter. The second term of the pair is a single word. The first is a series of words that, however, with respect to "helicopter," functions as a whole. Everything is clear, then, from the point of view of fantastic logic.

For a psychologist, the most interesting results are obtained, I think, when this fantastic "assignment" is given cold, without preparation, though not without a minimum of explanation.

Personally, having learned of this experiment from a schoolteacher in Viterbo whose name and address I have, unfortunately, lost, I tried to make use of it during an encounter with some second-grade children who were somewhat "blocked" in a pedagogical routine of the worst sort (copying, dictations, and the like). In other words, the worst conditions possible. I had tried in vain to get the children to create a story: a difficult enterprise when you show up suddenly, as a stranger, since it's hard for them to understand what you want. On top of that, I only had a few minutes at my disposal, since they were waiting for me in other classes. But I felt bad about leaving those children without giving them something besides the mere memory of a strange guy who tried to clown around by sitting on the floor, standing on a chair (actions necessary, in that context, to break though the bureaucratic atmosphere created by the presence of the teacher and the school inspector). If I had only brought along a harmonica, a fife, a drum . . .

I finally get the idea of asking if anyone feels like telling the story of Little Red Riding Hood. The little girls point to a little boy; the little boys point to a little girl.

"And now," I ask, after the little boy has finished rattling off the story of Little Red Riding Hood, not even the version that his grandmother must have told him at some point, but some bland nursery rhyme (no doubt a memory of a school play, poor thing), "now give me a word, any word at all."

They don't understand what "any word at all" means, naturally. We have to clarify. Finally they say, "horse." I can tell the story of Little Red Riding Hood who finds a horse in the woods, jumps onto its back, and gets to her grandmother's house before the wolf . . .

Then I go to the blackboard and I write, in a nice silence that—finally!—is full of expectation and warm as a little fire: "little girl," "woods," "flowers," "wolf," "grandmother," "helicopter." . . . I turn around. I don't even need to explain the new game. The more quick-witted children have already added two and two, and raise their hands. A wonderful story emerges, created by many voices, in which while the wolf is knocking at grandmother's door, he is discovered from the air by the highway patrol helicopter. "What's he doing? What does he want?" the agents ask themselves. And they swoop down, just in time to scare him off, right into the hands of the hunter . . .

We could discuss the ideological content of the new creation, but it's not necessary to right then. What has been put in motion is more precious. I'm sure that from time to time those children will ask if they can play the Little Red Riding Hood game again, with a new word: they've gotten to know the pleasure of invention.

An experiment in invention is valuable when children have fun, even if to reach this goal (the child as goal) the rules of the experiment itself have to be broken.

Propp's Cards

One characteristic aspect of Leonardo da Vinci's genius . . . consisted in his ability to consider, for the first time in history, a machine of any type not as a unique organism, an unrepeatable prototype, but as a combination of more simple machines.

Leonardo "deconstructed" machines, breaking them down into their elements. Into their "functions." And in this way he got to the point where he could study in isolation, for example, the "function" of friction, and this study led him to design spherical and conical bearings, and even blunted conical rollers for the operation of the gyroscopes that are indispensable for aviation, which have actually been manufactured only in very recent times.

In these studies, Leonardo was able to have fun, too. Recently a sketch of his for a pretend invention was discovered: "a shock absorber to control the fall of a man from a high place." You can see the man falling, where from it's not clear, and being braked by a system of interconnected wedges and, at the end of the fall, by a bale of wool, whose resistance to the impact is controlled and measured by another wedge. So it's probable that we should attribute to Leonardo the invention of "useless machines" as well, those constructed for fun, to follow a whim, those drawn with a smile, momentarily in opposition to and in rebellion against the utilitarian norms of technical and scientific progress.

Something like Leonard's deconstruction of machines into their "functions" has, in the realm of folktales, been performed on folktales by the Soviet ethnologist Vladimir Propp, in his work *Morphology of the Folktale*, as well as in his study "Fairy-Tale Transformations."

Propp is rightly famous for his book *The Historical Roots of the Wonder Tale*, in which he compellingly and, at least from a poetic point of view, convincingly puts forward the theory according to which the most archaic nucleus of tales of magic derives from initiation rituals in use in tribal societies.

What fairy tales narrate—or what, at the tail end of their metamorphosis, they hide—once occurred. When they reached a certain age, children were separated from their families and taken to the woods (like Little Thumbling, like Snow White), where the tribal shamans, dressed in frightening costumes with their faces covered by horrible masks (which for us immediately bring to mind sorcerers and witches), subjected them to difficult and often fatal tests (all fairy-tale heroes encounter these on their journeys). Where the children listened to tales of their tribal myths and were entrusted with weapons (the magic gifts that in fairy tales supernatural donors distribute to heroes in danger) and then finally returned home, often with another name (the hero of the fairy tale also sometimes returns incognito) and now mature enough to marry (as in fairy tales, which nine times out of ten end with a wedding).

The structure of the fairy tale repeats the structure of ritual. And it is precisely from this theory that Vladimir Propp (but not only he) derives the theory according to which the fairy tale began to live as such when ancient rituals disappeared, leaving only their narratives behind. In the course of millennia, narrators have been less and less faithful to the memory of ritual and more and more at the service of the autonomous needs of the fairy tale, which, as it passed from mouth to mouth transformed, accumulated variants, followed populations (Indo-European) in their migrations, absorbed the effects of historical and social mutations. In the same way, in the course of a few centuries speakers of a language transform that language until they give life to a new one: how many times has this occurred from the Latin of the late Roman Empire to the Romance languages?

In other words, fairy tales may have been born as they *fell* from the world of the sacred to the world of the profane, in the same way that what were in previous eras ritual and cultural artifacts *fell* and then landed in the world of children, where they were reduced to playthings. For example: dolls, tops. And isn't the same procession from the sacred to the profane at the origins of theater?

At their primitive, magical heart, fairy tales compile other secularized myths, adventure tales, legends, and anecdotes; they align magic characters with characters from the peasant world, such as the trickster and the fool. And thus a dense and complex magma was created, a tangled ball of a hundred colors of which, however—says Propp—the main thread is the one described above.

One theory is as good as another, and perhaps no theory is able to give a complete explanation of fairy tales. Propp's theory has a special allure because it establishes a deep link—there are those who would say at the level of the "collective unconscious"—between the prehistoric child who experienced initiation rites and the historical child who through the fairy tales experiences his or her first initiation into the human world. In the light of this theory, the identification between the young listener and the character of Little Thumbling in the fairy tale that his or her mother is telling has not only a psychological justification but a much deeper one, rooted in the dark depths of blood.

By analyzing the structure of the folktale—with particular attention to the Russian folktale (which in any case belongs largely to the same Indo-European heritage to which German and Italian folktales also belong)—Propp was able to formulate three principles: (1) "functions of characters serve as stable, constant elements in a tale, independent of how and by whom they are fulfilled"; (2) "the number of functions known to the fairy tale is limited"; and (3) "the sequence of functions is always identical."[1]

In Propp's system there are thirty-one functions; they, together with their variants and internal articulations, are sufficient to describe fairy-tale forms:

(1) Absentation ("one of the members of a family absents himself from home")[2]
(2) Interdiction ("an interdiction is addressed to the hero")
(3) Violation ("the interdiction is violated")
(4) Reconnaissance ("the villain makes an attempt at reconnaissance")
(5) Delivery ("the villain receives information about his victim")
(6) Trickery ("the villain attempts to deceive his victim in order to take possession of him or of his belongings")
(7) Complicity ("the victim submits to deception and thereby unwittingly helps his enemy")
(8) Villainy ("the villain causes harm or injury to a member of a family"); or Lack ("one member of a family either lacks something or desires to have something")
(9) Mediation ("misfortune or lack is made known; the hero is approached with a request or command; he is allowed to go or he is dispatched")
(10) Beginning counteraction ("the seeker agrees to or decided upon counteraction")
(11) Departure ("the hero leaves home")
(12) The first function of the donor ("the hero is tested, interrogated, attacked, etc., which prepares the way for his receiving either a magical agent or helper")
(13) The hero's reaction ("the hero reacts to the actions of the future donor")
(14) Provision or receipt of a magical agent ("the hero acquires the use of a magical agent")

1. Rodari quotes from Propp; I have used the English translation: *Morphology of the Folktale*, 21–22.
2. Here I have added to the short description provided by Rodari—"absentation," "interdiction," and so forth—the more descriptive designation from Propp's text (26–63).

(15) Spatial transference between two kingdoms, guidance ("the hero is transferred, delivered, or led to the whereabouts of an object of search")
(16) Struggle ("the hero and the villain join in direct combat")
(17) Branding ("the hero is branded")
(18) Victory ("the villain is defeated")
(19) Liquidation ("the initial misfortune or lack is liquidated")
(20) Return ("the hero returns")
(21) Pursuit ("the hero is pursued")
(22) Rescue ("rescue of the hero from pursuit")
(23) Unrecognized arrival ("the hero, unrecognized, arrives home or in another country")
(24) Unfounded claims ("a false hero presents unfounded claims")
(25) Difficult task ("a difficult task is proposed to the hero")
(26) Solution ("the task is resolved")
(27) Recognition ("the hero is recognized")
(28) Exposure ("the false hero or villain is exposed")
(29) Transfiguration ("the hero is given a new appearance")
(30) Punishment ("the villain is punished")
(31) Wedding ("the hero is married and ascends the throne")

Of course, not *all* of the functions are present in *all* fairy tales: in the course of the obligatory succession there are omissions, combinations, and syntheses, which do not, however, contradict the general sequence. A tale can begin from the first function, from the seventh or from the twelfth, but—if it is sufficiently ancient—it most likely will not then jump backward to retrieve the forgotten passages.

The function of "absentation," which Propp puts in the first position, can be carried out by a character who absents him- or herself from home for whatever reason: a prince who leaves for war, a father who dies, a parent who goes off to work (warning his or her children—and here we have the "interdiction"—not to open the door to anyone or not to touch something), a merchant who sets off on a business trip, etc. Each "function" can include its opposite: "interdiction" can be represented by a positive "order."

But we will elaborate our observations on Propp's "functions" no further except to suggest, for those who feel like it, an exercise: compare his sequence with the plot of any movie about the adventures of James Bond. It may amaze you to find a large number of them, in pretty close to the right order, a testimony to how alive and pervasively present the fairy-tale structure is in our culture. Much adventure fiction follows a similar pattern.

We are interested in the "functions" because we can use them to construct infinite stories, just as with twelve notes (disregarding the quarter tones and staying within the limited sound system of the West before the advent of electronic music) you can compose infinite melodies.

To test the productivity of the "functions," in Reggio Emilia[3] we reduced them to twenty, skipping some of them and substituting others with similar fairy-tale themes. Two artist friends designed twenty "playing cards," each tagged with a word (the generic title of the function) and an illustration that was either symbolic or a caricature, but in any case pertinent: "interdiction," "violation," "villainy or lack," "departure," "mission," "encounter with the donor," "magical gifts," "the villain appears," "diabolical powers of the villain," "duel," "victory," "return," "arrival home," "false hero," "difficult tests," "harm repaired," "recognition of the hero," "the false hero revealed," "punishment of the villain," "wedding."

Then, one group worked on producing a story structured on the twenty "Propp cards." I should add that they had a lot of fun, and that the end product had remarkable notes of parody.

I also noticed that for children it is easy to produce a fairy tale following the outline of the "cards," because every word of the series ("function" or "fairy-tale theme") is full of fairy-tale meaning and lends itself to an endless play of variations. I remember one original interpretation of the "interdiction": a father absents himself from home, warning his children not to throw flowerpots from the balcony onto the heads of passersby. And among the various "difficult tests," the obligation to go to a cemetery at midnight was not missing: the greatest example of terror and of courage, up to a certain age.

But children like to shuffle the cards and improvise rules: extracting three at random and building a complete story from them; starting from the last card of the series; dividing the deck between two groups and competing to compose two stories. Often a single card is enough to suggest a fairy tale. The "magic gifts" card was enough for a fourth grader to invent the story of a pen that did homework by itself.

3. Reggio Emilia is a small city in central Italy, north of Bologna, that became renowned from the 1970s on for its student-centered, experiential approach to preschool and primary education.

Anyone can make themselves a deck of "Propp's cards," twenty or thirty of them, or even fifty, if you choose: all you have to do is write the name of the "function" or "theme" on every card. Illustrations are not indispensable.

The game may recall, but erroneously so, the structure of a puzzle, where you receive twenty, or a thousand, out-of-order fragments of a single picture, with the task of reconstructing the entire picture, piece by piece. "Propp's cards," on the other hand and as has been mentioned, allow for the construction of an infinite number of pictures, since each piece does not have a single meaning, but is open to many meanings.

Why use "Propp's cards" and not cards that stimulate the imagination, or a group of images chosen at random, or a series of words taken from the dictionary? It seems clear to me: each "Propp's card" does not represent only itself, but an entire cross section of the fairy-tale world, a multitude of fantastic echoes for those children who have some familiarity with fairy tales, with their language and themes.

Each "function" is, moreover, rich in evocations of the personal world of the child. Children read "interdiction," or "prohibition," and the word immediately enters into contact with the experience they have of familiar "interdictions" ("don't touch," "don't play with water," "leave that hammer alone"). They dimly relive the first moments of their relationships with objects, when the only thing that helped them to distinguish between what was right and what was wrong was the maternal "yes" or "no." "Interdiction" is, for them, the clash with the authority, or authoritarianism, of school. But in a more positive sense ("interdiction" and "order" can be functionally equivalent), it is also the discovery of the rules of the game—"you do it this way, not that way," the encounter with the limits that reality and society impose upon their freedom, and one instrument of socialization.

The structure of the fairy tale not only follows—if we obey Propp—that of initiation rituals but is also repeated in some way in the structure of childhood experience, which is a string of missions and duels, or of difficult tests and disappointments, which follow certain inevitable itineraries. Nor is the experience of "magical gifts" missing from children's experience: they receive those of the Befana and Baby Jesus.[4] And their own parents have acted as "magic

4. The visit of the Befana is a popular version of Epiphany (January 6), in which an old woman—a sort of good witch—comes at night bearing gifts for children, just as the Re Magi did for the Christ child.

donors" for a long time, since they are capable of anything. . . . Children have long populated their universe with powerful allies and diabolical enemies.

And so it seems to me that fairy-tale "functions" help children, in some way, to shed light on themselves. And the functions are right there, tried and true and easy to use: to throw them away would seem like a needless waste.

I would like to add one last note to this chapter that is already too long.[5] It has to do with an observation that Vladimir Propp made when he studied the transformation of a particular theme in Russian folktales. He takes the theme of the "hut in the woods that stands on chicken feet," and he traces it as it concretely develops through its variants: by reduction (the hut supported by chicken legs, the hut in the woods, the hut, the woods); amplification (the hut in the woods supported by chicken feet, with walls of marzipan and a ceiling of cookies); substitution (instead of the hut a grotto, or a castle); intensification (an entire magical village). And we might also note how, in the way he lists typical variants, Propp ends up using almost the same terms with which Saint Augustine describes the work of the imagination, which consists, according to him, in the "disposition, multiplication, reduction, extension, ordering, and decomposition of images."

5. Rodari includes two notes, the second of which I have not included (a comment on an artist who has illustrated Propp's functions).

2

Giorgio Manganelli (1922–90)

The Milanese writer, essayist, and translator Giorgio Manganelli began his prolific professional life shortly after World War II, in which he came close to being executed as a Resistance fighter. Initially, he published translations from English and contributed to many of Italy's most important daily newspapers. His affiliation with the neo-avant-garde literary association Gruppo 63 was a formative influence on his subsequent writing, which distinguishes itself for experimentalism in form and content. His first work, *Hilarotragoedia* (Hilarious Tragedy, 1964), is a "little theoretico-practical manual" on death, heavily informed by Manganelli's own experiences with psychoanalysis and infused with the baroque wordplay and grotesquely black humor that would characterize much of his production. Several years later, Manganelli published the essay collection *La letteratura come menzogna* (Literature as Lie, 1967), in which he articulates his poetics and views on literature. Manganelli's attraction to the fantastic is evident in *Pinocchio: Un libro parallelo* (Pinocchio: A Parallel Book, 1977), as well as in *Centuria: Cento piccoli romanzi fiume* (*Centuria: One Hundred Ouroboric Novels*, 1979), a collection of one hundred unrelated, miniature (one- to two-page) "novels" that together form a sort of postmodern *Decameron*: a mosaic of themes, genres, and characters, from the mundane to the lofty and from the hyperrealistic to the marvelous.

Further Reading

Primary

Manganelli, Giorgio. *Centuria: Cento piccoli romanzi fiume*. Milan: Rizzoli, 1979. [source text]

Manganelli, Giorgio. *Centuria: One Hundred Ouroboric Novels*. Trans. Henry Martin. Kingston, NY: McPherson, 2007.

Secondary

Menechella, Graziella. *Il felice vanverare: Ironia e parodia nell'opera narrative di Giorgio Manganelli*. Ravenna, Italy: Angelo Longo, 2002.

Eighty-One (Ottantuno)

Translated by Henry Martin

This little parable uses a fairy-tale atmosphere and cast of characters to interrogate the ways in which we become locked into preestablished narratives and the "terrible tasks" that they ask of us, and whether it is possible to break out of these narratives.

In the city governed by the Bloody Princess, all the men fall sooner or later in love with her and present themselves at court to ask for her hand in marriage. She never says no, but poses a question to the man who asks for her hand in marriage: at times the question is complicated; at times it is simple, precisely like the questions asked in elementary schools. But no matter what the question is, the suitor will inevitably make an error, perhaps an irrelevant error, but an error which never escapes the Princess, and the suitor will be put to death. On the following day a new pretender will present himself, and will have no different a fate. In reality, the Princess is a tender and affectionate woman who would have no greater desire than to marry a fine young man who possesses neither title nor fortune, and to abandon her terrible task, since indeed it is nothing other than a task imposed upon her. The Princess, in fact, must obey a Bloody King, who supplies her with her questions, examines their solutions, indicates the inevitable error, and then, as well, imparts the order to proceed to the execution of the audacious suitor. But the Bloody King in turn curses his evil task and would hope for nothing better than to be able to read the classics, and to voyage in search of ancient cathedrals and books which men have forgotten. He would never wish the death of anyone, and not infrequently he sheds his tears along with his much loved Princess, but he must obey the Bloody Emperor. Every week the Emperor summons the King, and inquires as to how many men have been put to death, and in what way; and when the

King describes the horrid fate of those cautionless young men, the Emperor nods in assent as he listens, as though everything were going precisely as he desired; and in closing he congratulates the King, who in his heart of hearts is tearing his hair and cursing both the Emperor and himself. In reality the Emperor is a hearty, corpulent fellow who loves the hunt, and good rich foods, wine, and bouts of after-dinner song; he plays with the dogs and cats, and makes a point of being generous to the poor; but he too must obey. Every month he leaves his castle and travels to a place in the high mountains, at the mouth of a cave which he dare not enter; but standing in place on the threshold, he recounts aloud the number of people put to death and where and how. From inside The Cave a voice responds with growls and roars, and might even be the voice of a dragon, or of a volcano, or of a ghost. Strangely, that voice subsides into a kind of murmur, which has something kind about it. The Emperor then wraps his cape around himself and sets out again toward his castle, wondering who it may be he obeys, whether a demon or a god, and if what he obeys is itself a demon who obeys a god, or a god enslaved by the devil.

3

Roberto Piumini (1947–)

Roberto Piumini, author of children's and adult fiction and poetry, was born in Brescia in the northern Italian region of Lombardy. In much of his production he has reworked well-known fairy-tale types to explore various genres (ballads, theater, music) and to address contemporary concerns. His first work was the collection *Il giovane che entrava nel palazzo* (The Young Man Who Entered the Palace, 1978), and other original tales include *Fiabe per occhi e e bocca* (Fairy Tales for the Eyes and the Mouth, 1995), *Tre fiabe d'amore* (Three Fairy Tales of Love, 2005), the series *L'albero delle fiabe* (The Tree of Fairy Tales, 2009–), and *Le fiabe infinite* (Infinite Fairy Tales, 2011). Together with Lella Gandini, from 1995 to 2005 Piumini collaborated on a series of fairy tales from various Italian regions, rewritten and illustrated for children. A former teacher, Piumini has collaborated on projects aimed at the experimental use of narrative and language in the classroom; he also wrote for RAI television's *L'Albero Azzurro* (The Blue Tree), Italy's longest-running children's program. More recent works include *Shakespeare in versi* (Shakespeare in Verse, 2017) and *Alzati, Martin: Ballata di Martin Luther King* (Get up, Martin: The Ballad of Martin Luther King, 2018).

Further Reading

Primary

Piumini, Roberto. *Il cuoco prigioniero*. Rome: Nuove Edizioni Romane, 1985. [source text]

Piumini, Roberto. *L'Autore si racconta*. Afterword by Alessandra Avanzini. Milan: Franco Angeli, 2012.

Secondary

Salvadori, Maria Luisa. "Apologizing to the Ancient Fable: Gianni Rodari and His Influence on Italian Children's Literature." Trans. Alessandra Asteriti Mathys. *The Lion and the Unicorn* 26, no. 2 (2002): 169–202.

The Prisoner Cook (Il cuoco prigioniero)

"Il cuoco prigioniero" derives from one of the stories in Piumini's first work, Il giovane che entrava nel palazzo. *Although true fairy-tale magic is missing from this tale, it is substituted by the hero's marvelous skills, which in the denouement of the tale lead him to invent a new dish that holds "the colors of earth and the colors of the sea" and is "as hot as hell and as fragrant as paradise." The author also wrote a very popular theatrical adaptation of this tale, which inspired the children's opera* Il cuoco prigioniero *by Dimitri Nicolau (1978) and the 2004 film* Totò Sapore e la magica storia della pizza *(Savory Sal and the Magical History of Pizza, dir. Maurizio Forestieri).*

At the time when the Bourbon kings ruled Naples, there was an extraordinary cook named Antonio Gimbellino, though everyone called him Totò Sapore—Savory Sal. His dishes were so delicious that he was hired by the court, and there was no one more important than him in the kitchen of the royal palace.

His pasta dishes and his cakes were renowned, but Totò Sapore surpassed the cooks of the whole of southern Italy in virtually every sort of cooked food. The Bourbon kings were continually inviting foreign princes and nobles to Naples to taste his delicacies, and thanks to those exquisite dishes they were able to sign treaties and make lucrative business deals with them.

One day, however, the duke of Burgundy, protégé of the king of France and most distinguished guest, found a hair in his venison stew, and since his plate had been prepared exclusively by Totò Sapore, the cook was imprisoned to save the dignity of the Bourbons.

They put him, however, in a very large cell equipped with an oven and a stove, pots and a cupboard, and shelves full of everything one could wish for, which he used to continue cooking for the king and the court.

His imprisonment was special, but it was still imprisonment, and after some time Totò Sapore began to yearn for his freedom. And so he cooked a cake that was so heavy and indigestible that it would put a horse to sleep, but so good that no one would be able to refuse it. In fact, the prison guards, to whom he had given a taste of that prodigious dessert, had barely had the great pleasure of swallowing a mouthful when they collapsed to the floor, and Totò was able to escape through the alleyways of the city.

He stayed hidden for a week, cooking in the houses of relatives and friends, to their great enjoyment, but one day a marquis of the court was walking along the street with his soldiers when he caught a whiff of roast meat that was so enticing it couldn't have been made by anyone but Totò Sapore. In they came, off he went; got him! Totò was captured and locked up in a tall tower kitchen, this time without guards to eat his food and digest his tricks.

The court, which in the week following Totò Sapore's escape had decided to fast and do penance, naturally went back to having its meals prepared, and the dishes were lowered from the tower twice a day by ropes and pulleys. But there were no ropes and pulleys for Totò, for whom prison was an ever heavier weight.

One night he cooked up a huge pot of spaghetti to such perfection that it was both soft and resistant, flexible and compact, exactly as gourmands like it. Then he took that nicely cooked spaghetti and braided it into a rope that extended from the top of the tower to the ground. He slipped the rope and himself out of the opening where he usually handed out the pork roasts, lowered himself down to the ground, and once again fled through the alleyways of the city.

This time he stayed hidden for two weeks, but then the aroma of stewed peppers gave him away. In they came, off he went; got him! Totò was caught again and locked in an underground kitchen that was without guards but also without windows, and ventilated only by a chimney that was too small for him to pass through and in any case guarded by a bulldog.

Escaping just wasn't possible, but Totò Sapore didn't intend to end his life down there, hanging by a thread, and he decided to ask that he be either pardoned or put to death. And so he wrote a letter to the court that said:

"I ask your lordships to grant me a test. If I am able to cook, in less time than it takes to make a plate of pasta, a dish that is neither a first nor a second course, neither meat nor fish, that contains the colors of earth and those of the sea, those of war and those of peace, that is as hot as hell and as fragrant as paradise, as round as the world and harder to forget than an insult; and if this dish proves more pleasing than any other food to a hundred of the most finicky noblemen of the court, then let my freedom be given back to me. If this does not occur, let my head be cut off, for I do not intend for it to molder away in this cellar like a piece of cheese."

The king and his court read the message, were entertained by the pledge, and accepted. The next Sunday, Totò Sapore was supplied with what he had requested, and was left to cook. After not even ten minutes the king, the queen, and the three little princes were served five steaming plates, and the sovereigns ate with such gusto that they would not even answer the persistent questions of the hundred courtiers. In less than an hour steaming plates were brought to all of them, and every last one of them ate.

Then Totò Sapore came out, cleaning his hands on a dishrag, and said, "My lords, here I am: tell me whether as of today I may walk out of here with a free head or, instead, if you intend to free me of my head and my mind with a single blow."

Everyone laughed and applauded, and the king said, "Totò Sapore, you have kept your promise. No one here has any complaints about your dish, and indeed, we will ask you, now that you're a free man, to make us some more."

Then Totò, who already had the taste of freedom in his mouth and felt as generous as Saint Gennaro, took a low bow and returned to the kitchen to prepare another hundred Neapolitan pizzas.

4

Luigi Malerba (1927–2008)

Luigi Malerba, pen name of the writer and journalist Luigi Bonardi, was born in the countryside near Parma, Italy, and throughout his career wrote fictional works for both children and adults, as well as screenplays for Italian cinema. The fantastic and surreal figure prominently in his corpus, often taking expression in transgressive modern fables that incorporate icons of our times such as highways, skyscrapers, and computers to comment on the solitude and difficulty of communication that permeate everyday reality. For example, in *Mozziconi* (Mr. Butts, 1975), the protagonist throws his house and then the window itself out of the window in a fit of anger, after which he begins a new, freer existence under the bridges of the Tiber in Rome. In the same year his first volume, *La scoperta dell'alfabeto* (The Discovery of the Alphabet, 1963), was published, Malerba joined the Gruppo 63, an influential avant-garde literary movement advocating radical poetic experimentalism as a necessary reaction and antidote to the equally radical changes in Italian society in the direction of consumerism and conformity. The subsequent novels *Il serpente* (*The Serpent*, 1966) and *Salto mortale* (*What Is This Buzzing, Do You Hear It Too?*, 1966) established Malerba's reputation as one of the major writers of his generation; later prize-winning novels included *Il pianeta azzurro* (The Blue Planet, 1986) and *Le pietre volanti* (The Flying Rocks, 1992).

Malerba is the exceptional case of an author who wrote for adult and younger audiences with equal success. The later children's works *Mozziconi* (Butts, 1975) *and Storie dell'Anno Mille* (Stories of the Year One Thousand,

1977) highlight the search for fresh ways of envisioning the past and the present; *Le galline pensieriose* (Pensive Hens, 1980) are short aphoristic fables in the Aesopian vein, whereas *Storiette tascabili* (Little Pocket Tales, 1984) are absurdist parables on the paradoxes of modern consumerist society. The work most indebted to the fairy tale, whose marvelous dimension does not, in general, lure Malerba as much as the more realistic fable, is *Pinocchio con gli stivali* (Pinocchio in Boots, 1977). All of these works dissect and disrupt the languages of literary and political orthodoxy, encouraging their young readers to develop a critical perspective on the world around them.

Further Reading

Primary

Malerba, Luigi. *Pinocchio con gli stivali.* Milan: Mondadori, 1988. [source text]

Secondary

Accardo, Giovanni. "Le avventure della fantasia: I libri per bambini e per ragazzi di Luigi Malerba." *Studi novecenteschi* 23 (1996): 403–16.

Pinocchio in Boots (Pinocchio con gli stivali)

In the pastiche Pinocchio in Boots, *Malerba imagines that Pinocchio's adventures take a detour when the puppet opts out of entering the final chapter of* The Adventures of Pinocchio, *in which he meets the questionable fate of becoming a "respectable boy." After he escapes from his own story, Pinocchio's evolving narrative is interlaced with those of other classic fairy-tale characters, such as Little Red Riding Hood and Cinderella; the tale is used by Malerba not only to poke fun at the original Pinocchio's "noble" aspiration but also to contest fixed narrative roles and functions. Although this is a move common to rewriters of Collodi's classic, the puppet's encounter with the heroes and heroines of classic fairy tales is quite unique. Malerba also includes a theatrical version of the tale, which has been a popular choice for school performances in Italy.*

Toward the end of chapter 35 Pinocchio was swimming in the middle of the sea with his father Geppetto on his back. The sea was calm, the moon was shining, the Shark was sleeping, and Pinocchio was swimming. And as he swam along he was thinking that he really had no desire to move into the next chapter—the last one, that is—since in it he would become a respectable boy, and to him, a roughneck puppet, this did not hold the slightest appeal. But could he abandon his old father who didn't know how to swim, in the middle of the waves? Even if he was a roughneck, Pinocchio didn't feel that he could do something so revolting.

And so it was that in chapter 36 he landed on the beach with Geppetto, with the help of the Dolphin, and so it was that he went to live in the Talking Cricket's pretty little hut, and so it was that he found himself working for the farmer Giangio. After having woven sixteen rush baskets one evening,

Pinocchio fell asleep, and in his sleep—that is, in a dream—he encountered the Blue-ish Fairy, who gave him a long speech aimed at convincing him to mend his ways. And at that Pinocchio ran off in a great hurry, ditching both the Fairy and the dream.

"I'm happy as a puppet, and I don't want to become a respectable boy or a disrespectable one, for that matter," said Pinocchio to himself as he walked through the countryside with his wooden legs that went *click clack*.

But now he didn't know where to go. And the very last thing on his mind was finding a job, because he had discovered that working is tiresome. He would rather have preferred to act, sing, and dance, as a puppet is wont to do, and so he decided that since he had abandoned his own fairy tale the best thing was to find himself a place in another one.

After walking some distance with his wooden legs that went *click clack*, Pinocchio reached the woods and encountered the Wolf. The Wolf was waiting for Little Red Riding Hood, who was late.

When he saw Pinocchio show up instead of Little Red Riding Hood, the Wolf looked at him goggle-eyed. "What's your business in these parts?"

"I just happened to be passing through, by pure coincidence, and I thought I'd come and say hello. We can have a little chat, if you like."

"I've got things to do," said the Wolf.

"Can I be of any help?"

"No, it's best if you leave. I have an engagement."

"With Little Red Riding Hood"?

"If you know, why are you asking?"

"Because if you want, I can wait for her."

The Wolf snickered. "What have you got to do with Little Red Riding Hood? You wouldn't know what to say to her or what to do with her."

"Now just who do you think you are? I know Little Red Riding Hood's tale by heart. I know it so well that if you want I can take your place, for today. So you can have a rest."

The Wolf gave him a dirty look. "If I understand this correctly, you want to enter my fairy tale and take my place?!"

"For one thing, the fairy tale isn't yours; it belongs to everybody," said Pinocchio.

"But I'm the Wolf!"

The Wolf gave another nasty laugh, and Pinocchio understood that he had no intention of giving up his part in Little Red Riding Hood. But you never know, so he continued to insist.

"You're the Wolf and I can't argue with that, but what I'm proposing is that you let me play the role of the Wolf, just for once. Then I won't bother you anymore."

"And you want to play the part of the Wolf with that face? With that nose?"

"Your nose is long, too, almost as long as mine."

The Wolf wrinkled his nose and showed his teeth, which were as sharp as nails.

"Alright, let's do this, then," said Pinocchio. "Let me take the part of Little Red Riding Hood, and that'll be the end of it."

"But I eat Little Red Riding Hood up!"

Pinocchio started laughing.

"What's there to laugh about?" asked the Wolf.

"I'm up for being eaten."

"And in your opinion, I'm supposed to eat a wooden puppet? If you came here with the idea of pulling my leg, you better leave right now, and in a hurry."

Pinocchio didn't move.

"If I can't eat you," said the Wolf, "I can always give you a kick and break you into a thousand pieces!"

The Wolf lifted his paw threateningly. Pinocchio jumped back, but stood his ground.

"I was wrong to come to you," said Pinocchio. "The fairy tale where you play the part of the Wolf is named after Little Red Riding Hood because she's the protagonist, she's the one in charge. I'll go talk to Little Red Riding Hood."

"Now listen," said the Wolf, "the fairy tale may be named after Little Red Riding Hood, but until someone proves otherwise, I'm the one in charge here. I'm the Wolf, if you know what I mean."

"Then I'm going to sit right here and wait for Little Red Riding Hood. I won't do anything, I'll just look at you." Pinocchio sat down on a stone, folded his arms, and crossed his legs.

The Wolf moved toward him, growling. "You're bothering me!" Pinocchio jumped back again and went to sit on a stone that was a little farther away.

The Wolf scratched his head with a paw. He couldn't figure how to get rid of that pain in the neck.

"Tell you what," he said, "would you like to play the part of Grandmother? If you walk in that direction, you'll find her cottage at the end of the woods. Grandmother is so out of it that maybe she'll let you play her role. She's always tired, and she acts her part so reluctantly that maybe she'll be happy to have a little rest."

Pinocchio spit on the ground. "Who do you take me for? You know very well that I've always been the absolute protagonist of my tale, from the first page to the last! How do you expect me to settle for a minor part, and a boring one at that, like Grandmother's? I'm certainly not going to waste my time disguising myself as her. Let me come into the tale as Pinocchio instead; I can accompany Little Red Riding Hood to Grandmother's house, or I can meet her in the woods and accompany her to you; I can help her carry the food basket, keep her company."

The Wolf cut Pinocchio off. "Now listen to me, you pain in the neck of a puppet! You came here to create confusion and nothing else. Our fairy tale has gone on quite well for centuries and centuries just as it is. Whoever comes in now is going to disturb us. And we certainly don't want someone like you around, who's capable only of making trouble. So get out of here!"

"Colleagues shouldn't treat each other so rudely," said Pinocchio. "Colleagues?! To each his own," said the Wolf. "You should know that in fairy tales each character has its own function and that, therefore, neither characters nor their functions can be changed."

"If you let me come into the fairy tale as Pinocchio I swear that I won't change even a comma."

"You make me laugh with your promises!"

"Then let me be the Wolf! The important thing for the fairy tale is that everyone act their parts well. I was born to be an actor, trust me; once I even played a donkey, so you think I don't know how to play a wolf?"

"What does a donkey have to do with a wolf?"

"They're both animals."

"So?"

"So you're an animal, there's nothing wrong with that."

The Wolf's eyes turned red as fire. White foam started coming out of his mouth, and his whole body began to shake. He had never been treated like that by anybody, and he had to sit down because his head was spinning with rage.

Pinocchio understood that things were looking bad and that as soon as the Wolf calmed down he would attack him and tear him to pieces. And so he decided to leave—that is, to escape—and in fact, he escaped into the woods, leaping through the brambles with his wooden legs that went *click clack.*

After going a short way he met Little Red Riding Hood. "Where are you going, pretty little girl?"

"I'm taking these goodies to Grandmother. Who are you?"

"I'm Pinocchio, don't you recognize me?"

"No."

"I'm a puppet, and I know a lot of games to entertain children."

"I can see that you're a puppet, but I don't have time; I have to go because the Wolf is waiting for me and I'm already late."

To spite the Wolf, Pinocchio tried to convince Little Red Riding Hood to take another path. "If you come with me, I'll show you a shortcut, and you can get there faster."

"I can't," said the little girl, "I have no choice but to go this way."

"Why no choice?"

"Because that's what's written in the fairy tale."

Pinocchio tried again. "I know a place where we can find ripe blackberries. Do you like blackberries?"

"I sure do! But I have to go see the Wolf; he's waiting for me."

"But the Wolf is bad. Why do you want to go see him?"

"Because that's what's written in the fairy tale."

Little Red Riding Hood explained to Pinocchio that it was alright if she got there a few minutes late, but that she had no choice but to meet the Wolf and to go to Grandmother's, because that's what it said in the fairy tale.

That was enough. Pinocchio left, bored. Maybe he had chosen the wrong fairy tale: the Wolf was too bad and too presumptuous; and Little Red Riding Hood was too little and too annoying.

Pinocchio started walking again, and after walking on and on with his wooden legs that went *click clack*, he finally arrived at a castle where Cinderella's Prince lived.

"Now let's see," Pinocchio said to himself, "if the Prince is nicer than the Wolf and less annoying than Little Red Riding Hood. Usually princes are nice, at least the ones in fairy tales."

"A wooden puppet in my place?" said the Prince, opening his eyes wide with wonder when Pinocchio made his proposal.

"Just once," said Pinocchio. "In exchange I'll come and entertain your guests in the castle theater: I know how to sing, dance, and trip people. But you have to let me wear your footsteps at least once."

"Wear my footsteps?" asked the Prince.

"I meant to say wear your shoes. I made a mistake with the words."

"But you're asking me for something that's impossible! You forget that a prince is the son of a king, and that he's destined to rule. What would my father's subjects think of the heir to the throne if I gave up my place to a wooden puppet?"

"But we're talking about a fairy tale. You're a fairy-tale prince, your father is a fairy-tale king, and the subjects are fairy-tale subjects, too."

"Stop and think for a minute about Cinderella," said the Prince. "Do you think she would be happy to marry a puppet?"

"Anything can happen in a fairy tale."

"Even fairy tales have got to have their rules, otherwise they can't be told. I'm a prince and you're a puppet; to each his part."

"I've already heard this speech. But I could disguise myself, put on a moustache like yours, wear your cape, your boots, your spurs."

"You'd make even the ants laugh. You see," said the Prince patiently, "I've been acting my part with considerable effort for centuries, and, going by what everyone says, I've shown some talent. The fairy tale of Cinderella is quite ancient, whereas you, Pinocchio, were written just a short time ago. However hard you try, you would never be able to give your gestures and your words the right cadence and intonation. The part of the Prince can't be learned in a day, and it's not enough to wear a cape and boots. Everyone would realize it was a scam."

"Let me try."

"No, we must respect tradition."

"Forget about tradition."

"You see? You're too recent of a character to understand these things."

"I should have guessed that princes are all reactionaries, even fairy-tale princes."

"And I should have guessed that puppets are all pains in the you-know-what!" said the Prince, without losing his composure.

"I'm not offended even if you call me a pain in the you-know-what," said Pinocchio.

"And I'm not offended even if you call me reactionary," said the Prince.

"We're even, then."

"I never get offended," said the Prince, who wanted to appear more generous than the puppet.

"Can I insult you, then?"

"If you enjoy that."

"Unfortunately, I only enjoy insulting people if they get mad."

"How can a prince get mad at the words of a puppet? You should know that for centuries our court has kept jesters whose job consists of making fun of us and dishing out abuse. If you want, I can hire you as a jester."

"Either you let me into the fairy tale or I leave," said Pinocchio.

"Wait a minute, let me think, maybe there's a part that's right for you."

"Let's hear."

"You know when Cinderella runs away from the palace the second night?"

"Yeah; so what?"

"Cinderella goes out to the road; it's winter, it's cold, and the wind is blowing."

"So?"

"You could play the part of the wind."

"The wind?" Pinocchio was having trouble understanding.

"You could hide behind a corner of the palace walls and be the wind. It's easy; all you have to do is cup your hands around your mouth and shout 'Whooo! Whooo! Whooo!'"

"And that would be the part you're offering me in Cinderella?" Pinocchio sneered and made rude sounds with his mouth, his nose, and his hands, and then turned his back on the Prince and started to leave.

The guards planted themselves in front of him menacingly, lances in hand, ready to stop him and throw him in jail. But the Prince, who had a generous spirit, signaled to the guards to let him go.

After walking on and on with his wooden legs that went *click clack*, Pinocchio arrived at a mill right when the youngest son of the miller was complaining that all he had inherited was a cat. And right at that same moment the Cat was saying, "Don't worry yourself, dear master. All you need to do is find a sack for me and have a pair of boots made for walking in the woods, and you'll see that fortune has not treated you as badly as you think."

Pinocchio broke into the conversation. "If you're not happy that you inherited a cat, would you like to inherit a puppet that knows how to sing and dance, and can accompany you through the world and perform in town squares? Lots of money in that!"

The miller's young son looked down his nose at Pinocchio. "Do you know how our fairy tale ends? Right now I'm desperate and I don't have a cent, but soon I'll be very rich, and on account of this Cat here."

Pinocchio went over and whispered in his ear, "And I'll make you a hundred times richer!"

The miller's son, like all rich people, never felt rich enough, and seemed interested in Pinocchio's proposal. "And what do you plan to do?"

"What does it matter to you what I plan to do? I'm telling you that I'll make you a hundred times richer and super-richer than what happens in the tale of Puss in Boots."

"So what do I have to do?" asked the miller's son in a soft voice, so that he wouldn't be heard by the Cat, who was dozing nearby.

"You'd have to put me in the Cat's place and the Cat in the rabbit's place," said Pinocchio.

The miller's son moved closer to him and said, again in a soft voice, "I'll have to put the Cat in the sack, then."

"Exactly. And then you'll have to give me a pair of boots."

The miller's son pet the Cat a few times, and the Cat started to purr and then closed its eyes. The miller's son picked it up by the scruff of its neck and quickly stuffed it into a canvas sack, and then tied it at the top with a piece of twine.

"Do you know how to catch mice?" he asked Pinocchio.

"I'm a whiz at that," said Pinocchio, "but why do you care about mice? You don't want me to waste my time running after mice; I have to go to the King."

"That's right, you have to go to the King to bring him the rabbit," said the miller's son.

"To bring him the Cat," Pinocchio corrected him.

"I'm getting all confused," said the miller's son. "Things have been happening the same way here for centuries, and any change is confusing."

Inside the sack the Cat was swearing, snorting, sneezing, meowing. Pinocchio got a pair of boots from the miller's son, slipped them on his feet, put the sack on his back, and set off toward the King's palace on his wooden legs that went *click clack*.

When he arrived at the palace, the King's guards didn't want to let him in. They knew that a cat with boots and a sack on its back was supposed to show up there, but instead what they saw was a wooden puppet. But he had boots and a sack on his back, too.

The King consulted with his ministers, and his ministers consulted among themselves.

They finally decided to let the puppet in.

"Here you are, Your Majesty," said Pinocchio, who had memorized the words of the fairy tale, "a cat straight out of the cattery that the marquis of Carabas has directed me to present to you on his behalf."

"Tell your master," answered the King, "that I thank him and much appreciate his gift."

The King opened the sack, because that's what's written in the fairy tale. The Cat came out, ruffled and furious, and scratched everyone: the King, the ministers, the guards.

The King became terribly angry, because this wasn't what was written in the fairy tale.

Pinocchio was immediately grabbed by his feet and his nose, put into the sack, and tied up tightly with a sturdy piece of rope. Two mounted guards took him at a gallop back to chapter 36, to the exact point where he had escaped.

It took years for the fairy tale of Puss in Boots to be put back together again, and even today there's occasionally a mix-up.

5

Dacia Maraini (1936–)

Dacia Maraini, one of Italy's most renowned and prolific living writers, was born in Florence. She has authored novels, short story collections, theatrical works, cinematic screenplays, and essays, and regularly contributes to newspapers and journals. Active in feminist initiatives, in her writing she frequently focuses on female characters in their violent or alienating social and historical contexts, as well as on social outcasts and other vulnerable groups such as abused children. Her novels include *La lunga vita di Marianna Ucrìa* (*The Silent Duchess*), *Memorie di una ladra* (*Memories of a Female Thief*, 1972), the autobiographical *Bagheria* (*Bagheria*, 1993), and *Colomba* (Colomba, 2004). In 1973 she cofounded the women's theatrical cooperative La Maddalena in Rome, which staged her successful *Dialogo di una prostituta con un suo cliente* (Dialogue of a prostitute with one of her clients) in 1978. The stories of *Buio* (*Darkness*, 1999), which won the prestigious Strega prize, recount the lives of abused children, and the collection of fairy tales and fables *La pecora Dolly e altre storie per bambini* (Dolly the Sheep and Other Stories for Children, 2001) continues Maraini's attention to themes of social justice and childhood. More recently, Maraini revisited the fairy tale in her *Onda Marina e il Drago Spento* (Marina Wave and Fireless Dragon, with E. Murrali, 2019).

Further Reading

Primary

Maraini, Dacia. *La pecora Dolly e altre storie per bambini*. Milan: Fabbri Editori, 2001. 87–103. [source text]

Secondary

Schwartz, Cecilia. "Quando i grandi scrittori scrivono per i piccoli lettori: i casi Calvino e Maraini." In *Atti del VII Congresso degli italianisti scandinavi*, ed. Enrico Garavelli and Elina Suomela-Härmä. Helsinki: Société Néophilologique de Helsinki, 2005. 247–54.

A Family in a Shoe (Una famiglia in una scarpa)

In this ecological and pacifist fable, Maraini addresses the risks of burning bridges between the natural and human worlds. Significantly, it is the father who, with his violent and vindictive ways as an indiscriminate hunter, starts a war with the boars and ultimately threatens the integrity of his own family, until he is finally made to pay for his transgressions in a surreal final twist.

An entire family lived in a shoe: father, mother, and five children. The mother baked delicious pies, even if sometimes they exploded, launching newborn baby birds into the air. The fact of the matter is that she would leave the dough to rise on one of the eyelets of the shoe, and the sparrows found it so soft and cozy that they would use it to make their nests by digging a hole and burying their eggs there. Then, in the warmth of the oven, the eggs would mature and the baby birds, who felt like they were suffocating, would make the pie blow up.

The children of Mother Shoe were used to these explosions of baby birds, and they would push them affectionately in the direction of the window. In fact, they were used to playing with the woodland animals because the old shoe where they had gone to live had been abandoned at the edge of the forest. There was a den of a family of wild boars near the shoe, and the children often played hide-and-seek with them.

Father Shoe was obsessed with hunting. He would go out early in the morning and roam through the woods with his rifle on his back. The wild boars knew him well, and as soon as they heard him, they would greet him with a smile. They knew that no matter how passionate he was about hunting, he would never shoot a boar; they were friends, their children played together, and sometimes they would even take to dancing in the same little meadow on nights when the moon was full.

In fact, the shoe man would go hunting far from the woods near his house, often returning with wild hares hanging from his belt. And because of this the boars had gotten the impression that out of friendship and respect the shoe man would never kill a boar, not even an unfamiliar one.

This thought was shared by the shoe children, too, who slept at night in their bunkbeds in the toe of the shoes, which was the warmest part of the house.

When their mother wasn't making pies, she would go around and look for work. "I've always worked," she said, "and I don't see why I shouldn't continue to do so." She had a big belly because she was expecting her sixth child, and her husband would have preferred that she stay at home. But the woman was stubborn and would go out by herself every day, as if to say, "I'm a free woman, and I want to stay that way."

One morning, however, it happened that as the father was going out to hunt at around five o'clock in the morning, he found himself standing in front of a little boar who had just gotten up and was eating some lettuce from the family's vegetable garden. The little boar greeted him cheerfully, "Good morning, Mister Shoe. How are your children? Are you going hunting this morning again?" But the shoe man grew furious over that little theft and began thinking about how he had never approved of his children's friendship with those animals; and he raised his rifle and killed the little boar.

The next day a pack of boars broke into the shoe house and ransacked everything. The father wasn't there, and the mother was out looking for work. The children were still sleeping, except for the littlest one.

"Hi, what are you all doing here?" said the little one, his mouth dirty with chocolate. "Do you want to play?"

They didn't answer, and they continued to ransack the house. The little boy started to cry. The boars tied him up with rope and carried him off.

When the mother returned, she asked, "Where's the little one?"

"The boars took him," the others answered.

"To do what with?"

"They tied him up and carried him off."

The woman scratched her head. Then she remembered that her husband had shot a little boar with his rifle and grew worried for her child. "What should we do now?"

"Let's wait for Papa to come back," said the oldest of the children.

"Let's wait, then. In the meantime, I'll bake a pie," said the mother, and she mixed up the flour and put the usual ball of dough to rise on the balcony.

Toward evening the father came back and asked what had happened, since the house was all topsy-turvy. "The boars were here," answered the children, "and they carried off the little one."

The man didn't say a word. He took his rifle and went out, and the children and the mother put the house back in order.

At around two o'clock the man returned and told them he had gotten his revenge.

"But where's our child?" asked the mother.

"I don't know. I couldn't find him. But I did kill two more little boars."

"You shouldn't have done that. They'll be back again tomorrow and they'll take another one of ours," answered the mother. But the man didn't say a word.

The next day, as soon as the father went out hunting and the mother left to look for work, a pack of boars returned to the shoe house. They entered without permission, kicking in the fragile door that opened into the heel, and then took the youngest of the remaining children and carried him off.

When the mother came back, she said, "Where's my next-to-last son?"

"The boars took him," said the oldest.

"What should we do now? What should we do?"

"Let's wait for Papa to come back; he'll know how to avenge us," said the oldest son.

"But don't you understand that it'll be worse every time? At this point it's a war, and they won't stop. What am I going to do if they carry off all of my children?"

"Papa has a rifle. He's stronger than they are," said the oldest son, who had been promised a beautiful brand-new hunting rifle as soon as he passed this year's exams.

"Well, in the meantime I'll make a pie while we're waiting for Papa," said the mother, and she began to mix the flour. Then she put the dough to rise on the windowsill.

The father returned that evening, heard what had happened, and left again without saying a word, his rifle on his back. It was the middle of the night when he finally came back, his shirt stained with blood.

"Did you find our son?" asked the mother.

"No, but I got my revenge."

"Was it a good revenge?" asked the son, who was proud to have a father like that.

"Yes, I got revenge just as I wanted," answered the father, and he told them how he had killed another three little boars.

The next day was Sunday, and everyone in the shoe slept until late. When they woke up, they found their mother bustling about in the kitchen. She had put two pies in the oven to bake and was singing cheerfully. Even if every now and then she stopped in front of the window and looked out at the woods, thinking about her two children who had been taken prisoners by the boars.

That evening the father had invited some friends to dinner, a boar hunter with his wife and two older sons who already knew how to shoot.

At eight o'clock they all sat down at the table. They ate polenta and the meat of the boars that the father had killed with his rifle. They drank sparkling Piave wine, and by the time they got to dessert they were merry and satiated.

The mother brought the two pies to the table; they were topped by lovely golden crusts and were as lustrous and plump as church cupolas. The father went over to one of the pies with a knife and broke it open, and there was a cry of horror. There, under the pie's crust, was one of his two sons: tied up, floured, and browned like a well-baked biscuit. The father broke open the crust of the other pie, and they all jumped back from the table: the second child had also been baked.

"Now we're going to go and kill all the boars," said the father, grabbing his rifle. "You come along, too, friends, and you too, son; we have to teach them a lesson." And so the pack of men left in the middle of the night, their rifles on their shoulders. They were wearing rubber boots so that they could cross the swamp and leather jackets lined with fur to protect against the cold. They didn't say a word, but advanced through the freezing night with their heads down, off to get their revenge on the boars.

In the meantime, the mother was crying over the death of her two children. But as she was crying she became aware that one of her sons was looking at her as if he wanted to say something. Then she took a cloth and tried to clean the baked flour off him. Little by little she saw that under the crust his heart was beating. The boy was alive. She immediately untied both of them and sent them off to the bathtub so that they could get rid of all that baked stuff, and they both emerged from the water naked and happy to be at home. Their mother hugged and kissed them.

Late that night the men returned, their arms bloody. "We killed close to twenty baby boars. And this time we were able to get the mother and father boar. That'll teach them to take our children as prisoners."

"But they're alive!" shouted the happy mother. "Our two children are alive, there's no more need for revenge. Let's go make peace with the boars who are our neighbors."

"No, no peace," said the father. "They dared to attack our house and they have to be punished. Otherwise, they'll try it again soon," he said, putting away his rifle. Then he said goodbye to his friends and went off to sleep.

Two mornings later, when they woke up, they discovered that another of their children had disappeared. And this time no one had seen them come in. But they all thought that it had to have been them, the boars. The war showed no sign of ending.

The father took his still smoking rifle and said, "I thought I had killed them all. Now I'll have no peace until I exterminate every damn boar that lives around here."

"But why?" said the mother. "Your children are alive. They weren't killed. You, on the other hand, exterminated a whole family. What sort of revenge do you want to take?"

"They dared to take our other son, and I won't forgive them for that. I want to destroy them."

"You'll see that they'll return this one alive, too."

But he wouldn't listen to reason. He took the two older sons with him and went off to the woods in search of boars to kill.

Meanwhile, to lessen her suffering the mother got ready to make a pie. She mixed the flour, poured in the yeast, and set the dough out on the windowsill.

That evening the father returned with the older sons. All they had found was a baby boar, and the three of them had shot at it together. The spilled blood formed a long ribbon that extended from the woods all the way back into the shoe house.

At eight o'clock the whole family sat down at the table: they ate polenta and boar. Then the mother brought the nicely browned pie to the table. The father observed the dessert closely before he sunk the knife into it. "This pie is too small to be hiding a child," he commented, cutting it in half. Indeed, it was too small to contain a child, but big enough to hold the arm of the stolen son.

The father was furious and began to kick the pie, while the mother gathered up the cut-off arm and hugged it to her chest.

"From now on you won't be making any more pies," said the man to his wife, and fired a shot into the air as if he were putting a period at the end of his sentence.

The wife wasn't listening to him. She wondered how to keep that arm alive so that she could attach it back onto the body of her son. Just to be safe she sprinkled it with flour and sugar and put it in the oven, like she did with the pies.

The next day the man took some gasoline, poured it on the plants in the woods and set everything on fire. The trees began to shout, "We're burning, we're burning, help!" But the man wouldn't give up, and he continued to fan the fire and to light new ones until the woods was a single roaring flame. The smoke rose, and the poor beasts fled their dens; fathers and mothers together with their young ran, jumped, burned their tails, hurled themselves into the water of the lake.

In a few hours' time the fire devoured the whole forest, and in its fury it reached the shoe, too, swallowing it up in a single mouthful as Mother Shoe and her children fled toward the lake.

"Now what are we going to do, without a home?" she asked herself, crying.

"Did you see that? We killed them all off," said the man, and he sat down on the ground and smoked a cigarette.

"But now we're homeless, and thousands of innocent animals are in the same situation."

"What do I care? We showed them who's stronger. We massacred them. That'll teach them to raise their heads. Let's go look for another shoe."

"Just a minute," said the wife. "First I have to get my son's arm; it's still in the oven."

She started back toward the rubble of their house and found that the oven was still warm; inside it was the son's arm, floured and baked like a little loaf of bread.

While the husband was sitting peacefully on the charred meadow, smoking his cigarette, they heard a voice that said, "Some charity for a poor cripple!" The mother raised her eyes and saw the son who had been kidnapped by the boars coming toward her, thin as a rail and missing an arm.

She ran to him, squeezed him to her chest, and said, "I finally found you. I kept your arm so that I could attach it back on. I knew that you'd return."

But the boy didn't recognize his mother and father; in fact, he was looking at them with horror. "I'm your mama," she said, and he shook his head. "This is your arm; don't you recognize it?" And in answer the boy grunted.

The father grabbed him by the neck and took him to the lake's edge. "We're going to build a new house now," he said, "and you're going to help me. You're my son, the strongest one, and you'll have to pull your weight."

The son helped his father, but his movements grew stranger by the day. And his skin was growing dense with bristles.

"What's happening to our son?" said the man one day, looking at the boy's face, which reminded him of something familiar but something he hated, although he couldn't say what.

"He doesn't even want to taste my pies anymore," said the mother. "He left the arm to rot in a ditch. And he eats off the ground, like a dog."

"Wife, you know what our son resembles?"

"What?"

"A boar," said the man, desolately.

In fact, by then the child had fully become a boar. His mother hugged him, weeping, even though she saw that he had long, curved teeth. The father stood up to get his rifle. Then the boar spoke, and he said, "You love revenge more than your own son, and that's why you're destined to become a rifle. Just as I've been transformed into a boar, you'll become a rifle."

No sooner said than done: under the astonished eyes of his wife, the shoe man transformed into an enormous rifle made of iron and wood.

"And now I'm going to shoot you," said the rifle.

"Try to," answered the son.

The rifle moved, it wriggled, it gave a jump, but it wasn't able to shoot.

"A rifle can't shoot by itself," said the boar. "It needs a hand to press the trigger. So you just stay like that; good night, father!"

"You help me!" said the shoe man to his wife. "Shoot, press the trigger, don't you see that I can't do it myself? Don't let that boar insult me like that."

"That boar is your son," said the woman, and she refused to press the trigger. The rifle started shouting again, but the woman let it shout. She grabbed her boar son by the paw and headed toward the woods.

Appendix

ATU TALE TYPES

ATU 310: Basile, "Petrosinella"
ATU 311: Basile, "The Flea"; Gonzenbach, "The Bandit Who Had a Witch's Head"; Pitrè, "The Slave"
ATU 313: Basile, "Petrosinella"
ATU 326: Gonzenbach, "The Story of the Courageous Girl"; Calvino, "Dauntless Little John"
ATU 333: Calvino, "The False Grandmother"
ATU 327A: Rodari, "Nino and Nina"
ATU 328: Pitrè, "Tridicinu"
ATU 400: *Liombruno*
ATU 403: Straparola, "Biancabella"
ATU 403C: Gozzano, "The Silver Hare"
ATU 407: Calvino, "Apple Girl"
ATU 408: Gozzi, *The Love of the Three Oranges*
ATU 410: Basile, "Sun, Moon, and Talia"
ATU 425A: Straparola, "King Pig"; Pitrè, "The Little Mouse with the Stinky Tail"; Calvino, "The Crab Prince"
ATU 425B: *Liombruno*
ATU 425C: Calvino, "Bellinda and the Monster"
ATU 425D: Pitrè, "The Little Mouse with the Stinky Tail"
ATU 440: Capuana, "Ranocchino"
ATU 441: Straparola, "King Pig"; Capuana, "The Black Egg"
ATU 480: Pitrè, "The Ogress"
ATU 510A: Basile, "The Cinderella Cat"
ATU 510B: Deledda, "Our Lady of Good Counsel"

ATU 513A: Basile, "The Flea"
ATU 545A*: Gonzenbach, "The Story of the Courageous Girl"
ATU 545B: Basile, "Cagliuso"
ATU 554: Basile, "The Cockroach, the Mouse, and the Cricket"
ATU 559: Basile, "The Cockroach, the Mouse, and the Cricket"
ATU 563: Basile, "The Tale of the Ogre"
ATU 571: Straparola, "Adamantina"
ATU 571C: Straparola, "Adamantina"
ATU 653: Basile, "The Flea"
ATU 672: Gonzenbach, "The Snake That Testified in Favor of a Girl"
ATU 675: Straparola, "Crazy Pietro"
ATU 700: Capuana, "Cecina"
ATU 706: Straparola, "Biancabella"
ATU 709: Calvino, "Bella Veneiza"
ATU 710: Calvino, "Buffalo Head"
ATU 857: Basile, "The Flea"; Gonzenbach, "The Bandit Who Had a Witch's Head"
ATU 875: Gonzenbach, "The Clever Farmer's Daughter"
ATU 875A: Gonzenbach, "The Clever Farmer's Daughter"
ATU 877: Basile, "The Old Woman Who Was Skinned"
ATU 887: Straparola, "Biancabella"
ATU 891: Gonzenbach, "The Story of Sorfarina"
ATU 900: Straparola, "Biancabella"
ATU 1218: Morlini, "The Mother Who Left Her Son to Watch the House"
ATU 1533: Gonzenbach, "The Clever Farmer's Daughter"
ATU 1643: Pitrè, "Giufà and the Plaster Statue"

Selected Bibliography

This bibliography supplements the entries included in the sections on the individual authors. It is not intended to be exhaustive but meant to provide some basic resources that will help scholars, teachers, and students to further explore fairy tales and in particular the Italian tradition. For works by and on the authors included in this volume, see the Further Reading section in the individual chapters.

Fairy Tales—General (Collections and Criticism)

Anderson, Graham. *Fairytale in the Ancient World*. London: Routledge, 2000.

Ashliman, D. L. *Folk and Fairy Tales: A Handbook*. Westport, CT: Greenwood Press, 2004.

Bacchilega, Cristina. *Fairy Tales Transformed? Twenty-First-Century Adaptations and the Politics of Wonder*. Detroit: Wayne State University Press, 2013.

Bacchilega, Cristina. *Postmodern Fairy Tales Gender and Narrative Strategies*. Philadelphia: University of Pennsylvania Press, 1997.

Benson, Stephen. *Contemporary Fiction and the Fairy Tale*. Detroit: Wayne State University Press, 2008.

Bettelheim, Bruno. *The Uses of Enchantment: The Meaning and Importance of Fairy Tales*. New York: Knopf, 1976.

Bottigheimer, Ruth B. *Fairy Tales Framed: Early Forewords, Afterwords, and Critical Words*. Albany: State University of New York Press, 2012.

Bottigheimer, Ruth B. *Fairy Tales and Society: Illusion, Allusion, and Paradigm*. Philadelphia: University of Pennsylvania Press, 1986.

Canepa, Nancy L., ed. *Teaching Fairy Tales*. Detroit: Wayne State University Press, 2019.

Duggan, Anne, ed. *A Cultural History of Fairy Tales*. 6 vols. Vol. 1: *A Cultural History of Fairy Tales in Antiquity*, ed. Debbie Felton; vol. 2: *A Cultural History of Fairy Tales in the Middle Ages*, ed. Susan Aronstein; vol. 3: *A Cultural History of Fairy Tales in the Age of the Marvelous*, ed. Suzanne Magnanini; vol. 4: *A Cultural History of Fairy Tales in the Long Eighteenth Century*, ed. Anne E. Duggan; vol. 5: *A Cultural*

History of Fairy Tales in the Long Nineteenth Century, ed. Naomi Wood; vol. 6: *A Cultural History of Fairy Tales in the Modern Age*, ed. Andrew Teverson. London: Bloomsbury, 2021.

Duggan, Anne E., Donald Haase, and Helen Callow, eds. *Folktales and Fairy Tales: Traditions and Texts from around the World.* 2nd edition. Santa Barbara, CA: Greenwood, 2016.

Haase, Donald, ed. *Fairy Tales and Feminism: New Approaches*. Detroit: Wayne State University Press, 2004.

Hallett, Martin, and Barbara Karasek, eds. *Folk and Fairy Tales*. 4th ed. Peterborough, Ontario: Broadview Press, 2009.

Jones, Steven Swann. *The Fairy Tale: The Magic Mirror of Imagination*. New York: Routledge, 2013.

Lüthi, Max. *The European Folktale: Form and Nature*. Philadelphia: Institute for the Study of Human Issues, 1981.

Lüthi, Max. *The Fairytale as Art Form and Portrait of Man*. Bloomington: Indiana University Press, 1984.

Propp, Vladimir. *Morphology of the Folktale*. 2nd ed. Ed. Louis A. Wagner. Introd. Alan Dundes. Austin: University of Texas Press, 1968.

Propp, Vladimir, and Anatoly Liberman. *Theory and History of Folklore*. Minneapolis: University of Minnesota Press, 1984.

Röhrich, Lutz. *Folktales and Reality*. Bloomington: Indiana University Press, 1991.

Schacker, Jennifer, and Christine A. Jones, eds. *Marvelous Transformations: An Anthology of Fairy Tales and Contemporary Critical Perspectives*. Peterborough, Ontario: Broadview Press, 2013.

Tatar, Maria. *The Cambridge Companion to Fairy Tales*. Cambridge: Cambridge University Press, 2014.

Tatar, Maria. *The Classic Fairy Tales*. 2nd ed. New York: W. W. Norton, 2016.

Tatar, Maria. *Off with Their Heads! Fairy Tales and the Culture of Childhood*. Princeton: Princeton University Press, 1992.

Teverson, Andrew. *Fairy Tale*. New York: Routledge, 2013.

Teverson, Andrew, ed. *The Fairy Tale World*. New York: Routledge, 2019.

Thompson, Stith. *The Folktale*. Berkeley: University of California Press, (1946) 1977.

Thompson, Stith. *Motif-Index of Folk-Literature: A Classification of Narrative Elements in Folktales, Ballads, Myths, Fables, Mediaeval Romances, Exempla, Fabliaux,*

Jest-Books, and Local Legends. Rev. and enl. ed. Bloomington: Indiana University Press, 1955–58.

Uther, Hans-Jörg. *The Types of International Folktales: A Classification and Bibliography, Based on the System of Antti Aarne and Stith Thompson*. 3 vols. Helsinki: Suomalainen Tiedeakatemia, Academia Scientiarum Fennica, 2004.

Warner, Marina. *From the Beast to the Blonde: On Fairy Tales and Their Tellers*. New York: Farrar, Straus, and Giroux, 1996.

Warner, Marina. *Once Upon a Time: A Short History of Fairy Tale*. New York: Oxford University Press, 2014.

Ziolkowski, Jan M. *Fairy Tales from Before Fairy Tales: The Medieval Latin Past of Wonderful Lies*. Ann Arbor: University of Michigan Press, 2010.

Zipes, Jack. *Fairy Tales and the Art of Subversion*. London: Routledge, 2006.

Zipes, Jack. *The Golden Age of Folk and Fairy Tales: From the Brothers Grimm to Andrew Lang*. Indianapolis: Hackett Publishing, 2013.

Zipes, Jack. *The Great Fairy Tale Tradition: From Straparola and Basile to the Brothers Grimm: Texts, Criticism*. New York: W. W. Norton, 2001.

Zipes, Jack. *The Irresistible Fairy Tale: The Cultural and Social History of a Genre*. Princeton: Princeton University Press, 2012.

Zipes, Jack. *The Oxford Companion to Fairy Tales*. 2nd edition. Oxford: Oxford University Press, 2019.

Italian Fairy Tales—Criticism

Aprile, Renato. *Indice delle fiabe popolari italiane di magia*. Florence: Leo S. Olschki, 2000.

Boero, Pino. *La letteratura per l'infanzia*. Bari: Laterza, 1995.

Calabrese, Stefano. *Fiaba*. Florence: la Nuova Italia, 1997.

Calabrese, Stefano. *Gli arabeschi della fiaba: Dal Basile ai Romantici*. Pisa: Pacini, 1984.

Calvino, Italo. *Sulla fiaba*. Ed. Mario Lavagetto. Turin: Einaudi, 1988.

Campo, Cristina. *Gli imperdonabili*. Milan: Adelphi Edizioni, 1987.

Canepa, Nancy L., ed. *Out of the Woods: The Origins of the Literary Fairy Tale in Italy and France*. Detroit: Wayne State University Press, 1997.

Caprettini, Gian P. *Dizionario della fiaba italiana: Simboli, personaggi, storie delle fiabe regionali*. Rome: Meltemi, 2000.

Cocchiara, Giuseppe, and John N. McDaniel. *The History of Folklore in Europe*. Philadelphia: Institute for the Study of Human Issues, (1971) 1981.

Cusatelli, Giorgio. *Tutto è fiaba: Atti del Convegno Internazionale di studio sulla fiaba.* Milan: Emme, 1980.

D'Aronco, Gianfranco. *Indice delle fiabe toscane.* Florence: Olschki, 1953.

De Caprio, Caterina. *La tradizione del "cunto" da Giovan Battista Basile a Domenico Rea: Giornate di studio 19 e 20 Gennaio 2006, Palazzo du Mesnil.* Naples: Libreria Dante & Descartes, 2007.

De Gubernatis Angelo. *Storia delle novelline popolari.* Milan: Hoepli, 1883.

Gatto, Trocchi Cecilia. *La fiaba italiana di magia: Ipotesi di ricerca semiologica.* Rome: Bulzoni, 1972.

Getto, Giovanni. "La fiaba di Giambattista Basile." In *Barocco in prosa e in poesia.* Milan: Rizzoli, 1969. 379–401.

Lavagetto, Mario, ed. *Racconti di orchi, di fate e di streghe: La fiaba letteraria in Italia.* Milan: Mondadori, 2008.

Lavinio, Cristina. *La magia della fiaba: Tra oralità e scrittura.* Florence: La Nuova Italia, 1993.

Maggi, Armando. *Preserving the Spell: Basile's "The Tale of Tales" and Its Afterlife in the Fairy-Tale Tradition.* Chicago: University of Chicago Press, 2015.

Petrini, Mario. *La fiaba di magia nella letteratura italiana.* Udine: Del Bianco, 1983.

Rak, Michele. *Da Cenerentola a Cappuccetto Rosso: Breve storia illustrata della fiaba Barocca.* Milan: Mondadori, 2007.

Rak, Michele. *Logica della fiaba: Fate, orchi, gioco, corte, fortuna, viaggio, capriccio, metamorfosi, corpo.* Milan: Mondadori, 2005.

Solinas Donghi, Beatrice. *La fiaba come racconto.* Venice: Marsilio, 1976.

Italian Fairy Tales—Collections

Arbasino, Alberto, ed. *Favole su favole: Fiabe e leggende tradotte, trascritte e trasformate.* Cosenza: Lerici, 1975.

Bernoni, Domenico Giuseppe. *Fiabe e novelle popolari veneziane.* Treviso: Santi Quaranta, (1873) 2013.

Calvino, Italo. *Fiabe italiane.* Turin: Einaudi, 1956.

Comparetti, Domenico. *Novelline popolari italiane.* Bologna: Forni, (1893) 1968.

Coronedi, Berti Carolina. *Novelle popolari bolognesi.* Bologna: Forni, (1874) 1983.

Crane, Thomas Frederick, and Jack Zipes. *Italian Popular Tales.* Santa Barbara: ABC-CLIO, 2003.

De Gubernatis, Angelo. *Florilegio delle novelline popolari.* Milan: Hoepli, 1883.

Gatto, Trocchi Cecilia. *Le più belle fiabe popolari italiane.* Rome: Newton Compton, 2003.

Ghidetti, Enrico, and Leonardo Lattarulo, eds. *La bottega dello stregone: Cent'anni di fiabe italiane.* Rome: Editori Riuniti, 1985.

Imbriani, Vittorio. *La novellaja fiorentina con la novellaja milanese.* Milan: Rizzoli, (1877) 1997.

Nerucci, Gherardo. *Sessanta novelle popolari montalesi.* Milan: Biblioteca Universale Rizzoli, (1880) 1977.

Credits

Gianni Rodari

Original title "Nino e Nina," from *Venti storie più una.* Copyright © 1980, Maria Ferretti Rodari and Paolo Rodari, Italy; copyright © 2008, Edizioni EL S.r.l., Trieste, Italy. Translated and published by permission.

Original title "La casa di tre bottoni," from *Venti storie più una* Copyright © 1980, Maria Ferretti Rodari and Paolo Rodari, Italy; copyright © 2008, Edizioni EL S.r.l., Trieste, Italy. Translated and published by permission.

Original title "Pinocchio il furbo," from *Tante storie per giocare.* Copyright © 1980 Maria Ferretti Rodari and Paolo Rodari, Italy; copyright © 2008, Edizioni EL S.r.l., Trieste, Italy. Translated and published by permission.

Original titles "A sbagliare le storie," "Cappuccetto rosso in elicottero," "Le carte di Propp," from *Grammatica della fantasia*, copyright © 1980 Maria Ferretti Rodari and Paolo Rodari, Italy; © 2008, Edizioni EL S.r.l., Trieste, Italy. Translated and published by permission.

Gianni Rodari, e-book

"Nino e Nina," originally published in the Italian language in 1969 by Editori Riuniti in the collection *Venti storie più una.* Copyright © 1980 The Estate of Gianni Rodari. Translated and published in agreement with Piergiorgio Nicolazzini Literary Agency (PNLA).

"La casa di tre bottoni," originally published in the Italian language in 1969 by Editori Riuniti in the collection *Venti storie più una.* Copyright © 1980 The Estate of Gianni Rodari. Translated and published in agreement with Piergiorgio Nicolazzini Literary Agency (PNLA).

"Pinocchio il furbo," originally published in the Italian language in 1971 by Editori Riuniti in the collection *Tante storie per giocare.* Copyright © 1980 The Estate of Gianni Rodari. Translated and published in agreement with Piergiorgio Nicolazzini Literary Agency (PNLA).

“A sbagliare le storie,” “Cappuccetto rosso in elicottero,” “Le carte di Propp,” originally published in the Italian language in 1973 by Giulio Einaudi Editore in the collection *Grammatica della fantasia*. Copyright © 1980 The Estate of Gianni Rodari. Translated and published in agreement with Piergiorgio Nicolazzini Literary Agency (PNLA).

Luigi Malerba

Original title *Pinocchio con gli stivali*, copyright © Luigi Malerba Estate. Courtesy of the heirs. Translated and published by arrangement with The Italian Literary Agency.

Roberto Piumini

Original title *Il cuoco prigioniero* by Roberto Piumini, copyright © 2001 Giunti Editore S.p.a. Florence-Milan, www.giunti.it. Translated and published by permission.

Giorgio Manganelli

“Ottantuno” [# 81] by Giorgio Manganelli, translated by Henry Martin, from *Centuria: One Hundred Ouroboric Novels*, copyright © 1995 by Adelphi Edizioni, translation copyright 2005 by Henry Martin, all rights reserved. Published by McPherson & Company, www.mcphersonco.com. Reprinted by permission.

Dacia Maraini

Original title “Una famiglia in una scarpa,” from the collection *La pecora Dolly e altre storie per bambini*, © 2001 RCS Libri S.p.a. Milan; copyright © 2021 Mondadori Libri S.p.a./BUR, Milan. Translated and published by permission.

Italo Calvino

North America

“Dauntless Little John,” “The Crab Prince,” “Bellinda and the Monster,” “Buffalo Head,” “Apple Girl,” “Bella Venezia,” and “The False Grandmother” from *Italian Folktales*, selected and retold by Italo Calvino, translated by George Martin. Copyright © 1956 by Giulio Einaudi editore, s.p.a. English translation copyright © 1980 by Houghton Mifflin Harcourt. Reprinted by permission of Mariner Books, an imprint of HarperCollins Publishers. All rights reserved.

U.K. and Commonwealth, print

"Dauntless Little John," "The Crab Prince," "Bellinda and the Monster," "Buffalo Head," "Apple Girl," "Bella Venezia, and "The False Grandmother," from *Italian Folktales*, selected and retold by Italo Calvino, translated by George Martin. Copyright © 1956 by Giulio Einaudi Editore, s.p.a. English translation copyright © 1980 by Houghton Mifflin Harcourt. Reprinted by permission of Penguin Books. All rights reserved.

U.K. and Commonwealth, e-book

"Dauntless Little John," "The Crab Prince," "Bellinda and the Monster," "Buffalo Head," "Apple Girl," "Bella Venezia, and "The False Grandmother," *Italian Folktales*, selected and retold by Italo Calvino, translated by George Martin. Copyright © 1956 by Giulio Einaudi Editore, s.p.a. English translation copyright © 1980 by Houghton Mifflin Harcourt. Reprinted by permission of Penguin Books. All rights reserved.

North America

"The Forest on the Superhighway" from *Marcovaldo, or Seasons in the City* by Italo Calvino, translated by William Weaver. Copyright © 1963 by Giulio Einaudi Editore, s.p.a. English translation copyright © 1983 by Houghton Mifflin Harcourt Publishing Company and Martin Secker & Warburg, Ltd. Reprinted by permission of Mariner Books, an imprint of HarperCollins Publishers. All rights reserved.

UK and Commonwealth, print

"The Forest on the Superhighway," from *Marcovaldo, or Seasons in the City* by Italo Calvino, translated by William Weaver. Copyright © 1963 by Giulio Einaudi Editore, s.p.a. English translation copyright © 1983 by Houghton Mifflin Harcourt Publishing Company and Martin Secker & Warburg, Ltd. Reprinted by permission of Penguin Books. All rights reserved.

UK and Commonwealth, e-book

"The Forest on the Superhighway," from *Marcovaldo, or Seasons in the City* by Italo Calvino, translated by William Weaver. Copyright © 1963 by Giulio Einaudi Editore, s.p.a. English translation copyright © 1983 by Houghton Mifflin Harcourt Publishing Company and Martin Secker & Warburg, Ltd. Reprinted by permission of Penguin Books. All rights reserved.